A Garland Series

Foundations of the Novel

Representative Early

Eighteenth-Century Fiction

A collection of 100 rare titles
reprinted in photo-facsimile in 71 volumes

Foundations of the Novel

compiled and edited by

Michael F. Shugrue
Secretary for English for the M.L.A.

with New Introductions for each volume by

Michael Shugrue, *City College of C.U.N.Y.*
Malcolm J. Bosse, *City College of C.U.N.Y.*
William Graves, *N.Y. Institute of Technology*

Memoirs
of the
Twentieth Century

Being Original Letters of State
under George the Sixth

by

Samuel Madden

with a new introduction
for the Garland Edition by
Malcolm J. Bosse

Garland Publishing, Inc., New York & London

Bibliographical note:

*This facsimile has been made from a copy in the
Beinecke Library of Yale University
(DA486 M3)*

Library of Congress Cataloging in Publication Data

Madden, Samuel, 1686-1765.
  Memoirs of the twentieth century.

  (Foundations of the novel)
  Reprint of v. 1, 1733. Originally intended for
6 v. but no more were published.
    I. Title. II. Series.
PZ3.M2617Me 5 [PR3545.M3]   823'.5   74-170588
ISBN 0-8240-0570-8

Printed in the United States of America

Introduction

An ordained clergyman, minor playwright, and philanthropist, Samuel Madden wrote copiously on social, religious, and political topics of interest to conservative protestants of the day. He argued in Reflections and Resolutions proper for the Gentlemen of Ireland, as to their Conduct for the Service of their Country in 1738 *that the plight of Ireland could be remedied only through extensive education of its people, who were encouraged in their idle ways by their Catholic faith. In 1745 he produced a two thousand line poem with the assistance of Dr. Samuel Johnson in praise of Hugh Boulter, late Archbishop of Ardmagh. Madden's most ambitious work, however, was the* Memoirs of the Twentieth Century, *a book of political and religious prophecies of which only the initial 527 page volume of a projected six volumes actually appeared.*

Memoirs *is fulsomely dedicated to the Prince of Wales, known popularly as "poor Fred" because of his luckless life. Prince Frederick, hated by his father and destined to die before ascending the throne, is ecstatically called by Madden "Heir apparent of the best Man and Woman, the best King and Queen, that ever adorn'd a Family, or blest a Nation." In the ensuing Preface the author praises himself for entering the field of prophecy. The extravagance of Madden's language suggests irony, though one of the difficulties of this book is its tone, which hovers between straight-forward*

INTRODUCTION

seriousness and irony:

> *At the Worst, I shall be well treated by the World, as those exalted Spirits were, who discover'd the Antipodes, the Circulation of the Blood, the use of Telescopes and Barometers, of Printing and Sailing, the Loadstone and the Indies, who were so much despis'd at first, tho' so highly honour'd and regarded now.*

The narrator, not specifically identified with Madden, then claims that he painstakingly translated the work "from the English it was writ in," implying that radical changes in the language could be expected in the course of the next two centuries. After deriding those detractors whom he anticipates will attack his work, the narrator claims for himself a bloodline which descends from the spirit Ariel. It is this heritage that accounts for his knowledge of the future; a kindred genius singles him out and reveals to him the glories of twentieth-century England. Genii accomplished for the eighteenth-century writer of prophetic fantasy what the time machine and other technological gadgets do for the writer of science fiction in our own day. After telling the narrator about the future, the genius then hands over to him a number of letters which presumably will be written by his Great Great Great Great Great Great Grandson, destined to be "chief Minister in the End of the Twentieth Century." The reason for making these letters public, claims the narrator, is to show the present government how badly it has handled the ancestor of a great man who will rule England at the end of the world. This long winded preface is notable for flashes of wit and satire, as, for example, when the author

INTRODUCTION

pretends to have counted all the sentences, words, syllables, letters, and vowels in the entire volume in order to prevent imitation or bowdlerization of the text.

The format of the succeeding Memoirs *is epistolary; agents of the English government write reports to the narrator's ever-so-great grandson, describing conditions in Europe, Turkey, and Russia. Portions of the book become in effect travelogs and sober descriptions of customs in other lands. The dominant motif of* Memoirs, *however, is religion. Although Madden purports to deal with all aspects of life, his major interest, which assumes the intensity of an obsession, is the Catholic plot to take over England, the possibility of which would trouble English protestants until late in the century. Madden's fear and hatred of the Society of Jesuits turns prophecy into diatribe, indicating his true goal in this book is to proselyte against a contemporary foe rather than to anticipate actual changes in society. He spends considerable time ridiculing Catholic idolatry, a Protestant concern which he had inherited from the preceding century. In one long letter he has an English agent describe an auction of holy relics at St. Peters "on Monday the 25th of April 1998, from Nine in the Morning till eight at Night, and to continue till all be sold" (102). The following description of the objects is at once painstaking and bitterly satiric, a* tour de force *in the use of detail. In a twenty-five page inventory Madden reveals a vast, if prejudicial knowledge of catholic dogma. Some of the items that he mentions are "the Table on which Christ eat the last Supper, a little decayed . . . The Towel with which he wip'd his Disciples Feet, very rotten . . . Part of the Money paid Judas" (105). . . "the holy Linne-Cloath on which St.*

7

INTRODUCTION

John Baptist was beheaded, wants new Hemming and Darning . . . the brains of St. Peter, from Geneva" (106).

Midway in the Memoirs *a second preface of forty-one pages is inserted; once again the narrator defends his prophecies and identifies himself with great men of history, Socrates, Aristotle, Caesar, and Cicero, who presumably also communed with genii. Patently foolish though these remarks be, they emphasize the need for eighteenth-century writers to justify what they put on paper by claiming that their work was authentic, true, accountable. After this second preface Madden launches fresh attacks against the Jesuits and the Church, pausing intermittently for descriptions of French customs and for discussions of astronomy between an English envoy and the Turkish emperor. In these latter interviews Madden exhibits a fascination with the question of life on other planets. Late in the book a prophecy is made that the ten lost tribes of Israel will be rediscovered in the twentieth century, that they will "depart from the four winds under heaven and be gather'd unto the brethren of the dispersion at Jerusalem" (487), one of the few attempts at actual prophecy in the* Memoirs *and the one that has proved true. On page 505 begins yet another preface in which Madden argues once again for the authenticity of his book.* Memoirs *ends with a plea for political freedom, for scientific research, and especially for renewed efforts to convert Catholics from their evil ways.*

This long, disconnected, obsessive book reveals less of an eighteenth-century view of what the future held in store for England than it does of a particular man's fears and interests. Madden anticipates another eccentric writer, Thomas Amory, whose John Buncle, *a curious*

8

INTRODUCTION

mixture of pedantry and humor, reveals the temper of an unusual mind at the midpoint of the eighteenth century.

Malcolm J. Bosse

MEMOIRS

OF THE

Twentieth Century.

VOL. I.

MEMOIRS

OF THE
Twentieth Century.

Being Original LETTERS of STATE,
under *GEORGE* the Sixth:

Relating to the moſt Important Events in *Great-
Britain* and *Europe*, as to CHURCH and STATE,
ARTS and SCIENCES, TRADE, TAXES, and TREA-
TIES, PEACE, and WAR:
And Characters of the Greateſt PERSONS of thoſe Times;
From the Middle of the Eighteenth, to the End of the Twentieth
CENTURY, and the WORLD.

Received and Revealed in the Year 1728;

And now Publiſhed, for the Inſtruction of all Eminent
Stateſmen, Churchmen, Patriots, Politicians, Projectors,
Papiſts, and Proteſtants.

In SIX VOLUMES.

VOL. I.

Μάντις ἄριστος ὅστις εἰκάζει καλῶς.   Eurip.

Bon Dieu! que n'avons nous point veu reüſſir des conjectures de ce temps
là comme ſi c'euſſent eſlé autant de Propheties?
La Mothe Le Vayer Diſcourſe de l'Hiſtoire. Tom. 1. p. 267.

Hoc apud nos quoque nuper ratio ad certum produxit. Veniet tempus,
quo iſta quæ nunc latent, in lucem dies extrahat, & longioris ævi dili-
gentia. Ad inquiſitionem tantorum ætas una non ſufficit, ut tota cœlo
vacet. Itaque per ſucceſſiones iſta longas explicabuntur. Veniet tempus, quo poſteri noſtri tam aperta nos neſciſſe mirentur, non licet ſtare
cœleſtibus, nec averti: Prodeunt omnia; ut ſemel miſſa ſunt, vadunt.
Idem erit illis curſus, qui ſui finis. Opus hoc æternum irrevocabiles
habet motus. *Senecæ Nat. Quæſt.* lib. 7. cap. 25.

LONDON:

Printed for Meſſieurs OSBORN and LONGMAN, DAVIS, and BATLEY,
in *Pater-noſter-Row*; STRAHAN, and CLARKE, in *Cornhill*;
RIVINGTON, ROBINSON, ASTLEY, and AUSTEN, in *St. Paul's
Church-Yard*; GOSLING, in *Fleetſtreet*; NOURSE, by *Temple-Bar*;
PREVOST, and MILLAR, in the *Strand*; PARKER, in *Pall-Mall*;
JOLLIFFE, by *St. James's*; BRINDLEY, SHROPSHIRE, and SMITH,
in *Bondſtreet*; and GOUGE, and STAGG, in *Weſtminſter-Hall.* 1733.

To His Royal Highness

FREDERICK LEWIS,

Prince of Wales, *and Earl of* Chester, *Electoral Prince of* Brunswick Lunenburg, *Duke of* Cornwall *and* Rothsay, *Duke of* Edinburgh, *Marquiss of the Isle of* Ely, *Earl of* Eltham, *Viscount of* Launceston, *Baron of* Snaudon *and of* Renfrew, *Lord of the Isles, and Steward of* Scotland, *and Knight of the Most Noble Order of the Garter.*

May it please your Royal Highness,

IT *would be highly proper even in a Stranger to Dedicate a Work, where the Growth of the Protestant Interest in* Europe, *and the Happiness deriv'd to these Nations from your Royal House do so often occur, to that Prince who will one Day wear the Title of the* Defender of our Faith, *as well as prove the Ornament of that Crown he is to inherit; and that Succession of our Princes, which he is e-*

A   *qually*

qually born to perpetuate and adorn. But in one that has so long liv'd under, so often admir'd and experienc'd the happy Influence of that Conſtellation of Virtues, (if I may so ſpeak) which exalts you as much above other Princes, as your Birth does above other Men, it would be equally inſenſible and ungrateful to have applied to any other Patron.

It is to be fear'd indeed, that the Work which I have the Honour to preſent to You, muſt ſeem leſs agreeable to your Royal Highneſs, who so frequently converſe with the great Genius's of Greece and Rome ; to You, Sir, who do not only ſteal many early Hours from the Pleaſures of the Court, to give to their Labours, but whoſe conſtant Practice it has been, like Francis the Firſt, to ſpend ſome time every Night before you Sleep, in attending to a Gentleman, whoſe Office it is to read them to you then for your Amuſement.

But, as I have long obſerv'd, the Candour of excuſing any unavoidable Errors is more a-greeable both to your natural Temper and your ſettled Judgment, than the ſeverer Delicacy of cenſuring them ; so I muſt own I have with ſome Pleaſure taken hold of this Opportunity of giving vent to the ſtrongeſt Paſſion of my Heart, that Veneration or Admiration
rather

rather of your Royal Highness, which my Personal Knowledge of your Heroick Qualities, have imprest in the most indelible manner on my Soul.

Possibly I had been less liable to Censure, if I could have contented my self with paying You in private the secret Homage of my Heart, without giving any publick Testimony of that infinite Regard which I pretend to bear You.

Professions of this kind from a Subject to a Prince seem generally too Interested, to be very Sincere; and we may say of most of them, as well as of the false Patriot's Love for his Country, that, like some matrimonial Smithfield Bargains, tho' much Affection is pretended, there is no more meant by it, than a good Settlement for one's Family.

Nay in this case, the very Tribute of our Praise which we pay to such exalted Benefactors, is seldom taken by the World as current Payment, but is suspected to be mixt up with the basest Alloy. For Praise is so generally the common Incense offer'd up by the Idolaters of Power, that many Men are from the same Principle grown as perfect Infidels in matters of Panegyrick, as some pretend to be in Religion; who because they see so many false

Gods

Gods *fet up for the publick Worfhip of the World, and ador'd with fo much outward Profeffion of Zeal and Ardour ; conclude, that all is but Mummery and Hypocrify, that is paid even to the true One.*

But if the Conduct of my Life cannot fecure me from an Impeachment of this fort, your Royal Highnefs's uncontefted Virtues fo univerfally acknowledg'd by all, will furely ftand as the ftrongeft Proof, that the higheft Profeffions of Veneration and Gratitude to fuch a Prince, may well be confiftent with Sincerity of Heart, and unfufpected of the little Arts of fawning Sycophants.

And indeed, one may as well charge a Man with Hyprocrify, for profeffing the Religion of his Country, as tax him with Flattery who owns himfelf an Admirer of your Royal Highnefs. For certainly as the one is as univerfally given into as the other by all our People; if it be Flattery, it is the Flattery of a Nation, and fhould no more be objected to a particular Perfon, than the Anglicifms of our common Speech, fince 'tis the Language of the Country, and in the Mouths of all.

For who is there, Sir, in the moft diftant Corner of thefe Nations, that is fo infenfible

of

of his own, or the general Happiness, as not to regard you with the sincerest Love, when you are only considered as the Heir apparent of the best Man and Woman, the best King and Queen, that ever adorn'd a Family, or blest a Nation: As their Son, who have so frequently given us the most delightful Prospect this World can afford, the Joy of seeing that infinite Desire of doing Good, which has so remarkably distinguish'd their Lives, join'd to as unlimited a Power of exercising it, by contriving for the Happiness and relieving the Miseries of Thousands: As their Son, I say, who have by so many Proofs, taught their Subjects no longer to consider a numerous Family as an intolerable Burthen, while they see such repeated Instances of their Solicitude to lighten it by particular Bounties, so many Laws to provide in general, for the Ease and Maintenance of the poorest of their Subjects, as well as such a parental Tenderness for every Calamity that befalls the greatest of them.

Your Royal Highness appears in a most amiable view, even to every common Eye, that regards you merely as a Descendant from such Princes, who have made the Happiness of their People the solid Basis of their Throne; who have govern'd us so, as to be Examples to all

good

good, and Reproaches to all bad Rulers, and in a Word, whose Love of Justice, and Benignity of Spirit, whose natural Goodness of Heart, and hereditary Hatred of Oppression, have secur'd the same Blessings to their Subjects who live under a despotical Government, which we enjoy from them under a free One.

But how infinitely dearer, Sir, must you be to those who are inform'd of your amiable Character from others, or are so happy to observe you at a nearer Distance, and are as it were grown familiarly acquainted with that Complacency of Manners, that Candour and Openness of Soul, that winning Condescension, that fearless Courage, that Elevation of Mind, and Generosity of Heart, join'd with that filial Piety and Sweetness of Temper, which have made you, like Titus, *the Delight of Humankind.*

With what Pleasure to my self, with what Joy to others, have I been able to produce a thousand instances of this Nature, and convinc'd the most Incredulous, that tho' you promis'd such prodigious things in your Youth, as would have bankrupt the Virtue of any other Prince to have made good; yet your Reputation, how glorious soever then, like the dawning of the Morning, was but the glimmering of

that Day, which is now haſt'ning to its Meri-
dian height of Splendour.

    'Tis *the peculiar Happineſs of your Royal*
Highneſs's Character, that there is nothing ne-
ceſſary to be concealed in it ; and that, tho'
there are few Princes, who muſt not have a
Veil thrown over one half of theirs, in order to
commend the other, who muſt not, like Hanni-
bal, *be drawn in Profil to cover their blind*
ſide, there are no Deformities, or accidental
Blemiſhes that need to be diſguis'd in Yours.
But if there were, your Royal Highneſs is ſo
entirely in the Poſſeſſion of the Eſteem of Men,
that your very Imperfections would appear
not only pardonable, but even amiable ; and
indeed, as to behold You is ſufficient to make
You lov'd, ſo to know You perfectly is the ſu-
reſt Method to make You admir'd.

    And to ſpeak the Truth, in what other Lights
can we regard a Prince, who at an Age when
others ſeem but to enter upon Life, has ſo happi-
ly emulated his Royal Father, as to have done
more generous, more beneficent Actions, than
he has liv'd Days; nay, more than would ad-
orn the Annals of the longeſt Reigns? But I
forget, that it is not allowable for me even to
give the leaſt hint to others, of thoſe ſecret De-
poſitories of your extenſive Charities in this

*World, which are entirely paid to him, who
only can and will reward them openly in the
next.*

*I shall therefore stop my Pen, — nor had
I indulg'd it so far, had I consider'd how greatly what I have already said might offend that
Modesty, with which you conceal the best A-
ctions with the same Care that others endeavour to hide their worst ; or to express the
noblest Quality (which to my shame I recol-
lect too late) in the meanest Poetry,*

> 'Tis thy peculiar Grace, Great Prince, 'tis thine,
> Like rising Suns to blush because you shine!

*I shall therefore turn the poor imperfect
Tribute of my Praise, into what will become
me more, my sincere Prayers for you; that
you may so go on to copy all the Virtues of that
best of Men and Princes, your Royal Father,
that when worn with Cares and Years, God
shall call him from that Crown he now adorns,
to an eternal one, You may so fill his place,
and so become in his stead a Father to your
People, as to make his glorious Memory neither reproachful to You, nor too often honour'd
with the Tears of your Subjects.*

*May You then reap the happy Fruits of all
your Royal Virtues and his Majesty's prudent
Coun-*

Counfels and perpetual Labours for the general good of his Kingdoms, and may they both concur to make us the happieſt of Nations, and the beſt of Subjects under a race of Princes, againſt whom the little Clamours and Arts of Faction at Home, will be as impotent and contemptible, as the inveterate Malice of Rome, and the Enemies of our Peace Abroad.

In thoſe Halcyon Days may God fo bleſs your Reign as to give you no other object of your Cares, but to preſerve to us thoſe Bleſſings of Unity and Concord (the Seeds whereof are now fo happily fown and growing up in our Land) and to encourage the Improvement of the riſing Arts, and patronize the learned Sciences, till they gain new Life among us, and grow in proportion cultivated as our Manufactures, and extended as our Trade. In a word, may the Happineſs of your People be then fo univerſal and compleat, that your charitable and generous Spirit may fearch with equal Difficulty for diſtreſſed Families to relieve, as for Enemies to convert or pardon; and to fum up all, may you then fo fecond the preſent pious Cares of your Royal Parents in combating the Vice and abandon'd Wickedneſs of a degenerate Age, that your Piety may ſhield us from the Vengeance of Heaven, if ever our Virtue

and

and Religion should sink to a lower Ebb than they are fallen to at present.

And thus in Virgil's *noble Prayer for young* Augustus, *I commit your Royal Highness to the Protection of the Almighty.*

Hunc faltem everfo Juvenem fuccurrere feclo,
Ne, Superi, prohibete.

I am with the utmost Submission,

Your ROYAL HIGHNESS's

January
25, 1731,

Most Obedient

Most Devoted

Humble Servant

A MO-

A Modest

PREFACE

Containing

Many Words to the Wife.

BEING about to deliver to the learned World in thefe Letters, one of
the nobleft Prefents that ever was
made to it, I muft own, I have been as
much perplex'd how to introduce them
properly, by a *Preface* worthy of them, as
Cervantes himfelf, when he fell on that which
ftands before his inimitable *Don Quixote*, or
as *Thuanus* was how to begin the firft Sen-
tence of his Hiftory, which we are told,
coft him fo many painful Hours, before he
could fettle it to his Mind.

I queftion if *Malherb* who fpent a Quire
of Paper, in finifhing his Simile of *Phillis*'s
gathering Flowers in a Garden ; or the illuftrious *Balzac* who us'd to take a Week to
write a Letter in, for fear of the *French* Cri-
ticks ; ever toil'd more than I have done,
to give full Satisfaction in this Introductory
Dif-

Difcourfe, to the profound Readers and
Judges of thefe Times, who have the Glory
and Advantage of being Witneffes to the
birth of this admirable Production.

For, alas! People are fo capricious, that
as they often take good or ill Impreffions
of others at firft fight, fo they will frequently reject the moft excellent Piece without
looking into it, if the Preface be difagreea-
ble to them. If therefore, I fhould ftum-
ble in the Threfhold, and introduce this
Work as injudicioufly as *Ovid* is faid to have
done moft of his, the confequences may be
very untoward; and as I write this poor
Prologue, without the leaft Affiftance from
that fuperior Nature, from whom I receiv'd
the Volumes it ufhers into the World, I
am much perplext left I fhould not appear
equal to the task.

I will not fay with the *Spaniard*, that I
would willingly write it with the Quill of a
Peacock, becaufe it has Eyes in it, but I would
rather exprefs my Zeal and Concern for
what I am here undertaking, in the words
an Author, (who will appear before the
Year 1739) paints the behaviour of a diftrefs'd Suppliant in, that addreffes to a
fevere and cruel Judge,

—— her

----- *her humble Prayer,*
And as a moving Preface dropt a Tear.

Be it as it will, I can only ufe my beft Endeavours to convince the World, what a Treafure I have here offer'd them, and if they will not regard my fervent defire to ferve them, but defpife the labour I've been at, in bringing thefe firft Fruits of a much greater Harveft to the publick ufe, I muft acquiefce, and be content with the Honour and Misfortune, of being the firft among Hiftorians (if a mere Publifher of Memoirs may deferve that Name) who leaving the beaten Tracts of writing with Malice or Flattery, the accounts of paft Actions and Times, have dar'd to enter by the help of an infallible Guide, into the dark Caverns of Futurity, and difcover the Secrets of Ages yet to come.

I am fenfible that all extraordinary Difcoveries in their firft Propofal, are lightly regarded and hardly credited, and I am prepared for it; yet, if Men will but be prevail'd upon to confider, of what uncommon ufe thefe may be, I hope I fhall be able to fay enough in their behalf, to procure them at leaft a candid Reception, if not the moft generous Welcome.   I

I expect this the rather, becaufe I freely confefs, that what I now publifh, is but introductory to many other Volumes, fo copious and full of matter, that they will almoft deferve the name of the *Hiftory of the* XXth *Century*; and which I hope Perfons of Tafte and Judgment, will therefore receive with all that Regard, not to fay Refpect and Veneration, fo prodigious a Work will appear entitled to.

Nor fhall any flight Difappointments herein difcourage me from Printing them; for how ungratefully foever the prefent Age, thro' Blindnefs or Envy may receive thefe vaft Lights; yet, I fhall be fufficiently comforted with the Confcioufnefs, that my declaring the future Births of fuch great Events, will be regarded by the coming Ages, as my having in fome meafure fown the Seed of them, in the Bofom of a well cultivated, tho' an unthankful Soil : Befides, at the worft, I fhall be as well treated by the World, as thofe exalted Spirits were, who difcover'd the *Antipodes*, the Circulation of the Blood, the ufe of Telefcopes and Barometers, of Printing and Sailing, the Loadftone and the *Indies*, who were fo much defpis'd at firft, tho' fo highly honour'd and regarded now. It

It is true as a mere Publifher, (which I only fet up for) it may feem too arrogant, to rank my felf with fuch illuftrious Company ; but if it is confider'd, that without my generous Benevolence to Mankind, thefe mighty Treafures and Difcoveries I beftow on them, had never feen the Light, and that I have here convey'd to them the great Secrets of Futurity, in fo plain and open a manner, that this Age may fay, (tho' contrary to the receiv'd Axiom of the Schools) *de futuro contingenti eft quoad nos determinata veritas*, I hope, I fhall not appear too affuming. Nay, I have yet the merit of infinite Toil to plead, fince I can fairly aver, that the tranflating this Work, from the *Englifh* it was writ in, (*viz.* the *Englifh* that will be fpoke in the XXth *Century*) was a task fo painful and difficult, that no unenlighten'd Mind could have perform'd, and which even I my felf had mifcarried in, without the fuperior affiftance that my good Angel afforded me.

A Task fo laborious! that befides this being the fecond Time of my Writing to the Publick, * which according to Cardinal *Be-*

* See my Works, three Volumes in *Quarto*, Printed for Mr. *Lintot*, 1720. *N. B.* There are fome fets in Royal Paper for the Curious.

rule's

rule's Opinion, (who thought we fhould i-
mitate our Saviour, who is never faid to
have writ but once before, and once after
his anfwer to the *Jews*, who brought the
Adulterefs before him) is full enough for
any good Chriftian; tho' I were more fecure of receiving all poffible Favour and
Honour for my Toils than I am, yet I
doubt whether I fhall ever venture on a
third Sally, in any other Performance, tho'
my Modefty and Indolence fhould occafion
ever fo much Grief to Pofterity.

As to this particular Work, I muft indeed
be greatly difcourag'd by the World, if I fupprefs the Sequel of it, which I propofe by
proper intervals to communicate to them,
tho' I will not anfwer, how far their receiving this Book I now offer them, with Contempt and Difregard, may make me ufe the
fame Haughtinefs the facred *Sibyl* did to
Tarquinius Superbus, and after burning all
the remaining parts which I defign'd for
them, make them pay as high a price for
this Volume, as on a contrary demeanour
I defign'd to allow them the whole for.

But as I flatter my felf, fuch Fears are
very groundlefs, I fhall fay the lefs on that
Subject. I fhall rather hope, as thefe Papers
are

3

are defign'd to enlighten the Nations of the Earth, they will be treated with the utmoft Admiration and Reverence; nor need I from any unjuft Imagination of their ill reception, threaten the World, as *Apollo* did on the ill Fortune of his unhappy *Phaethon*, to leave it hereafter in eternal Darknefs, as a juft mark of my Refentment, fince I am perfuaded all that have Eyes will fee and applaud the Light I am lending to them. Naturalifts tell us, that fetting up a burning Torch in fenny or marfhy Grounds, is a fure Method to fhut up the clamorous Throats, and filence the Croaking of Frogs; and I hope the amazing Splendour and Brightnefs of this Work, will have the fame happy effect on my envious Maligners, and quiet the noify Tongues of dull Objectors.

Not that I expect to have it treated at firft Sight, as well as it deferves; for as all who fet up for extraordinary Difcoveries that are reveal'd to them, ought to be receiv'd with Diffidence, and hearken'd to with Caution, I make no doubt, but many People may be ready enough to fufpect me as an Impoftor, in thefe I am communicating to them. And I almoft imagine my felf engag'd, with one of my Readers

B of

of this Character, in such a Dialogue as *Ho-race* represents between *Ulysses* and *Tiresias*, who pretended to reveal Things to come.

Num furis ? an prudens ludis me obscura ca-nendo ?
O Laertiade, quicquid dicam, aut erit, aut non :
Divinare etenim magnus mihi donat Apollo.
Quid tamen ista velit sibi Fabula, si licet, ede.

But as I am determined to give such Rea-ders and all Men, so full, and fair, and con-vincing an Account of my self and that ce-lestial Spirit I receiv'd these Papers from, and to answer all Objections so entirely, as to put Ignorance, and even Malice it self to Silence: I am confident, the ingenuous and candid part of the World, will soon throw off such mean narrow spirited Suspicions, as unjust and ungenerous. I am willing the important matters reveal'd to me, may stand as publick and severe a Trial, as those of St. *Bridget* did before the Council, and have the Truth fully examin'd and search'd into, e-ven by the strict Rules Chancellour *Gerson* prescribes for hers and all such Examinati-ons, in his Treatise *de Probatione Spirituum*, where he most gravely and judiciously ad-vises, that all Persons (Layman, Nun, Monk

or

or Friar) who pretend to Revelations of any kind, fhould give a fatisfactory Account, 1*ft*, From whence it is. 2*dly*, What it is. 3*dly*, Why it is. 4*thly*, To whom it is. 5*thly*, How it is, and 6*thly*, Whence, or from what place it is reveal'd.

To this end therefore, and that the Reader, my dear and kind and learned Reader, may the better underftand the Nature and Value of the Prefent which I make him; I fhall obferve the following Method: *Firft*, I fhall give fome Account, both of my felf and my good Genius, from whom I receiv'd it. 2*dly*, I fhall mention the Reafons of my publifhing it, and alfo my Care and Conduct about it. 3*dly*, I fhall anfwer all kind of Objections, that are or can be made, againft this wonderful Treafure I am putting into their Hands, and *laftly*, I fhall give my Friends, (my great, wife and numerous Friends) the learned World, (the good, judicious and learned World) and Pofterity, (our noble and excellent Pofterity worthy of their admirable Anceftors) fome Cautions about it, and fo leave it to its Fate.

As to the firft point then, I muft own that I am defcended in a direct Line by the Mother's fide, from a Son of that famous

Count

Count *Gabalis*, in the 17th *Century*, whofe Hiftory is in every ones Hands, and whofe Wife, as all true Adepts know, had Carnal Knowledge of, and was Impregnated by a certain invifible *Dæmon*, that call'd himfelf *Ariel.* I hope as this extraordinary particularity was the Cafe of *Plato, Appollonius Tyanæus,* the Earl of *Poitiers,* and other great Perfonages; and as the Marefchal *de Baſſompiere* in his Memoirs, is fo candid as to confefs it alfo, of one of the Heads of his Family; it will not be confider'd as infolent or conceited in me, that I have own'd this Circumftance, efpecially fince in all Probability, 'tis not a little owing to it, that I am able to enrich the World at prefent, with thefe Works, worthy of fo celeftial an Origin.

I was born alfo under the moft fortunate of all Planets, and to make my Nativity ftill more Happy, in one of the *Ember*-Weeks, and with a Cawl, or certain Membrane about my Head; both which as the learned Jefuit *Thyræus,* (an Order I particularly Reverence) obferves, in his Tract * *de apparitione Spirituum,* are Circumftances, that render

---

* Cap. 14. Num. 346.

such

such Children more likely than others, to gain the Acquaintance and Familiarity of the *Genii* defign'd for their Conduct. Nay, I was born under that Afpect of the Heavenly Bodies, which *Ptolemy* in his 4*th* Book of his *Quadripartite*, and 13*th* Chapter, affures us, generally confers this ineftimable Privilege, having had the Moon, that great *Domina humidorum*, in Conjunction with *Sagittary*, Lady of my Actions, not to mention, left it fhould look too like Vanity, fome other as favourable, tho' lefs credible Circumftances.

But to pafs to more material particulars of my Hiftory: I came into the World Heir to a good Family and Fortune, as well as a deal of Pride and Ambition, to diftinguifh my felf from the common Herd of Mankind. In order therefore, to gratifie this reigning Paffion, after quitting the Univerfity, and determining any Profeffion to be below my regard, both as taking too much Time, Thought and Reading to mafter, and a deal of mean Art, or good Money to fucceed in ; I refolv'd as a fhorter way, to raife my felf above the thoughtlefs Crowd of Gentlemen, to fpend one third of my Fortune in Travelling, and feeing and ob-

B 3   ferving

ferving fomething more, than my Country-
Seat and Neighbours in Summer, and *London* in the Winter, could furnifh me with.
This I did for three Years, and came Home
as perfectly improv'd as any fine Gentleman of
my Time in an utter Contempt of *Tramon-
tane* Barbarity, an abfolute Averfion for my
own People, Climate and Country, and a
thorough Infight into all the little learned
Cant of Priefts and Religions of all kinds.

On thefe deep laid Foundations, I com-
menc'd a fage Politician and Patriot: I bought
a Seat in Parliament at a fair Purchafe, for
a good deal of Beef and Ale for the Mob,
and a round Sum of Money to the worthy
Electors, and determin'd to grow great by
Voting according to my Confcience, and as
the beft Arguments fhould be offer'd me in
Favour of thofe two dangerous Monofyllables, *Yea* and *No.*

Accordingly all the Time I fat there as
a *Senator,* I never gave a fingle Vote, without a fubftantial Reafon of one kind or another for it, and endeavour'd to think a certain great Patron (I had devoted my felf to)
in the Right, whatever fide of the Queftion
he took, and fhew'd a generous Violence
in fupporting all the Meafures he purfued,

as

as the beſt and wiſeſt in the World, and particularly while he diſtinguiſh'd himſelf as an
Enemy to the Miniſtry, whom we were to
overturn and ſucceed. But in ſpite of all
the fortunate Conſtellations I was born under, being entirely diſappointed in theſe glorious Hopes, it luckily happen'd my Patron
fell in with the Court-Party, and got a very
comfortable Poſt to live honeſt by ; and
as I found my ſelf, by the ſacred Ties of
Love to my Country and my Family,
oblig'd to turn with him ; I us'd my humble Endeavours to ſecond him, and to obtain ſome of thoſe many honourable Em-
ployments, with good Salaries for doing nothing, which I was aſſur'd by my great
Friends, I could not fail of.

To this end, I became as violent for the
Court, as ever I had been againſt it, and to
ingratiate my ſelf the more with the Miniſtry, I kept up an extravagant Table, and a
Crowd of humble Admirers of my Eloquence to eat at it, among whom I cenſur'd
our Oppoſers as Fools or Knaves, rail'd at the
Minority as Tools or Villains, and after con-
futing all their Arguments, to the Satisfaction of my Gueſts while they were eating,
crown'd my daily Victories, with drinking
Confuſions of all kinds.　　B 4　　On

On thefe excellent Foundations, I built up a World of Hopes, and afkt for every thing I knew I deferv'd, making a Confcience of aiming at any thing further, and was happy enough to receive many fair Promifes and good Looks, not only from my Patron, but my Patron's Patron's Patron, who was a very great Man indeed. I was trufted with feveral Secrets before they were in Print, and affur'd of fucceeding to many tolerable Places, before they were vacant ; and was fo much confider'd, that I never afkt for any thing, that I did not get a diftant Promife of, or a very civil Excufe for being refus'd it. This kept up my Spirits, and quickned my Zeal for feveral Seffions, till finding my Equipage and Table, my Elections and living like a Man of Confequence, had funk another third of my Eftate, I began to be fo importunate for fomething, as foon as I found I had little or nothing left, that tho' I was willing to take any Place during good Behaviour, which by a fair Computation I might have purchafed the yearly Value of in Land by half what I had fpent in the Service, yet I found my felf fo utterly unfecure of any thing but fincere Promifes, which I knew it difficult

to

to fubfift my Family on, that I defperately
broke with my Patron, and all my dear
Friends the Courtiers, and fet up once more
for a good Confcience, on the other fide.
But, alas! I foon found this was the worft
tim'd ftep I could have taken, for it both
ruin'd my Character with the World, and my
Tradefmen loft me my Election the next
Parliament; and in a Word, left me to
brood over my own Refentments, Difappointments and Defpair.

Under thefe unlucky Circumftances, the
Town not agreeing with my *Conftitution*,
I retir'd to the Country, to the Ruins of my
Eftate, of which I had fold two Thirds, to
pay off the Debts thefe Schemes in Politicks
had brought on me; and becaufe I could
not with Eafe look back on the World, I refolv'd to look forward, and confider what
might happen, fince I abhor'd to reflect on
what had.

The Truth is, my dear Reader, tho' I
blufh to tell it, my Difappointments and Difcontents wrought fo violently on my Pride
and Choler, which were the two chief Ingre-
dients in my little carnal Tabernacle, that
renouncing all my former Engagements in
Favour of our civil and religious Rights, as
Britons

Britons and Proteſtants, I gave my ſelf up Body and Soul, to a little ſorry melancholy Faction, who only ſubſiſt themſelves, like the *Cevennes* in *Languedock,* on a ſeditious Sermon now and then, and a few comfortable Viſions, Rumours and Hopes, of gratifying their private Reſentments at the price of the publick Ruine.

Indeed I muſt own, I had ſome Scruples of Conſcience at firſt, on this extraordinary Converſion that was wrought in me; but when I reflected on the Expences I had been at, to obtain Promiſes that were forgotten, and ſecure Places I now ſaw poſſeſt by others; when I compar'd the Ruins of my Fortune, with my old Rent-Rolls, my paſt Debtors with my preſent Creditors, and my former Hopes with my preſent Deſpair; I at once broke thro' all my Oaths of *Allegiance,* and thought my Revolt the leſs diſhonourable, ſince I had taken them but about ſeven or eight Times, and I ſaw ſeveral Men of Honour, engag'd in this Faction againſt the Government, who had taken them on at leaſt twenty different Occaſions.

In a Word, my Reſentment ſoon quieted my Reaſon, and I began to hope for a thouſand Scenes of Confuſion and Deſtruction to
my

my Country and the Royal Family, and to
fee their Labours to make us happy, luckily overturn'd by fome fortunate Calamities,
which might deftroy their Intereft with the
People. By fome fuch defirable Accident,
I flatter'd my felf, that by God's Bleffing on
our honeft Endeavours, in bringing it about
and improving it, we might all mend our
Circumftances, and that poffibly for
my part, I might thus recover my E-
ftate, from the Rogue who bought it, by
turning *Papift* in fome glorious Revolution
in the *Chevalier*'s Favour.

To indulge my Spleen and Melancholy
the more, I gave my felf up Night and
Day to reading for feveral Years: And becaufe I defpis'd the little narrow beaten
Paths of common Scholars, I ftudied all hidden Sciences, from Magick to the *Jewifh
Cabala* and the Philofopher's Stone, and
particularly turn'd my felf to Aftrology
with vaft Application, in hopes to find fome
propitious Influence from the Heavens, to
favour thefe reafonable Expectations, fince
I faw with Sorrow there was little to be
hop'd for from the Earth.

I made a great Progrefs, efpecially in
this laft noble Science, and flatter'd my felf,
that

that I had found out fome favourable Conjunctions in the Planets above, that might
be too ftrong for all the united Interefts of
the beft Man and Prince and the happieft
People among the Nations below.   When
behold one Night, which I fhall never forget, and *Great Britain* muft ever remember
with Joy, (it was on the 20*th* of *January*,
1728,) as I lay in my Bed, agreeably footh-
ing my Spleen, with thefe pleafing Profpects
I had been contemplating in the Stars;   I
was furpriz'd to fee my Door which was
faft lock'd, and my Curtains which were
clofe drawn, opening fuddenly of themfelves, and a great Light filling my Chamber, in the midft of which I faw a beautiful Appearance of fomething like what we
ufually imagine Angels to be.

   I began to fancy my felf in the famous
Van Helmont's Condition, who fays, * he
once plainly faw his Soul in an hu man Shape,
but, as he modeftly fpeaks, without diftin-
ction of Sex; or like that *Pifander*, who, as
a certain *Greek* Author tells us, was afraid
of meeting his own Soul, which he apprehended would appear to him feparated from

* Chap. I. p. 9.

his

hisBody, and play him a fcurvy Trick. But
I had not time enough for many Reflections,
for while I lay filent with Wonder and
Surprize, he inftantly rais'd me up by the
Hand, told me he was my good *Genius,* and
was come to fhew me nobler Profpects, that
fhould be deriv'd to me and my Family, as
well as my Country, from the prefent Royal
Line and their Pofterity, than thofe I was
drawing from my miftaken Principles in Political Aftrology. He affur'd me, if I would
be directed by him, he would give me fufficient Lights to convince me, that there never could be a greater Blefling beftowed on
a Nation, than thefe Kingdoms receiv'd when
the Royal Line of *Hannover,* was by the Favour of Heaven plac'd on the Throne, to be
the Source of a long Series of Profperity,
Wealth, Peace and Glory to us, if we would
but be content to enjoy it with common
Senfe and Gratitude. He added much more
on this Head, and concluded with promifing
to keep up a conftant Communication and
Correfpondence with me; and to give me at
once fome little Intelligence of the great E-
vents that would happen under their glorious
Goverment, not only to my Country but even
my ownHoufe andDefcendants, he made me

a

a prefent of feveral large Volumes of thefe
Letters, which, he affur'd me, would be writ
by or to my Great Great Great Great Great
Grandfon, who would be chief Minifter in
the End of the Twentieth Century, and to
deal plainly with me, as far as he could guefs,
in the laft days of the World.

The Joy! the Surprize! the Tranfport!
thefe Words gave me, is not to be expreft:
And as *Kircher* told *Schottus* *, he was cur'd
of a deadly Difeafe, by dreaming he was
madePope, and receiv'd the Congratulations
of all Kings and Nations, while he iffued
out Bulls and Decrees for new Laws, new
Churches, new Saints, and new Colleges, with
vaft Joy, and awaken'd after a long and
happy Reign perfectly recover'd; fo I found
in an inftant all my Difcontents in Politicks
vanifh'd and remov'd by thefe real Vifions,
my good Genius had communicated to
me. I accordingly receiv'd this prefent,
as an immediate Bleffing from Heaven, and
after affuring him in the moft folemn manner how fincerely I renounced my former
Principles, I enter'd into a long Dialogue
with him, both as to the prefent and future

* *Gafpar Schotti Phyfica Curiofia,* Lib.. 30.

ftate

ſtate of Things, and learnt from him Secrets as important as the Ruine or Safety of
Crowns and Empires can make them, and
by the Communication of which, to the
chief Miniſters of ſuch Princes as can gain
my Eſteem, and particularly of my own,
he aſſur'd me, I might with good Huſban-
dry, raiſe a Fortune whereon to ſubſiſt my
Family with Honour and Affluence, till my
Deſcendant ſhould be Prime Miniſter under
George the VI.   Every one may imagine,
how eagerly I liſtned to all this, and how
eaſily a Mind thus illuminated, with Views
of ſo glorious a Change, in my own and my
Family's future Circumſtances, would lay
aſide its former Principles and Prejudices, as
I immediately did, with a thouſand Thanks
to my good Genius, for all his Favours, and
as many Entreaties for his future Correſpondence, which both on my own Account,
(as he was pleas'd to expreſs himſelf) and
my Relation to Count *Gabalis*, he kindly
promiſs'd, and has ever ſince often made
me happy in.

　　He had no ſooner left me, than I began
to read over the Volumes he had given me,
with all the Delight which I hope the World
will receive from that part of them, which

with-

with his Confent and Affiftance, and by the Advice of my learned and ingeniousFriends, I have refolv'd to communicate to them, as a moft ineftimable Treafure. I have made no other Change or Alterations in them, than the tranflating them into the *Englifh* of thefe illiterate Times oblig'd me to, except where the Secrets of crown'd Heads and prime Minifters, or the good or ill Conduct of the Friends or Enemies of my Country and fome great People at home, made it neceffary to leave out either whole Letters or particular Paragraphs, which fhou'd be referv'd in Secret, for the Ufe and Service of the Crown and my own Family, and not expos'd to publick view.

And thus having given my dear Reader, as full an Account as I judg'd proper, both of my felf and my good *Genius,* and the Prefent he made me, (for of my conftant Correfpondence fince with him, I fhall fay nothing here) I fhall now proceed, to mention my Reafons for publifhing this Work, and alfo my Care and Conduct about it.

And the firft I fhall affign is, that I really believ'd I fhould do an Injury to the World, to the Commonwealth of Learning, and above all to my Country, if being thus
en-

enlighten'd, and having such wonderful Discoveries revealed and intrusted to me, I did not give them some Foretast of these surprising Scenes, which Fate is to open to Mankind, in future Ages.

Nor was this all, for to say the Truth, when I saw evidently in these Papers, that the World and my Descendant's Ministry would end together; I was the more willing to have my Fame and his laid open to the present Age, since it was impossible for future Times to do us Justice, by assigning us that shining place in History, which Printing these Volumes will so fully entitle us to. Those great Persons, whose Writings or Actions distinguish'd them so much in former Ages, have had a large recompence made them, by the Honour and Applause that has long been heap'd on them; but as my Fame had been entirely conceal'd, and his reduc'd to take up with the short-liv'd Applause of a few Years, in his old Age, the Dregs of Life, and the last Moments of the World, I resolv'd to be before-hand with the Glory of my self and Family, and to enjoy some part of our Reputation before we had earn'd it. And while I make this sincere Confession, let me take this opportu-

nity

nity, to exhort thofe few great Spirits, who are thirfting after Glory, to redouble their Speed to perpetuate their Fame, and do greater and more glorious Things than have yet been attempted ; that thereby they may the fooner obtain that reward of their Merit, and raife thofe Monuments to their Memories, which at beft they fee, muft fo fuddenly perifh in the common Ruine, and be loft for ever in the general Deftruction of all Things.

Another Motive I had for making thefe Papers publick was, that by magnifying the Glory of fucceeding Minifters, I might fink and leffen the Reputation of thofe, that at prefent fit at the Helm, fince they have been fo regardlefs of all true Merit, as to do little or nothing for me or my Family. I faw it in vain to attempt their Ruin by downright Railing, throwing Dirt at random, and calling them at all Adventures Rogues and Knaves in Print; for they have fo deluded the People, by the curfed Succefs of their Adminiftration, that they will not liften any longer to general Declamations, to witty Infinuations or the boldeft Satyrs, without fome few real Facts to vouch them, and prove they are well grounded. Now as

I found

I found this an insuperable difficulty, since they manage with such vile Art, as to keep all Proofs of that sort from our Knowledge, so I knew no better method to vilify their measures, and serve his *Majesty* and my *Country*, then shewing the World, that notwithstanding the popular Cry of the Prosperity of our Affairs, there will, some Ages hence, be much greater and more successful Ministers than they are, and who, by the by, may then remember to their Posterity, the little respect these Gentlemen pay one of their Ancestors now, whom (out of that Modesty so natural to all great Spirits) I shall not mention here.

Another reason, which, I must own, induced me to present the World with this Work, was, that the busy inquisitive Sages and Politicians of these times, may have some more Employment given to their restless Tempers. For as *Charles* II. by publickly setting up new Systems of *Philosophy*, diverted his unmanageable Subjects from disturbing the ancient Forms of Government, and by amusing them with searching into the Revolutions of the Heavens, kept them from contriving new ones upon Earth ; or (not to grudge the Reader another instance of equal

force)

force) as by settling our banish'd Felons in the new World, and employing them sufficiently there, we keep our selves pretty quiet at Home in the old one; so I hope that these ungovernable and satyrical Observers, who not content with censuring and decrying all that past in former Ages, turn themselves to ridiculing and contemning all that is done in this, may be kept from overturning the Peace of these our Days, by being employ'd on the Secrets of Times to come. Besides I find it is by no means sufficient, for the elevated *Genius's* of this Age, to know all that *may be known:* This is too easy a Conquest for their superior Strength, and they gloriously aim at being Masters of all that is *not to be known.* As I pay the highest Veneration to such exalted Spirits, I have done what Man could do, (aided by the Discoveries of my good Angel) to let them see all that is to be in Art or Nature, till the Dissolution of both, and have resolv'd to gratifie them with some considerable Hints of what will happen at the general Conflagration, when they, this Earth, and even Time, and all their learned (their exquisitely learned) Labours, shall be no more!

I am

I am fenfible, an Author fhould obferve as proper Seafons for his Productions, as the fkilful Hufbandman or Florift for their Seeds; and I am of Opinion, I could not have prefented this curious inquifitive Age, with a Work more admirably calculated, to amufe and employ their vaft Knowledge and deep Referches, and divert them from lefs ufeful, tho' more dangerous Enquiries, which they are of late fo profoundly taken up with.

In the laft place, my dear Reader, when I confider'd that the great *Auguftus*, as *Suetonius* tells us, neither neglected his own nor other Mens Dreams, concerning himfelf or his Affairs, and confequently whatever related to his Country, or the whole World which was his Empire ; * *Somnia neque fua neque aliena de fe negligebat* are the Hiftorian's Words when I read in the great *Artimedorus*, that it was the Cuftom of the Antients, that whatever any one had dreamt of the Publick, relating to the Commonwealth, he fhould publifh either by the Voice of the common Crier, or by a written Table fet up to the view of others; † *moris antiqui fuit, ut quicquid quifque de republica fomniaffet, illud vel Præconis voce, vel Pittacio, hoc*

---

* In Augufto, Cap. 91. † Lib. 1. Cp. 2.

eft,

eft, tabula quadam defcriptum indicaret, I thought it a criminal Action to conceal fuch important Difcoveries as had been intrufted to my Care.

Befides, how do I know, but the bringing *thefe* to Light, may in fome meafure be a means to preferve our Country from all the Confufion and Madnefs, which the reft of the World will be involv'd in; and continue us in that happy Situation, and that Spirit of improving our Laws, Arts and Manufactures, which I have fhewn we fhall enjoy in the following Centuries, when the other Kingdoms of the Earth are to labour, as it were, in actual Convulfions, and be jumbled together, like the Mountains and Plains of *Jamaica* in the dreadful Earthquake in 1692.

As to my Care and Conduct in this Edition, I fear indeed how great foever it has been, Men will be difpleafed with me, as having beftowed much lefs on it, than fo invaluable a Treafure will feem to have deferv'd. Some will cenfure me for having conceal'd and fupprefs'd many important Secrets, relating to our publick Affairs and Minifters, Peace and War, the Trade of the Nation, and the Conduct of the Throne; without confidering the dangerous Confequences,

quences, of making such matters publick, as well as the particular Interest I may have, to keep them by me in *petto*, till proper Conjunctures.

On the other hand, many great Men will blame me, as *Alexander* did *Ariftotle*, for communicating too many of such hidden Mysteries, such *Arcana imperii*, to the Knowledge of the Vulgar. For my part, I have acted with the utmost Caution in suppressing or publishing any Particulars, and as it is to be fear'd, if after all my Care this Book should grow too common and be in every one's Hand, it may be applied to ill purposes, by letting the meanest of the People see, *uti digerit omnia Calchas*, I have given order to print but fifty Copies, which I compute will answer the number of Persons in *Great Britain*, who are *Wife* and *Honeft enough* to be trufted with such a Jewel.

I have also gone further, and that Posterity may not be impos'd on, by any spurious Additions, Forgeries or Obliterations in this admirable Work, I have with great Labour number'd and reckon'd up the whole of what is in it, which is a safer and fairer Way than a Table of Contents, which our modern Publishers tack to their mangled Vo-

lumes.

lumes. I find therefore that there is in this Collection, (Publifh'd, and to be Publifh'd) 28,967 Sentences that have meaning in them, 1,232,356 Words, 2,125,245 Syllables, 6,293,376 Letters, and thro' the Roughnefs of our barbarous Tongue, but 2,992,644 Vowels, (exclufive of *y* and all Dipthongs) as any careful Reader may find, who will caft them up with equal Diligence.

Poffibly it may feem a little arrogant and conceited, that I fhould have taken. fuch Pains herein, but if we confider, that the *Turks* have done as much for their *Alcoran*, and that the learned *Rabbies* among the *Jews* value their *Talmud* fo highly, as to fay, that miftaking a Letter in it, is enough to deftroy the World; I hope, I may be indulg'd, if not applauded for my Care, in a Work in the *Englifh* Tongue, where it may happen that the Lofs a of Word in it, may be of vaft Damage to our native Country, which all Men among us are fo defirous to ferve.

And now, after fo candid an Account as I have laid before thee, one would think, my dear Reader, I might fhut up this Preface, and have nothing more to do, than receive the tributary Thanks and Homage

of

of Mankind, for fo glorious a Prefent as I here make them, for the common G ood; but alas! I find the envious World, has cut out a deal of other Work for me, and that I muſt anſwer a Crowd of malicious Obje-ctions, which my learned Friends aſſure me, are levell'd againſt this unparallel'd Per-formance, by thoſe who ſaw it in Manu-fcript.

But as this is PREFACE enough of Con-fcience for one Time, I muſt ſay with St. *Auſtin* when he us'd to cut his Sermons in-to two, *Parcite mihi fratres, non dicam vo-bis quod ſequitur* ; and beg the Reader to indulge me in a Liberty always allowed great Writers, of treading in unbeaten Paths, and for my Eaſe and his own, as well the Novelty and Boldneſs of the Stroke, to pardon me if, like the Adventure of the *Bear* and the *Fiddle,* I break off here a little abruptly, and (as I have reſolv'd for a *Coup d'Eclat* to make three PREFACES to this glorious Work) fend him for the Se-cond and Third to the Middle and End of this Volume.

M E-

MEMOIRS

OF THE

TWENTIETH CENTURY, &c.

To the Lord HIGH TREASURER, *&c.*

My Lord,   *Conſtantinople, Nov.* 3, 1997.

I HAVE, according to the Commands your Lordſhip honour'd me with by Captain *Milton,* by the way of *Vienna* in *September* laſt, ſo far preſs'd the Concluſion of the Treaty grounded on the new Stipulations, that I think it is as good as finiſhed, and that our Trade ſhall be as much favour'd here, as by his Majeſty's Authority and Influence and your Lordſhip's Care, it has been in all other parts of the World.

The

The only Difficulty that remains, proceeds from the 4*th* and 5*th* Articles, which the Grand Vifier feems to think too highly honourable for our Nation, and derogatory to his own, judging it hard that their Ships of War, fhould in their own Ports and Seas, ftrike their Flag to ours and falute them, (as by the 5*th* Article is provided) with double the number of Guns.

However, thefe Points are fo gently canvaft by them, that I fee evidently they defign not to infift on them, and I make account, we fhall in a little time mutually fign, and that our Cloath and Manufactures fhall hereafter have no unreafonable Duties impos'd on them, as thofe of other Nations have; who muft therefore vend theirs at great Difadvantages. I fhould be tempted to be exceeding vain on my happy Succefs herein, but that it is fo evident my carrying all my Points here, is owing to no Dexterity of mine, but to the Wifdom and Courage of his Majefty's Meafures, the Strength, Loyalty and Wealth of his Subjects, the Terror which his Fleet fpreads over the Ocean, and the Care and Policy of his Minifters, and above all your Lordfhip, who now fo happily prefide over them.

The

THE long Intimacy and Friendſhip you have honour'd me with, as well as the Relation I have to your Noble Family, will prevent any Suſpicion of Flattery, when I aver to your Lordſhip, that the News brought me by Mr. *Milton*, of your being declar'd Prime Miniſter and Treaſurer by his Majeſty in Council, was to me the moſt agreeable I have heard this twenty five Years that I have reſided here. At the ſame Time I can ſay with Truth, that the Satisfaction this gave me, took not its riſe from any private Views as to my own Intereſts, which I neither want nor deſire to encreaſe in the World, but from the aſſured Hope I have, that our native Country ſhall hereby be highly advantag'd.

It is a peculiar Felicity that attends your Lordſhip's Promotion; that it happens when our glorious *George* VI. hath by the Succeſs of his Arms oblig'd his Enemies to accept the Terms he was pleas'd to preſcribe them, and that after having humbled *France* ſo far, as to oblige her to give up all her Ports in the Channel, even *Dunkirk* and *Calais* it ſelf into our Hands, and taught all the Powers in *Europe* the Reſpect and almoſt Dependance they owe us; your ſacred Maſter's

fter's Cares and Yours, will now be almoſt
ſolely confin'd, to the keeping the general
Peace we are in with all Nations ſafe and
undiſturb'd, and to promote our Trade
wherever our Induſtry and Profit can extend
it.

But your Lordſhip is too uſefully employ'd with ſuch Cares, to liſten to my awk-
ward Compliments how ſincere ſoever, and
therefore I ſhall leave them ; and ſince you
are pleas'd to think I am capable of giving
you ſome Light into the State of Things
here, which by my long reſidence I muſt
have ſome tolerable Knowledge of, I ſhall
obey your Commands herein with the ſmall
Abilities I am Maſter of.

I ſhall not trouble your Lordſhip with any
hiſtorical Events relating to theſe People,
ſince the *Ottoman* Line was extinguiſhed in
Mahomet IX. and the *Tartar* Race ſucceeded.
This was many Centuries ſince foretold, as
well as the Decline of this great Empire, and
that a *Mahomet* would be the laſt of that
Family, as it has really happened. *Juxton,*
the laborious Writer of the 19*th Century,* has
given us ſo full a Detail of their Affairs, that
they are known to all the learned World as
well as your Lordſhip ; I ſhall therefore only
dwell

dwell on such Facts and Alterations as are
of a later Date, and confin'd within the
Year 1949 and this present Time, which are
worth your Curiosity; and which the *Memoirs* of my two Predecessors in this Post,
which have fallen into my Hands, and my
own Experience have given me a fuller Acquaintance with.

Your Lordship is no Stranger to the vast
Alterations which the coming in of the *Tartar* Line has produc'd, and above all in Matters of Religion. For as the *Mufties* and all
the Heads of their Clergy, have been still
the *Grand Seignior's* Countrymen, as fearing
to place natural *Turks* in so high a Trust,
the Zeal to the *Mahometan* Religion and
Discipline, has been thence greatly slacken'd,
both in their Priests and People, which was
anciently so hot and violent. By this means
there succeeded in its stead a dead Palsy in
their Faith, which has almost been destroy-
ed betwixt *Christianity* and *Deism*. It
is incredible, my Lord, what an Harvest
Christian Missionaries and *Jesuits* have reap'd
thereby among this People. For being dis-
guis'd as *Physicians, Mathematicians, Astrologers,* nay, as *Janizaries* and *Spahies,* as well
as under the appearances of all kinds of the
best

beſt ſorts of Trades, (and ſome of them e-
ven by the *Pope*'s Connivance circumciſed
and acting the part of *Turkiſh* Prieſts,) they
got ſo throughly both into the Knowledge
and Confidence of all Kinds and Ranks of
People here, and eſpecially the better ſort,
that under pretence of propoſing their own
Doubts, they ſoon overturn'd the eſtabliſh'd
Religion, in the Minds of all Perſons eminent for their Poſts or Learning.

They conceal'd the *Chriſtian* Truths at firſt
under the pretended Name of *Serabackzi* or
Enthuſiaſts, till at length their Doctrines got
Admiſſion into the *Seraglio*, by the means of
the *Renegedo Vizier Ibrahim*, in 1955 or
56, who they ſay, to make amends for his
Apoſtaſy, gave this Sect (whoſe Deſigns he
was not only fully acquainted with, but alſo conducted) all poſſible Countenance and
Encouragement. By his means it was, that
ſo many *Printing-Preſſes* were diſperſ'd thro'
the whole extent of the *Ottoman* Empire,
thereby ſupplanting and almoſt extirpating
the infinite Crowd of *Scribes* and *Hogies*, who
liv'd by writing the Books of the Law and
the heaps of Comments on the *Alcoran*, and
conſequently were the hotteſt Zealots for the
Glory and Honour of *Mahometiſm*.

With

With the fame Views he put down the *Minarets* and order'd all to be called to the *Mofques* at the Hours of Prayer, by founding their wind Inftruments and beating of Drums. By this means he oblig'd the *Miffionaries* by filencing the blafphemous Proclamations of the *Muezins* or Criers from the *Minarets*, who us'd to call the *Turks* to their *Naama* or Prayers; and alfo made the People lefs zealous and furious, for the Honour of their Prophet and his Religion, who us'd to have their Ears ftill dinn'd, and their Zeal inflam'd with the proclaiming their *Mahomet* for the Prophet of God.

With the fame fubtle management, he confin'd to their own Towns all the vagabond *Dervices*, who us'd to run thro' the Provinces poffeft with the hotteft Spirit of *Mahometifm*, and turn'd many of the Monafteries of thofe lazy *Drones* (who had all the Zeal and ignorance of our worft kind of Monks in them) to *Caravanferas* or Inns for Travellers, or elfe into *Timariots* to maintain fuch a number of Soldiers.

He fent fuch Orders thro' the Empire and appointed fuch faithful Minifters to execute them, (many of whom were difguis'd *Chriftians* and even Jefuits,) that the open Profeffi-

D

on of *Chriſtianity*, was ſo far from being *penal,* that under pretence of the *Chriſtians* being uſeful for the Arts and Sciences, the Trade and Plenty they brought with them wherever they came, they were even reſpected and regarded, provided they were not natural *Turks* or converted *Renegadoes.* Nor was this Work leſs ſubtilly carried on by the free Trade for all ſorts of Wines, thro' the Dominions of the *Grand Seignior;* the Drinking of which was ſo univerſally conniv'd at, that in the open Taverns in every Village, the *Turks* would be ſeen all Day carouſing and fuddling in defiance of their *Alcoran.* Nay, ſome of them have been heard in the Freedom of their Cups, to ſpeak contemptuouſly of the ſtupid Prophet, who thought, (they ſaid) by the blind Hopes of an imaginary Paradiſe above, to deprive them of the only Heaven Men could enjoy below, a cheerful Bottle, and an open-hearted Friend.

But what help'd to introduce the *Chriſtian* Religion ſtill further, was the Cuſtom he eſtabliſh'd during his Miniſtry (almoſt as long as the two great *Kuperlies* in the 17*tb Century* joined together) and which has been kept up ever ſince, of ſending Ambaſſadors to all the Courts of *Europe;* theſe were accompanied

panied with a great Train of the Sons of the *Baſſa*'s and chief Men in the Empire, who re=turn'd Home improv'd indeed, but often by the Addreſs of the *Miſſionaries* (who waited ſtill on the Catch for them) ſo prejudiced a-gainſt *Mahometiſm*, and ſo in Love with the noble Arts forbidden by their Prophet, as *Painting*, *Sculpture*, *Architecture*, and above all the delicious *Vine-Preſs*, that it is incredi-ble how far the ſecret Infection is ſpread, and how likely ſuddenly to break out into a violent Diſtemper in the State.

The Tranſlation of ſelect Parts of the Bible with uſeful ſhort Notes licens'd by the Pope, and alſo the number of *Arabick* and *Turkiſh* Books which the *Printing-Preſſes* diſperſt a-mong them, help'd on the *Miſſionaries* marvel-louſly; for they were ſo ſubtilly compos'd, as to ſhake and undermine the falſe Religion, and ſecretly to prepare the People for op'ning their Eyes to the Truth. Indeed, as to outward Pro-feſſion *Mahometiſm* ſtill ſhews its Face, but 'tis juſt like the *Pagan* Religion under *Ju-lian* the Apoſtate, the Religion of the State but not of the People; one third of whom are either ſecretly or avowedly *Chriſtians*, another third *Deiſts*, and hardly as many ſincere *Mahometans*. What adds to the

wonder

wonder is, that all this has been effected chiefly by the Means and Management of the *Roman* See, who tho' she has almost renounced the Faith her self, yet out of political Views labours to encrease her Converts here.

This is an odd Scene of things, my Lord, and yet as true as 'tis surprising, and I doubt not in a few Years we shall see, that as the old Empire of the World forsook *Rome* to settle in *Constantinople*, so Religion possibly before this *Century* expires may do the same; and as the *Pope* is almost turn'd *Pagan* or *Turk*, the *Mufti* will set up for *Patriarch* of the *Eastern* World, and the great Head and Father of the *Christian* Church here.

What the Consequences of so prodigious a Revolution may be, I shall not presume to hint, to so exquisite a Judge of such things, as your Lordship is confessedly allow'd to be; and therefore leaving them to your own judicious Reflections, I shall only observe, that had *Great Britain* continued her Care and Protection of the *Grecian* Church, with her true *Christian* Zeal, possibly we should have made as large an Harvest of Converts in *Turky* as by our Supineness and Negligence the Jesuits have done.

But

But leaving this for another Occafion, I fhall proceed to give your Lordfhip fome Account of the State of their Army and Soldiery, their Trade and Revenue, their Laws and Cuftoms at prefent; fince the faid Period of 1949, to which my Predeceffors *Memoirs* and my own little Experience neceffarily confines me.

It is certain then, my Lord, that both the Spirit and Courage, as well as the Difcipline of their Soldiery, has been fenfibly declining ever fince the coming in of the *Tartar* Race, and efpecially within this laft 150 Years, provided we always except the fmall Interval of Vizier *Ibrahim*'s Adminiftration.

This has been chiefly owing to their taking in all forts of People (and efpecially natural *Turks*, married Men and Tradefmen) for Money into the Body of the *Janizaries*; who us'd formerly to be compos'd of *Chriftian* Children taken Captives, and bred up in the ftrict Difcipline and School of the *Seraglio*, in all manly and warlike Exercifes.

It muft be confeft alfo, that the fecret fpreading of *Chriftianity* among their People and the Soldiery, has not a little contributed hereunto; for as the Succefs of their

D 3

Arms

Arms has ever been the great Source of the
Propagation of their *Faith*, it is not to be
wonder'd at, if thofe who had privately made
a Defection from this laft, did not fight with
the utmoft Refolution and Obftinacy, for the
Power and Glory of a *Mahometan* Emperour.

But the dreadful Cuftom of giving the
Soldiery fuch perpetual Largeffes, and as it
were, rewarding their Seditions whenever
they refolved to depofe one and fet up another Emperour, (and confirm or deftroy the
Grand *Viziers* and Principal *Baffa's*, as the
Fancy took them) abfolutely overturn'd what
little Spirit, Virtue or Difcipline was left a-
mong them. Let us join to this abomina-
ble Infolence, the horrible Licence of daily
guzling Wine in the Streets, and almoft the
very *Mofques* of *Conftantinople*, and their
Debaucheries of all kinds that accompany'd
it, and we need not feek for any other caufes of their furprizing Degeneracy.

Some indeed, have alfo accounted for it
from their frequent Defeats in their Battles
with the *Germans* and the *Poles*, and their
being fo often vanquifh'd by both the *Mufcovites* and *Perfians*, who have all of them
ftrip'd this Empire of fome of its ftrongeft
For-

Fortreffes, and richeft Provinces. But it is plain thefe were not the Caufes but the Effects of their decay'd Valour and Difcipline, by which they have by degrees loft all their Conquefts in *Perfia*, and their Territories round the *black Sea*, together with the greateft part of *Tranfilvania*, *Moldavia* and *Wallachia*, and almoft to the Gates of *Adrianople*.

Nor is it their Land Forces only that have thus declin'd, for their naval Power which was anciently fo formidable is now fo prodigioufly funk, fince the Defect of their Fleet by the *Englifh* Squadron in 1876, and in the Sea-fight with the *Dutch* ten Years afterwards, that befides their lofing both *Crete* and *Cyprus* to the *Pope* and *Venetians*, they have loft all Intereft and Influence, with their old Dependants of *Tunis* and *Algiers*. Nay, the very Knights of *Malta*, have fince fo often burnt and taken their greateft *Galeaffes*, that their few Gallies and Ships of War that remain to them, dare hardly fail now out of fight of the *Dardanelles*, to collect the little Tribute of the neighbouring Iflands, which are every Day revolting to them and the *Venetians*, and refufing the Payment of their old *Capitation Tax*.

After

After mentioning this I need not add that their Trade which in the 18*th Century* was in so poor a Way, and yet before 1876 was in so flourishing a Condition, is now entirely sunk and fallen into the Hands of the Merchants of *Great Britain.* For a great while indeed, they applied themselves to it with more than ordinary Vigour, and by being Masters of the best Ports in the *Mediterranean,* and by the Assistance of their Harbours in the *Red Sea,* open'd an easier and quicker Passage to the *East Indies,* than the *Christians* could have, who are forc'd to sail to them by the tedious and hazardous Navigation of the *Cape of Good Hope.* It was easy with such Advantages to have engross'd the whole Trade of the *East,* and under-sell both the *British* and *Dutch* Merchants in the *Mediterranean;* but the Unskilfulness of their Mariners, the Weakness of their Vessels, with the natural Indisposition of the *Turks* to long Voyages, and the Toils and Hazards of the Sea, prevented their carrying these Designs so far as they might have done. But besides this, our visiting them with our Squadrons, and shutting up the *Dardanelles,* and at last our falling on their Fleets and destroying some

of

of them, foon made them furrender up their
Pretenfions to that Branch of Trade, and
indeed all others into our Hands; where I
hope they will long continu eto improve,
and efpecially if this Treaty be once agreed
to in all its Articles, as I doubt not, it will
very fuddenly.

I have but little to fay of the Revenues
of this vaft Empire, fince I propofe not to
write to your Lordfhip, what is to be found
in every printed Account of them, but only
fuch Alterations as are of more modern Date,
and little known in *Europe.* It is certain
within this laft forty Years, they have applied themfelves much to raife them, even
beyond the exceffive Bounds of the late
Emperours, who feem'd to ftrive to make
up by new Taxes, the loft Revenues of their
old Provinces, torn from them on every
fide.

They have laid immenfe Excifes on all Eatables and Drinkables, and exceffive Cuftoms
on all Imports and Exports except our *Britifh* Manufactures, on all Mills, Taverns, and
every Trade, not only fubfervient to the Pleafures but the Conveniences and even Necef-
faries of Life. They have befides loaded
their Lands with great Impofitions, and laid

Taxes

Taxes on every Acre plow'd or dug, on e-
very Cow, Horſe, Bullock, Sheep, Goat, Aſs
or Camel throughout the Empire. Beſides
this and the *Pole-Tax*, every Houſe, Boat
and Ship, and every Marriage pays ſo much
to the *Grand Seignior*; the Births indeed
are Tax-free, to encourage them to breed ;
neither do they pay for their Burials for a
very good Reaſon, the *Grand Seignior* being
Heir in effect to every Man that dies in his
Dominions. There are alſo Taxes on Paper and Leather, and in one Word, on every
thing neceſſary to Health or Eaſe, or even
Life it ſelf, and if it were poſſible, I am
perſuaded, they would Tax the only Bleſſings they enjoy here, their Air and Sunſhine. Yet with all this grinding the Face
of the miſerable oppreſs'd Subject, theſe Revenues are ſo ill manag'd, and the Officers
employ'd in the Collection of them, ſuch
wicked Stewards to their cruel and rapacious Maſters, that hardly one half is brought
into the Treaſury of what is paid them. Indeed if it were not for the vaſt hereditary Revenue, the *Baſſa*'s are obliged to pay in from
their ſeveral Provinces, over and above all
theſe Taxes, and the immenſe Wealth that
the dayly Forfeiture of their Heads, to their
Ma-

Master's Avarice or Jealousy brings in; this unweildy dispirited Empire would almost sink, for want of vital Nourishment.

Under all this Oppression, there is not one found who dares even lament his own and Fellow-subjects Misery, or who will not pretend at least to Glory, in calling himself the *Grand Seignior*'s Slave, and owning that he has no title either to his Life or Liberty, his Lands, House or Substance, but from the sole Will of his mighty Emperor. A Reflection which I cannot make, but with the honest Joy every *Britton* must feel, who sees himself secur'd by Laws of his own making, in his Liberty, Life and Property, above the Reach of the highest Power and the strongest Arm; and in Peace and Security under his own *Vine* and *Fig-tree*, enjoys from the best of Constitutions, and (the usual and natural Consequence thereof,) the best Princes, all the Blessings Men can ask for as *Freemen* and *Christians*.

O Fortunati nimium, sua si bona norint,
Angligenæ!

I shall detain your Lordship no further, than with two or three Words, as to some con-

confiderableAlterations of late Years in their
Laws and Cuftoms, by which they have endeavour'd to retrieve the Virtue and Majefty of this falling Empire, and which they
owe chiefly to the Skill and Ability of the
Renegado Vizier *Ibrahim*, who flourifh'd in
the middle of this *Century*. Many of them I
fincerely wifh with fome Alterations could
betranfplanted into our Country and Con-
ftiution, and, if that Excefs of Liberty we
abound in would allow it, I doubt not we
fhould find our Account in them.

The firft I fhall touch upon is the Method he took to cure the Defects of their
Difcipline and Courage, which he found fo
low, and endeavour'd to raife fo high.   To
effect this, he divided all the Troops into
Battalions and Squadrons of about 1000 or
1500 Men. Each of thefe Bodies were raifed from one particular Province, whofe
name they carried, from whence alone their
Officers and Recruits came ; and confequently whenever they fought, the Glory
or Difgrace of the Country to which they
belong'd, and where they were born, was
directly concern'd.   By this means both
Men and Officers fought ftill with the greater Emulation and Defire of diftinguifhing
them-

themselves and their Country by their Valour; and also Recruits were more cheerfully and willingly rais'd, being sure to be sent
to assist their own Country-Men and Ac-
quaintances.

Nor was there any Danger of such Bodies uniting in Seditions in their own Province, being never disbanded; nor yet abroad
in the Field, where their Strength was so small
and inconsiderable, in respect of the whole
Army, and their Country still answerable for
their Conduct.

In the next place, (besides the popular
Tenets of the *Turks*, that every one's Fate is
writ on his Forehead, and is inevitable, and
all who die in the War go strait to Paradise)
he took care to breed up a contempt of Death
or Danger in them, by remitting the half of
all Taxes to the Widows and Children of
the Slain, and by doubling the Pay of all
that were wounded in Battle, as well as by
allowing an annual Stipend for Life, to all
who lost their Limbs, Eyes, or were any
ways disabled. This he settled according to
the following Table; for one Eye 5 *l.* a Year
of our Money for Life, for both Eyes 12 *l.* for
the right Arm 5 *l.* the left 3 *l.* for both 12 *l.*
for their Hands something less, but with little

tle difference. For one Leg 2 *l.* 10 *s.* for both Legs 6 *l.* and the fame for a Foot or both Feet, or with a very fmall Difproportion, according to the Danger and Suffering of the Soldier. Nay, fo careful was he of Men fo difabled, that if any one offered to wound, hurt or even ftrike a Soldier thus maim'd in the Service of the Empire, he was inftantly fentenc'd to lofe his Hand for the Offence; which was a feverer Penalty than he incurr'd, if he had ftruck an *Iman* or a *Cady*; as they call their Priefts and Judges.

By this means, my Lord, it is incredible for a while, with what Zeal his Troops us'd to rufh into the Battle defpifing Wounds; or rather wifhing for them, as the very Road to Preferment and Reward. Nor did his Care end here, for out of the choiceft and beft Troops, he form'd two great feparate Bodies of *Infantry* and *Cavalry* of 5000 Men each, of the braveft *Veteran* Soldiers, who receiv'd double Pay, and were fworn on the *Alcoran* never to turn their backs in Battle, till they had Orders to Retreat, or that two Thirds of them were kill'd, and then to yield and be immediately ranfom'd, with twice the Number of the Enemies Troops. To keep them in this fevere Difcipline

cipline, all Officers of his Forces both *Jani-zaries* and *Spahies* were intirely chofen out of thefe two Bodies; which were in like manner ever recruited out of thofe Men who had ferv'd longeft and diftinguifh'd themfelves moft, in every Provincial Corps in the Army.   A method which had he liv'd to have kept up, (for it fell with him) might have bid fair for the Recovery of all the Territory and Glory, they had loft before in fo many unfuccefsful Battles, and had probably coft the *Chriftian* Powers, infinite Blood and Hazards to have furmounted. Af-ter all, my Lord, the Oath thofe Troops took was ftill lefs than the *Roman* Gladiators obli-ged themfelves to perform, who us'd frequent-to fell, not the Hazard but the certain Lofs of their Lives, for fmaller Advantages.

Till this great Man found a Remedy for it, the *Turkifh Cavalry* were generally of lit-tle Service, for tho' their Horfes were fine and beautiful to the Eye, they were light-limb'd and fo thin-bodied and Fleet, that they were ftill ready to yield to the Shock of the *European Cavalry*, and to truft to their Speed to fave themfelves; but by banifhing thofe fort of Horfes, and obliging them only to ufe the largeft and weightieft that could be

found

found, he taught his Troops to truſt no more to the Swiftneſs of their Horſes, but their Strength and the Weight of them, and their Swords, to the infinite Service of the Empire.

Another Method he took to improve the Soldiery, was frequently imploying them to ſhoot at Marks for Rewards, whence he made them excellent Marks-men with their Guns, when employed againſt their Enemy; ſaying often to them, " it was ridiculous a " Soldier ſhould not ſhoot as well as a Fow-" ler, ſince the one ſhot for his Life, and " the other only for his Diverſion or a little " ſilly Gain ". Nay, he carried this even to his *Cannoniers*, who by this means in his time, us'd to ſhoot as true, as with a *Harquebuſh* or *Muſket*.

Nor were his Cares and Skill in Civil Affairs leſs conſiderable than in Military Matters, for to him alone are owing thoſe excellent Regulations (which the *Chriſtian* World would be happy in) as to the Proceedings and Deciſions of all Judges, who preſided in Law-ſuits and Proceſſes, in their judicial Courts.

By them, a Bribe being fully proved to be taken by any Judge, was Death without
Remi-

Remiſſion, and Forfeiture of all his Subſtance, half to the *Grand Seignior*, and half to the *injur'd Party*. Nay, whenever Judges decided any Controverſy, they were obliged by him to give their Reaſons on which they grounded their Judgment, to both Parties in Writing; and as there was ſtill an Appeal allow'd to a *Cadeliſker* at *Conſtantinople*, appointed ſolely to receive ſuch Decrees; if there was found either great Ignorance, or the leaſt evident Fraud or Malice in the Deciſion, the Judge was inſtantly ſummoned and examin'd, and if guilty condemned to pay the whole of the Value he had given his Decree for. A Precedent, my Lord, I fear we dare not hope to ſee follow'd, no more than that he eſtabliſh'd concerning Perjury, by which all falſe Witneſſes were for the firſt Offence condemn'd with forfeiture of Goods for ten Years to the *Gallies*; and for the ſecond Offence, to be torn in pieces by Horſes tied to their Limbs. He alſo forbid all Perſons but the Soldiery, to carry any Weapons about them by Night or Day, on pain of Death; by which means Robbery and Murders were in a great meaſure prevented, or the Malefactor more eaſily detected; and, which was ſtill more uſeful,

E   he

he made an Intention to Rob or Murder, if
fully and evidently proved, equally penal
with the having put the defign in Execution.
Nay, fo far did the rigour of Juftice carry
him, that any kind of Fraud or Collufion, to
cheat or deceive another, or even denying
or avoiding artfully a juft Debt, was made
as punifhable, as if the Offender had actually attempted a Theft of equal value.

He went further yet, and with the Spirit
of the ancient *Spartans*, if any Perfon could
juftly impeach another of evident Ingratitude, he gave up the Offender to him into
Slavery, for fo many Years as might bear
fome proportion to the Heinoufnefs of
the Offence he was Convicted of. Befides, he
inforc'd that excellent Law which had grown
obfolete, that every *Turk* fhould effectually
learn fome Trade, by which he might preferve himfelf from Want, which he eftablifhed with fuch Vigour and Care, as was never before feen in this Empire. A Law, my
Lord, which if it were paft in *England,* as
to the Children of the ordinary People, would
deliver us from thofe Shoals of Beggars,
Thieves and ufelefs Idlers, which are the
greateft Curfe of our Country.

The

The late Emperour *Achmat* made also some Laws, (how ineffectual soever they proved) that deserve our Notice at least, if not our Imitation ; as that, by which, for his short Reign, he effectually cur'd the growing, Crime of *Suicide*, by Forfeiture of Estate and Goods, and ignominiously exposing the Bodies of the Deceas'd unburied to the publick View. He also ordered the substituting perpetual Slavery, as the Penalty of most Crimes formerly punish'd with Death, not excepting even Theft and Adultery ; and prohibited all Playing (which spread prodigiously among the *Turks*) either at Games of Hazard or Skill, on pain of the severest corporal Punishment.

'Tis to the same Emperor, that they owe those excellent Laws against Drunkenness, that occasions so many Quarrels and Murders, and destroys so many Families by Poverty and Disease ; as also the appointing Clerks of the Market in all Places of the Empire, to prevent Extortion of Prices from the Poor, and to seize on such Meat for their use, or condemn it to the Fire, which should be found unwholsome or unmerchantable. It was he also, who sentenc'd all owners of Houses, which happen'd by their neglect to

be

be set on Fire, to make good half the Damage they bring on their Neighbours; and that all Slaves who by Negligence endangered an House by Fire, (tho' it should be extinguished) shall be branded on both Cheeks with a red hot Iron, and their Noses cut off as a Mark of perpetual Infamy.

It is certain, my Lord, many of these Laws seem too severe; but indeed, that is no more than what is necessary in *Turky*, both from the Nature of the People, and also because such numbers of them are now no ways restrain'd by the Injunctions of their Prophet, (which they consider no longer as the Commands of God, but the meer Inventions of Men,) and must therefore be the more severely watch'd over by the Hand of Justice, and the most sanguinary Laws. A Reflection which while I am making, I can't but turn my Eye and Thoughts, with Grief and Shame on the *Christian* World, where I fear the same Necessity will call too soon for the same Severity; while we behold so many Miscreants, slighting the Restraints of our holy Religion, and deriding the Faith and Principles, that us'd to Influence the Piety of their less corrupted Ancestors.

But

But I detain your Lordſhip too long, with theſe unimportant Matters, to which I could add much more of the ſame Nature, if I durſt flatter my ſelf that they deſerved your Attention.

In the mean Time, as I have the Fortune to be much in the good Graces of the *Grand Seignior*, and am often ſent for to entertain him with Accounts of *Europe*, and the Advancement of *Arts* and *Sciences* there, which he Admires without underſtanding them ; and as I have particularly made great Impreſſions on him, in behalf of our *Aſtronomy* : I muſt beg you will ſend me one of the beſt new Teleſcopes you can poſſibly procure, for I ſee it will be matter of infinite Delight to him.

When I have the Honour to receive your further Commands, I ſhall venture, if you deſire it, to proceed to continue your Trouble in Reading, and the Pleaſure I take in Writing any thing, you will vouchſafe to peruſe.

In the mean Time I humbly take my leave, beſeeching your being perſuaded of my ma-

naging

naging the Treaty, with my beſt Care and A-
bilities, and my ſhewing my ſelf with the utmoſt Zeal and Reſpect, both to my *King,* my
Country, and your *Lordſhip,*

a moſt faithful Subject,

Friend and Servant,

S T A N H O P E.

✧ ✧ ✧ ✧ ✧ ✧ ✧ ✧ ✧ ✧ ✧ ✧ ✧ ✧ ✧

To the Lord T R E A S U R E R, *&c.*

M Y L O R D,   *Rome, Nov.* 7, 1997.

YOUR ſecond Expreſs which followed cloſe on the Heels of the firſt,
found me here juſt ſettled in a moſt hand-
ſome and convenient Houſe, aſſign'd by
his Holineſs a Day or two after my firſt
Audience, on the *3d* Inſtant, which paſt to
my entire Satisfaction. The *Pope,* to ſay
'Truth, how heartily ſoever he wiſhes our
Deſtruction, as the great Bulwark of the
Proteſtant Cauſe and Intereſt; yet is ſo
ſenſible of his Majeſty's Wiſdom and Power, and the vaſt Aſcendant his Fleets and
                                        Arms

Arms have procur'd him, over all the Affairs in *Europe*; that he shews the greatest Readiness to comply with all our Demands, and puts the best Mien on it he can. He has already confirmed *Civita Viechia* a free Port for us, and restor'd all our Privileges in the *Adriatick*, and has engag'd that after the next Consistory he holds, which will be in two or three Days, no *British* Subject shall be liable to the *Inquisition*. A Bull is to be publish'd accordingly; and in a Word, he has complied with all the less important Articles I was commanded to insist on.

Matters standing thus, I see nothing to hinder our Squadron, to sail directly from *Leghorn* according to their Instructions, and have signified as much by this Express to Admiral *Mordaunt*; being persuaded that there will not the least Objection or Obstacle arise in these Affairs, from the *Roman* See.

In the mean Time, I shall use my utmost Industry to observe my Instructions, to get the best Intelligence possible, of all the dangerous Intriegues of this overgrown State; and give the fullest Lights, and use the fittest Means I can reach to, to enable his sa-

cred

cred Majefty, by your Lordfhip's wife Counfels, to difappoint and overturn them.

Tho' I am fettled here but a few Weeks,
I have not been afleep, but purfuant to the
5*th Article* of my Inftructions, have applied
my felf where I was directed, as well as to
the *Imperial* and *French* Ambaffadours here.
I live already in no fmall Degree of Intimacy and Confidence with them; as they
affure me, they have in Command from
their Mafters to do, on their parts with me,
and which your Lordfhip well knows their
own Interefts tie them to.

By their Informations and my Intelligence
from the other Quarter, I hope to be able to
obferve your Directions, and anfwer your Enquiries concerning this tow'ring See, or rather
this new Empire of the *Vatican* as they u-
niverfally, and too juftly call it here; which
is rifen of late to fo prodigious an height,
that it feems not only to rival, but out-grow
the moft extended Limits of old *Rome*, in
the fulleft Glory of its Strength.

I fhall therefore endeavour to lay before
your Lordfhip's difcerning Eye, the whole
Plan of this *fpiritual Monarchy*, and the
Pillars on which it is built; which we fhall
find fubfifts no longer, as Cardinal *Sancta
Croze*

Creze told *Thuanus*, (*Aulæ noſtræ Majeſtas ſtat tantum famâ & patientiâ hominum*) but on the deepeſt and beſt laid Foundations Men can lay, by vaſt Riches, incredible Policy, and the greateſt armed Strength in *Europe*.

When I have done this to the beſt of my poor Capacity, I ſhall, as your Lordſhip directs me, examine whether his Holineſs ſtill purſues his prodigious Views, in Caſe of the preſent Emperour's Demiſe; and what reaſonable Hopes his Majeſty may entertain, openly to thwart or ſecretly to undermine them.

Your Lordſhip's Knowledge of the Affairs of *Europe* in the 19*th Century*, as well as the preſent Times, is too extenſive, to allow me to dwell long on thoſe terrible Wars and Diviſions, between the *Emperour*, *France* and *Spain*; which with the unhappy Diſſenſions here, gave the Jeſuits ſo far the Aſcendant in the *Conclave* at that time, as to blind the Eyes of the Cardinals, to take that fatal and deplorable Step, of placing *Paul* IX. a Jeſuite on the *Papal Throne*.

Nor is your Lordſhip leſs appriz'd of all the dreadful Train of Conſequences that follow'd, to the infinite Increaſe of the Power

of

of that afpiring Order, and thro' their means of the *Roman* See. Hence it came that after they had by degrees made themfelves Mafters one way or another, both of *Savoy*, *Naples*, and *Tufcany* in lefs than fifty Years; they brought even *Venice* it felf with all her Policy, to be with her Territories but a fort of *Ecclefiaftical Fief* to the *Empire* of the *Vatican*.

In a little Time they actually tore from them, *Brefcia*, *Crema*, and *Bergamo*, with their Dependencies, as having been anciently united to the *Millanefe*, which they were long poffefs'd of, by the Ceffion of the Emperour *Charles* IX. in 1845. The *Polefin* they wrefted out of their Hands, in the Wars that broke out foon after, between *Innocent* the XV. and the *Senate*; who after the fatal Battle of *Verona*, had like to have loft all their Dominions on the Continent, if they had not fav'd them by that infamous Peace, which has in a manner made them Vaffals to this See ever fince.

Thefe are Events which fill the Hiftories of thofe Times, and all that read them, with Amazement; tho' I doubt not but your Lordfhip's Wifdom confiders them, but

but as the natural Confequences of the Power of that Church, which being entitled to feize or purchafe every thing fhe can lay her Talons on, and unable to alienate any thing fhe has once poffefs'd, muft necef- farily have been forefeen, (if Men had Eyes) to be fecure in a few Ages of becoming Mi- ftrefs of the World, as fhe has now in a manner made her felf, by enflaving *Italy.* A Truth, which even the Blindnefs of the laft Age, might have difcern'd with half an Eye, tho' the *Pope* had not been believ'd by them, to have the Keys of Heaven and Hell abfolutely in his Difpofal. For this Pri- vilege alone as it tied all pious fcrupu- lous Minds faft to *Rome,* fo the other as to this World, where her Power muft be ever neceffarily encreafing, could not fail to join ftrongly to her, all daring and ambitious Spirits, by the Riches and Poffeffions, fhe could tempt them with, to her Interefts. The Policy of this See had, for many Ages perpetually employ'd her *Ecclefiafticks* to preach up to the People in all parts of the Earth, the vaft Superiority of the fpiritual Office of Priefthood, above that of the Tem- poral one of a worldly King. They advanc'd the Prieft, as taking care of the immortal

Part

Part the Soul, infinitely above the Prince, who only had Authority over their Bodies; and as they had perfuaded them that the pooreft Friars, were the *Mofes* and *Aarons* fent and commiffioned by Heaven to be as Gods to Kings *, (who were really but the *Pharoahs* of the World,) they had gain'd a much greater Influence over the Minds of Men, than their Governours. On thefe deep Foundations the Jefuits took care to build the prodigious fuperftructures of Wealth, Territories and Power; and join'd to that notional Empire, which ties down Mens Minds and Confciences, thofe additional Strengths and Buttreffes, that might prop it up, when length of Time and encreafe of Knowledge fhould threaten it's Fall; and by every worldly Motive, fecure Mens Hands and Paffions, and earthly Interefts to fupport and keep it ftanding.

But thefe are Reflections which lie too open to your Lordfhip's Mind, to allow of my dwelling long on them, and it will be fufficient to fay, that as they have ever fince had the ableft Hands and the wifeft Heads to employ them; they have fo far eftablifh'd their Ufurpations, during the Diftractions

* Exod. Ch. VII. Ver. 1.

of

of *Europe* and *Italy* which they artificially fomented, that they have taken such Root, as will probably keep them secure from tumbling in the greatest Storm.

But let us carefully view the several Steps and Measures they have made use of towards the maintenance of this Power they have arriv'd at; and your Lordship will soon see the Apprehensions of the deep rooting of their Strength, to be more than probable.

And in speaking to this matter, I shall not once touch on that prodigious Authority which they have ever claim'd, of disposing of the Crowns and Empires of the World, as they find good for the Service of the Church and their spiritual Kingdom below: This they have exerted these two last *Centuries* in all the Plenitude of their Power: And I shall only dwell on such worldly Schemes and Methods, which have rais'd this Order to be Masters of the Earth; without which power of the Sword, that of the Keys (in these Days especially) would have signified little.

And first then, they are not only Masters of *Italy*, excepting *Piedmont* and that part of *Savoy*, which *Geneva* and the *Swisse Cantons* conquer'd and keep in spite of them, to the great Joy of the *Chriſtian* Princes; but they are Maſters of it more ſtrongly forti-fied, better furniſh'd with Magazines, and better guarded with a ſtanding Force of near 130000 *Veteran* Troops, than ever the World yet ſaw it. But beſides this, with the Forts and Hands of *Italy*, they have by the *Pope*'s Authority amaſs'd toge-ther, all the Wealth of it's Churches, the Hoards of it's Convents and Monaſteries, and all the votive Plate, Images, Jewels and Riches of *Loretto*. Theſe, under Pre-tence of ſaving them from the Fury of he Wars, and the Plunder of Hereticks, they have treaſur'd up in the Caſtle of St. *Ange-lo*, to the Value of near 150 Millions, as Men generally compute it. A Fund which in ſuch Hands, and under the Management of ſuch artificial Craftſmen, is able not only to keep up an invincible Army as they perpetually do, but even to buy off the ve-nal Faith and Forces of half the Princes of *Europe*, to their ſide.

Along with this immenſe Treaſure, the Pope and this Order (for they are but one and the ſame Body and Intereſt) have from their Provinces in *Africk*, their Territories or Empire rather of *Paraguay* in *America*, and

and their Revenues from *China*, a Fund so prodigious, that it exceeds all Belief, or even Computation; the neat Produce from *Para-guay* alone, after all Deductions, amounting to near three Millions. To add to these, the Computation of all the Revenues of *Italy*, and their vast Estates in the different Parts of *Europe*, would be a needless La-bour; since every one may see, as plainly as your Lordship, that they are already Masters of a Treasure, sufficient to carry on the lar-gest Designs, that their Ambition or even their Religion (as they have drest up Reli-gion) can prompt them to.

But they have Forces still unmentioned, that are equal to their Riches, for my Lord, you, who know the Courts of *Europe* so in-timately, can vouch, that there is hardly a great Person in them, who has not a Je-suite for his Confessor, nay his Director. How few of its crown'd Heads are there, whose Prime Minister is not either a Car-dinal Jesuite, or so absolutely under the In-fluence of the *Pope*'s Nuncio, that they may be said to be entirely govern'd and directed by them, and the perpetual Couriers and Coun-cels that are sent hourly from *Rome*, where the Nephew or Cardinal *Padrone* dictates

mea-

meafures to *Europe*, as if he were a fifth *Evangeliſt*.

By theſe means it is, that they have en-tirely excluded all Princes from intriguing in the *Conclave*; for tho' they ſometimes leave the Nomination of fit Perſons to the ſacred Purple (provided they are Jeſuits) to crown'd Heads; yet are there no longer *Spaniſh*, *French* or *German* Cardinals in the World, ſince whatever Nation they belong to, they are abſolutely and ſolely Jeſuits and nothing elſe. Thus by confining the Cardinalſhip and Popedom to their own Order, they have been able to avoid two Rocks, namely, long and factious *Conclaves*, and ſhort Reigns. For it is not now as it was formerly, that he who went in there *Pope*, came out *Cardinal*, but even during the *Pope*'s Life, they ſettle by Agreement the next Succeſſor, with-out Violence and Party-Feuds, and enter the *Conclave* for a few Days for Form's ſake, and generally take care to chuſe a middle-ag'd and healthy *Pope*, by which they are the more enabled to execute their Schemes and build up their Power.

Nay, ſo indolent are the Princes of *Europe* grown and ſo little jealous of their old Rights, or at leaſt ſo conſcious are they of
their

their want of Power to influence Elections, that 'tis grown a common Maxim with them, that *Popes* refemble Houfes, which 'tis better generally to buy ready made, than to be at the Expence and Care in making and raifing them, fince often they do not like them, when the top Stone is plac'd on the Building. And here indeed, is the great Source and Fountain of their Strength, for chiefly by this Canal (the Popedom) that feeds their leffer Streams, are the great Promotions, Rewards and Preferments, not only in their own but all other Courts, deriv'd to the Friends of the Society; and by them are the fmaller Rivulets fupplied, and the Land water'd and enrich'd, by their wife and artful Diftribution. Thus are all kept in awe by hopes of Preferment of one kind or another. *Omnibus una quies, Venter!* All that ftick to them zealoufly and ferve them faithfully, being fecure of Rewards and Advancement, whatever Profeffion or Employment they follow.

From fuch plain Facts as thefe, it is, my Lord, that moft People are convinc'd, that over and above the Crowds of great

Men

Men, that are lifted openly in this Society, there are ftill a much greater Number, who are fecretly Jefuites in private, and *ex Voto* as they call it. Nay, the World is much deceiv'd if they have not, by this fubtle Method as many Generals at their Devotion, in the Service of other Princes, as they keep in their pay in *Italy*, and their Territories abroad.

With fuch incredible Affiftances, is it any thing wonderful, that they have been able to divide and diftract the *Proteftant* Powers, to corrupt and pervert fome of them, perfidioufly and atheiftically to break thro' Oaths, and the moft folemn and facred Engagements, and to embrace the *Romifh* Communion; and purchafe off the poor diftrefs'd Branches, of the *Greek* and *Armenian* Churches, to fubmit to their Authority, and obtain their Protection at the Price of their Faith.

For my part, my Lord, when I fee them poffefs'd of fuch Power and Policy together, when I fee all the Cardinals, Fathers, Prelates, nay, all the Orders of their Church, all the Minifters of their Princes, (not to fay the Princes themfelves,) abforb'd and funk into this one prodigious

gious Body ; I cannot but admire at
their Prudence or rather the Providence
of Heaven, that keeps them from being
as absolute Masters of this World, as they
give themselves out, (and are believ'd) to be
of the next, in spite of their flagitious A-
ctions, and the open and flagrant Wickedness
of their Conduct.

These Articles, my Lord, which I have
been insisting on, are the great Engines
by which this vast Machine has gain'd,
and now continues to exert its Strength;
and let me now hint some others as useful, tho' seemingly more weak and contemptible, which this Church makes use
of by her inferior Dependants.

And First then, there is not an Art
so mean, which these Jesuits do not
stoop to, if it can be of use to them.
With this View, besides their being the
general Bankers and Traders of the World,
they have unjustly, and by the vilest
means engross'd all the Schools and Colleges of *Europe*, and the sole Education
of the Youth there. From among those,
they pick and garble all the choice Spirits and promising Genius's ; whom by
Places in their Universities and Prefer-

ments

ments when they leave them, and every Allurement that fuits their natural Temper and Difpofitions beft, they tie faft to themfelves, either as Friends or Members of their Society.

But they ftoop lower yet, for as they alone, or fuch as they licenfe, are allowed the Privilege of being Confeffors, (that is Spies over all Mankind) by the *Bull* of *Clement* XIV. in 1862; fo they do not only thus keep an infinite afcendant, over the Minds of Princes and all in Authority, but they even preferve their Empire with the lower Ranks and Degrees of Men; to the pooreft Tradefmen, the common Soldiers, and the very Porters and Rabble of the Streets, who are all oblig'd to Confeffion at leaft once a Month, or to be Excommunicated and Outlaw'd.

In the next place, my Lord, as by the fame *Bull* they are conftituted fole *Inquifitors*, and thereby have intirely routed their old Rivals the *Dominicans* and fecular Clergy; they have thence got an unbounded Power, of ruining the Fortunes and deftroying the Lives, of all that offer not openly to oppofe, (which were vain) but even to
cen-

cenfure them. For as by their Arts
they have turn'd the holy Office of
the Inquifition (as they ftyle it,) into a
meer Engine of State, to take off under
Colour of Herefy, all of whom they,
or the Prince conceive the leaft Jealoufy; fo the Awe which by this Method they ftrike their Enemies Minds
with, can only be equal'd by the Hopes and
Encouragement, they give their Friends
both Laity and Clergy, by efpoufing and
ferving their Interefts and Advancement,
per fas & nefas, Right or Wrong.

By the fame *Bull* they alone are privi-
ledg'd to Exorcife the Obfeft, which gives
them an huge Appearance of Sanctity with
the Crowd, as if none but they among the
Regulars, were able to combat with, and
overcome the Rage and Fury of the Devil; and what adds not a little to their
Veneration, tho' others are allowed to
marry People, which they never do (poffibly as fearing they may gain more Enmity
and Curfes, than good Will and Thanks
by it) yet they alone are empower'd to
examine into, and grant Divorces where
they fee caufe, which makes them not a
little confider'd and applied to.

F 3   But

But as tho' thefe were but fmall Honours, which the holy See has heap'd on
them, they are conftituted alfo fole Licen-
fers of Books, by which means nothing appears in Publick, but what is feafon'd to
their Palate, and drefs'd up by their fpiritual Cooks fo fkilfully, as to pleafe their
Society and the relifh of the World. And
it is worth your Lordfhip's Notice, that
fince 1862, there has not one Book either
in Divinity or Hiftory (for on other Subjects
they are very indifferent) which has feen
the Light, but what have been wrote by
the publick Profeffors in thofe Faculties;
fo that both prefent and future Times,
muft either take up with the falfe Lights
they prefent them with, or fearch out Truth
from a few private conceal'd Manufcripts,
which it will be difficult, if not impoffible
to come at.

This brings to mind, what *Pafquin* faid
on this Occafion, that his Holinefs had
made his good Brethren the Jefuits, fole
Spectacle-makers to the World; by which
means they were impower'd to make all
things in Print, appear dark or clear, fair
or foul, great or little, as they pleas'd to
reprefent them to the Eyes of others.

But

But to preferve and maintain their Power yet further, as all other *Ecclefiafticks* are but little Agents and under-work Men to them, fo the Cures in remote places are ferv'd by fuch; while the crowded, and moft frequented Pulpits are ftill filled with Fathers of the Society, who are the popular Preachers admir'd and ador'd by all. Nay, to infinuate themfelves the more with the Crowd, they affect to appear the Champions and Defenders of their darling Doctrine of the Immaculate Conception; in favour of which a *Bull* was at laft procur'd for them, in fpight of the *Dominicans* Oppofition. By this means they pretend to be fo peculiarly favour'd by her, as to receive particular Revelations from Heaven, nay, to work miraculous Cures and Converfions, and to be enabled as it were, to infpire the dulleft Children with Learning, by her Bleffing on their Prayers and Labours, all which extraordinary Gifts none of the other Orders have dar'd to fet up for, or rival them in this laft *Century*, whatever they us'd to do in the former ones.

Nay, fo peculiarly does fhe protect them, (as 'tis generally faid) and believed, that if any great Sinner enters into their Order, he either

ther

ther dies by her Means, or amends his Life perfectly in six Months; and as there has not these fifty Years, been one Jesuit accus'd of any Crime whatever, so it is well known, that for fifty Years before, none were accus'd who were not acquitted, and whose Accusers did not die some violent or sudden Death, by her vengeance and the judgment of Heaven; tho' Hereticks, like your Lordship, may impute it to another cause.

In the last place, their Numbers and political Correspondence are of vast service to them, for tho' there are computed to be near 170,000 known Jesuits in *Europe* alone, all of whom by their Friends and Relations strengthen their Party; yet are matters so regularly order'd, that each Member once a Week, gives an Account of his Conduct and Observations to his Rector, and he to the College, each College to the Provincial, each Provincial to the *Nuncio*, and each *Nuncio* to the *Pope*, who is always General of the Order. Their Numbers are also as exactly distributed, as the regular Forces of a Prince, and even in *Great Britain*, if my Intelligence be good, there are not less than 1300 quartered in different Places and Disguises; some of
them

them as Tradefmen, *Valet de Chambres*,
and Clerks, and not a few as Preachers and
School-mafters, among our unhappy and
unreafonably divided Sectaries.

I fend enclos'd a Lift of 75 of thefe Traytors
Names and laft Places of Refidence; and I
need not caution your Lordfhip, not to be
impos'd on by Proofs of their being zealous
Proteftants in their general Converfation,
or keeping no Fafts, nor regarding *Lent*,
&c. for they have full Difpenfations for
thefe ufeful Acts of *Hypocrify*.

And thus, I fhall fhut up this tedious
Account, of this prodigious Society, which
I believe will be found to have fully deferv'd the Title, fo long fince given it, of
the *Monarchia Solipforum*. Sure I am, this
vaft Encreafe of Power, has done as much
harm to the Health, not to fay the very
Being of the *Chriftian* Church, as the Swel-
ling and Over-growth of the Spleen does to
the Human Body, which waftes and con-
fumes in proportion to the Size and Excefs
of the other.

After what I have laid before your Lordfhip, I fear it will appear, that there is too
much Ground for my being fent hither;
and to apprehend that his Holinefs will
be

be able to purſue, (tho' I hope unſucceſs-fully,) thoſe prodigious Views which the Im-perial and *French* Ambaſſadors are ſo much alarm'd with; and both eſtabliſh the *In-quiſition* in *France*, and in caſe of his Im-perial Majeſty's Death, endeavour, if poſſible, to be choſen Emperour. This laſt is the more to be fear'd, becauſe he has ſo far influenc'd the Electors already, as to refuſe to chuſe a King of the *Romans*, and it is by all agreed here, that as *Charles* V. one of the ancient Heroes of the 16*th Century*, actually laid his Schemes to be choſen *Pope*, tho' he could not carry it; ſo the *Pope* could not do better for the good of *Chriſtendom*, if he made Reprizals, now when it is more than probable he may not be diſappointed.

Of the eleven Electors, the two laſt of which were made entirely by the Intrigues of this Court, it is certain he has the five Eccleſiaſticks at his Devotion, both as they are all Jeſuits, and alſo as they expect the Purple for their Attachment to him; and tho' the other ſix ſeem determined to op-poſe him, yet alas, what a weak Security is a little *German* Truth and Virtue, when tempted by all the Arts, and Wealth, and
Power

Power of this See. The Imperial Ambaſſador aſſures me, that he has actually offer'd the Electour of *Bavaria* to make him a King, and be acknowledg'd as ſuch by all the crown'd Heads in *Europe* that are *Catholicks*, if he will Vote for a Perſon he ſhall propoſe, and with ſome Aſſurances that it ſhall be a *German*. But how far this, and eſpecially the laſt Particular, can be depended on, and if true, how far his Electoral Highneſs's Virtue may outweigh his Vanity, which has ſo long thirſted after this airy and empty Title, we muſt wait on that great Diſcoverer *Time* to unriddle.

However, amidſt all our Apprehenſions, it is ſome Comfort that his Imperial Majeſty's Health rather improves than declines; and tho' the ſtrong and hale Complexion of his Holineſs, bids fair to ſurvive him, yet it is poſſible the Goodneſs of Heaven may interpoſe, for the Peace and Liberty of *Europe*, which if this terrible Intrigue ſhould ſucceed, would be greatly endangered. It is moſt ſure his *Britannick* Majeſty is conſider'd here, as the greateſt Obſtacle to all theſe Schemes of the *Papal* Ambition; and how far the daily Terror of our
Fleet

Fleet on this Coaſt, and his Majeſty's Arms, Conduct, and perſonal Bravery, (hereditary to his Houſe) may intimidate and cool the Ardour of his Hopes, is not eaſily to be imagin'd. In the mean time, as to the other Particular, this Court ſeems reſolute in ſetting up the *Inquiſition* in *France*, and has actually ſent an Expreſs laſt Week, by the way of *Lyons*, to order the *Nuncio* to make the moſt preſſing Inſtances, that it may be no longer delay'd; and if this be complied with, the Slavery of that unhappy Nation is compleated, who long ſince have had no other Remains of their ancient Liberty left them but the Freedom of their Tongues; whereas this infernal Office, like *Satan* who invented it, will accuſe them for the very Guilt of their Thoughts too.

A Proceeding ſo much the more ungenerous and unjuſt, as it oppreſſes a Nation, to whoſe Valour and pious Aſſiſtance, the State and Grandeur of this *See* is ſo highly indebted; but as the great *Cornaro* ſaid once, *that Ingratitude is the Vice of Prieſts,* ſo this will be but one of many Proofs, that it is a Crime that deſcends *ex traduce,* and is hereditary to the *Popedom,* if I may uſe ſuch an Expreſſion of an elective Kingdom.

The

The Study of Antiquity which is the reigning Paffion of this Court, has put his Holinefs on an extraordinary Project, which is to be executed early next Summer; and that is, to cut a new Bed for the *Tiber*, by a vaft Canal from its old Channel, thro' the deep Valley hard by the *Poute Molle*. As it is expected, (befides, the Convenience of raifing the Banks of the River, and fecuring it from future Inundations) that prodigious Quantities of Antiquities of all kinds will be found by this Method, and much more than will anfwer the Charge; they propofe to fpare no Expence, in executing the Defign with Care and Expedition, before the great Heats endanger the Health of the Inhabitants, from the Stench of the Filth and Slime of the River.

I forgot to mention to your Lordfhip, that I was fhewn here Yefterday, an old Gentleman who is actually the lineal Defcendant of one of our ancient Kings, who abdicated his Throne thro' a violent Averfion to the Northern Herefy, and his Zeal to this See; and yet, fo grateful are his good Patrons the Jefuits, that he is no farther confider'd here then as a Piece of Antiquity, which they keep to mor-

mortifie themfelves with in *Lent*. They allow him 2000 *l*. a Year, aud a beneficial
Place, of firft *Valet de Chambre* to his Holinefs. He feems to be a grave heavy Man,
and very conftant at his Breviary, neither
he, or his Father ever took the Title of
King on them ; he is near Eighty, and
has a very bad Afpect. He keeps no Attendants but a few Highland Gentlemen,
and has fuch a faturnine melancholy Severity of Manners, that he converfes with none
but a Rabble of *Scotch* and *Englifh* Jefuits,
and now and then an *Italian* Painter or
Fiddler. He is certainly Great Great Grandfon, to the Perfon who is once or twice
mention'd in the Hiftories of the glorious
Reigns of *George* II. and *Frederick* I. under
the Name of the Pretender. He was never
married but has five illegitimate Children ;
two Sons, one of whom is Bifhop of *Como*,
the other is a Colonel in the *Pope*'s Service,
(but I know not whether Horfe or Foot,) and
three Daughters, who are Mother Abbeffes
to three *Nunneries* of very large Revenues.
I faw him at the *Opera*, for he is a great
Lover of Mufick, and we converfed together near an Hour in *Italian*, having no
Englifh.

So

So fall the Idols and the Slaves of Rome.

I am afham'd to have detain'd your Lordfhip fo long and fo unprofitably, and therefore fhall only add, that as I fhall faithfully purfue my Inftruƈtions here, fo I hope my Zeal for my Country, and Attachment to your Lordfhip, ftand in need of no Profeffions, and efpecially from one, who has fo often facrific'd his Fortune and Intereft, to the little Services he has been fo happy to render to both, and to the Honour of being

My Lord, your Lordfhip's, &c.

HERTFORD.

I Write this with Mr. *Secretary's* Cypher, having unhappily miflaid the one you order'd for me.

To the Lord HIGH TREASURER, &*c.*

MY LORD,   *Mofco, Nov.* 29, 1997.

IN my laft of *September* 25, which carried my fincere Compliments on your
happy Advancement, and being declar'd
Prime Minifter and *Treafurer* ; I fent you
the fulleft Accounts I was able of the State
of Things here, and the good Condition
they ftand in, by our laft Treaty of Commerce. This Court indeed, has not forgot
the fatal Blow we gave their Naval Power
in the *Baltick* formerly, and the great Reftraint we keep them under ever fince ; yet,
as they fee there is no hope of bettering
their Affairs, by living on ill Terms with
us, they feem determin'd to try to gain
upon us, by all the Friendfhip and Favour
they can fhew us in our Commerce here.
I fhall omit no Opportunity, to improve
this good Inclination towards us according
to my former Inftructions, and your Lordfhip's Commands; and as this People are
vaftly

vaſtly improv'd every way, have made great
advances in all polite Arts, as well as the
learned Sciences, and are grown conſiderable in the World, by their Arms, Conqueſts
and Riches ; I doubt not but we ſhall find
our Account, in keeping up a conſtant In-
tercourſe of Friendſhip and Amity with
them. The great Caravan for *China* went
off Yeſterday, with near twenty *Britiſh*
Merchants in their Company, all provided
with ſufficient Paſs-ports, and allowed the
ſame Privileges with the *Czar*'s Subjects ;
and I hope in time, to ſee this Branch of
our Commerce turn to greater Account,
than it has been repreſented to the Com-
miſſioners for Trade in *London.*

Your Lordſhip, who is ſo well acquainted
with the vaſt Encroachments, this powerful
Empire has made, on all her Neighbours
round her, both on the ſide of *Turky*, *Poland*, *Sweden* and *Perſia*, and how dangerous an Enemy, and uſeful a Friend ſhe may
prove, to the Affairs of *Germany*; can never
want Inclination to tie the *Czar* to our Intereſts, by all ways and methods that in
good Policy we can make uſe of.

All the crown'd Heads in *Europe*, except
Sweden who is at War with them, have

G   Envoys

Envoys or Ambaffadors conftantly here to this end, tho' fome of them, as *France* or *Spain*, have little or no Trade with them, and therefore your Lordfhip's Refolutions to keep a conftant Refident here, which has been fo much neglected of late Years, is certainly extreamly neceffary. Your Informations of the great Influence the prefent *Pope* and his Jefuites have gain'd here, are but two well grounded, and I make no doubt, but in a little time, if they go on as they have of late Years, by bribing the leading Clergy and Nobility, by Places and Promifes of Preferment, and by keeping up a conftant Body of *Miffionaries* to difperfe their Opinions among the People and lower Clergy; but this Church and her Emperour and Patriarch, will be more obedient Sons to the triumphant *Latin*, than they were to the militant *Greek* Church.

I have nothing more to add to my laft Difpatches, but to fhew my Obedience to your Commands, in procuring you as exact an Account as I could, of the Affair which you fay has made fo much Noife in *London*, to wit, the *Laplanders* Sun-fhine. It is certain then, my Lord, that this matter, which begun about twenty Years ago, near

Novo-

Novogorod, is fpread to feveral Parts of *Mufcovy*, and is likely to grow in Fafhion at Court.

It took it's rife from the *Knez Peter Kikin*, who living near *Novogorod*, about the Year 1971, hir'd a Couple of *Laplanders* that were Brothers, for Servants. As their Mafter was fond of Gardening, and had got a *Gardener* from *Mofcow*, he put one of thefe *Laplanders* to work there under him; and the *Gardener* often complaining of the Climate, the Fellow told him if his Mafter would give him Money to bear his Charges, he would bring him a *Laplander* that with his Affiftance, would make Sunfhine for him. This he averr'd fo frequently and fo pofitively, that at laft it was told his Mafter; who after examining the Fellow, and knowing it was ufual with the *Laplanders* to fell Winds, refolved to make a Trial of this Method, tho' new to him. In a Word, he fent and had the Perfon hir'd and brought from *Lapland*, who perform'd all that his Countryman and Affiftant undertook for him, and even exceeeded his Mafters fondeft Imaginations. Tho' *Novogorod* lies in the Latitude of 56 Degrees, yet by the perpetual Sunfhine thefe

Creatures

Creatures produc'd in his Gardens, he had
in Time as Choice Peaches, Nectarines,
Figs, and Grapes, nay Pine-apples (as I am
affur'd) as could grow in *France*, at leaft in
the more Northern Parts of it. Nay, he got
fome of the tendereft Plants and Flowers
which before he never durft venture out of
his Green-Houfe till *June*, to thrive and
flourifh in the open Air from *March* till
November; which is longer by much than
they dare keep out their Orange Trees at
Verfailes.

This look'd fo like a Fable, that I could
fcarce give it Credit, till I enquir'd of feveral Perfons of the greateft Worth and Honour here, who all agreed in averring it to
me; and that feveral *Mufcovite* Noblemen
had actually got *Laplanders* by the Means
of this Fellow, who by their amazing Art
of making Sunfhine (for I know not what
other Term to ufe) had as fine Gardens for
choice Fruit, Flowers, and exotick Plants,
as any Gentleman in the Neighbourhood of
Paris. They nam'd at leaft a Dozen to me,
that made Ufe of this wonderful Method,
fo that there was no Room to doubt of the
Fact; and being refolv'd to give your Lordfhip the fulleft Satisfaction I could, I fet out
the

the latter End of laſt Month, to ſee the Seat
and Gardens of *Knez John Petrowiſky,*
who has two of the moſt famous *Laplanders* in all *Muſcovy.*

I was receiv'd there with much Civility,
he being prepar'd for my coming, and as the
Knez ſpoke *French* very well, I enter'd into a long Dialogue with him on this ſurprizing Affair, of which I ſhall now relate
to your Lordſhip the chief Particulars. The
Laplanders are extremely reſerv'd, in communicating the leaſt Circumſtance of their
Art to any one; nor will they allow any
Man, no not the leaſt Child, to be in the
Garden while they are about their Buſineſs, ſo that there was no talking to themſelves upon it. The *Knez* told me that
with great Difficulty he procur'd his *Laplanders* to leave their Country. That he
was forc'd to allow them Cloaths, Brandy, Rain-Deers dry'd Fleſh, and Marrow,
(their favourite Diſh) which he brings yearly from *Lapland,* beſides Tobacco and ready Money, to the Value of at leaſt 90 *l.*
Sterl. by the Year. That there muſt alway
be two of them, neither of which can perform the Operation alone, and that they
will not leave their Country without bring-

G 3   ing

ing a Wife with each of them, fo that it is
extremely expenſive to get them or keep
them. They are alfo exceſſively humour-
ſome, and will neither eat with others, or
let any but their Wives dreſs their Food for
them, and upon the leaſt Ill-humour they
will leave the Garden without Sunſhine for
ſeveral Days, nay a whole Week; but by
that Time the Fit is generally over, and
they fail to Work readily of themſelves.
That about three Years ago being diſ-
guſted for not having Rain-Deers Fleſh in
ſufficient Plenty, they left his Gardens without Sun for near a Fortnight, in the midſt
of a terrible Seaſon of Froſt and Snow, and
the Wind all that while in the North. That
he had like thereby, to have loſt moſt of his
foreign Plants and Flowers, ſeveral of
the tendereſt of which actually died; and
the reſt had followed, but that he got his
Laplanders in good Humour and recovered
them, by giving them fine Weather for ſeveral Weeks, and pruning away all that was
decay'd of them.

He told me his Men generally made three
Acres of Sunſhine in a Day, but that few
others could come up to that, and many
not over one or one and a half. That by
their

their Contract they oblig'd themselves, to continue the Sunshine for seven Hours each Day, and when they were not lazy, would often give them eight or nine Hours; but in very foggy or rainy Weather, and especially, if accompany'd with great and high Winds, they would often toil for the whole Morning, without any tolerable Benefit. He said he had an hundred Times, seen them at Work from the Windows of his Apartment, and that they did all by the Beating of a Drum, and burning some particular Herbs, and especially wild Moss and Mint, and singing some odd Kind of Songs, which he knew not what to make of, but he believ'd they were no Psalms. He concluded with saying, that he would not prevent by an ill Description, the Pleasure of my seeing Things with my own Eyes, for if I would stay there that Night, I should survey every Thing next Morning, as soon as I pleas'd.

I very cheerfully accepted the Offer, and tho' I rose before it was clear Day-light, I was hardly dress'd till he call'd me into his Bed-Chamber, and plac'd me with him in the Window, to behold this astonishing Scene. There I saw at about a hundred Yards Distance the two *Laplanders*, who seem'd to

be

beat their Prayers, for they were both on their Knees. He assur'd me they were every Morning, an Hour and an half before Sunrise constantly employ'd thus, murmurring something in a low mournful growling Tone, (which I heard, tho' faintly from the Window,) and reeling their Bodies back and forwards, and often beating their Foreheads violently against the Ground. He told me that the Place in the Garden, was a little Circle in one of the Walks, which they had planted round with their own Hands with Sun Flowers, common Daffadills, Marygolds, and red Daisies; under the Roots of which, they had buried many Skeletons of several Kinds of Birds, and that they allow'd no Body by their good Will, to walk or sit down in it, and much less to dig or break the Ground.

In a little Time, I perceiv'd they begun to alter their Motions, and heard a Noise of a Flint and Steel in striking Fire, which he told me they were now busy about, and preparing their Moss and Herbs and stretching their Drum. In some Minutes I plainly saw it was so, by a little Smoak arising from a small Heap, they had made in the Garden Walk; and no sooner did the Smoak appear, but they both fell a singing with a low

low hoarfe Voice, one of the vileft Songs for Words and Mufick I had ever heard. One of them who held the *Kannus* or Drum, all the while beat on it, firft low and foftly, and then by Degrees louder and quicker, and again with all his Force, till at laft a little Blaze began to appear; upon which they got on their Feet, ftamping fo violently on the Ground, that I could hear them to the Window, and dancing and finging as furioufly, as if they had been diftracted. They then fell to running in a Circle round the Fire, and ftill the Fellow who had no Drum threw fomething in the Flame; they feem'd to be Things with Knotts on them, bawling lowder than ever, every Handful he caft on it, while the other ftill beat the Drum higher and fiercer.

This was all I could perceive they did, for above an Hour by my Watch, and then they both drop'd down befide the Fire, which went out of a fuddain, and there they lay as if they were dead or afleep; and the *Knez* affured me the Operation was over, and bid me wait and fee the Succefs. It was a dark cloudy Morning, as generally at that Time of the Year (the End of *October*) the Mornings are here, and as little Apperance of the Sun,

Sun, as if it had not rifen that Day; and yet in lefs than half a Quarter of an Hour, I perceived the Clouds break into a little fmall Aperture, as regularly as if one would draw the Curtains of a Bed, and a lovely Gleam of Sunfhine burft on the Garden, as bright and as fair as if it had been in Summer. Immediately I perceived the *Lap-landers* get up and rub themfelves, as Men would do after a fevere Sweat, and then they retired immediately out of the Garden, whither I went down with my *Mufco-vite* Landlord.

I was not a little amaz'd at the Novelty and Surprize of the Thing, and had no great Inclination to go into the Sunfhine, which I look'd on as of the Devil's making, and could not help thinking of the *Spanifh* Proverb of *going out of God's Bleffing into the warm Sun*. But my Landlord laught at my Superftition fo heartily, and pull'd me into it fo merrily, that I was afhamed of my felf. I look'd round me and furveyed the Ground on which the Sun fmote with remarkable Warmth; and to the beft of my Judgment I verily believe therewere about threeAcres thus enlightned, while all the reft of the Garden about them, as well as the whole Country, was

covered

covered with a dark mifty Fog; and what amaz'd me above all, and convinc'd me there was fomething fupernatural in the Matter, it continu'd fo all the reft of the Day.

I fpent fome Time in it with my good *Mufcovite*, who was very induftrioufly fhewing me his choiceft Trees, Flowers, and exotick Plants, and telling me whence he had got them, and how well they throve with him; tho' I only anfwer'd him with a few Monofyllables now and then, fo much was my Mind taken up, with what I had feen thofe Devils of *Laplanders* perform. He perceived my uneafinefs, and tho' he laughed heartily at me, he was fo civil as to take me into the Houfe to breakfaft with him. There I found his Lady and Family, who fell on talking as familiarly of their *Laplanders*, and how happy they were in them and their Sunfhine, as if they had only been commending their dry Wood, and the Fire which was blazing finely in the Chimney.

I threw off my Surprize by Degrees as well as I could, and heard all their Difcourfe of the *Laplanders* and their Way of Living; and above all of their Drum and the Herbs they made ufe of, both which my

Land-

Landlord undertook to fteal me a Sight of,
tho' there is nothing the *Laplanders* are fo
jealous of, as that any one fhould fee or
handle either, and above all their *Kannus* and
the Hammer they beat it with. However, to
oblige me he fent for the poor Creatures, and
by giving them a great Cup of Brandy a-
piece, he got them to fpeak to me and ferved as Interpreter between us. But the Truth
is, they were either fo referv'd, or fo ftupid, that I could learn nothing from them,
but that their Names were *Undo Marki*,
and *Riconi Norki*, and that their good Mafter had brought them out of their fweet
Country, and gave them good Brandy,
Money, Tobacco and dry'd Rain-deer,
for making his Sunfhine. I afk'd them
how they made it, and they laugh'd juft
as a Dog grins, and faid *Kannus, Kannus,*
meaning their Drum, and that was all I
could underftand from thefe *Deep A-
depts* in Sunfhine, who in a little Time
thought fit to retire, to fleep off their Brandy. They were low, fwarthy, ill-looking
Creatures, very lean, and ftooped much,
and hardly ever took off their Eyes from
the Ground.

In

In a little Time my good *Mufcovite* followed them, and was not long away, till he returned with a World of Joy in his Face, and their Herbs, Drum, and Hammer in his Hand, which he had ftole from them while they were fleeping. I look'd at them and examined all very curioufly. The Herbs feemed to be chiefly Mint, Rofemary, Lavender, and wild Thyme, mix'd with a good deal of Mofs and fome Feathers, and all appear'd to be fprinkled with Blood, probably of fome poor Birds they had murder'd, with a great deal of Injuftice, to ftrengthen the Charm. The Drum is oval, about fixteen Inches one Way and twelve the other; and there were painted on it feveral Figures of Men and Beafts, two or three Sorts of Birds, a great many Stars, and the Moon in the Middle of them, and at leaft a Dozen Reprefentations of the Sun, all very ill-favouredly painted, and feem'd to be drawn on the Skin of the Drum with Blood.

The Hammer was of Bone, and about feven Inches long, and fomething like a *Roman* T, or rather like the young Branches or Sprouts, of the Velvet Head of a five or fix Year old Buck, with us in *England* in

June,

June both of them feem'd exactly to anſwer the Defcription *Scheffer* gives of them in his Hiſtory of *Lapland,* which is too curious a Book, not to be well known to your Lord-ſhip, for the many rare and uncommon Ac-counts of that Country, which are contained in it. I am perſuaded upon reading over his Work, that this Drum, and thoſe de-fcribed by him, are much the ſame, except the Painting of it; and befides their Man-ner of beating on it, feem'd to have a pretty cloſe Refemblance with that he defcribes.

I was ſo free with my obliging Landlord, as to aſk him if he did not think it was a Sort of Magical Incantation that his *Lap-landers* us'd, and if he believed it was by the Aſſiſtance of the Devil they made their Sunſhine, or ſuppos'd it lawful to make Uſe of ſuch Helps in obtaining it? But he anſwered me only with a loud laugh, and aſſuring me he believ'd there was no ſuch Thing in the Matter; and tho' for his Part he had other Thoughts, yet moſt of the Noble *Muſcovites* in that bad Cli-mate, had ſuch a Paſſion for Gardens and good Weather, that they would almoſt be oblig'd to Magick for them, rather than want them.

In

In ſhort, my Lord, I left him in his Sunſhine very happy and contented, and took
my Leave much indebted for all his Civilities,
and ſet out for *Moſcow*. I fell to conſidering all the Way of this new Method of making Sunſhine, and what Uſes it might be applied to, if ever our induſtrious Merchants,
ſhould ſhip it off and with a fair Gale purchas'd in *Lapland*, ſail directly for *England*,
like *Ulyſſes* carrying all the Winds in his
Bags. What Gardens ſhould we ſee riſing
up on every Hill under the Direction of theſe
lovely *Laplanders*, with all the Fruits, Trees,
and Flowers of *France* and *Spain*, and even
the *Eaſt* and *Weſt Indies*. How many Cures
might our *George* the Sixth make, by ſetling
a few Acres by the Year on our Hoſpitals for
the Sick, and our Mad People in Bedlam;
and how many of our fair Ladies, and nice
peeviſh fine Gentlemen, would be ſet free
from their Spleen and Vapours, by ſetting
out a reaſonable Proportion for St. *James's*
Park and the Mall, not forgetting his own
Royal Gardens and amiable Family. How
many fretfull uneaſy Husbands and Wives,
melancholy Lovers, and ſullen Beauties, not
to ſpeak a Word of our gloomy Sectaries and
four Catholicks, diſcontented Courtiers that
                                    loſe

lofe Places, and zealous Patriots that want them, would he recover to plain Senfe and good Humour, by this lovely Cordial.

If he would fettle an Acre or two on our Profeffors of Aftronomy, what clear Accounts of our Eclipfes fhould we have for the future, without the old lazy Excufe of dark Days and bad Weather; not to mention a Syllable of the clouded Brows, and the filent fplenetick Tempers of our Univerfity Men, that would be finely clear'd up by it.

In fhort, my Lord, I begin to be reconcil'd to this Affair, and tho' the Devil fhould have a little Hand in it, we might eafily get an ingenious Jefuit to bring us off that Scruple, by two or three learned Doctors Opinions, and a few good Diftinctions with Probability in them. We fhould by the Help of thefe honeft Drummers, be able to make our Air and Weather above Stairs as eafily and as conveniently, as thofe ingenious underground Philofophers the *Miners,* can below Stairs; who by mere Perflation and Ventilation, as they term it, that is by letting Air in and out as they find proper, produce a kind of actual Circulation of it, and make it thicker or thinner, as they find beft for their Bufinefs.

I muft

I muft take Leave to be merry on this Subject with your Lordfhip, to make Amends for the Fright it gave me; and if we once fall to Dealing with thefe admirable Fellows, we fhall foon be no longer fatisfied, either with the Earth, or Sun of our Forefathers, but by the Help of their Improvements in our Fields and Gardens, we fhall get, as it were, *new Heavens, and a new Earth*, as St. *Peter* fpeaks. We fhall certainly have the Advantage of the good Catholicks, in taking up with this Scheme, for they will probably be fearful of dealing with thefe fame Lords of the Air, *propter metum Judæorum*, and left the Clergy and Inquifition talk to them about it in private. Befides, they will probably ftick to their old Way of Weather-making by Proceffions, and carrying about the Shrines and Relicks of their precious Saints, which we all know by Experience, never fail to produce Rain or Sunfhine on all publick Occafions, as the Prieft and People defire them; and may with proper Regulations, be made Ufe of in the Way of Gardening, for the Service of private Gentlemen, that have ftrong Faith and large Fruiteries.

H   The

The Ancients keep a great Noife with their Witches charming down the Moon, and the Prieft of *Jupiter Lycæus* caufing Rain when he pleas'd, by dipping a Branch of Oak in a certain Fountain, whofe Name I've forgot. The *Jews* boaft as loudly of *Judah*, that by unloofing one Shoe, brought a heavy Rain down in a Drougth; and that had he untied the other, it would have caus'd a fecond Deluge; but none of them could come up to thefe fame *Laplanders*, that make the Sunbeams brighten the Face of Nature, where they direct them.

The famous *Swedifh* Prieft and Inquifitor, *Joannes Nider*, tells us, indeed, (in his 4*th* Chapter of his Tract about Witches,) that the learned Judge *Peter Stadelein*, condemn'd an old Witch for caufing Tempefts; who confeft, on the Torture, that fhe did it, by invocation of the Devil in the Field, and facrificing a black Cock, and throwing it up to him in the Air, which when the Devil feiz'd, he immediately began the Storm. This was extraordinary enough, my Lord; but to oblige him to give us Calms, and as bright glorious Seafons in the Night of Winter, as others enjoy in the Morning or Noon of Summer, is an honeft

Sort

Sort of Magick that deferves publick Premiums, inftead of Punifhment, and excels all that ever yet appeared in the World. Even our learned Countryman, *Roger Bacon*, tho' he declares he could undertake to raife artificial Clouds, and caufe Thunder-claps to be heard, and Lightning to flafh in our Eyes along with them, and then make all end in a Shower of Rain, could never pretend to any Thing like thefe extraordinary Gentlemen; and therefore, my Lord, I leave it to your prudent Confideration, whether I had not better treat with a Colony of *Laplanders*, to come and fettle with their Drums in *England*, than fpend my Thoughts and Time, with keeping fair Weather with thefe buftling bluftry *Mufcovites*.

But I muft grow ferious when I fpeak on fo important a Subject as our good Agreement with *Mufcovy*, which in fo many Views, is of the higheft Confequence to *Great Britain*. But as it becomes not me to dictate to your Capacity and Experience, and as I have Reafon to hope, you think the fame Way that I do on this Occafion, I fhall not trouble you with a long Detail of Reafons and Motives, to perfuade us to cultivate the *Czar's* Friendfhip. It becomes me better to fay, that

whatever

whatever Commands your Lordſhip honours me with at this Court, I ſhall labour to perform with all my little Strength and Ability; as being conſcious I am ſerving the beſt of Princes, the moſt generous and diſintereſted Miniſter, and where they are well govern'd, the wiſeſt and braveſt Nation, that ever gave Laws to the Earth and the Sea. I am, with the greateſt Reſpect,

My Lord, Your Lordſhip's, &c.

C L A R E.

To the *Lord* H I G H T R E A S U R E R.

My L O R D,   *Paris, Dec.* 16, 1997.

YOUR laſt Diſpatch of the 8*th*, found me juſt return'd from viſiting our Sea-Ports, and their Garriſons in this Kingdom, all which I left in perfect good Order. The new Works at *Calais* to the Seaward, have much improv'd that Port, and in the loweſt nepe Tides at *Dunkirk*, our Ships of War of forty Guns can go out and come in in without any Hazard; the Benefit of which I need not mention to your Lordſhip.

Indeed if the eager Zeal of our Anceſtors, had not with ſo much Induſtry ruin'd this Haven, while it was in the Hands of *France*, we might have ſav'd a vaſt Sum in Repairing it now; and with half the Expence made it a better and ſafer Port, than at this Time can be hop'd for. All the *Britiſh* Garriſons, both Men and Officers, are in perfect good Health and Order, well fed, cloath'd, and paid, and made a fine Appearance; eſpecially when compar'd with thoſe of the *French* in the Towns I paſt thro', which were as naked and lean as Beggars. This is certainly very impolitick in this Crown, for when Troops are ſo ill paid and fed, they will never have Heart and Spirit in Time of Action; and tho' 'tis peculiar to the *Turkiſh* Soldiers, to carry a Spoon tied to their Swords, as Travellers aſſure us; yet in Effect all Soldiers do ſo, and never fight well for a Prince that feeds them ill, and neglects to keep them well. *France* and *Spain* have a long Time been remarkable for this Miſmanagement, and have paid dearly for their Neglect, by ſo many terrible Loſſes as they have met

H 3   with

with for thefe laft fifty Years, and yet the *French* feem no way induftrious to reform it.

As to the wretched State of Things here, which your Lordfhip is pleafed to demand an Account of from me, it is almoft as bad as their greateft Enemies can defire. For thefe many Years paft, partly by the Ravage which both Famine and the Plague made with them, their unfuccefsful Wars with *Germany*, and our Ruining their Naval Affairs and cramping their Trade, they have been much on the Decline. Befides the Quarrels *Lewis* the nineteenth and his prefent Majefty have had with the Papal See, (when the *French* King would fain have acted the Part of *Henry* the Eighth in *England*, and renouncing the Pope's Authority, feized on all the Wealth and Revenues of the Abbies and Monafteries) ended fo difgracefully for this King, and their Holineffes have held fo fevere an Hand over him ever fince, that his Affairs have gone very untowardly. He was forc'd to give up his Patriarch of *Paris*, (which as your Lordfhip knows he fet up as our Metropolitan of *Canterbury)* into the Pope's Hands, who as he had been the prime Contriver of the Scheme was burnt for an Heretick; and in fhort, the Clergy and Peo-

ple

ple joining with the See of *Rome*, cut out such Work for him, that he was sufficiently humbled, and glad to buy his Peace, with giving up the Regale and the Loss of two or three, strong frontier Towns in *Dauphine*, which the Pope keeps as Keys to enter the Gates of *France* from *Italy*, now that most of *Savoy* is his own.

Nor on the Side of *Spain* are the Affairs of this Crown any Thing better, for tho' in the last Wars between the Crowns, both made a mighty Noise of their Advantages, singing *Te Deum* for every little Village they took on either Side, just like the *London* Prize-Fighters, that with Drums and Trumpets proclaim each little Cut they give each other; and tho' *France* especially pretended, that the *Spaniards* were not able to stand before them, yet on the upshot of the Matter, when they made the Peace that has lasted ever since, *Spain* forc'd them to very inglorious Conditions. Your Lordship is perfectly well appriz'd, that they are as ill circumstanc'd on the Side of *Flanders* and *Germany*, where they have lost both *Lisle*, *Mons* and *Doway* to the *Dutch*, and *Strasburg* to the Emperor; so that all their Conquests in the 17*th* and 18*th* Centuries, that cost them such vast Sums, and such

H 4   Numbers

Numbers of Men, are vanifh'd into Smoak
and gone, and the Pope is now the entire
Object of the Fears of *Europe,* inftead of the
conquering *French.* The Truth is, this
Nation does not feem form'd for Empire, and
tho' they've often made mighty Efforts, and
great Conquefts, they never preferve them.
They feem to traffick for Provinces, as *Bufbe-
quius* tells us the *Turks* do for Birds, to take
them and buy them, juft to let them go again,
and that they may thank them for their Liberty. His prefent Majefty, *Lewis* the twentieth, does not feem fufficiently refolute, or
able, to mend the ill Pofture of his Affairs;
and if he were, his Clergy and People feem
no ways defirous to difoblige the Pope, by
ftrength'ning the Hands of their Prince;
and what is worfe, they are jealous the King
would take a fevere Revenge, for their joining with *Rome* againft him, if he fhould
once recover his former Power.

Befides, tho' the King is not fifty, he is
grown a little crazy, and leaves his Affairs
to his Minifters, who are more defirous
to manage Things well at home, and remedy the Diforders that cramp their Adminiftrations, than quarrel with their Neighbours who ufe the Nation ill. Thus it is with
great

great Difficulty, we have been able to influence them, to think of coming to an actual Rupture with the Pope, tho' he treats them so ill, and tho' we pay them such high Wages for it. As the King also has been always a very weak Prince, and extremely amorous, and entirely under the Management of one Miſtreſs or another by Turns, so he is now more so than formerly, which is a dead Weight on his Government. Every reigning Miſtreſs introduces a new Set of Miniſters and Officers; and this has often occaſion'd vaſt Convulſions at Court, where the Fall of every Favourite brings on the Ruin of all his Dependants; which is but a Sort of Copy of the Cuſtom *Herodotus* tells us the *Scythians* had, where when the King died, all his chief Officers were of neceſſity to be ſlain, and accompany him to his Grave.

Judge, my Lord, if the natural Conſequence of this muſt not be, That his Majeſty will be very ill ſerv'd, and have only mercenary rapacious Miniſters to manage his Affairs, when he neither ſhews Prudence in chuſing, nor Conſtancy in ſupporting them; and indeed the *French* Nobility have plaid their Game accordingly. The whole
of

of their Endeavours, under several Admini-
strations, for two Thirds of his Reign, has
been to pillage the Kingdom, whether Affairs went well or ill, being like some Mills I
have seen on the *Seine,* that will grind and
get Toll both with Flood and Ebb.

In the Mean-time this unhappy Kingdom
has been paying severely for these Misma-
nagements; tho' every Ministry, in their Turn,
have been applauding their own Conduct,
and on every little Occasion crying up their
happy Times, and striking Medals to the
Glory of their King. And certainly if future
Historians were to plan out their Chronicles
of these Days from such Vouchers, they
would represent this Monarch as considerable
an Hero; as the present Writers (if they impar-
tially represent the Distractions of his Councils, the Defeats of his Troops, the Loss of
his Provinces, and the Cries and Sufferings of
his opprest Subjects) must paint him a weak,
unfortunate, and contemptible Tyrant.

It is true, indeed, Mr. *Meneville,* who
is a wife and able, tho' a corrupt Minister,
and those who are at present at the Helm
with him, (and depend on Mrs. *Duvall,* the
reigning Mistress) as they seem to have an
absolute Ascendant over him, and are likely

to

to keep it, have manag'd him and his Affairs, these last four Years, something better than their Predecessors, and are endeavouring to bring Things into tolerable Order; However, after all, they have chiefly aim'd at keeping the Clergy a little humbler, and calming the Parties and Factions in the Kingdom; and by stopping the Mouths of the boldest and most seditious Leaders by Preferments, making every one pay more Submission to the King's Decrees and Authority.

Tho this has not sufficiently quieted the Provinces, yet at Court they have taught them all, to speak entirely the King's Language and Sentiments; where (as in *Copenhagen* every body's Clock and Watch is set to go exactly with the King's great Clock at the Palace) all are ready to answer his Majesty and his Ministers as submissively, as *Menage*, an antient *French* Writer tells us in his Time, the Duke *D' Usez* did the Queen Regent, who when she ask'd him what Hour it was, answer'd, Madam, what Hour your Majesty pleases.

This great Work, tho' it be but half done, would never have been brought about barely by Preferments and Places; for I can assure your

your Lordſhip, it has coſt immenſe Sums too, which they have been forc'd to fleece the People for, to buy off their Demagogues, ſo that they whip the Subject with Rods of their own making. And indeed the *Ratio ultima Regum*, which us'd to be plac'd as the Motto on the Cannon of this King's Predeceſſors, ought to be taken off and plac'd around his Coin, as the chief Specifick of the preſent Times, for Submiſſion and Obedience to the Authority of the Crown.

Their great ſtanding military Force, has alſo with the Help of theſe Lenitives, gone of late a good Way to re-eſtabliſh Peace and Order, in the Room of their former Confuſion and Diſtractions. By the Means of ſo conſiderable a Body of Troops as they keep up, they at once over-awe their Enemies and the *Pope*, from attempting new Diſturbances; and alſo ſilence the loud *Orators* whom he prompts, from thundering in their Pulpits to ſtir up the People, as effectually as *Lewis* XIV. us'd to drown the Speeches of the *Huguenots* at the Scaffold and the Gibbet, with the Noiſe of the Drums, leſt their Words ſhould make too ſtrong Impreſſions on the Crowd, by repreſenting how Religion and its true Profeſſors were injur'd,   Such

Such miferable and deftructive Meafures is Tyranny, and its deteftable Advocates forc'd to make ufe of, to fupport its own Violence, and chain down that natural De-fire, which the great Author of Mankind has plac'd in every Breaft, to weaken or over-turn it. Whereas, if Princes would act with the Spirit of our glorious King, or his Roy-al Anceftors, and make the Laws of the Land, the Rule of their Government and the People's Obedience; nay, if they would act barely as honeft Men, with a common Regard to Confcience and Juftice, how hap-py would Mankind be? What would then become, my Lord, of Generals, Officers, and Soldiers; of Infantry and Cavalry, Ar-tillery, Powder-Mills, Gun-Smiths, Sword-Cutlers, Spies, Informers, Jefuits, and Af-faffins?

But Sycophants and Flatterers, that are ever buzzing about the Ears of great Prin-ces, knowing it is impoffible otherwife to fupport themfelves, and the defperate Mea-fures they put their Mafters on, are ftill per-fuading them they can never reign effectu-ally, but when they tyrannize abfolutely. To this End it is, that they fo immenfely en-creafe their Troops, to tie the Subjects Chains and

and Bondage fo faft, that 'tis dangerous at
laft even for the Prince to unloofe them, if
Pity and Humanity fhould encline him to
it. Thus they ftrain the Cords of Government, fo far beyond their natural Strength,
that fooner or later they break of themfelves,
and end in the Deftruction of thofe Sycophants; who, while they pufh on Princes to
aim at enlarging their Power, (juft as the Devil deluded our firft Parents) by telling them
they fhall be as Gods on Earth, turn them
into Devils, and occafion their irretrieva-
ble Ruin.

The Mifery of this poor People, that
groan under fo many Burthens, is incon-
ceivable; they pay Taxes for all that they
eat or drink or wear, to an exceffive Degree,
even to their Salt and Bread; nay, they pay
for every Beaft that they keep, even to plow
their Land, for every Arpent (equivalent almoft to our Acre) when plow'd, and for e-
very Mill that they grind their Corn in, for
the Houfes, or Cottages rather, they live
in, and the very Fires in them which they
warm themfelves by; and alfo for every
Marriage, Chriftening, and Burial in their
Families. Thefe Taxes are every Year encreafing, and indeed, like *Virgil's* Torrent,
the

the longer they run, the more they swell
and enlarge, till at last they lay waste whole
Countries, like an Innundation, sweeping
away both the Substance, Houses, and Inhabitants of the Land.

By this Means the Poverty, especially a-
mong the lower Sort, is so excessive, that
they want even the common Necessaries of
Life; nor is it possible, in some Provinces,
to prevent a general Desolation, without
a Remission of many of their burthenous
Gabells, unless some of those miraculous
Showers should be procur'd them by the Jesuits, which *Livy* tells us were sometimes
sent the *Romans* by their Gods, that rain'd
down Corn and Flesh and Milk among
them.

In the midst of this Misery, the Luxury
of the Nobility and Gentry is increas'd beyond all Bounds, as if they were not only
insensible of, but even rejoyc'd in the publick Calamities of their Fellow-Subjects.
Their Tables are cover'd with such Profu-
sions of Expence, in all Sorts of Delicacies,
that it exceeds the Riot and Revelling of
Greece and *Rome*, flush'd with the Glory of
their Conquests, and corrupted with the
Wealth and Spoils of the World. The stat-

ed

ed Hours of dining and supping are absolutely laid aside, and thro' a silly Affectation of mimicking their Princes, People of Distinction oblige their Cooks, to have a Dinner still ready at all Hours when they call for it, thinking it only fit for Tradesmen and Rusticks to dine at set Times. Nay, I can assure your Lordship, some are grown to such Excess and Folly, as to buy no Flesh of Beeves or Sheep for their Tables, that have not their Hair and Wool close shaven off, and curried with Pumice-Stones, to make the Meat sweeter and higher relish'd.

Nay they have, in Imitation of the Ancients, brought into Fashion, the sowing and cultivating the famous *Silphium* of the *Persians*, with which they feed these Sheep, and make them extremely fat and high tasted; and many mingle *AssaFœtida* with their finest Sauces, which they reckon gives them a more exquisite Flavour, than the Spices and Ambergreace of their Ancestors. They have in all great Houses also, several different Sorts of Cooks, that preside over the particular Provinces of Luxury; as Cooks for Soops, Cooks for roasting, Cooks for boiling, Cooks of the Fishery, as they call them here, Cooks for Ragooes and Fricassies, Cooks for bak'd

and

and ftew'd Meats, Cooks, Confectioners, and Cooks of the Paftry. They have carried this wretched Pleafure of their Palates fo far, that there are few Noblemen who do not, like *Fulvius Hirpinus**, keep an *Efcargatoire*, or Snail-Houfe, where they feed their Refervoirs of Snails, all the Year, on the choiceft and fineft Herbs, Fruits, and Flowers, for making their exquifite Ragoos, which this Nation is fo ridiculoufly fond of; and have even brought the Breed of Pullets from *Malabar* to *France*, becaufe their Flefh is reckon'd prodigioufly fweet and delicious, tho' the outward Skin and the Bones are as black as Jet, as Dr. *Frier* tells us in his Travels. One would think, my Lord, after indulging themfelves in fuch amazing Extravagancies this Way, they would not give into any other; and yet the violent Paffion for Gaming, in both Sexes, runs fo high, that the Honour and Modefty of the one, and the Fortune and Eafe of the other, are entirely facrificed to it. It eats up even their State, and their belov'd Equipage; and devours their favourite Embroidery and Jewels. The only Refource the Ladies have, under the difmal

---

* Vid. Pliny, L. IX. C. LVI. & Varro, L. III. C. XIV.

I   Ravage

Ravage that attends this bewitching Madnefs, is to proftitute their Perfons to the
fortunate Conqueror, and at the dreadful
Expence of all that fhould be dear to them,
to prevent the irreparable Deftruction that
muft otherwife confume, like Fire, their
domeftick OEconomy, and the Fortune of
the Family. A Practice which I fear fpreads
too faft in fome Countries, as well as here,
and puts me in Mind of what *Tacitus* fays
* of the *Germans* Love of Gaming in his
Time, that when they had plaid away all their
Money, they then fet their Liberties and their
Bodies at Stake, which became the Property
of the Conqueror. The Men indeed have
fometimes the happy Confolation, by turning
Villains and Sharpers, to repair the Ruins of
their Eftates, by preying on the Ignorance
and Inexperience of others; but furely, to
an honeft and ingenuous Mind, there is no
Ruin can befall a Man equal to this, where
the Repairs of their Circumftances are owing to the Sale of their Reputation?

I know not, my Lord, whether it be an
Alleviation of the Crime, or an Aggravation
of it, that this fatal Luxury and immenfe
Extravagance is not fo much owing to the
Humour of the People, as the Policy of the

* De mor. Germ. C. 24.

Court;

Court; but certain it is, that this is the main Fountain of all the sad Disorders. Frugality and OEconomy are the great standing Fences against the shining Temptations of ambitious Princes and designing Ministers, and therefore there is a Necessity of breaking thro' them, by rendring them unfashionable, and consequently ridiculous. The great *Machiavels* in the Art of Ruling, know too well the Force of this Reasoning; a luxurious Gentry must be expensive, if expensive needy, if needy they must run in Debt, and if indebted, they must either give up their Pleasures, or take Places and Preferments to support them, that render themselves Slaves to the Will of their Master, who is thereby Lord at once of their Honour and Liberty, and in them a fair Purchaser of that of his People.

Behold at once, my Lord, the fatal Market of the Freedom of this Nation, and all their boasted Parliaments Rights and Privileges, which they once enjoy'd in as full a Proportion, as our own happy Countrymen. But while we lament their miserable Conduct, let us rejoice at our own, and the Blessings that, under Heaven, we owe to that glorious Race of Heroes, under

I 2   and

and by whom we ſtill poſſeſs thoſe invaluable Bleſſings, which the falſe Ambition of our neighbouring Princes, and the thoughtleſs Vanity, Pride, and Folly of their Subjects, have extirpated.

But I have detain'd your Lordſhip too long with theſe grave Reflections, and ſhall therefore reſerve any further Accounts of this People, and the Conduct of the Miniſters here, who ſeem deſirous of improving the preſent State of Things, till the next Diſpatch I have the Honour to ſend you. Poſſibly in caſe what I now ſend be not diſagreeable to you, I may be able, in my next, to entertain you better on this Head. In the mean Time, it cannot fail to give your Lordſhip ſome Satisfaction, to ſee this great Kingdom, that for ſo many Years was ſtill enterprizing on the Liberties and Dominions of her weaker Neighbours, and laying Schemes for the Ruin of *Great-Britain*, (as the main Step to the Empire of the World,) fallen now from the Object of our Fears, to that of our Pity.

I am ſenſible, your Lordſhip's great Wiſdom and Experience, knows all theſe Things that I have wrote on this Subject, or that I am able to write on it or any other, infinitely

nitely better than I do. But you will be fo
juft to confider, that I have herein rather
obey'd your Commands, than follow'd my
Inclinations, being fenfible I have as little
Defire as Ability, to fpeak or write on fuch
weighty and difficult Matters, but when
I am enjoin'd it by your exprefs Direction.

I fend herewith two little manufcript Trea-
tifes, remarkable for their Oddnefs and Novelty, and more to gratify your Curiofity,
than pleafe your Taft. One of them is
wrote by Monfieur *Perault*, firft Surgeon
to the King; it is entitled, *An Effay on
Circumcifion and Embalming*. On the firft
Head he endeavours to prove, that it is vaftly ferviceable to Health, in many Refpects,
efpecially in warm Climates, and particularly that it is a great Extinguifher of Luft,
and chiefly for that Reafon enjoin'd the
Jews, and therefore advifes the Renewing
that Ufage now. In the other Treatife, he
fhews the Satisfaction it would be for great
Perfons, inftead of throwing their Friends
and Relations, to rot and corrupt in Vaults
and Graves, to keep them in a decent Repofitory, where they might furvey the very Perfons and Features, of the whole Race of their

I 3   Anceftors

Anceftors, as little disfigur'd as an *Ægypti-*
an Mummy. He undertakes to do this in
the greateft Perfection, and propofes it to
the Publick for their Encouragment, tho'
his Friends have, with much ado, prevail'd on him not to publifh it. Your Lordfhip fees, however, thefe Gentlemen are
not fatisfied with the Work we cut out for
them, which our Debaucheries and Luxury has made but too confiderable; but they
are for beginning with us from the Birth,
and following our wretched Carcaffes, even
after our Death.

The other Manufcript is a fhort Hiftory
of, about, an hundred Men, remarkable
for their great Wealth in this laft Age, in
Paris. He firft gives a fevere, but feem-
ingly an impartial Account, of the vile Arts
by which they obtain'd their Riches; of
their feveral Cheats, Extortion, Oppreffion,
fordid Avarice, flavifh Toil, and mean
Drudgery; their flattering the great, or
ruining the Poor, by which they had rifen
in the World. He there fhews the Pain
and Uneafinefs they went thro'; the Undu-
tifulnefs of Children; the ill Conduct of
their Wives or Widows; the Deaths of their
favourite Sons, or their dying Childlefs, and
　　　　　　　　　　　　　　Strangers

Strangers poffeffing their Subftance; or at leaft an extravagant Heir fquandring it fafter in bafe Methods, than they rais'd it. In the Conclufion he fhews how few of their Families or Fortunes remain at this Day, and how much fewer of them had the Honefty or Virtue to leave, even the twentieth or fortieth Part of what they had, to publick Ufes, or the Poor.

The Book is rather an ufeful Subject, than a well writ Treatife; but I wifh it were tranflated into *Englifh*, and ten Thoufand of them prefented to the rich Men of our Age; who, with fo little Regard to the publick good of their Country, or thinking of making generous Foundations of their own, or contributing to thofe of others, go on continually in thofe beautiful Expreffions of the *Pfalmift, to heap up Riches which they cannot tell who fhall gather.* It is not to fee the Light here, it being dangerous to publifh it, for fear of provoking the Refentments of fome Perfons, whofe Relations are hardly treated in it, tho' I am told, with great Juftice. 'Tis writ by Father *Meron* a *Capuchin*; but this I tell only to your Lordfhip. The Jefuits are feverely fatyriz'd in

I 4   it,

it, for their Avarice, which makes it dangerous for the Author to own the Writing it.

When I have obey'd your Commands, as to giving you fome Account of the poor Duke *D' Aumont*'s Fate and Character, who has been fo differently reprefented to you, I fhall put an End to this tirefome Letter. It is certain, he died the firft of this Month at his lovely Retirement in the Country, but not of Poifon, as your Lordfhip mentions, but of a Fit of the Apoplexy, which took him off in a few Hours.

He was unqueftionably a Gentleman of the moft uncorrupted Integrity, the greateft Abilities, and the moft univerfal Genius, of any Minifter of State this Nation ever bred, not excepting that Hero of the Antients, Cardinal *Richlieu.* With all thefe Advantages, he carried himfelf in fo haughty and arbitrary a Manner, with his late Majefty, who favour'd him, and his Enemies that envy'd him, that he made his Merit and great Qualifications almoft ufelefs to his Country. His Honefty had the Appearance of Oftentation and Infolence, (tho nothing was further from his Heart) and his Capacity and Knowledge, feem'd to wear an affuming and fupercili-

ous

ous Air. He affected a Sincerity and Severity, that continually alienated the Hearts of the Courtiers from him. Not content to be unblameable himfelf, he thought to brow-beat Corruption and Immorality, in all that had any Thing to do in the King's Affairs; by reproaching them openly with any ill Conduct in their Lives and Manners. He was not fatisfied in excelling all Men in the greateft Talents for the Camp, or the Cabinet, for Books or the World; unlefs he could drive Ignorance or Infufficiency from the Court, by fevere Upbraidings of the Weaknefs, or Miftakes, the Folly, Incapacity or Vices of many in the Crowd of Pretenders there to Place and Power.

It was eafy, my Lord, to fee the Confequence of fuch a Conduct muft be the Ruin of him who gave into it. And indeed tho' Heaven feem'd for fome Time to declare in his Favour, againft the Malice of the World, and to labour for his Eftablifhment, by many Succeffes abroad; yet, on the firft Turn of the Tide, by the Lofs of the Battle at *Strafburg*, the whole Kingdom, or in other Words, all that was vicious and bad in it, feem'd, with one Voice, to cry out againft him, and call for his Deftruction; and even
Lewis

Lewis the Nineteenth, his Mafter, tho' he efteem'd him, was fo fick of his intolerable Virtue, that he readily abandon'd him to the publick Hatred.

He was turn'd out of any Share of the Adminiftration, banifh'd the Court, and confin'd to his Country Seat for Life, where he gave himfelf up, with infinite Relifh, to a few worthy Friends and his Studies; and where he writ thofe Memoirs of his Time, which I fent your Lordfhip, and which alone will be a lafting Proof of the Virtue and Capacity of the Man. It is certain, if he could have pardon'd his Mafter's and his Courtiers Vices and Follies, or his Enemies evil Arts to defraud the Crown, by the Mifmanagement of the Finances, and the ufual Corruptions in the Officers of the Army, he might have rul'd the one, and triumph'd over the others; but he was too much in haft to do good, and too violently virtuous to reform a corrupt World, which he profefs'd to abhor. I remember a great Man one Day fpeaking of his Vigilance, Dexterity, and his equal Zeal and Capacity to ferve his Mafter, and clear the Court of fuch troublefom eVermin; compar'd his Fate to the Duchefs of *Chevreufe*'s Cat, who having broke her Leg,

by

by a Fall in the Cellar, was the next Night bit to Death, and almost devour'd by the Rats, she had so often been labouring to destroy.

I am impatient for your Lordship's next Dispatches, and doubt not but this Court will oppose, with Vigour, the setting up the Inquisition, in spite of the Intrigues of the Nuncio, and his humble and pious Masters, the Jesuits; in which, according to my Instructions, I have and shall continue to express his Majesty's and your Lordship's zealous Concurrence and Assistance, by all proper Measures, and am, with the highest Deference and Esteem,

My Lord,

Your Lordship's, &c.

H E R B E R T.

To

To *the Lord* HIGH TREASURER.

MY LORD, *Rome, Jan. 7, 1998.*

BY the laſt Courrier, my Diſpatches carried you a full Account of the fair Proſpect of Succeſs I have for all my Negotiations here. The Bull mention'd therein, ordaining that no *Britiſh* Subject ſhall any longer be judg'd liable to, or hereafter be ſeized by the Inquiſition, having paſt the uſual Forms; has delivered already many of our Countrymen from the Harpies of that Court, and ſecur'd them from it's terrible Judicature for the future. The Emperor's happy Recovery, has, at preſent, pretty much ſuſpended all our deſign'd Proceedings, to prevent the Intriegues of this See, in order to place his Holineſs on the Imperial Throne; and above all, as the Elector of *Cologne* has luckily broke with this Court, I hope we ſhall have Time to take ſuch Meaſures, as ſhall effectually ſecure *Europe* from ſo terrible a Blow.

In

In the mean Time, I haſten this by a very worthy *Engliſh* Gentleman, Mr. *Lumley*, which brings you an Account of as extraordinary an Undertaking, as this Court has ever attempted, tho' it ſeems to be the natural Soil and Climate for Projects of all Kinds. In ſhort, 'tis nothing leſs than ſelling by publick Auction all the vaſt Collection of Relicks, which were brought hither many Years ſince, at different Times; and particularly, when the Treaſures of *Italy* were heap'd up in the Caſtle of St. *Angelo.*

This amazing Event, of ſelling publickly thoſe venerable Remains, which the Bigottry and Zeal of their Anceſtors had ſo long held ſacred, is entirely occaſion'd by the Avarice and Prodigality of the Cardinal *Nephew* ; whoſe Expences are as unbounded, as his Paſſions and Extravagancies, which this Sale is deſign'd to ſupply. It is palliated indeed with the Pretence of diſperſing ſuch holy and precious Things, thro' all Chriſtian Nations, to encreaſe their Devotion and Piety, which might otherwiſe ſicken and flag, for want of ſuch extraordinary Incentives, but I have told your Lordſhip the true Cauſe.

It

It is generally believ'd that this Defign will bring in vaft Treafures to the Cardinal *Nephew's* great Relief and Comfort; and as the Pope's managing Temper, and the reft of the Cardinals high Regard for ftrict OEconomy, prevent his fquandring the Treafures of the See; they have complied with this Project, to raife a large Sum out of this holy Trumpery, which they were fick of, and which they found the Devotion of the *Italians* growing very cold to. I remember to have heard, that in the Beginning of the 16*th* Century, *Vergerius,* who was afterwards the Pope's Nuncio in *Germany,* was employ'd by the Elector of *Saxony,* to buy up for him many Relicks of the Saints in *Italy.* Accordingly he bought feveral, but before the Relicks had been fent to *Germany,* *Luther's* Books and Doctrines began to fly about, and leffen'd the Value of fuch delicate Wares fo far, that the Elector order'd him to fell them with great Lofs, and poffibly that is one Reafon that occafions the prefent Sale, fince *Italy* begins to defpife them.

The Catalogue is not yet printed, but I have procur'd the Original from the Imperial Ambaffador, who defigns to lay out great Sums on them, and what follows I
have

have copied and translated very faithfully
from it, adding some few Notes of my own,
in Hopes it will both surprize and entertain you.

I can venture to assure your Lordship,
that whether the Relicks in the Catalogue be
really genuine or no, there are none in it,
which have not actually been maintain'd,
by the gravest Writers of this Church, to
have been preserv'd in the Places, from
whence they are said to be brought, and which
were not religiously venerated, not to say,
ador'd there. Indeed the good Jesuits may
have falsified some of them, to make their
Collection more glorious, and raise the larger Sum; yet I have Faith enough to believe they are fully as authentick, as most
of the Originals, which these poor Catholicks, in different Places, preserve so religiously, and attribute so much Sanctity, and
even Miracles, to.

But I will detain your Lordship no longer
from perusing the Catalogue, than to say, I
omit the Preface, because it only contains a
fulsome, affected Declamation on the Veneration due to Relicks, on the vast Preference these deserve above all others; the
pretended Reasons of their being exposed

l

to

to Sale, in order to diſperſe them more
equally thro' the Chriſtian World, and the
unqueſtion'd Authority theſe ought to have,
with all good Catholicks. For theſe, my
Lord, are all voucht (as the Preface ſpeaks)
by the Pope's authentick Inſpection and Direction, confirm'd by his annex'd Bull,
(which I alſo omit) and verified before the
Conſiſtory of Cardinals, by the due and legal Proof, of having paſt untouch'd and un-
damag'd, in the Trial by Fire. ----But I haſten to the Catalogue, which follows. -- --
A Catalogue of the moſt ſacred, and emi-
nently venerable Relicks, of the holy *Roman*
Catholick Church, collected by the pious
Care of their Holineſſes the Popes, the moſt
auguſt Emperors, Kings, and Princes, Po-
tentates, and Prelates of the Chriſtian World,
and ſeveral of them brought to *Rome,* by
the vaſt Care and Expences of the moſt Reverend Fathers, the Jeſuits. All which are
now to be diſpos'd of by Auction, for the general Benefit and Emolument of the Chriſtian
World, at the Church of St. *Peters* at *Rome,*
on *Monday* the 25*th* of *April* 1998, from
Nine in the Morning till eight at Night, and
to continue till all be ſold. *N. B.* The
whole of theſe ſaid moſt precious Relicks,
                                                    with

with their proper Vouchers and Certificates of Verification, and his Holiness's Bull for their being true authentick Originals, may be viewed and examined, (but not handled) at the Church of St. *Peter's* aforesaid, by all Ambassadors, Prelates, and Persons of Quality, and proper Credit, Condition, and Character, till the Day of Sale.

The Ark of the Covenant, the Cross of the good Thief; both somewhat Worm-eaten. *Judas's* Lanthorn, a little scorch'd. The Dice the Soldiers play'd with, when they cast Lots on our Saviour's Garment; from *Umbriatico* in *Calabria*. The Tail of *Balaam's* Ass, that spoke when she saw the Angel. St. *Joseph's* Ax, Saw, and Hammer; and a few Nails he had not driven, a little rust eaten. St. *Christopher's* Stone-Boat, and St. *Anthony's* Mill-Stone, on which he sail'd to *Muscovy*. The Loaves of Bread turn'd into Stone by St. *Boniface,* on a Soldier's denying him a Piece of them when he was starving, for which he suffer'd Martyrdom, as a Sorcerer. Our B. Saviour's Teeth, Hair, and *Præputium (Emptum Charovii)* another *Præputium (Emptum Aquisgrani)* brought thither by an Angel from *Jerusalem. N. B.* In all such Cases

K   of

of Duplicates equally well vouched and verified, it is left to the Faith of the Buyer,
which deferves the Preference; but the *Præputium* vouch'd by Cardinal *Tolet*, to be
kept at *Calcata*, in the Church of St. *Cornelius* and *Cyprian*, and that other of *Podium*,
as well as that preferv'd at *Antwerp*, and
vouch'd by *Theobald* Archbifhop of *Bifonti*,
John Bifhop of *Cambray*, and confirm'd by
Pope *Eugenius* and *Clement* VIII. fince
they are all three alfo approv'd by Miracles,
are left uncenfur'd to the Piety and Veneration of the Faithful; it being certain, that
the fame Power that maketh his Body to be
and exift, at the fame Time in different
Places, may exert it felf in like Manner, as
to this moft precious and holy Relick. Several Drops of *Chrift*'s Blood, on different
Occafions, as his Circumcifion, bearing his
Crofs, and his Crucifixion, purchafed at a
vaft Price, and brought by the Fathers, the
Jefuits from *Rochel*; feveral fmall Phials of
it from *Mantua*; larger Veffels of it from
St. *Euftachius*'s in this City of *Rome*. Mix'd
with Water, as it came from his Side, from
St. *John Lateran* in this City. His Cradle
and Manger very old. *Ditto*, a Pale full of
the Water of *Jordan*, where he was baptiz'd,

tiz'd, fresh and clear to this Day (*emptum Cassini.*)   The Water-Pots of the Marriage at *Cana* in *Galilee.* N. B. These are not the Pots shewn at *Pisa (Cluniaci & Andegavi)* but the true original ones.   Crums of the Bread that fed the 5000 *(Romæ ad Mariæ Novæ.)* A Bough of the Tree carried by *Christ* entring *Jerusalem* in Triumph, the Leaves almost fresh still ; from *Spain (ad Salvatoris.)* The Table on which *Christ* eat the last Supper, a little decayed ; at *Rome* St. *John Lateran.* Some of the Bread which he broke then; from *Spain ad Salvatoris.* The Cup he then drank out of and gave to his Disciples (*ad Mariæ Insulanæ* near *Lyons.)* The Sacrament of his Body and Blood (from *Brussells.)* I assure your Lordship, this is neither more nor less than a plain small Ivory Ball.   The Towel with which he wip'd his Disciples Feet, very rotten, *(Rome.)* Part of the Money paid *Judas. Malchus*'s Lanthorn, some of the Panes crack'd, and the Door quite decay'd, from St. *Denis.*

The following most holy and precious Relicks were brought to *Rome*, by the blessed Father *Francis Visconti*, by Order of the Pope, from *Aquisgranum* or *Aken.* Part of

the

the Wood of the Crofs, a little decay'd, and a Nail of the fame. Some of the *Manna* in the Wildernefs, and of the Bloffoms of *Aaron's* Rod. Part of the *Sudarium*, of the Reed, and Spunge of our Saviour. A Girdle of our Saviour's, and another of the Virgin's, little worn. The Chord with which *Chrift* was bound at his Paffion, very frefh. Some of the Hair of St. *John* Baptift. A Ring of the Chain of St. *Peter*. Some of the Blood of St. *Stephen*, and the Oyl of St. *Catharine*. The Arm of St. *Simeon*, ill kept. The Image of the bleffed Virgin, drawn by St. *Luke*, the Features all vifible. The Relicks of St. *Spes*, or St. *Hope*. Some of the Hair of the Bleffed Virgin. One of her Combs, brought originally from *Bafançon* in *Burgundy*, and twelve Combs of the twelve Apoftles, all very little ufed, originally from *Lyons*. The *Indufium* or Shift, of the Bleffed Virgin, when our Saviour was born. The Swathes in which our Saviour was wrapt the Night of his Nativity. The holy Linnen-Cloath upon which St. *John* Baptift was beheaded, wants new Hemming and Darning. The Cloath with which our Saviour was cover'd, when he hung on the Crofs. The Brains of St. *Peter*, from *Geneva*. Note, thefe are the individual Brains which

which that Arch-Heretick *Calvin* declar'd were a mere Pumice-Stone, sinning against God, the holy Apostle, and his own Soul.

The following most venerable Relicks were bought at, and brought from *Prague* to this City, by the Reverend Father *Priuli*, Jesuit commission'd and authoris'd by the Pope. The Head and Arm of the blessed *Longinus*. Some Relicks of *Abraham*, *Isaac*, and *Jacob*, very old. The Arm and some Part of the Body of *Lazarus*, ill kept and smells. Two Pieces of two Girdles of the Blessed Virgin. A Part of the Body of St. *Mark*, and a Part of his Gospel, of his own Handwriting, almost legible. A Piece of St. *John* the Evangelist's Coat. A Piece of the Staff of St. *Peter*, and another Piece of the Staff of St. *Paul*. A Part of St. *Peter*'s Chain. A Finger of St. *Ann*. A Part of the Blessed Virgin's Veil, as good as new. The Head of St. *Luke*. It is true, there is also another in this Catalogue, but both are so amply verified, nay avouch'd by daily Miracles, that his Holiness leaves it undecided; betwixt God and the Buyer be it. Some of the Relicks of St. *Catharine* of *Alexandria*. The Head and Finger of St. *Stephen*, 'tis suppos'd to be his middle Finger, but that is doubtful. Here endeth the Collection of

K 3   Relicks

Relicks from *Prague*. The Staff deliver'd
by our Lord to St. *Patrick*, and with which
he drove all the venemous Creatures out of
Ireland. Eight *Veronicas*, or holy Hand-
kerchiefs of our Lord's, one from *Turin*, another from St. *John de Lateran*, and a
third from St. *Peter*'s in this City, another
from *Cadoin* in *Perigort*, a fifth from *Befan-
çon*, another from *Compeigne*, a seventh from
Milan, and another from *Aix le Chapelle*.
It is as impossible as unjust, to decide which
has the best Title to be the real one, since
they all have been received from Age to Age
by the Faithful: but as that of *Cadoin* hath
fourteen Bulls in it's Favour, and the rest but
one or two, (tho' that of *Turin* produceth
four in it's Behalf) we leave it undecided.
This we do the rather, as the Prayers and
Devotions of the Pious have probably sanctifi-
ed them all equally; and moreover, it is possible that they have been miraculously mul-
tiplied by the Goodness of God, for the Support and Aid of the Faithful, as the Loaves
and the Fishes were to the hungry *Jews*.
The most holy Fore-Finger of *John* the Baptist, with which he pointed to *Christ*, saying, *Behold the Lamb of God*, &c. brought
from *Jerusalem* to *Malta*, by the Brothers
of

of St. *John*'s Hofpital, and fince to this City. The holy *Sindon*, or Linnen, in which *Chrift*'s Body was buried, from *Turin*. The Difh in which *Chrift* eat the Pafchal Lamb, made all of one Emerald, from *Genoa*. A Nail of our Saviour's Crofs, fix'd formerly on the Church Roof of *Milan*, and brought hither: Another, being one of thofe which the Emprefs *Helena* order'd to be wrought up into the Cheek of a Bridle, for the Emperor *Conftantine*; and a third which was thrown into the *Adriatick* Sea in a vaft Storm, to appeafe it, as it actually did. Taken up fince in a Fifherman's Net, and brought to this City. The Stone upon which *Abraham* offer'd to facrifice his Son; and another Stone on which our Lord was plac'd, when he was prefented in the Temple. The Top of the Lance with which *Chrift*'s Side was pierc'd. The Smock of St. *Prifca*, in which fhe was martyr'd 1700 Years ago, fomething decay'd. A Thorn of that Crown of Thorns which was put on our Saviour's Head. The Head of the Woman of *Samaria*, who was converted by our Saviour, decay'd, but plainly an Head ftill. The Arm of St. *Ann*, Mother of the Bleffed Virgin; and the Chain of St. *Paul*.

K 3 *Scala*

Scala Sancta, or the twenty eight Steps of
white Marble which *Chrift* was lead up in
his Paffion to *Pilate*'s Houfe, and on which
vifibly appear the Marks of his Blood; fent
by *Helena* from *Jerufalem* to the Emperor
Conftantine. A Picture of our Lord, faid
to be begun by St. *Luke,* and finifh'd mira-
culoufly by an Angel; or (as others fay) St.
Luke preparing to draw it, and falling to
his Prayers to God, that he might draw his
Son aright, when he arofe, he found the
Picture finifh'd. The holy Crib of our Saviour's. The Pillar at which he was whip'd,
the firft of thefe very old and tender.

Here follow fome moft venerable and
precious Relicks, brought hither from *Venice*
by the aforefaid Father *Francis Vifconti.*

Some of our Saviour's Blood, gather'd up
at his Paffion, with the Earth it was fpilt
on. A Thorn of the Crown of Thorns.
A Finger of St. *Mary Magdalen.* A Piece
of St. *John* Baptift's Skull. A Tooth of St.
Mark, a little rotten; alfo one of his Fingers, and his Ring with a Stone in it. A
Piece of St. *John* Baptift's Habit. Some of
the Virgin's Hair. The Sword of St. *Peter,*
very rufty and old. A Piece of *Chrift*'s
white Robe when he was fet at nought by
Herod.

Herod. One of the Stones wherewith St. *Stephen* was ftoned. Some of St. *Jo-feph*'s Breath which an Angel enclofed in a Phial, as he was cleaving Wood violently, which was fo long ador'd in *France*, and fince brought to *Venice*, and from *Venice* to this City. The Head of St. *Denys*, which he carried two Miles after it was cut off under his Arm, praifing God all the Way, and faying, *Glory be to thee, Lord.* The Rock which *Mofes* ftruck in the Wildernefs, with the three Holes in it of the Diameter of a Goofe Quill, out of which the Water iffued for the 600000 *Ifraelites* and their Cattle. Here endeth the Lift of the Reliques from *Venice.*

A Piece of the Rope *Judas* hang'd himfelf with, from *Amras* near *Infpruck.* Part of the Crown of Thorns from *Paris.* Several fingle Thorns from different Places, *Compoftella, Tholoufe,* and this City, to be fold feparately. The Reed given our Lord for a Scepter *(Romæ* St. *John Lateran.)* His Holy Crofs, a great Part of it from *Jeru-falem,* more of it from *Conftantinople,* more from *Paris.* A large Crucifix made of the Wood of it *(Romæ).* Several Nails belonging to it, two of *Rome,* two from *Venice,*

one

one from *Colen*, two from *Paris*, one from *Sienna*, one from *Naples*, one from St. *Denys*, one from the Carmelites at *Paris*. *N. B.* We fay in this as aforefaid, Which are the right Nails, he only knows, whofe Body they pierced; but the Vouchers and Certificates for all are to be feen, proved, and examined, let the Purchafers determine according to the Truth. The Title faftned to the Crofs, fair and legible, and thought to be *Pilate's* Hand Writing, from *Tholoufe*. The Spunge that was dipt in Vinegar, and given to our Lord; *Rome*. From *Caffini* another. The Point of the Launce, three of them, one originally of *Rome*, another from *Paris*, a third from *Xaintonge*, all properly voucht and evidenc'd. The Church herein decides nothing, but modeftly faith, *Caveat Emptor*. The Footfteps which our Lord left in the Rock on his Afcenfion; *Rome*. The Marks of his Seat made on the Rock by his refting; from *Rheims*. Four Crucifixes, whofe Beards grow regularly, feven that have fpoke on feveral proper Occafions; ten more, that have wept often and bitterly upon *Good-Frydays*, and the Succefs of Hereticks, in their Wars with Catholicks. Five others

that

that have ſtirred and moved on different Accidents, four of them equal to any in the Chriſtian Church; ſix more that have groan'd, ſmil'd and nodded, all voucht authentically, very little inferior to the former, except the freſheſt being the laſt made. Another Crucifix, which having had it's Leg broke by accident, ſtunk ſo grievouſly, that all in the Church were forced to hold their Noſes for the Stench, till proper Remedies being applied, the Bone knit again, tho' the Place where the broken parts join'd, is ſtill viſibly thicker and larger, and that Leg near two Inches ſhorter than the other. Another Crucifix from *Trent*, under which the Synod was ſworn and promulg'd, and which bow'd it's Head to teſtifie the Approbation which it gave to the learned Decrees of that Holy Aſſembly. *N. B.* As no Man could ever tell what this Crucifix was made of, ſo it is much doubted by the Faithful, if ever it was made with Hands; it worketh unheard of Miracles. Another Crucifix from St. *Dominick the greater* in *Naples*, which ſpoke one Day to St. *Thomas Aquinas, Thou haſt well written of me,* Thomas. Another from the Church of the *Benedictines* in *Naples,* which

which held twice two long Converfations
with his Holy Vicegerent, Pope *Pius* V.
of bleffed Memory; and another of St. *Mary* of the *Carmelites* of the fame City, which
bowed it's Head at the Sight of a Cannon
Bullet which was fhot at him in 1439, (when
Don Pedro of *Arragon* befieg'd that City)
and only ftruck off the Crown. *N. B.* To
cover his Head, being very bald, there is
a Peruke of the Hair of the Virgin fitted
to it, to be taken off in hot Weather.
An Image of *Chrift* made by himfelf, and
fent to King *Abgarus* from St. *Silvefter*, in
the Field of *Mars* in this City. Another
made by Angels, from the Chapel of the
Sancta Sanctorum in this City, and a Crucifix which was begun to be painted by *Nicodemus*, but finifht by Angels; from the Cathedral of St. *Martin* in *Lucca*. *N. B.* All
thefe Crucifixes have wrought incredible
Miracles within thefe laft fifty or fixty Years.
Large Parcels of the Bleffed Virgin's Hair,
all of one Colour, from *Paris* and feveral
Places lefs known, and much of it of this
City. Great Quantities of her Milk gathered from many Places. Some Butter
and a fmall Cheefe made of it, that never
decays or corrupts, from *Mexico* in *America.*

ca. Her Slipper, and one of her Shoes.
N. B. This is the original Shoe, which the
famous *Rivet,* in his Apology for the Virgin
(*Lib.* 11. *Chap.* 1x.) was poffeft of, and had
the Figure of it grav'd, and publifht with
Licence ; and in the middle of the Sole
this is written, *The Meafure of the moft
Holy Foot of our Lady* ; and then follows,
Pope John XXII. *hath granted to thofe who
fhall thrice kifs it, and rehearfe three Ave
Maries with Devotion to her bleffed Honour
and Reverence, that they fhall gain* 700
*Years of Pardon, and be freed from many
Sins.* I muft add here, my Lord, what all
the learned, and even thofe who have only
feen the Cut of it publifht by *Rivet,* know
to be true, that the exact Meafure of this
bleffed Shoe, is juft feven and a quarter of
our Inches ; which I hint to your Lord-
fhip, becaufe fome well-fhap'd Catholick
Ladies, may be much rejoyced in cafe their
Feet fhould tally with this Meafure. Her
Needle, Thread, and Quafillum, *(Halæ.)*
Her Picture by St. *Luke* (*Romæ ad Mariæ
Inviolatæ.*) Another by the fame Hand of
that Holy Evangelift (*Romæ ad Mariæ novæ.*)
A third from *Cambray. N. B.* Tho' fome
Catholicks maintain St. *Luke* only painted

one

one, yet as thefe are each of them unqueſtio-
nably voucht, and that allowing St. *Luke* was
a Painter, as well a Phyſician, it is but reaſonable to ſuppoſe he ſhould have painted
more than one; his Holineſs, by the an-
next Bull, has thought it expedient to warrant them all for Originals, of the ſame
divine Pencil. St. *Michael's* Dagger and
Buckler *(magni Michaelis apud Carcaſſonen-
ſes.)* St. *John Baptiſt's* Face, very little the
worſe for the keeping, *(Cambiis ad Joannis
Angelici.)* The Hand, and part of his Head,
without a Face, from *Malta.* Others *ditto,*
from *Nemours.* His Brain very well dried
and preſerv'd *(Novii Rantrovienſis.)* His
whole Head *(Rome,* from the Convent of
St. *Silveſter.)* As to theſe two Heads, the
pious Reader is referred to the foregoing
Apology for the two Heads of St. *Luke.*
It is true, *Gregory Nazianzen* has declared
that his Bones were burnt by the *Donatiſts,*
ſo that nothing remain'd but a Piece of his
Skull; but 'tis abſur'd to compare the Authority of him, or one Hundred ſuch Fathers, with the Authority of the Church,
and her ſacred Traditions. At the ſame
time, far be it from the Modeſty of the
Holy See to maintain he had two, but
both

both are so amply voucht and verified, that 'tis presumptuous to decide for either. Let us say rather with Cardinal *Baronius* in the Sentiments of a truly pious Mind, allowing a Mistake in such cases, *Quicquid sit, fides purgat facinus.* It is not the Head of the Saint we adore, but the Faith for which he died. Behold, my Lord, what a delicate Plaister of Faith here is for the Wounds of Idolatry. A second Fore-finger of St. *John Baptist*, with which he pointed at our Saviour, and said, *Ecce agnus Dei*, &c. from *Tholouse.* As good an one from *Lyons.* Another from *Florence* wants the Nail. Another from *Genoa* mightily damaged. *N. B.* Tho' these are not maintain'd to be Forefingers, yet they are indubitably the real Fingers of the Saint, and be they anathema and accursed who say otherwise, wounding the Sides of the Church thro' these her blessed Reliques. His Ashes *(Rome* St. *John Lateran.)* More of them from *Genoa* very safe and dry. Some of the Blood of our Saviour as he hung on the Cross, gathered in a Glove by *Nicodemus*, which being thrown by him into the Sea, for fear of the *Jews*, was cast up after many Ages on the Coast of *Normandy*, and found out by a Duke

Duke of that Country as he was Hunting, by the hunted Stag and Dogs all kneeling quietly about it. From the Abbey *du Bec* in *Normandy*, which the Duke built for it, and where it was kept till now, and the said History recorded. St. *Peter* and St. *Paul*'s Bodies mixt together, one half belonging to St. *Peter*'s, the other half from St. *Paul*'s at *Rome*, both equally weigh'd and divided by Pope *Silvester*. *N. B.* That Moiety at St. *Peter*'s (with some other precious Reliques) is not to be dispos'd of to any Person whatever, but to remain to the Church. Both their Heads, from St. *John Lateran*, (*Rome*.) A Toe, a Finger, and a Slipper of St. *Peter*, all in good condition (*Rome*.) His Episcopal Chair wants a Foot. His Vestments want mending and darning greatly, but dangerous, the Cloth is so sadly decay'd. His Rochet, which he always us'd to say Mass in, and especially in this City, when he was here, much torn and greatly damag'd by Time, (all at *Rome*.) Another Chain, and another Sword of this blessed Apostle's when in Prison, (all at *Rome*, from St. *Petri ad Vincula*.) A Shoulder of St. *Paul*'s (*Rome*.) St. *Bartholomew*'s Body. Three of them, one

one from *Naples*, another fully as well faved from St. *Bartholomew*'s in this City, and a third from *Tholoufe*, very tender, and not well dried, but plainly his own. *N. B.* Thefe different Bodies are as hard to have any thing determin'd about them, as the Dupli-cates aforefaid. They are well voucht by ancient and unqueftionable Tradition, and all proper Depofitions and Certificates; and it fuits better with good Faith and good Manners, to leave fuch perplext Difficulties in fufpenfe, as the Holy Church, and our Religious Anceftors have deliver'd them down to us, (however ambiguous and in-comprehenfibly obfcure) than that the Te-merity of thefe Days fhould overturn the Piety of the former. Let the Buyers exa-mine and judge to the beft of their Faith and Knowledge, and remember as they are bleffed who believe tho' they faw not, fo much more bleffed doubtlefs are they, who believe pioufly and candidly, even againft that which they do fee. The Skin which was flay'd off this bleffed Apoftle, in a fad condition, and fomething rotten; from *Poitiers.* Another of them, probably from one of the aforefaid Bodies, but wants the

L   But-

Buttocks, tho' better preferved by a great deal (*Rome.*) St. *Matthias*'s Head (*Romæ Petri ad Vincula.*) His Rib, Shoulder, Arm, one Foot, and a Piece of another, all of them moift kept, and ftrong fcented (from *Paris Aquæ Sextiæ*, and other Places of equal credit.) Another Skin of St. *Bartholomew*, in all human probability flay'd off one of the Bodies aforefaid (from *Pifa.*) His Head, and another Member, but hard to fay what it is, 'tis fo much disfigur'd by Time, and the zealous Devotions of pious Pilgrims and Vifitants (from *Pifa* alfo.) St. *Mathew*'s bleffed Bones (*Treviris.*) His left Arm (from *Caffini.*) His right Arm (*Romæ ad Marcelli.*) Another Arm (*Romæ ad Nicolai.*) We have faid enough on thefe Duplicates already. The compleat Body of St. *Anne*, the Bleffed Virgin's Mother (*Aptæ oppido Provinciæ.*) Another from *Mariæ Infulanæ*, *Lyons.* Her Head (*Treviris*) another. Other Heads (*Tureni apud Juliacenfes.*) A third (*Annabergæ oppido Thuringiæ.*) We have faid above, what is abundantly fuffi-cient to eafe the Minds of truly pious, tho' fcrupulous Chriftians, concerning thefe δυσνόητα, thefe vexatious Difficulties. The

faithful

faithful and fincerely religious Perfon will
afk no more hereupon; and to Schifmaticks,
Hereticks, and Unbelievers, we fpeak not,
as gangren'd Members cut off from the Body of Holy Church, to their eternal Deftruction.

St. *Magdalen*'s Body (*Veffali prope Altiffi-
odorum.*) Another Body of hers; but as this
is not well voucht, having but twenty Depofitions, and thofe not fully confirm'd by
oral Tradition, and the conftant Teftimony
of the Church, and the Devotion of her
faithful Sons; we candidly and ingenuoufly
declare, our not being perfectly fatisfied in
this particular Relique, which yet we would
not caft out, left we fhould fcandalize the
devout Catholicks who have fo long vene--
rated it; (*apud San. Maximinum oppid. Provinciæ.*) Her Head, and the Mark of the
Blow, given her by our Lord on the Cheek
when fhe would have toucht him, when he
faid, *noli me tangere*, the Blow very plain
ftill. The Head out of order. Great Quantities of her Hair, near twenty Pound from
many Places. *N. B.* Tho' this Quantity is
large, there is nothing therein to give the
leaft Offence to the Faithful; for on all

dead

dead Bodies, and much more on thofe of the Saints, the Hair, even after Death, grows moft exuberantly, by which means probably thefe Quantities have been produced. The holy fpoufal Ring with which the Bleffed Virgin was efpoufed to *Jofeph*, for which the *Clufians* and *Perufians* waged fuch Wars here in *Italy*, as Hiftory mentions; (from *Perufia*.) The Bodies of the three Kings, or Magi, *Melchior*, *Jafpar* and *Balthafar*, all perfectly frefh and fair, and good liking from *Colen* or *Cologne*. Three other Bodies of the fame Kings, fully as fair and as well preferv'd, except the Nofe, the right Eye, and a part of the left Foot of King *Jafpar*; (from *Milan ad Euftorgii.*) We fhall be altogether filent on thefe fix Bodies belonging (that is, univerfally agreed by infallible Tradition to belong) to thefe three Kings; and fhall content our felves with referring the Pious Reader, and efpecially if a Purchafer, to the foregoing Apologies. Bleffed be the pious Care of the Emprefs *Helina*, to whom we and the Chriftian Church are indebted for thefe precious Reliques, by her fending them to *Conftantinople*; and furely it is much better to have

fix

fix Bodies difputing for this Honour than none at all. The Knife ufed at the Circumcifion of our Lord; (from *Compendium*.) The Stone on which St. *Peter*'s Cock crew, and the Column which was cleft afunder, from top to bottom on the Day of the Paffion, and the Stone on which *Pilate*'s Soldiers caft Lots for *Chrift*'s Garments; (all from St. *John de Lateran* in this City.) St. *Stephen*'s Body (from St. *Stephens* at *Rome*,) Several Parcels of the Bodies of the Innocents from *France*, *Germany*, and *Italy*. *Tefticuli eorum* (from *Friburgh* in *Brifgaw*.) St. *Lawrence*'s Body (from his Church in this City) together with a Veffel full of his broil'd Flefh, and another full of his Fat when broiling on the Fire (from the fame.) The Gridiron on which he fuffer'd Martyrdom, and the Coals wherewith this bleffed Martyr was broil'd to death for the Faith, (from St. *Euftachius*'s in this City.) Four Bodies of St. *Sebaftion*; one from St. *Lawrence*'s in this City, another from *Soiffons*, a third from a Town near *Narbonne* his native Country, and the fourth from *Pelignum apud Armoricos*. 'Tis not to be denied, thefe undiftinguifhable Duplicates do return

too

too frequently, but our former Defences, and the Confusion and too forward Zeal of thofe darker Times, muft (and if he be Faithful and Pious) will content the Reader and Buyer. Let us only add, which is a Point full of Comfort, that the Prayers of the Church, and the Devotions of her Religious Children, have fo far confecrated the Miftakes of their Forefathers, that all muft allow, that each of thefe Bodies have wrought moft prodigious Miracles, of which the proper Certificates remain with each of them. An Head of the fame glorified Saint, at St. *Peter*'s in this City. Another Head of his, belonging moft certainly to one of the above Carcaffes, (from *Magdeburg*.) A third Head of his, in like manner (as is to be believed) fever'd from another of the faid Bodies, procur'd from the *Dominicans* at *Tholoufe*, who recover'd it at the immenfe Expence, of a tedious Law Suit. Four of his Arms, one got from the *Dominicans (Andegavi.)* A fecond from *Tholoufe (ad Saturnini.)* A third from the Town *Cafedei* in *Avernia.* And a fourth from *Monbrifon.* Several of the Arrows he was fhot and cruelly martyr'd with; *(Lambefii*

befii in *Provincia.*) More of them, from the *Auguftine Fryers* in *Poitiers.* Several Chefts full, of the 11000 Virgins, from *Colen, St. Deny's,* the Monaftery of *Marcian* in *Flanders,* and many other Places, where the Bodies of thofe wonderful Saints were difperft. The Bones of *Abraham, Ifaac* and *Jacob,* very found and well kept (*Romæ Mariæ fuper Minervam.*) One of *Aaron's* Rods (*Paris ad Sacri Sacelli.*) *Solomon's* Candleftick, from *Prague.* Some of the Oyl of the Holy Sepulchre's Lamp, which every *Eafter Sunday* blazes up of its felf, before the Eyes of the truly Faithful, got from the Altar of St. *John.* The Ring of St. *Thomas a Becket,* the Bleffed Martyr, who rebell'd againft his Prince, to ferve the Holy See and the Caufe of Truth. His Rochet fprinkled with his Blood when murder'd, fo as never to be wafht out. His Hair Shirt, the fame which *Gononus's Chronicon* affures us, the Bleffed Virgin fow'd herfelf for him, and then hid it under his Bed; all from the Monaftery of St. *Martin* in *Arthoife,* with an authentick Catalogue of Sixty Seven Miracles wrought by them. St. *Apollonia's* Head and Arm, one Jaw,

L 4   and

and feveral of her Teeth from two or three different Churches in this City. Her Mouth, Part of her Jaw, and one of her bleffed Teeth, from *Volaterræ* in *Etruria*. Several more of her Teeth, and her lower Jaw, from *Bononia*, where they us'd to be folemnly venerated the 9*th* of *February* each Year by the Pope's Legate, or Vice-Legate. A Part of her Jaw from *Antwerp*, where frequent Miracles were wrought by it. A Part of her Tooth from *Mechlin* and feveral whole ones from *Flanders*. A remarkable Portion of her lower Jaw from *Artois*. Four other Teeth, a Rib, another Tooth and her Shoulder-blade from *Colen*. Another Jaw from the *Carthufians*, a Tooth from St. *Maurice*'s Church, and another Lower Jaw from St. *Alban's*, all in the fame City. Another of her Teeth and fome other bleffed Reliques of her's, from the Church of St. *Roch* in *Lisbon*, and from *Placentia* in *Spain*. St. *Anthony*'s Beard from *Colen*, and a remarkable Part of his Head. His Tongue, bleffed for ever, from *Padua*. N. B. This is the fame Tongue which St. *Bonaventure* 30 Years after his Death, found in his Afhes ftill frefh and full of Juice and Blood; which,

which, before the Magistrates, he reverent-
ly took up and kiss'd, saying, *O blessed
Tongue, which always did bless God, and
taught others to bless him; now it appears of
what Merit thou wast*; and so deliver'd it
to them to be laid up again with his holy
Ashes, as the famous *Mendozius* tells us.
The Hay found in the Cratch where our
Saviour was laid, call'd the Holy Hay;
(Brought from *Lorain.*) *Moses*'s Horns, which
he had coming down from Mount *Sinai*,
and the Tail of the Ass our Saviour rode on,
got from *Genoa*; and a Pair of *Joseph*'s
Breeches, very old and much worn, from
Aix. The blessed Navel of our Lord, from
St. *Mary del Popalo* in this City, and the
Skin or Pannicle, that came out of the most
holy Body, of the Blessed Virgin with our
Saviour, when he came into the World,
from the Church of St. *Mary* the Greater,
in the same City. The Stone, on which the
same Blessed Virgin used to wash our Saviour's Linnen, brought from *Constantinople.*
A Tear which *Christ* shed over *Lazarus*, en-
clos'd in a little Crystal by an Angel, who
made a Present of it to St. *Mary Magdalen.*
Another from the *Benedictins* Convent, at
Vendome in *France.* *N. B.* This is the

7   very

very Tear, which the learned Pere *Mabillon* writ so admirable a Treatise in Defence of, to the Honour of God and holy Church.

But, my Lord, I propos'd to entertain you, and I am but tormenting you with so hideous a Recital of the superstitious Dreams and Inventions of these formal Hypocrites; whose Godliness is Gain, and who, under the Pretence and Cloak of exterior Sancti-ty, and an high Veneration for such holy Trumpery, seek only Wealth, Ease, and Profit, and make a God of their Belly and their sacrilegious Gain.

I shall therefore leave the bulky Remains of this amazing Catalogue, till I know how your Lordship relishes this Taste of it, which I send you; and shall only mention to you, that from the Beginning to the End of it, on the strictest Examination, I don't recol-lect one Relique, the original of which at least, has not been actually venerated, and almost worship'd, this several hundred Years, by this blinded and deluded People; except that one of the Cheese and Butter made of the Virgin's Milk, which is said ne-ver to corrupt, and to have been brought from *Mexico.* Among all the rest, there
are

are but a very few, which I have not been
at the Pains to fearch for, and have really,
with thefe Eyes, feen in different authentick
Lifts of Reliques fhewn at *Rome*, and other
Places; and either mention'd by her own
Writers, or Men of Honour and Truth, that
affert they have feen them in their Travels.
So that I can aver, there are few or none
inferted in this Lift, which were not publickly known, and expofed to the Veneration of pious Catholicks. I have made bold,
to add a few ludicrous Notes to feveral of
them, that deferv'd much feverer Remarks,
on fuch horrible Impoftures and Fables.
For, alas, if all thefe Reliques, and the infinite Number of Miracles wrought by them,
were fairly to be examined, and call'd to the
Proof, before equitable Judges, as the Temples in *Greece* and *Afia*, who fet up Afy-
lums, were by the *Roman* Senate in *Tiberi-
us*'s Time; how many of them would be o-
blig'd, either quietly to give up all their
Pretenfions, or to maintain them by fome
filly old Tale or other, as moft of the Defenders of the Temples were forc'd to do, as
Tacitus affures us in the Third of his Annals, *Cap.* 60, 61, 62.

But

But if this were the Cafe, this jugling Church, which, like a true Quack, makes Ufe of Infallibility and Authority as a certain cure for every Sore, has provided a fufficient Remedy, tho' all her Reliques fhould be prov'd counterfeit; and that is by determining, that fuch fuperftitious Reliques may really work actual Miracles, becaufe the good Intentions of thofe, who pioufly have Recourfe to them, procures them that Blefsing from God, as a Reward of their Devotion. She actually teaches this Doctrine, my Lord, which folves all Difficulties on this Point, and what is more, fhe is believ'd on it; her Confidence in deceiving, and the Credulity of her People in believing, anfwering like two Tallies, and makes one often remember the famous Axiom, *Homo eft Animal credulum & mendax.* In the mean Time, what a Crowd of terrible Reflections, muft this Scene of Things raife in every honeft and ingenuous Breaft, to fee this infallible Church abufing the Purity and Excellence of our Faith, and the common Senfe of Mankind, with impofing on them fuch an Heap of fenfelefs Fictions, and filly Bawbles, not only for their Belief, but even

even for their Veneration and Homage·
With what Indignation ! with what Resent-
ment! with what honest Scorn ! must every
considering Christian, that has not blindly
given up his Senses and Reason (the only E-
vidence to which our Blessed Saviour appeal-
ed for the Truth of his Miracles) to her
groundless and usurp'd Authority, look on
such horrid Trifling both with our Religion
and Understanding?

Can one bear, without Grief and Torment of Heart, to see this Church of *Christ*
exceeding in the Foppery and Folly of such
Conduct, the greatest Absurdities of the
Heathen and *Turkish* Superstition; and at the
same Time, by infinite insidious Arts and
horrible Treasons, as well as furious Perse-
cutions and open Wars, attempting daily
against the Authority of all Protestant Princes, and the Peace and Prosperity of their
Subjects in this World, and giving up both
of them in the next to eternal Damnation,
for daring to question her Power, or dissent
from her Opinions?

After saying this, can I add, (without la-
menting the Blindness! the Meanness! the
Dishonesty of Mankind !) that Popish Princes
will

will probably, for political Views and worldly Motives, never fail to combine together
in fupporting her Authority, tho' in their
Hearts they may defpife or renounce it; and
confequently they will in all Likelyhood, by
enlarging her Power, and joining in the
Schemes of her infinite Policy, perpetuate
their own unreafonable Slavery, and her re-
diculous Empire, to the End of the World,
and this wretched Scene of Wickednefs and
Folly and Falfehood below! I am,

My Lord, Your Lordſhip's, &c.

HERTFORD.

I beg the Favour of your Lordſhip to
tranfmit to me a regular Lift of the Temporal Peers fummon'd to this Parliament,
his Holinefs having defir'd to fee it.

👑👑👑👑👑👑👑👑👑👑👑👑👑👑👑

To the Lord HIGH TREASURER.

MY LORD,   *London, Chelſea, Dec.* 19, 1997.

I Had the Pleafure of your Difpatches, of
Nov. 3*d*, fome Days fince, and am thus
early in returning my Thanks, where I hold
my

my self so much oblig'd, both for your Care of the Publick and of me. Your Congratulations on my Advancement were very welcome, for from one so sincere and candid, as I have ever found your Excellency, even Compliments pass for Truths, and we think our selves oblig'd to give Credit to them. At the same Time, my Lord, you have not forgot *England* so much, by your long Residence at *Constantinople,* but that you must know, there can be no great pleasure to preside over the Councils of a People, that may almost be called a Nation of prime Ministers; that examine and suspect every Thing, and yet are never pleas'd or in good Humour, and least then, when they can find nothing to blame.

Your Accounts, of the State of Things in *Turky,* were most entertaining; his Majesty did you the Honour to hear your Letters read, and to express some Satisfaction in them; and therefore you must hasten to us the Remainder of your Observations, that we do not overpay for the Pleasure, by too long Expectation.

Mr. *Secretary* will, by this Night's Express, by the way of *Vienna,* communicate to you
his

his Majesty's Pleasure, in Relation to the Treaty, and the Approbation which all the Steps you have hitherto taken, have met with here. His Majesty has particularly order'd me to assure you, that the Bishops and Papa's of the *Greek* Church, shall be honour'd with his Protection and Favour; and all that are Needy and sincerely Scrupulous to submit to *Rome*, shall have proper Pensions to prevent their making Shipwreck of their Faith, and selling their Birthright, like *Esau*, for a little Food to sustain them. I think there has been an inexcusable Negligence, in the Ministry here (tho' I know not realy at whose Door to place it) in Relation to that unhappy neglected Church; which has neither had any Benefit drawn from our Protection at the Port, nor the least Care shewn, by sending Missionaries of our own, to prevent the Artifices of the Jesuits, and keep her steddy to her Principles, as a Sister Church, who has ever abhor'd to join in their Communion. This is a Defect, which all Protestant Churches have much fail'd in, and our own as much as any; but I hope in Time to see this amended, with many other Irregularities, if Providence

shall

fhall be pleafed to lend me Opportunity and Power.

I fhall be much oblig'd to your Excellency, if you can inform me if Mr. *Biron* or Mr. *Pearfon,* have recover'd any choice Manufcripts, either *Greek* or *Arabick,* or valuable Medals, or any Rarities or Curiofities in their Travels, which I procur'd his Majefty to fend them abroad for, when I was only principal Secretary of State. I thank you for the Curiofities you fent me, and to engage you to this Kind of Traffick, I have given Orders to fend you, by the *Turky* Fleet, an excellent Hogfhead of *Carolina,* (our own Plantation White-Wine) and three or Four fine Pieces of Damafk, made of the Silk of that Country; both which we have brought to that Perfection there, as is of vaft Advantage to *Great Britain,* as well as the Colony.

Since you think it will make the Grand Seignior encourage Aftronomy, I have alfo fent you one of the compleateft largeft and beft reflecting Telefcopes in *London,* which we make with fuch exquifite Skill and Contrivance, that they exceed tenfold all thofe that were ufed by the Aftronomers in the laft Age. Tho' it be but of a moderate Length, yet

M   it

it is altogether as good as the largerOnes; and
the Expence of fixing it up, much lefs; and
you may difcern evidently with this, not only
the Hills, Rivers, Vallies, and Forefts, but real
Cities in the Moon, that feem nearly to refemble our own, and what is ftill more, even
Mountains and Seas in *Venus* and the other
Planets. Nay fome of our Aftronomers have
gone fo far, as to aver, they could diftinguifh
the Times of Plowing, and Harveft there,
by the Colour of the Face of the Earth, and
to fpecifie thofe Times, that others might
make a Judgment of their Obfervation, and
have maintain'd, that they have plainly feen
in the Moon, Conflagrations, and the Smoak
arifing from them.

As I fancy there is more of Imagination
than of Truth, in fuch Opinions, I would
not have your Excellency quarrel with this
I fend you, if it does not perform all thefe
Miracles. I will affure you, beforehand, you
will find it magnifie to fo prodigious a Degree, as will perfectly aftonifh you, as much
as you are us'd to Telefcopes; while it gives
you fuch evident Demonftrations, that all
the Planets are not only habitable, but inhabited. I fhall defire you only, while you
are enjoying thofe Pleafures, to remember,
that

that you are chiefly indebted for them, to the Bounty and generous Encouragement, with which our Royal Master contributed to the Project, for improving them so highly, without which, they would never have receiv'd the Perfection they have gain'd.

As Mr. Secretary will entirely take off my Hands, to Night, the Province of the Statesman and the Minister, your Excellency will pardon me, if I only entertain you very poorly *on Philosophy*, and as a Brother Virtuoso, with some small Accounts of what Improvements have been made here in the polite Arts; and also, how far our Trade, and both the Laws and Manufactures of our Country, are advanc'd and regulated within these twenty-five Years, since you left us.

That I may prepossess your Excellency in the best Manner I am able, in Favour of our Improvements here, I shall begin my Account with those elegant Arts, you have so long admir'd and cultivated, Painting, Sculpture, and Architecture; which, tho' greatly encourag'd by his Majesty's Royal Ancestors, have been shewn such extraordinary Favour and Protection, under this Reign, that there have not only Salaries been allow'd to Professors,

M 2

feffors, in each of them, but a Fund of
5000 *l. per Ann.* eftablifh'd by Subfcription
of his Majefty, and the Nobility and Gentry, which is divided equally on his Majefty's Birth-Day, in *December*, to the three
beft Pictures, Statues, and Houfes, that have
been made in *Great Britain* in that Year.
Tho' his Majefty fubfcribes 1500 *l.* a Year,
he has but one Vote in determining who beft
deferves the Premiums; and that Parties
and Factions may be excluded, and only
Merit confider'd, all the Subfcribers are engag'd, on their Honour, not to folicit any
Member for his Vote, and as all is perform-
ed by Balloting, it is generally agreed, that
nothing can be manag'd with greater Candour and Impartiality.

By this fingle Method, we have made
Great Britain, the Seat of thefe lovely Arts,
and have drawn hither, the firft Mafters of
the World, to contend with Emulation for the
generous Rewards, which our Country beftows
on their Labours and Merit. I do affure
your Excellency, it has fuch an Effect here,
that I am confident, we have better new
Pictures and Statues in *Great Britain,* than
in all *Europe* befides; and perhaps *Italy* her
felf, will not, in a little Time, be able to
excel

excel the Palaces we have built here, since this Scheme has taken Place. In Sculpture, particularly, we have so far excelled, that no Nation comes near us in cutting in Granite, Serpentine, or Porphyry; and we alone have the Art of Working in that hardest of Stones, the Bisaltes, by the Help of Emery, prepar'd in the new Method; and by having probably found out the Secret of tempering our Steel, after the Manner of the Ancient *Greeks* and *Romans.*

I am sorry to tell your Excellency, that we have gone as great Lengths as to Music, but without assigning Premiums, and am afraid you will put me in Mind of *Cicero*'s Maxim, in his Treatise *de Legibus, Mutatâ Musicâ mutantur Mores,* and the Rule he lays down for it, which is worth the Consideration of every Nation, *Curandum itaque est, ut Musica quam gravissima & sedatissima retineatur.* It was with this View, that several of his Majesty's Royal Predecessors, peremptorily drove the *Italian* Opera and Music twice from *Great Britain,* and forbid their acting in their Theatres, in St. *James*'s Square and *Kensington,* as enervating our Spirits, and emasculating the *British* Genius. *George* III. would never allow

allow it to be us'd in his Troops, or by any Officers in them; and with Difficulty let it be retain'd in the Church Service, and Anthems.   Some States have prohibited the Study and Practice of Mufick; with the fame Views; and the *Spartans*, your Excellency knows, made a Decree againft *Timotheus*, for improving foft Mufick, and yet we have run into a Paffion for it, with that Violence, that it has not only thriven at the Expence of the good Senfe, and, almoft, the Valour of our Nation, but has, in fome meafure, fupplanted our Ambition, and our Thirft for Wealth and Power.

The Fiddle, particularly, has fo far got into the Hands of our Gentlemen, that, I fear, they will at laft forget the Ufe of their Swords; and am jealous, they will fet up, in Time, a new Sect of vifionary Religionifts amongft us, who will worfhip nothing but that ador'd Inftrument, tho' at the fame Time, every one knows, 'tis as rare to fee a good Fidler without a poor Underftanding, as it is in *Ireland* to fee an Harper, that is not blind.   It is certain, however, that they have brought the Improvement of it here to a vaft Pitch; but your Excellency obferves, that this is rather what I am afham'd,

fham'd, than proud of, being heartily concern'd to fee our brave People rivalling the
Eunuchs of *Italy*, in fo trivial an Excellence,
to fay no worfe of it.

Let me lead you now by the Hand, into the Royal College of St. *George* at *Oxford*, which, tho' founded by his Majefty's
Anceftors in the Eighteenth Century, has
been fo vaftly improv'd, and it's Revenues
fo far encreas'd, by the King our Mafter,
that we may almoft call it his own Foundation. Your Excellency was well acquainted with it in your Youth, and therefore, I
fhall only mention to you, fuch Additions,
and new Regulations, as have been made
there of late Years. I fhall begin with
the great Square, all built by his Majefty, which he nam'd the College of the
learned World. Here there are Apartments for Twenty-fix Fellows, who muft
be learned Foreigners in Diftrefs, chofen by
the Votes of the Nobility, Bifhops, and
Heads of Colleges, fignifying by a fign'd
and feal'd Certificate, that the Perfon to be
elected, is a learned Foreigner in Diftrefs,
whom they think beft deferving the vacant
Fellowfhip, which is worth 50 *l.* the Year,

and

and Diet, and is conferr'd on him who has the moſt Votes.

In the old Square, adjoining to this, there are Lodgings for four new Profeſſors, who have each of them 150 *l.* a-piece *per Ann.* The Firſt profeſſes and teaches Agriculture and Gardening, and has (near the College) twenty Acres of Ground, which he employs in ſmall Parcels, under the Plow and Spade, in different Methods and Experiments, in thoſe two uſeful Arts; and has ſtill a Number of Scholars, who are bred under him, to whom, in foul Weather, he reads Lectures; and in fair Day's he inſtructs them, in all the practical Methods, neceſſary to the Improving the Culture of the Field and the Garden. They are to aſſiſt him in all his Experiments to that End, which he is oblig'd to publiſh each Year, with their Succeſs or Failure, and the probable Cauſes and Reaſons of both. The King's, and all Noblemen's Gardener's are bred here; and all young Gentlemen, who come to the Univerſities to learn nothing, are oblig'd, before they take any Degrees in Arts they are perfect Strangers to, to ſpend ſix Months under this Profeſſor, in order to make them know ſomething.   The

The fecond is called the Weather Pro-
feffor, and tho' this was eftablifh'd in 1840,
yet as his Salary was trebled from 50 *l.* to
150 *l.* I reckon him with the others. He
is oblig'd to keep exact Diaries and Indexes
of the Wind and Weather, of all Storms,
Drougths and Rains, and the antecedent con-
comitant and confequent Circumftances, as
well as the Pofition of the Planets; and collect all other Symptoms indicative of the
Changes of the Air and Weather, with Deductions and Conjectures as to all Dearths,
great Crops, healthy Seafons, and epidemical Diftempers, and the Caufes and Remedies of Famines and popular Sickneffes.
He is to enter his Obfervations in regular
Calendars, and to add Differtations on all,
and particularly on the Caufes of fuch Accidents, as are occafion'd by Heat or Cold,
Rain, Froft, Snow, Lightning, Blafts,
Mildews, biting Winds and fcorching Suns;
and to fet down the probable Extents of
Coafting Winds, Rains and Snows, and to
keep three Clerks at three different Diftances
of at leaft Eighty Miles afunder to purfue the
fame Methods exactly. ꝉ He is alfo to keep
carefully, and obferve conftantly, his *Statical
Hygrofcopes,* as to the Moifture and Drynefs of
the

the Air, how far full or new Moons, and the menftrual or annual Spring-tides, the Multitude or Fewnefs of the Solar *Maculæ*, the Approach of Comets, the Afpects of the Planets, their Eclipfes, Conjunctions, *&c.* appear to affect our Atmofphere in this particular. He is to attend with the fame Exactnefs his Weather Engines to exprefs the Strength of the Winds, by their lifting up fuch and fuch Weights; and meafure the Quantities of Rain that fall throughout the Year, the Thicknefs of the Ice, and Depth of Snow, the Length, Breadth, and Force of Earthquakes, as well in his Neighbourhood as by his Correfpondents throughout *Great-Britain*, and the neighbouring Coafts of *France* and *Ireland*, and whether they move as is fuppofed generally from Eaft to Weft, or how otherwife.

Six Volumes in Folio of thefe Calendars have been publifht from 1840 to 1991, at the King's Expence lately, and it is incredible what a Certainty we are come to in thefe Matters, and the Advantage thereby, as to Sieges, Campaigns, Harvefts, Journeys, Sailing of Ships, Inundations, and Tempefts ; it being certain from them, that every Revolution of *Saturn*, we have the fame

fame Weather exactly, or with very fmall
Variations. A Difcovery, which your Excellency fees at one Glance the Importance
of, tho' I fear, as 'tis probable the World
will not hold out many Centuries longer,
this will be like coming to a great Eftate
when one is paft Seventy, and has no Hopes
of enjoying it. The laft I fhall mention to
your Excellency, are the two Profeffors of
Trades, and Mechanical Arts. Thefe divide
all the moft myfterious Trades between them,
fuch as Dying, Weaving, Tanning, Turning, Carpenters, Mafons, Painters, Brewers, Bakers, Spinners, Miners, Wheel, Mill
and Ship-wrights, Printing, Glafs-making,
and fuch like; and are oblig'd to infpect
into all poffible or probable Methods to improve thofe in his Province.

Each Year they give in their Obfervations
or Inventions to the Board of Trade, who,
after examining into them, and confulting
thereon with the Hall of Tradefmen in that
Myftery, give Orders for its being followed
and obferved by them and their Apprentices,
and publifht, if proper, for the common
Good. The Profeffors muft be Mafters of
Arts in one of the Univerfities, and well
vers'd in Experimental Philofophy, and muft
                                    every

every feven Years, prefent his Majefty with an Hiftory of the feveral Trades in their refpective Provinces, and the Improvements made in them by their Care and Infpection. I cannot detain your Excellency too long, or I could reckon up many prodigious Advantages the Publick has gain'd, by light'ning the Labour, fhort'ning the Road, removing old Miftakes, and fupplying new Methods and Inventions, to the feveral Trades and Manufactures of thefe Nations.

Thus I have gone thro' the new Profeffors our Royal Mafter, following the Steps of his glorious Anceftors, has fo generoufly and fo happily eftablifht. The Queen indeed, who is the beft of Princeffes, and a fecond *Caroline* or *Elizabeth*, would have had his Majefty found a Profefforfhip of Piety, fince there was ne'er a one in either Univerfity; but he told her pleafantly, There were fo many Profeffors of that Kind already in the World, and fo few who put what they profeft in Practice, that he would not hear of it, till that matter fhould be amended. But to fhew your Excellency how much the learned World is indebted to his Majefty's Cares, I muft defcribe to you the Royal Printing-houfe which he has erected and endow'd,

endow'd, and which ftands in the middle
of the noble Square where your Excellency
and I lodg'd. It is of *Portland* Stone, built
on fuch vaft maffy Vaults, and with fuch an
huge Profufion of convenient Offices of all
kinds, and Apartments for the Printers, Cor-
rectors, and Servants, and makes all together
fo auguft and magnificent an Appearance,
that *Sheldon*'s Theatre would appear but as
a Cottage by it. There is 500 *l. per Ann.*
iffuable out of the Treafury to the Foundation, befides the Benefit of all Copies they
print. They muft ufe no Types or Paper
but of the beft kind, and they work Night
and Day, relieving each other by turns, and
are to forfeit 5 *s.* each for all Erratas, fo
that their Copies are reckon'd the moft correct extant. Over the great Gate there is a
large Infcription in a vaft Marble Table, in
which the Caufes of the Foundation are declared to be, the Service of Religion, the
Good of the State, and the Benefit of the
Learned World. Then it goes on to fay,
that as the Number of Books is infinite, and
rather diftract than inform the Mind, by a
mix'd and confufed Reading, fome being well
writ, but ill Books, others good Books,
but ill writ; fome hudled up in hafte,
others

others ftinking of the Lamp; fome without
any ftrength of Reafoning, others over loaded with Arguments, half of which are in-
fignificant ; fome Books being obfcure
through too affected a Brevity, others per-
fpicuous through an unneceffary Redundan-
cy of Words (like a bright Day at Sea, where
yet there is nothing to be feen but Air and
Water ;) fome treating on Subjects that
thoufands had handled better before, others
publifhing ufelefs Trifles, becaufe new and
unthought of by others; fome Writing as
if they had never read any thing, others as
if they writ nothing but what they read,
and then borrowed; therefore his Majefty
decrees, no Book fhould be printed within
thofe Walls but the Works of the Ancients,
and fuch only as fhould be voted moft proper,
by two thirds of the Colleges in his two
Univerfities, and confirmed by the Lord
Chancellor, and Arch-bifhop of *Canterbury* for the Time being.   I have dwelt the
longer on this noble Defign, becaufe I had
the Honour to propofe it to his Majefty, and
the Happinefs to bring it to Perfection for
the good of Mankind; and I muft now lead
your Excellency, to take a View of the noble Square that furrounds the Royal Print-
ing-

ing-Houſe, which is all new built ſince we lodged in it. It is divided now, beſides a large Houſe for the Provoſt, into twenty different Buildings, each of which belongs to a Fellow, and contains Apartments for twenty Scholars who are his Pupils, and live with him as in one Houſe, of the Door of which he keeps the Key, as alſo of all their Chambers. By this Means, as none can go in or out but with his Knowledge, and by his Leave, ſo nothing can be privately tranſacted or conçeald in their Chambers, which he enters by his Key at Pleaſure, thereby ſhutting out idle Viſitors, and Cabals; and to prevent all Intriegues with Women, none are allow'd to come into the Houſe. This Rule extends to all Relations except Mothers, and to their very Servants, who are all Men.

To each Building there is a large Hall, where Morning and Evening his Pupils meet, and ſtudy under his Eyes four Hours, writing down his Lectures from his Mouth, or contracting the Authors he gives them; and each *Saturday* they are examined the Repetition of the whole. For each Morning or Evening Lecture the Tutor is abſent, there is treble the Sum due for each Day's Tuition deducted

deducted, which enſures their Attendance. There are each Year four Examinations of the whole Body of Scholars in publick, divided into four Claſſes, and each Claſs into five Diviſions. The Examination laſts two Days, four Hours in the Morning, and four in the Evening, each Day. The twenty Fellows are the Examiners, and return Judgments of each Scholar's Anſwering on their Oaths, and the five beſt Anſwerers in each Diviſion are paid 5 *l.* each in Books, and their Names hung up in the great Hall for ten Days, and oppoſite to them the Names of the five worſt Anſwerers. After four compleat Years they take their Degrees of Batchellors, except ten of the worſt Scholars in each Claſs, who are conſtantly ſtopt for at leaſt one Year more.

After taking their Degrees, their Studies are continued in like manner preciſely, as when Under Graduates; when they are lecturʼd and examinʼd by the Profeſſors, with equal Severity and Conſtancy, and not allowʼd to idle in private. The firſt of *Auguſt*, each Year, if there are any vacant Fellowſhips, thoſe Graduates that pleaſe ſit for them, and are examinʼd ſix Days, and eight Hours each Day, by the publick Profeſſors, who,

who, upon their Oaths, nominate the beſt Anſwerers, and diſtribute in like manner 40 *l.* apiece of the Royal Annual Bounty to thoſe who miſs, but appear to deſerve theFellowſhip.

After eight compleatYears, they commence Maſters, and are diſmiſt the Society, if they deſire it, with proper Teſtimoniums of their Behaviour and Scholarſhip; and if they continue in theSociety, are allow'd 20*l.* aYeareach, from the Royal Bounty, and are oblig'd to attend the Profeſſors ofDivinity, Mathematicks, Hiſtory, and Civil Law, each of them, two Hours every Day at their publick Lectures for four Years, and then they are declar'd *Emeriti,* and honour'd with larger Teſtimoniums, betake themſelves to their ſeveral Profeſſions in the World.

This truly Royal Foundation, of which I omit many ſmaller Particulars, coſts his Majeſty about 3000 *l,* aYear, beſides the Expence of a Regal Viſitation every three Years, when the Morals, Learning, and Diligence of the Provoſts, Profeſſors, and Fellows, are ſeverally enquir'd into, and all Offenders, either ſtrictly caution'd, remov'd, or expell'd.

The Numbers of admirable Scholars that this Society has ſent into the World, and their having deſervedly obtain'd, a large Share of

N   all

all Preferments in Church and State, is the best and plainest Evidence that the Foundation is well modell'd, and will save you the Trouble of my enlarging further on it, unless I venture to add, that were the Discipline of our other Colleges proportionably strict, and the Premiums and Allowances more enlarg'd, it is impossible but a Nation so capable of exerting it's natural Turn for Letters, would send out more exalted Genius's, and excellent Scholars, than we have of late done.

But the Delight I take in this Subject, and my Desire that your Excellency should have your full Share in it, has run this Letter into an unexpected Length, especially from my weak Eyes and Hands. It has perfectly tir'd me, and as the Reader is generally sick, by the Time the Writer is weary, I shall cut off half the Trouble I propos'd to give you, in relation to our late Improvements, as to our Trade, Manufactures, and Laws; and shall reserve those for the next Dispatch, I have the Pleasure to send you.

Since I wrote this, Mr. Secretary tells me he has drawn up his Majesty's Commands for you, in relation to the poor deserted *Greek* Church, and the State of all Affairs where you are; to which I have nothing to add, but my

best

beſt Wiſhes for their Succeſs, and my earneſt
Entreaties for your Diligence and Vigilance,
that nothing may diſappoint the Hopes your
Excellence has given us, and the kind Expectations I have ever had, of the ſkillful management of all Matters, that are to paſs
through your Hands.   When you receive the
Carolina Silks, and White-wine, pray let me
know ſincerely how you approve of them,
for they are much admired here.

All your Relations in this Family kiſs your
Hands, and your good Lady's, and long for
your return once more to them and your
Country, where there is no Man more deſirous, not only to ſee but to ſerve you, than,

My Lord, Your Excellencies moſt, &c.

N——M.

To the Lord HIGH TREASURER.

MY LORD,

Moſco, Jan. 27, 1997.

I Have the Pleaſure of your Commands by
Mr. Secretary of *January* the 3ᵈ, and am
highly delighted that I have in ſome meaſure
anſwer'd your Expectations by mine of the
29ᵗʰ of *November* laſt; and as I ſhall faithfully
purſue my Inſtructions, and particularly the
Hints in Cypher, ſo if any thing new ariſes, I
ſhall

ſhall uſe my beſt Diligence to give the ear-
lieſt Intelligence, and in the mean time ſhall
act as my preſent Lights ſhall direct me.

I find your Lordſhip conſiders me as very
little employ'd here, ſince you ſeem deſirous
I ſhould explain to you, upon what Grounds
the common Opinion hath prevail'd, that the
Muſcovites, who have ſo long adhered to the
Greek Church, are now, as it were, with all
their Sails, a Trip bound for *Rome.* You deſire I ſhould alſo inform you at large, by
what Methods the Jeſuits have been able to
overcome, that violent Averſion which has ſo
long been manifeſted, againſt them and their
Communion here; and above all, what Alterations they have been able to bring about,
in order to make the Doctrines and Rites of
this Church, compatible with theirs.

I will make no Apologies for my Inability
to perform this Taſk, ſince you have enjoyn'd
it me; and ſhall endeavour to lay the whole of
the Jeſuits Plan before you, as I have been
ſhewn it here by a very conſiderable Perſon,
that you may gratify your Curioſity fully,
and judge if I am right in my Conjectures,
in ſaying *Venient Romani,* as the *Jews* ſaid
of old; and that the *Greek* Church will ſoon
veil her Mitre, to the Pope's Triple Crown.

It

It muft be confeft indeed, that the Jefuits herein have proceeded with their u-
fual fubtlety and caution, and have not
hitherto attempted in an avowed manner
the leaft publick ftep to oblige this Church
to own her Subjection to that of *Rome*. As
they know the general ftream of the People's affection, as well as of the inferior Clergy, went violently againft them; they have
taken their meafures accordingly, and have
done all they could to remove that Averfion: while at the fame time, they have by
a thoufand methods, fecured to themfelves
the Czar's favour and protection, as well as
the Patriarchs, the two Metropolitans, and
moft of the Bifhops, and the Chiefs and
Heads of the regular and fecular Clergy.

They have managed this point fo well,
that they are more refpected at Court than
is eafy to be credited, and have fuch intereft
with the Nobility, that no man can fucceed
with them, but as he is favoured and recommended by thefe pious and worthy Fathers. It is true, indeed, they owe this
kind reception to the vaft intereft this Court
finds they have all over *Europe*, and if that
were weakened or overturned, probably
they would foon fink here alfo; but as there

O   is

is little danger of that, and as they are on
all occafions vaftly ferviceable to the Czar's
affairs, both at home and abroad, it is certain their power will rather increafe than
leffen here.

In the mean time, they make the utmoft
ufe of what they have, to bring over more
and more the whole body of the Clergy to
their Party, that by them they may gain on
the People, and by degreees prepare this
Church to receive the Yoke on her neck,
which fhe has fo long, and fo obftinately
renounced.

To oblige the Clergy in the moft fenfible
manner, they have perfuaded the Czar to
eftablifh in different parts of the Empire,
near two hundred Schools for the *Mufcovite*
Youth, and efpecially the Sons of the Clergy; and to fettle the annual Præmiums on
the feveral Univerfities, for fuch of them as
diftinguifh themfelves by their parts and
diligence: and at the fame time, they have
thofe Schools, and Univerfities, and Præmiums, entirely under the management of
perfons folely dependant on them.

By this means, fuch principles are in-
ftilled, fecretly and imperceptibly, into the
Youth of the Empire, as neceffarily beget a
                                    horror

horror of Schism, a love of Union, and a high veneration for the authority and doctrines of the Church of *Rome*.

But as these counterfeit Fishers of men are generally observed not to do their work by halves, they have taken measures yet more effectual, to oblige both the People and Clergy for ever. There are, my Lord, numbers of poor mortals in this Nation, who being able just to read the service of the Church in their own tongue, and a translation of St. *Chrysostome*'s Homilies into it, to the People, get into Priests Orders, like the sons of *Eli*, to gain a piece of bread; and yet the provision made for them is so small, they are disappointed even in securing that, and are almost starving two thirds of the year. There are in the Czar's Dominions four thousand Parishes in these circumstances, where the priest was in this wretched scituation; and yet by his Majesty's personal contributions, and by a regular tax of the tenth penny on all ecclesiastical preferments, which they procured to be voluntarily laid on, by the Patriarch, Bishops, and richer Clergy, whose livings exceed a hundred pounds *per annum*, there is a fund raised, with so generous and christian a spirit, that their poor

brethren

brethren, who were daily in danger of perifh-
ing, and Religion with them, for want of
fupport, are delivered from the contempt and
mifery of their condition, and have now full
forty pounds *per annum*, fettled for ever
on each of their Livings.

While they thus provided for the poor
and the ignorant, they have not forgot the
richer and more learned Clergy; and as
they have their fpies and emiffaries every
where, whenever they find a man of real
merit confin'd to a parifh in fome remote
corner, out of the eye and notice of the
Court, where he is obliged to wafte his life
in inftructing his *Ruffes* (the moft ftupid of
rational Creatures) like a fecond St. *Francis*
preaching to the rocks in a defart; they take
care, if they find him a friend to their Order, or can make him fo, to have him removed to fome happier fcituation.

Judge, my Lord, what an influence this
muft give them on poor *Ruffian* Monks, who
though they are regular enough in their
lives, and are good men at their breviary;
yet, I fancy, when they pray, may now
and then, as Naturalifts fay of the Came-
leon, look at the fame time with one eye to
Heaven, and with the other on the Earth,
where

where eafe and convenience are pretty induftrioufly fought after. Nay, they have
even taken care of their interefts, if I may
fo fpeak, after their death; and have obtained a Law, that their Widows, if poor,
fhall enjoy one year's full profit of their
Husband's living, after his deceafe, or ten
pounds *per annum* for life: So that here is
another deep obligation laid on this powerful body, and by men that are little in-
clined to favour a married Clergy.

I fhall continue, my Lord, a little longer,
to make thefe Jefuits panegyrick (and certainly, if they did thefe good things to a
good end, they would deferve a much nobler one than I can honour them with;) for I
muft confefs, the Conftitutions they have
introduced into this Church, as to Bifhops,
are worthy the virtue and piety of the apo-
ftolick Age. For in the firft place, they
have obtained a Law, that no Bifhop fhall
be capable during life, of being tranflated
from the firft See he is appointed to fill, (except when he is removed to be Patriarch)
but he is married as effectually to his Church
as to his Wife, and can never efpoufe another. The *Ruffian* Bifhops formerly were
ftill changing their fcituations, and driving

O 3   about

about in their coaches, like the *Tartars* who lived perpetually in carts, journeying from one place to another for better grafs, when they had eat the pafture bare where they had firft fettled; but they have taught them now, like *Iffachar*, to know that Reft was good (at leaft in one fenfe) for them, and made them both remember and prac-tife the good old Monkifh maxim,

Si qua fede fedes, quæ fit tibi commoda fedes,
Illâ fede fede, nec ab illa fede recede.

By this Law they have obtained two good ends. Firft, that the Bifhops fhall not dan-gle perpetually after the Court, but fhall be lefs flavifhly dependant on the Czar, (who before ufed to manage them as he pleafed, and fet their tongues to go fafter or flower, as we do our Clocks, as he found moft convenient) and in confequence here-of, that hereafter they fhall be more incli-nable to the intereft of the Pope, and his ecclefiaftical Authority, when once it fhall be eftablifhed here. This was certainly a moft impolitick ftep for this Court to make, but it is grown a maxim now in this, as well as moft Governments in *Europe*, that

where

where the Jesuits are obliged, every thing is done with prudence; and this original error sanctifies all others that flow from it.

In the second place, by bolting the gate against all future preferments, they have effectually provided that the Sees shall be faithfully watched over, and constantly resided on, to the infinite emolument of the Christian Church, and the several Cures dependant on their Bishopricks.

This your Lordship will certainly allow to be an excellent regulation, and yet I have another to mention, nothing inferior to it, which is established by the same Law; and that is, that every Bishop shall on the death of any of his Clergy, before he gives away his Living, publickly receive the Sacrament in his Cathedral Church, and in the view of all his Congregation, solemnly swear on the Evangelists, that he will collate to that Living no Relation, nor be moved by any respects to solicitations of others, or blood or affinity, or any worldly regards, *nec prece nec pretio*, but the service of God, and his true Religion; and shall then and there (I am repeating the words of the Law to your Lordship) on the place name the person to whom he resolves to bestow it. A

O 4   secu-

security so strong and binding, to have piety, learning, and true merit only considered in such sacred preferments, that if it prevailed through the whole body of the Popish Church, or indeed in any other, would soon give them strength and credit sufficient to baffle and overturn all their adversaries, and almost give countenance and authority to the worst and weakest Doctrines she could maintain. Behold here the noblest provision for learning and merit! but the difficulty that still remains, is to find either of them in *Russia*. My Lord, they have taken effectual care, even of this almost insurmountable evil; for besides the new Præmiums they have got established in the Schools and Universities, which are able to rouse and awaken the drowsiest natures, the Bishop is obliged to keep a constant Library (appropriated to, and belonging to the See) in good order and condition, for the use of his Clergy; and in their turns of seniority, to have six of them residing in his house for twelve calendar months, reading under his direction for at least eight hours every day.

By this means learning, that is, some reasonable degree of it, is become more general

ral among the Clergy who formerly could hardly read their Liturgies; and furely if this obtain'd in our Country, it would be of much greater fervice than our larger libraries are, which like armories have few or no arms kept for conftant fervice, but are really more for fhew than ufe, and to give an air of ftrength and fuperiority to our Neighbours and Strangers that vifit them.

And becaufe formerly the *Ruffian* Clergy like the reft of the *Greek* Church entirely neglecting preaching, never making Sermons but twice in the year, on the Firft of *September* when their year begins, and St. *John Baptift*'s day, they have by their influence and authority in many Dioceffes prevail'd on the Bifhops to oblige their Parifh Priefts to preach at leaft the firft Sunday in every month, and to leffen their labour thofe days they have order'd them to abbreviate the tedious Liturgies of the *Greek* Church, and thereby prepar'd them for the fhorter and much eafier one ufed in the *Latin*. It is certain indeed, with all this care and reading the *Ruffian* Sermons are miferable Performances; for tho' they are kept by turns thus conftantly poring in their Bibles and Comments on them, and

eternally

eternally turning over the beſt of the ancient Fathers of the *Greek* Church, they
do not ſeem to reliſh, or at leaſt to digeſt
them well; and if I may be allow'd the levity of the expreſſion, they drink Wine,
but they piſs Water.

But methinks, my Lord, I perceive an
Objection ready to be offer'd here, and
which yet I will undertake the good Jeſuits ſhall effectually anſwer ; and that is,
that by theſe excellent Inſtitutions they ſeem
to have cut ſhort their own power of providing for the Friends of their Society and
Faction. No, my Lord, never doubt them,
they are not ſo ſhort-ſighted; for tho' they
concern themſelves leſs in the ſmaller Preferments, they induſtriouſly take care of all
that are conſiderable, and particularly as to
the Biſhopricks they let no Man ſtep into
the pooreſt See of this Church, whom they
cannot abſolutely depend on as a Creature
of their own.

There are in all Churches, and eſpecially
in this, a kind of very managing and ma-
nageable Divines, who pay their court to
intereſt and power, wherever they find it,
by a ſervile obſequiouſneſs in proſtituting
their Pens and their Pulpits to defend or ex-
plode

plode all Tenets as they are convenient or improper for the prefent times, and the prefent views of their mafters. They are a race of creatures who are ftill mighty fticklers for all feafonable local Truths and temporal Verities, and are too often found to be the ufefulleft tools that ever were fet at work by the wife *Matchiavels* of the world: However the malice of fome envious people nick-name them fometimes the Profeffors of the *Engaftromythick* Divinity, and rail at them a little feverely as teaching trencher Truths, and writing and preaching from that lower kind of Infpiration which has fet fo many great Souls at work, and fills the head from the fumes of the belly.

Out of this illuftrious body thefe good Fathers fail not with infinite skill and care to garble fuch Spirits as they find entirely devoted to their fervice, and ready to act the part of meer machines, to be directed and managed as they fhall find proper to employ them; and of this clay, thus temper'd and prepar'd, are the choice veffels of the *Ruffian* Church, her holy Bifhops and Fathers conftantly made.

Next

Next to this great circumftance (which is ever a *conditio fine quâ non*) there are two material confiderations that have perpetually influenc'd their choice of fit Perfons to fill the vacant Sees, both which deferve your Lordfhip's confideration.

The firft is, that fuch as are of the families of the Nobility, and related nearly to the great Knezzes and Officers at the Court, or in the feveral Provinces, fhall ftill be preferr'd to thofe that are meanly born, tho' fuperior to them in parts and learning; by which rule they tie down their relations to fupport their defigns, and approve of that great revolution they have projected.

The fecond is, that unmarried and childlefs perfons fhall always be pitch'd on; becaufe tho' they find it impracticable to introduce Celibacy among the inferior Clergy (who by the Canons of the *Greek* Church muft be married before they take orders, and can never marry again being widowers) yet by this method they have fufficiently eftablifh'd it among the whole Order of Bifhops. Hereby they have brought them to conform to the *Latin* Church in a material article, and by being childlefs, made them lefs tied down in their families

3   and

and fortunes to the Civil Powers, and likelier and abler with their Wealth and Intereft to fupport the Ecclefiaftical Eftate, to
which they are fo nearly related.

A rule, my Lord, which, if it obtain'd
in the *Greek* and Proteftant Churches,
which allow marriage to their Clergy,
would at leaft have this good confequence,
that men of the greateft Talents, and blefs'd
with a fpirit and genius fit for governing
others, would live unmarried, and prepare
themfelves by times for fuch important
trufts; and alfo the little ftream of wealth
which is yet left undrain'd and allow'd to
feed the conveniences or neceffities of their
Prelates, would not fo often be entirely funk
in filling up the private ponds and canals of
a family, but be more generally difpers'd
to enrich the face of their country, to the
profit and fervice of the publick. But as
thefe reflections are fitter for a different
place, I fhall difmifs them, to mention to
your Lordfhip another maxim by which
thefe good and pious Fathers prepare the
way for the papal authority; and that is, by
encouraging learning among the Nobility
and Clergy of *Ruffia*.

This

This would be a very unlikely Engine for them to work with, if they did not confine it in proper bounds and limits; but as there are few Printing-preſſes here, and moſt of them ſet up by themſelves; and ſince they are in a manner the ſole importers of books; they take heed, while they cheriſh and reward Scholars, to furniſh them only with ſuch Authors as are either ſecretly or openly conducive to theſe ends. Thus in *Ruſſia*, as in many other places, Men read not to direct themſelves in forming juſt thoughts and opinions of things, but to confirm them in thoſe which they have already taken up, or in favour of which their Intereſt or their Paſſions are ſtrongly engag'd. As to this people, it is beyond all queſtion, the Jeſuits could not have ſo effectually broken down (the main fences between the *Greeks* and *Latins*) the Zeal and Ignorance of the Laity and Clergy, as by this limited kind of learning; which is as different from true knowledge, as the light of a lanthorn that juſt directs us in the night in the path we deſire to walk in, is from the light of the Sun that opens the whole face of the Creation to our view.

Let

Let us now pafs from their management of the Clergy, to confider the mixt body of the people in general; and we fhall find there three powerful caufes, that are perpetually at work to bring about the ends which the boundlefs ambition of this fociety, and the empire of the *Vatican* are ever perfuing.

The firft of thefe is, removing a fcandalous practice that prevail'd, as all hiftorians tell us, for many ages in this country, of the landlords obliging all their poor vaffals to work on Sundays as much as other days, to the intolerable burthen of their tenants, to the utter breach of the Laws of God, and the fcandal of thofe of Men. Their remedy indeed has little regarded the former of thefe, but has entirely removed the latter, which was nearer their hearts; for by a new conftitution of the Czar's, and a Canon of one of their Synods, they have ordain'd, that on Sunday no perfon fhall be allow'd to labour, but fhall fpend the day, after attending divine fervice, entirely in fports and diverfions of all kinds. As this was known to be their work, it is incredible what favour and refpect they have gain'd by it among all the lower ranks of people;

who

who ufed to abhor the leaſt communication and correſpondence with them.

As this artifice takes in all the herd of
the lower people, the ſecond reaches to
thoſe who are eaſier in their circumſtances,
and endeavour by their induſtry to enlarge
their fortune.   To gain theſe, as the good
Fathers are the great Bankers and Traders
in the Catholick world, (where they have
labour'd to ſupplant both the *Dutch* and
us) ſo they have with great expence and
gain eſtabliſh'd trade and manufacturies in
the chief towns of this vaſt Empire, and have
taught the *Ruſſians* to extend their commerce and bring in wealth to their country
in a ſurprizing manner.

How far this muſt endear them to all, is
eaſily conceiv'd; and therefore I ſhall paſs
on to the laſt main cauſe that favours their
deſigns, and that is the univerſal Deiſm that
has infected ſuch crowds of perſons confiderable for rank, power, and fortune in
this nation.   This epidemical plague has
ſpread moſt unaccountably among them
from ſeveral ill-grounded and ſhameful
cauſes, the falſhood and folly of which
we are not to examine now: but it has
prevail'd ſo here, that even thoſe who ſtill
                                    pre-

preferve fome remains of refpect for our holy Faith, indulge themfelves in picking out
of it and their particular fancies and prejudices, a mix'd Olio of a Religion of their
own, which deferves to be compar'd to nothing fo properly as that of their neighbouring *Tartars*, the *Morduites*; who are both
circumcis'd and baptiz'd as *Jews* and *Chriftians*, and yet are abfolute Pagans in
their worfhipping and facrificing to Idols.
Nay, I have known Great Men here, remarkable for more Learning than generally
falls to the fhare of Noblemen in *Ruffia*,
who were credulous enough to allow a thoufand hiftorical abfurdities in Authors of credit on the flighteft evidence, who believ'd,
or affected to believe nothing in the Bible,
tho' fupported by the ftrongeft.

Such an odd unaccountable way of thinking have fome Minds contracted, that refemble the Dead Sea, as *Mandeville* defcribes it, on which Iron would fwim, but
a Feather would fink immediately. How
far this deluge of Infidelity, overfpreading
and overturning the old Foundations fettled
here in this Church, may contribute and
give opportunity to the building up the papal Authority amidft the ruins and deftruc-

P   tions

tions of both, I need not obferve to your
Lordfhip, who have fo thorough an infight
in the dependance and confequences of fuch
things. Thus far it is obvious to remark,
that in fo terrible a confufion, *Rome* and the
worft of her corruptions will be preferred
by the Clergy themfelves, and all that have
any remainder of Piety left, to no Religion
at all; and even the debauch'd and immoral part of Men who have none, and find
it neceffary to keep up fome outward profeffion in the world, will come into the
change as the beft and fitteft they can find
for their purpofe. And indeed it muft be confeft, there is no Religion upon earth, where
believing or doing fo little, will fo effectually
ferve the turn (if men will be filent and
obedient) as that of the Church of *Rome*,
and thefe good Fathers with their diftinctions
and abfolutions.

But while I fay this I would not be underftood, my Lord, as if I gave credit
to the reports that are fpread here, as if the
Jefuits fecretly favour'd the growth of this
devouring peftilence. Tho' we well know
by fad experience in *Great Britain*, what
horrible fects and herefies their emiffaries
fow'd among our anceftors, in the calami-

tous confusions of the seventeenth Century, in hopes to overturn *our* Church and restore their own ; yet I am unwilling to believe they can be possess'd with so infernal a spirit as that of *James Mora* the Surgeon and *William Platen* of *Milan*, who conspir'd to poison and infect the Citizens in the time of the Plague, in order to make themselves masters of their Fortunes, as an old Author tells us in his Travels *. However I think I may without breach of charity say, that they would rather even Deism or Mahometism should prevail, so they could at last establish themselves, than that the *Greek* Church should flourish in opposition to *Rome*, and keep their ador'd St. *Nicholas* in his post of Porter of the gates of Heaven, in contempt of St. *Peter* whom they have plac'd there.

And thus I shall put an end to this account of their Intrigues here, and their Schemes for obliging and serving the *Russian* Church and Clergy, in order to enslave them; and must own, there are some things they have done as to this last particular, that with proper Abatements I would rejoice to see copied in our own Kingdoms, whenever the

P 2 wisdom

---

* Addison's *Travels in* Italy, page 39.

wifdom and piety of our excellent Sovereign fhould judge it convenient.

Where truth allow'd it, I have given them their due praifes, and fhould be forry to fpeak of them with any unreafonable bitternefs and feverity. I admire the great Talents, Learning, and Wifdom of that prodigious fociety as much as any man, where they are applied (as they ought folely to be) to the good of Mankind, and the glory of our Creator. But to fee fuch excellent inftruments turn'd to corrupt our Morals, to wound Religion, and raife Factions, Schifms, and Rebellions in the earth to ferve their own ambition, muft raife every one's indignation. 'Tis a deteftable perverting of Wit and reafon, and all the powers of the human mind, from the noble purpofes they were given us for by Heaven, to the worft that can be fuggefted by Hell; and bears a near refemblance of their practice who make ufe of that foul of vegetation, and bafis of nutriment, the Nitre of the Earth, to convert it into gunpowder for the deftruction of their fellow-creatures.

It is true they pretend the good of mankind, and the peace of the Church, are the great views which all their toils and labours

are

are directed to; tho' they make ufe of fuch
infernal methods to arrive at them, as plainly
fhew 'tis the power and empire of *this* world
they aim at. If they made a good ufe of
their power where they are mafters, Men
would certainly oppofe them with lefs violence than they do; but alas, they are perpetually employing it where they dare, to per-
fecute and torment their Chriftian brethren
for the leaft uneffential differences in opinions : condemning them to dungeons
and tortures, and delivering them up, as far
as they are able, both to temporal and eternal fire. The favage nations in *America*
indeed, are faid to make war on their neighbours, who do not ufe the fame cuftoms
and fpeak the fame language; but thefe
Gentlemen go a few fteps further, and per-
fue you to the death, nay beyond the grave,
becaufe you do not think as they do (a
matter in no man's power) in fpeculative
points of their own contriving and impofing.
For after all, my Lord, they have not only
made a perfect manufacture of this commodity, but a monopoly too, and have manag'd with their *Faith*, as to the world, as
the *French* King has done with his falt as to
his fubjects. At firft it lay ready in every

creek, a plain useful healthful commodity, which all that pleas'd had for taking up, till by his absolute power the King seizes it solely into his hands, makes it up his own way, and refines it as he thinks proper; and then orders every one, on pain of death, to take such a proportion of it as he thinks necessary for them, whether they want it or no, or whether they will or no; and forbids under severe penalties that any that's foreign should be imported, and punishes all that make use of any other (tho' ever so much better) that is privately brought in by strangers.

But my zeal to satisfy your Lordship's curiosity on this subject has made me go somewhat beyond my own intentions, and I fear a great way beyond your desires. I will not encrease my fault by a long apology, and how ill soever I may have executed this, I shall wait with impatience for some new occasion of obeying any other commands you have for me, and every opportunity of shewing my self with great respect and submission,

My Lord,

Your Lordship's, &c.

CLARE.

To the Lord High-Treasurer, &c.

My Lord,

Constantinople, Feb. 25. 1997.

I CAN never sufficiently thank you for the pleasure I received from your Lordship's of Novemb. 29. from London-Chelsea, and the agreeable accounts you gave me in it, that my little Services here are acceptable to his Majesty and your Lordship; and above all, that the King condescends to entertain himself with the imperfect accounts I am able to send from hence.

Your Presents were most welcome to me, and especially, the glorious Telescope you have honour'd me with, which I shall in a few days set up conveniently enough. The Grand Seignior has already heard of it, and has resolv'd to have it brought into the Seraglio for his entertainment; which I am much rejoic'd at, you may believe, for the reasons I gave you. When he has seen it, I shall write to your Lordship a full account of all passages. Your Carolina White-wine was admirable, and the Silks much applauded here.

I

I hardly know which to admire moft,
your prodigious Prudence, that has fo greatly improv'd that drooping Colony in fo
fmall a time; or your Goodnefs, that after
fo long an abfence can continue to remember me in fo obliging a manner. But tho'
I have lefs fhare in it as to any pleafure or
expectation of my own, your Lordfhip's
moft exact and minute account of all the
furprizing improvements made in the poli-
ter Arts, and thofe noble marks his Majefty
has given of his zeal for Learning, gave me
the higheft fatisfaction: and I am confident,
all who have any regard to what our Country owes him, will never fail to exprefs a
due fenfe of the bleffings they receive from
him, and to befeech Heaven to continue
long to us a Prince, who feems born for the
good of his fubjects and the world.

I am glad I can now affure his facred Majefty and your Lordfhip, that at laft the
Treaty is perfected in every article, as directed in my laft inftructions in Mr. Secretary's Cypher. The Grand Seignior order'd
the Vizier to fign them laft Tuefday, as he,
accordingly did; and by this fafe convey-
ance I tranfmit them for your perufal, and
doubt not but your Lordfhip will be pleas'd
to

to fee our Trade here fo happily eftablifh'd, and that no weaknefs or inability of mine, has been able to difappoint the prudence and wifdom of his Majefty's and your Lord-fhip's Meafures.

I have fpoke to the Patriarch and feveral of the *Greek* Papas or Priefts in a body here, and they have affur'd me they will tranfmit their thanks in a particular Addrefs to his Majefty. Their miferable condition made the mention of Penfions highly wel-come; and indeed if fome of our learned Clergy and Books could be fent hither, to concert meafures with them, it might pro-duce uncommon confequences in favour of our Church, and to the prejudice of the Papal See, who fo ridiculoufly ftiles herfelf *Catholick*, tho' her dominions are nothing equal to thofe of this Church in *Europe* and *Afia* as to extent, and very little fuperior as to numbers of people. And now, my Lord, I return with all fubmiffion to ob-ferve your commands, to make fome addi-tions to thofe imperfect Obfervations I had the honour to tranfmit you from hence re-lating to thefe people. But while you in-creafe my defire, you almoft take away the power of obeying you, by letting me know

I

I am writing every word under my royal Maſter's diſcerning eye. This over-awes and
damps my mind: for alas! what am I able to
write, that can be fit to be heard or conſider'd
by ſo great a Prince, by ſo great a Judge as his
Majeſty? But your Lordſhip's deſires, which
are to me in the place of the moſt abſolute
commands, oblige me too ſtrongly, to ad-
mit of any excuſe to diſobey them: and
therefore as I have already ſpoke ſufficiently
on the ſubjects of their Army, Navy, Trade,
and Revenue, and have alſo touch'd on ſeveral new Cuſtoms and Laws eſtabliſh'd a-
mong them of late years; I ſhall go on to
take notice of ſome others, that as yet I have
left unmention'd. And the firſt I ſhall point
to, are ſeveral Regulations formerly quite
neglected here (which poſſibly may not be
be unuſeful to our ſelves or neighbours hereafter) in relation to the Plague.

Your Lordſhip, who is ſo perfectly acquainted with the cuſtoms and uſages of
all Nations, is by no means a ſtranger to
the ſtupid contempt and indifference which
this Court uſed to ſhew formerly on this
occaſion; and though they ſaw every year
ſo many millions ſwept away, by the ravage of that epidemical evil, yet ſo blindly
were

were they given up to their prejudices of Predeſtination, and that every Man's Fate was wrote in his forehead, that they never took the leaſt meaſures for the common good and ſafety of their Subjeɛts. But as experience (the fond wife of Wiſemen, and the ſcornful miſtreſs of Fools) has ſufficiently convinced them of their error, they have of late iſſued ſeveral Orders relating to this ſubjeɛt, that are not unworthy your Lordſhip's conſideration, if ever the crying Sins and Immorality of our times ſhould call down this ſevere chaſtiſement on our Country.

I ſhall not need to take notice to your Lordſhip, that in all Countries, and eſpecially in *Turky*, whenever that calamity falls on them, one fifth of the People generally periſh, and conſequently that this is a vaſt drawback on the ſtrength of the Empire, and the increaſe of their Subjeɛts, and therefore that the ſevereſt Laws are requiſite to remedy ſo dangerous an evil. As they are fully convinced of this now, they have eſtabliſhed ſuch Orders throughout the Empire, as they judged moſt neceſſary to prevent the ſpreading of ſo fatal a Contagion, and decreed that the moſt ſevere

2   Qua-

Quarantines muſt be obſerved in all Sea-
Ports, whereby it ſhall be death for any
Mariner or Paſſenger to come aſhore, and
ſufficient rewards eſtabliſhed for every perſon
who ingenuouſly diſcovers the infection of
any Ship, and the heavieſt forfeitures in caſe
of concealment. That all Cuſtom-houſe-
Officers ſhall have the ſame rewards, who
diſcover any ſhip to be infected, and forfeiture of place and goods, if they connive
at, or conceal ſuch Infection: and that all ſhips
where one fifth part of the crew are ſick,
ſhall be judged as infected, and perform
the moſt rigid Quarantine accordingly.

Thus far they ſtrive to ſhut out the danger by Sea, and at Land they have taken
as great precautions, both to prevent its
leaſt approach, or, if it appears, to ſtop its
courſe; and in caſe it ſpreads, to put all poſſible bounds to its raging fury. As to the
firſt of theſe, the late Emperor *Achmet* ordered that the whole Quarter called the
Janiſarchi where the Linnen and Woollen
Drapers, and the Druggiſts lived, (and where
by reaſon of the moiſt earth near the Sea-
ſhore, and the rotting of the vaſt heaps of
drugs thereby, and the aptneſs linnen and
woollen packs have to retain infectious qualities,

lities, the Plague generally firſt broke out) ſhould be removed into different parts of the ſuburbs, and adjacent villages, in the beſt air, and only one of thoſe Trades to be aſſigned to each ſtreet. The ſame order obtains as to all Apothecaries, Brewers, Bakers, Tallow-Candlers, Butchers, Dyers, and ſuch trades, which are apt to infect the air, and injure the health of great Cities, and are therefore obliged to live at a convenient diſtance from *Conſtantinople*: which I wiſh heartily were obſerved in every Metropolis in *Europe*, as well as in *London*, ſince I am confident it would make them abundantly more pleaſant and healthful. There are Clerks of the Market alſo ſettled, who watch carefully that no corrupted or unwholeſome meat, fuſty corn, or rotten or decayed fruits or roots, be ſold to the People, under ſevere Fines; nay, they are obliged alſo to deſtroy and bury thoſe hideous tribes of wild dogs that run about their ſtreets; and have even laid a tax on all houſes that keep cats in them (though this laſt is ſo great a favourite with the *Turks*) thoſe creatures being reckoned to contribute much to the ſpreading, if not to the breeding, infectious diſtempers. Beſides
thefe

thefe precautions, all common Beggars,
Gypfies, and Dervifes, who live on alms,
are banifhed this City on pain of Death;
their ufual naftinefs and diftempers having juftly rendered them fufpected: and alfo
all perfons are obliged to bury their dead at
leaft feven foot under ground. Nay though
they keep publick Scavengers to carry away
all filth and naftinefs, yet every Houfe-
keeper is to have the ftreet clean fwept before his door, and in fummer time fprinkled with water to cool the air.

But in the fecond place, my Lord, if the
Infection breaks out, each diftrict has publick Searchers appointed to attend it, who
remove all the fick who are neceffitous to
publick Hofpitals, where they are well
looked after; and oblige the richer fick to
live retired in the remoteft part of their
houfes, under the care of the publick Phyficians of that diftrict, who are in fufficient
numbers obliged to attend them, at the general charge of the Inhabitants, on pain of
the Galleys. All fick houfes are marked
with black ftrokes, to the number of the
fick in them, and two flaves fet to watch
them by turns night and day, and to bury
all that die, in their yards or gardens ten
foot

foot deep, with all their clothes and bedding, it being death to fell, or even conceal the leaft part of fuch goods, as they ufed to do.

In each diftrict there are Cadies and publick Officers appointed to examine daily if the publick rules are obferv'd both as to Phyficians and Apothecaries, Searchers, Watchmen, and the Sick they are to attend; and to order all proper food and provifions for fuch houfes as are fhut up, and to oblige all fuch attendants on the Sick to carry white wands in their hands, that all may avoid them. It is true indeed they are under fome difficulties to provide a fufficient number of Phyficians for all diftricts, and the Phyficians here are really very ignorant creatures; but then by their frequent experience in this epidemical diftemper, and the general rules that are printed and difpers'd among them, every little Quack, Druggift, or Apothecary is able to difcharge his duty tolerably in this point, tho' perhaps in no other.

Laftly, my Lord, if the Plague in fpite of all this care fpreads thro' the City, all publick concourfe, even at markets or the mofques, is prohibited, and no perfon allow'd

allowed to walk the ſtreets without ſome
ſtrong-ſcented herbs in their hands to ſmell
to, or tobacco in their mouths or noſes, and
all publick houſes are forbid the ſale of any
thing within doors.   No Magiſtrates whatever are to leave the City, but muſt aſſem-
ble once every day, to iſſue neceſſary orders, and puniſh all Offenders without mercy.   They are to keep guards of Janiſaries
in every proper poſt, and to make vaſt fires
in all great ſtreets and ſquares, to purify the
air, and in a word, to ſee nothing omitted
for the publick benefit.

By theſe methods, my Lord, it is incredible how many millions of his ſubjeſts
lives this good Emperor has ſaved, many of
which, if eſtabliſhed as laws in *Europe*,
would keep us from thoſe diſorders, and
panick fears which attend us when this publick judgment viſits us for our ſins, as it has
more than once this laſt Century.   In this
view I have troubled your Lordſhip with
this tedious repetition of ſome of the moſt
conſiderable of them, which have been
praſtiſed of late ſo ſucceſsfully throughout
this Empire.

It is certain, ſuch care is more neceſſary
in this age than ever, when Men and Women

men are obferv'd to grow barren, and to have fewer children than their Anceftors. Whether this proceeds from a deteftable pronenefs to the unnatural Sin, or at leaft to Whoredom, or from the wafte and ravage which Luxury, Voluptuoufnefs, and Debauchery of all kinds have made in our bodies, or the dwindling and decay of Nature, that is wafted and fpent with its own labours, or, which is moft likely, from all together; I leave to your Lordfhip to decide, and to the Governors of Nations to provide againft: for as their Strength confifts in the numbers of their fubjects, fo their Lives feem to want and deferve more care than ufual.

But I fhall quit this melancholy topick, to obferve fome more agreeable regulations which have obtained here, that might be of fervice to our Country, if introduced among us, either by Laws, or Cuftom, the ftrongeft of Laws.

And the firft I fhall take notice of in this light, is one which has contributed to raife this City from its Ruins, and the obfcurity of its dark, narrow, and irregular Streets, to the beauty and uniformity which appears in every quarter of it: and that is, that even

Q   in

in its fmalleft ftreets, and much more in
its larger ones and open fquares, all houfes
whether great or fmall, muft be built of
one equal heighth and uniform model, as
to doors, windows, and cornifhes, according to the publick plan, fettled by the
Grand Seignior's Architect.

By this method the meaneft ftreets are
kept fo even, ftraight, and with fo regulated a neatnefs and proportion, for the pooreft Citizens and the greateft, and are
fo properly fuited to and matched with
the adjoining dwellings, that they make
a moft pleafing profpect to the eye. I
have often reflected, that if this had been
fettled but fifty years fince with us, we
fhould have by this time a very different
City, and lefs of that fhocking mixture of
good and bad, high and low, old or new-
fafhioned houfes, which deform our ftreets
and fquares, and look more like ill-forted
different fized Ships, of all burthens, and
built by feveral Nations, when they lie at
anchor in our Harbours, than Houfes of the
fame City and People.

Another method I fhall hint to your
Lordfhip, is that of the publick Schools,
which are ufed here of late for inftructing
the

the youth in wreftling, leaping, vaulting, fwim-
ming, riding, fhooting, and fencing, which
has prov'd of vaft ufe in making them active,
ftrong-limbed, and able-bodied. This is of
fuch infinite fervice to Mankind in the various accidents of Life, that it were to be
wifhed, we, who have fo many fchools for
the improvements of our Minds, would have
fome to provide for the fervice of our bodies; and not leave fuch matters to chance,
or the humour of Children, who feldom
mind them or practife them, but with danger or hazard, for want of care and skill to
direct them.

The next particular I fhall mention, is a
Law that obtains here as to houfes already
built, but extends not to future buildings,
whereby all homefteads in every City, Town,
or Village, where any houfe falls down, and
continues four years in ruins, are immediately forfeited to the Grand Seigniot, and
fold at a low price to any Perfon, who will
oblige himfelf to rebuild it. By this fingle
rule they have kept their Towns from that De-
folation which ufed to lay them wafte; and if
this were extended in our Country to forfeiture or fine, from the Tenant to the
Landlord, and then in feven years to the

Q 2   King

King, it might keep up at leaft our prefent
Tenements in repair, which are gone to
ruin in fo many of our Towns, to our great
detriment.

I know not whether fo abftemious and
regular a perfon as my conftitution and
courfe of life have obliged me to be, may
venture to mention another Cuftom which
univerfally prevails here, fince the ufe of
Wine has been fo general; and that is, that
the *Jews* are entirely poffeft of the monopoly of Wine in this Country, who are
found by experience to fell it pure and un-
mixed. This practice they give into out of
principle, the Law of *Mofes* ftrictly forbid-
ding all mixtures; and as they fcrupuloufly
adhere to it, and dare not violate it, they
are obferved to keep it unadulterated, as it
comes from the Vineyard. How far this
might deferve to be encouraged in *Great-
Britain*, where we confume fo much Wine,
and fo abominably brewed and compounded, by the tricks and impofture of our Merchants; or how far at leaft, thefe Brokers
of the World, who lie fucking the life-blood
of our Trade, might be made ufeful in this
branch of our Commerce, I leave to your
Lordfhip's confideration, who knows fo
well

well how much the health and lives of the Subjects are concerned in it, as well as the Excise on the confumption.

I have but one thing further to offer to your Lordfhip, and I fhall quit this fubject for a while; and that is, the fevere Penalties that every one is liable to, who is found in the ftreets of this City after one a-clock at night. I am very fenfible this would be very difagreeahle to a Nation like ours, that glories in the very abufe and exceffes of Liberty; but whether the confequences of fuch a regulation amongft us, by preventing Murders, Robberies, and Debaucheries of all kinds, would not make abundant amends for the reftraint, I am more in doubt than poffibly your Lordfhip may be, when you ballance the two Evils together.

I fhall take the hint from hence to turn to another fubject, and fhew your Lordfhip that though it muft be owned that there are fome advantages in this abfolute Monarchy, which ours, as a limited one, is deprived of; yet they are fo trivial and inconfiderable, in comparifon of the miferies that accompany it, that they deferve not to be mentioned. Nay, if I might trouble your

Q 3　　　　　Lord-

Lordſhip with my ſmall judgment in Politicks, I am of opinion, that no ſenſible, not
to ſay no juſt and generous Man, would rather chuſe to govern an Empire of Slaves,
as this is, than a Nation of Subjects, as ours,
merely upon the principle of eaſe and ſafety to himſelf, and ſecurity to his Family.

For tho' Men here are ſuch vaſſals to power, that, like the *Chæroneans* in *Bœotia* of
old who worſhipped *Agamemnon*'s ſceptre,
(as made by *Vulcan* for *Jove*, and brought
from Heaven by *Mercury*) they make Gods
of their Rulers; yet their Hiſtory ſhews us
how often they have ſerved their Emperors
whom they worſhip, as the poor Heathen
did his Idol that he prayed to ſo long in
vain to eaſe his miſeries, that at laſt in a
rage he broke it to pieces.

As on every little ill-ſucceſs or ill-humour of the People, the heads of the Baſſas are made a ſacrifice to them, ſo on all
greater misfortunes or miſconduct abroad,
we ſee how inſolently and violently the rage
of the Commonality and Soldiery breaks
out againſt the Emperors themſelves. They
then depoſe one and ſet up another, according as their Paſſions or Caprice directs them,

and

and take a full revenge for their intolerable flavery, by ufurping as unjuftifiable a
power to themfelves. How often, my Lord,
fince I have been Ambaffador here, have I feen
the worft and loweft of the People demand
and obtain the heads of the wifeft and the
beft of the Baffas, on falfe and ill-grounded
furmifes? and this with fuch univerfal fury,
that one would think the vengeance of Heaven fell on thefe Infidels, like *Mofes*'s great
miracle on *Pharaoh*, when the duft of the
Earth was turned into Lice that fwarmed
every where, crawling into the Palaces of
Kings, and defiling and devouring the Princes of the Land.

It is true indeed, I have fometimes known
thefe terrible Seditions of the People occafioned by real dangers of the State, which,
like the Geefe in the Capitol, they have
faved by their noife and clamours, when
thofe who fhould have been their beft
watchmen flept. But they have ftill been
attended by fuch dreadful confequences
to their Governors, as may make their Suc-
ceffors tremble to confider, that the rage of
their Subjects, like the authority of their
Emperor, is not circumfcribed and bound-

Q 4   ed

ed by fettled and regular Laws, but their own wills.

A reflection which more or lefs there is too much ground for in all abfolute Monarchies, but efpecially in this; and muft make every wife Man chufe to govern a People, who are bound by Rules they have freely confented to, and have no temptations to break through from their own intereft, than to rule over them by an abfolute authority, which muft ever be precarious, in proportion to the People's temptations and advantages to overturn it.

Befides, though in the hands of a good Prince the People feldom fuffer by a Defpotical Government; yet his Virtue will be no defence to him, if his Arms prove unfuccefsful abroad, or his Adminiftration by unforefeen accidents prove unfortunate at home; neither of which opportunities are often neglected by his oppreft Subjects, or left unrevenged by Civil Wars or Infurrections, which feldom end but in his ruin, or his Minifters.

Whoever looks into the Hiftory of this Empire, will be convinced by numberlefs inftances of thefe truths, and will find in *them,* arguments fufficient to convince the

3   moft

moſt abſolute Princes, that they would be happier in a more limited Government, and make them not only privately debate, like *Auguſtus*, how to moderate their tyranny, but publickly ſet on foot ſo noble and generous a deſign. I am perſuaded, were the Grand Seignior to travel over, as a private perſon, the wide depopulated Waſtes of his Provinces, and with his own eyes behold the Cruelty, Extortion, Oppreſſion, and Injuſtice, which, under the cover of his authority, his Governors, Cadies, and Officers, make uſe of to enrich themſelves, and plunder his wretched Subjects; his good-natured and generous temper would be affected in the tendereſt manner by it. But while he ſits in his Palace or Camp, ſurrounded by his great Baſſas, he muſt hear with their ears, and ſee with their eyes, whatever is offered to his conſideration; and to propoſe the leaſt abatement of the miſery of his People, would be regarded only as undermining his power, which at preſent rather wants props to ſupport it.

In all abſolute Monarchies where I have been, the inhuman treatment of the ſubjects has ever ſtruck me in the moſt ſhocking manner; and ſurely, to ſee Wretches,

whom

whom the Prince who tyrannifes over them, calls his Fellow-creatures, and fometimes his Chriftian Brethren, us'd with lefs mercy or humanity than the beafts of the field; muft fill every one, who has any bowels of pity in him, with horror. Indeed the lovely climates where Tyranny has generally feated herfelf in the World, feem to make fome amends for the mifery of thofe who groan under the burthen of fuch fevere task-mafters. But to behold it deftroying the peace and happinefs of the Northern Parts of the Globe, is to fee upon Earth a lively image of Hell, that is, Woe, Punifh-ments, and Mifery in the midft of an un-comfortable gloom and darknefs, without the leaft glympfe of hope from the mercy of Heaven, or the fmalleft relaxation from their own complaints, or the wearinefs of their cruel tormentors, who muft fhare in the tortures they are made minifters of.

Many people have wonder'd how fuch Governments find fubjects to live under them, and have generally accounted for it by the love of one's Country, which runs thro' all. But can Debtors love their Goal, or Felons their Dungeon? No certainly, my Lord; and therefore it muft be accounted

counted for, partly by the care thefe greedy
fhepherds take, that as few as poffible of the
flock they are to fleece ftray from them; and
partly, from feeing few of their neighbours
much eafier; and laftly, from their being
teather'd up by little domeftick ties and relations, and by cuftoms and languages that
are ufed by them, and thought barbarous
by others.

I am affur'd, that about fifty years fince
the Inhabitants of the Ifle of *Scio* found out
a middle way (which few I doubt will dare
to imitate them in) to put an end to their
flavery under the *Turks*. For having fevere
new Taxes laid on them, and on being unable to pay them, finding their Wives, and
Friends, and Children carried away for
Slaves; they all, Men and Women, bound
themfelves by the fevereft penalties to make
their Commonwealth, as *Florus* fpeaks, *Res
unius ætatis*, and to put an end to their
Slavery by having no more Children. It is
certain they kept up this refolution fo many years, that their Mafters were glad at laft
to prevent the utter depopulation of the
place, to remove their obftinacy and defpair
by abolifhing the new Gabels. This was
certainly a degree of refentment and refolution

lution greater than ever was known in former Ages, and infinitely beyond the generous Fury of the people of *Saguntus* the *Roman* Colony in *Spain*. For they only burnt themſelves, their Wives, Children, and Wealth, rather than be taken and enſlav'd by their Enemies; but theſe calmly and deliberately perſiſted in cutting off all their Race, and delivering themſelves without violence or rage in a calm, quiet and regular method, from an inſupportable Tyranny, which at laſt they conquer'd by a noble Deſpair.

But it is time I ſhould take your Lordſhip from ſuch diſagreeable Scenes of the miſery of theſe States, to acquaint you with the happineſs of a Commonwealth, which, next to your native Kingdom, you love above all others; and that is, the Commonwealth of Learning. It is with the higheſt pleaſure I ſend you two of the nobleſt Manuſcripts which poſſibly the Spoils of the Eaſt or Weſtern World could furniſh me with, and which our Royal Maſter's generous allowance for ſearching out and buying up all choice Manuſcripts throughout this Empire, has enabled me to lay now at his feet, through your Lordſhip's hands.

They

They are both in *Arabick*, and as far as I can judge with my little skill in that language, wrote in a good ſtyle, tho' probably in the tenth Century. They are perfect and tolerably well preſerv'd, though ſuch Treaſures deſerv'd infinitely greater care. The firſt and ſmalleſt is a Tranſlation of ſeveral of *Cicero's Tuſculan* Queſtions, which we have already ; and thoſe two invaluable Books of his *De Gloria*, the original of which was preſerv'd, as *Paulus Manutius* and ſeveral Authors tell us, till the ſixteenth Century, in the Library of *Bernard Juſtiniani*; and probably ſtolen from thence by *Alcyonius* the Phyſician, who is ſaid to have deſtroy'd them, and inſerted a great many paſſages out of them in his Treatiſe *De Exilio.* If I had the good fortune to have *Alcyonius's* Work here, I could ſoon inform your Lordſhip if the Phyſician was indeed the Plagiary he was ſuſpected to be: but as I want that Treatiſe, I muſt leave that diſquiſition to your Lordſhip's care.

Beſides this, there is at the end of the Manuſcript a Treatiſe of his *De Vita beata,* that ſeems admirable in its kind, but 'tis imperfect. I ſhould regret this as a great loſs, if the joy of recovering the reſt allow'd me;

me; where tho' his admirable Style is ftill wanting, yet his manner of handling thefe noble Subjects, and the Reafonings and Images he adorns them with, is ftill preferv'd, and now happily reftor'd to us.

But I haften to the other larger and in my poor judgment a more defirable Treafure; which is a fine *Arabick* Tranflation, by one who calls himfelf *Abumepha Nezan Ali*, of that noble Hiftorian *Trogus Pompeius*, who writ the Hiftory of the World in forty-four Books, in fo elegant and admirable a ftyle and manner, under *Auguftus*. Your Lordfhip well knows, that this admirable Work was mangled and epitomis'd by *Juftin*, and how that wretched Abbreviation occafion'd the lofs of his noble performance; like *Pharaoh*'s lean kine devouring the fat and well-favour'd ones of their own fort. The Tranflation feems well perform'd, and has fome good Notes added to it, and feems to have been wrote in the ninth, or at leaft in the beginning of the following Century, by the hand and ftyle, which anfwers that Age. I have look'd over it carefully, with what little judgment I have in fuch things, and cannot without indignation obferve what Treafures of Antiquity

tiquity

tiquity and History, as well as Geography;
and what material Paſſages and Actions,
untouch'd by all other Writers but the learned and judicious *Trogus*, his poor and un-
skilful Abbreviator has ignorantly and care-
leſsly paſs'd over unmention'd. This excellent and admirable Perſon, to whom Hiſtory and the learned World were ſo much
indebted (tho' they ſo ill repaid the debt,
by ſuffering him to periſh) was, as he tells
us in his forty-fourth Book, a noble *Roman*,
originally deſcended of the *Vocontii* in the
Narbon Gaul, and whoſe Godfather of the
ſame name was declar'd a *Roman* Citizen
by *Pompey* the Great in the *Sertorian* War.
His Uncle commanded a Squadron of Horſe
in the War againſt *Mithridates* under the
ſame General, and his Father ſerv'd under
Caius Julius Cæſar, both as a Commander
and his chief Secretary of State and War.
Judge, my Lord, with what tranſport of
heart I ſend you this incomparable Author,
to be reſtored by you and our Royal Maſter's cares to the Commonwealth of Learning, which has too long mourn'd for his
loſs.

I beſeech your giving the ſtricteſt orders
to ſome able hand, to have him tranſlated
into

into an excellent *Latin* Style; tho' it will be impoffible to equal that of his own inimitable Elegance, which we have loft for ever.

I muft in juftice to the care and judicious conduct of Mr. *Weft*, who carries this and them, acknowledge, that 'tis to his induftrious and unwearied labours, next to his Majefty's bounty, that we are indebted for the recovery of this invaluable Jewel. He found it, and the Tracts of *Cicero*, cover'd with duft and moldinefs in the *Armenian* Monaftery at *Etchmeafin* near *Rivan* in *Perfia* : and on this and many other accounts I zealoufly recommend him to your Lordfhip's favour.

He affures me, Mr. *Pearfon* is ftill in that Country on the fame account; and gives me hopes we may yet be able to retrieve fome other valuable Authors, among the old *Arabick* and *Perfian* Manufcripts that lie difpers'd in the neglected Libraries of many Monafteries there, and in the Eaftern Countries.

Will your Lordfhip forgive me, if I encreafe the length of this tedious difpatch, by accompanying thefe ancient rarities with a modern one, that was perfectly fo to me,
tho'

tho' I have fo long refided here, and which I met the other day at a Cady's houfe in *Pera*, where I went on fome bufinefs.

It was a Man of the famous *African* Sect of *Mahometans* that are called *Bumicilli*, of whom I had heard fo much from common report, and the Writings of Travellers, without ever meeting one of them before. They fet up for a very religious fort of people, who have a knowledge of, and converfation with aerial Beings, and are engag'd in perpetual war with the Devils, who are ftill ranging about the Earth and the Air, in order to tempt and hurt Mankind by all the arts and methods they can contrive.

However, it is certain thefe Gentlemen of the *Bumicilli* Sect are at bottom but a fort of vagrant thieves, who go round this vaft Empire under this pretence, and either beg or fteal all the pence they can from the deluded people. I am affur'd they have by thefe means greatly enrich'd themfelves, and their Society; who have by fuch collections thus gather'd, founded great Convents, and got large Poffeffions, to enable them to continue their conftant wars with all wicked Spirits with vigour and fuccefs.

R   Me-

Methinks, my Lord, one may fee here, with half an eye, a perfect picture of that illuftrious religious Society, who owe their rife to the holy *Loyola*, and who profefs all kinds of labour and toil, both as Exorcifts, to drive out evil Spirits, and to extirpate imaginary Herefies and Hereticks, and defeat all fuch emiffaries of the Devil, who diftract their infallible Church.

I faw this Creature from my window in the ftreet, laying manfully about him with all his might, (for he was a tall ftrong black fellow) and beating the air like a Bedlamite, with a long Pike he brandifhed about his head, and frequently pufh'd moft furioufly with; traverfing his ground, now running forwards and fhouting, and then giving back, and appearing forely hurt; and anon, recovering himfelf, and feeming to fall anew on his foes. The people of the houfe told me he was a moft holy Man, and had defeated all the Devils in that neighbourhood fo fortunately, that they liv'd much happier and holier than formerly; and that it had coft them very little money for fo great advantages. I found my felf obliged to give them a paient hearing; and efpecially feeing all the teo-

ple

ple in the ſtreet ſeem'd to be of their mind, by the zeal and joy they ſhewed whenever their heroick Combatant appear'd to get the better of the imaginary and inviſible Devil he was engag'd with: for I need not aſſure your Lordſhip, that whether he apprehended being oppreſs'd with numbers, or having foul play ſhewn him, or other reaſons beſt known to himſelf, the Devil was ſo cowardly as never once to let himſelf be ſeen by us, who were gazing on this furious engagement.

After I had look'd on this fine battle, with equal amazement and delight, near a quarter of an hour by my watch, I ſaw our Warriour, to the great concern and trouble of all his religious Spectators, fall down on the earth as in a ſwoon. There he lay a long time, and the Cady, in whoſe houſe I was, being a very zealous and ſincere Muſſulman, ran out into the Street, with tears in his eyes, and with all the concern and care imaginable had him brought in. He made him be laid gently on a Sofa in the room where I was, and had two or three Slaves, ſometimes throwing cold water on his face, and ſometimes rubbing his limbs, and endeavouring to bring him to life.

As

As fenfible as I was that it would difpleafe, I could not help asking the Cady
in the ear, if it was poffible he could think
all this any thing but a meer cheat to get
money from them; and indeed all the people before our faces (as the cuftom is on
thefe occafions) had put money into the
Combatant's bag which hung at his back.
Notwithftanding all this, he lift up his
hands and eyes at my infidelity, reproach'd
me with our credulity as to miracles in *Europe*, and our falfe Church, tho' we would
believe none in the true one; and to convince me of my miftake, and open my
blind eyes (for fo he call'd them with fome
fury) he made the flaves pull off the wretch's
clothes, and fhew me the black-and-blue
marks he had receiv'd in the combat, and
which appear'd plentifully all over his arms,
ba k, and fides.

The truth is, tho' I well knew, and had
been told, that their way is to make fuch
marks by cords, and actual blows they give
themfelves in the night-time, in order to
impofe on the croud; yet finding the good
Cady fo violent, I was oblig'd to feem a-
mazed and convinc'd, and to give my affent
to a number of ftories they told me of the

3

battles

battles this holy Man had fought with unparallel'd fuccefs with a great many Devils, to
the peace and comfort of all true Muffulmen in thofe parts. I was even under a
neceffity to applaud his courage and fanctity
as the reft did ; and at laft, when they had
recover'd their Warriour out of his counterfeit fwoon, I very humbly fat down, and
eat and drank with him and the Cady,
liftning attentively to his accounts of his
long warfare with different Dæmons, and
to fhew my firm faith in all he related, and
entirely appeafe the Cady, I gave him a
Zequin for his further encouragement in fo
ufeful a method of ferving his Prophet, and
the good Muffulmen in *Turkey*.

Was this a wonderful fcene or no, my
Lord? and is there not matter here for fine
reflections? However, my Lord, I fhall
cut them fhort, having fo long trefpafs'd on
your patience already, and fhall leave you
to make your own remarks on the wretched
impoftures, and the filly credulity of that
noble, that wife, that rational creature Man!

I expect in fome little time to be fummon'd to the Seraglio to fhew the Grand
Seignior your admirable Telefcope, of which,
probably, I may give your Lordfhip fome

R 3

account

account in my next; and in the mean time I muft acquaint your Lordfhip, that I find two or three packs of fome of our beft deep-mouth'd fouthern Hounds would be a moft acceptable prefent to his Highnefs. If you would procure fome able and skilful Phyfi-cian to come and attend the Grand Seig-nior, I am empower'd to affure him of 30 Purfes at leaft (or 15,000 Ducats) befides Prefents, with all poffible good treatment, and to be *Hachim Bachi* or chief Phyfician. As this I find would be a moft agreeable Ob-ligation, I recommend it to your Lordfhip's care to procure fuch an one: and indeed the favour and complaifance that has been fhewn to his Majefty's defires in our late Treaty, deferve all the returns we can make them.

I referve my Compliments for another opportunity, and, if I may fay fo, for ano-ther fort of Man than your Lordfhip; to whom, and all your excellent Family, I and mine are,

My Lord, your Lordfhip's, &c.

STANHOPE.

PREFACE

the Second.

IT is not without a mixture of ſhame
and ſorrow, my dear Reader, that I
am forced to take thee from the delightful Entertainment which thou haſt been taſt-
ing in theſe admirable Letters, and the a-
mazing Scenes of Futurity diſcover'd in
them; to return to ſo inſipid an employment, as my anſwering all objections againſt
this Work. But there is no help for it ;
and ſince the World (as ſome ill Paymaſters
ſerve their Workmen) loves rather to rail at
the performance and skill, of the wiſe Authors who labour for its ſervice, than to
pay them their wages; I muſt do my beſt
to anſwer all its Accuſations and Cavils.

I

I shall not expostulate here against the ingratitude of such treatment. I shall take a nobler revenge, than upbraiding or reproaching them for it: and that is, by shewing the Folly, Stupidity, and Ignorance of all they are able to urge against me! Against me, did I say? against that exalted Spirit, that seraphick immortal Being from whom I receiv'd it!

The first Objection then, and which I find most insisted on, is, That there are no such Beings assign'd to attend Mankind, as good or bad Angels or Genii; and that therefore all I have said on that subject, must be meer Invention, that I may not use so vile a word as Falshood.

These Objectors are very violent, but altogether as blind and ignorant; and I may say of them as *Momus* did of the Bull, that he was a stout pusher, but he wanted an Eye in his horn, it being his way to shut his Eyes when he pushes, as one would think these poor people do.

For it has been the common opinion of all Nations, of all Religions, of all Ages, that every Man had a good Angel attending him. 'Tis true indeed, we must except a little Sect among the *Jews*, from this general
ral

ral account: but till we are in danger of becoming a Nation of *Sadduces*, I hope we fhall have little regard for their Error. All the *Pharifees* in the ancient *Jewifh* Church, who were follow'd by infinitely the largeft, and wifeft part of that people, did not only maintain the exiftence of Angels, but many of them believed every Man had two af-fign'd him, the one good to protect him, the other bad to record his faults, and be his accufer. Nay, fome of their Doctors made thefe Angels to refemble exactly thofe whom they thus attended; and afferted, that as it was *Efau's* Angel, who wreftled with *Jacob*, it was for fear of being known, that he would fain have perfuaded *Jacob* from keeping him till the morning, which however he could not fucceed in, and fo was difcovered by the Patriarch.

Some of them carried this point fo far, that I can produce proofs from their beft Authors, (however fome *Rabbies* may deny it) that they ufed to pray on all occafions, to their guardian Angels to protect them; and applied to them to this end, even in the very act of relieving Nature*: a time when
in

* Vide *Ceremonies of all Nations, for thofe of the* Jews *Prayers.*

in every one's opinion, but *Thomas d'Aquinas*'s, the body is too much taken up, to leave room for pious Meditations, or Ejaculations of any kind, unlefs in cafes of painful coftivenefs, or violent fluxes.

The very *Turks* and *Perfians*, and all the Heathens that overfpread the Eaftern parts of the Earth, acknowledge this great Truth; and tho' they fhut their eyes againft fome of more importance, yet are afham'd to deny one fo glaring and manifeft as this; and furely my Adverfaries will not have us fhew ourfelves greater Infidels than thefe, let things go ever fo ill with fome conceited Men among us as to believing. Nay, the *Mahometans* do not only allow two Angels to Men, to attend on them during their Lives, but even after their Deaths, they affign to each wicked perfon two black Angels, whom they call *Mongir* and *Guavequir*, to fit by him in his Grave, and torment him there till the Day of Judgment; or if good, two white Angels, one of which lays its arm under his head, and the other fits at his feet, and fo protect him moft quietly, till Domefday difcharges thefe trufty Watchmen. It is true, we fhould not build too much on the *Turks* opinion herein,

the

the good *Mahomet* having been so very li-
beral of his Dæmons, as to assign an evil
Angel, (a matter of Faith to all his Followers) to every single Grape. But tho'
he may have overstrain'd that point a little,
yet still he has but followed the general
opinion of Mankind: for many Nations in
different parts of the Earth, do not only
allow Angels to Men, but even to the four
Seasons of the Year, the four Gates of Heaven, the four Quarters of the World, the
four Rivers of Paradise, the four Winds, the
seven Planets, the twelve Months of the
Year, the four Elements, the twelve Signs
of the *Zodiack*, and the twenty-eight Man-
sions of the Moon. To the very Days of
the Week, and every particular Hour of the
Day and Night, they assigned a presiding
Angel, as these ignorant Objectors might
read (if they could read such things) in all
occult Astrologers, and great Philosophers;
and particularly in the *Elementa Magica*
of *Petrus de Abano*, where their names are
specified, and joined regularly to their several Offices.

Certainly therefore, as almost all the
known Nations of the Earth, not excepting
the

* *Apud Corn. Agrip. de occulta Philosoph.* p. 342. Edit. *Lyons.*

the Atheifts of *China* and *Siam*, have maintained this opinion, I might, had I wanted
ftronger proofs, fairly infift that it muft
be true; and lay it down as no ill axiom
for thefe fceptical doubters, *Quod præfcrip-
tione valet, ratione valet.* But I fhall argue more fairly with them, and fhall undertake to fhew them, firft, that the learned
Heathens, and fome great Rabbies; and
fecondly, that many of the Fathers, and
all the *Roman,* and truly Catholick Infallible Church, have ever maintained this
doctrine; and fhall give fome known inftances from learned Writers in both.

Among the firft, both *Homer* in feveral
places of his *Iliad* and *Odyffea,* and *Hefiod,*
in his *Moral Poem,* appear plainly of this
opinion; and the latter has even affigned
the number of good Angels*, appointed to
attend Mankind. In the little that we have
of the Works of *Menander,* there is a full
proof that he gave into the fame fentiments;
for in one of his fragments he afferts, that
every one from his birth has a particular
Dæmon affigned to take care of him. *Pythagoras,* who dogmatized in the fixtieth
Olympiad, and whofe fchool lafted to the
nine-

* Vid. *Hefiodi Opera & Dies,* ad lin. 252.

nineteenth generation; and *Plato,* who flourished above thirty Olympiads after him,
(as *Diogenes Laertius* tells us*) and all their
Disciples taught this; and especially among
the *Platonists, Maximus Tyrius, Plotinus,*
and *Jamblicus.* This was also the universal
doctrine of the *Stoicks,* as one might easily
shew by numberless proofs; but it will be
sufficient to point out *Seneca's* hundred and
tenth epistle to *Lucilius,* where this is a-
bundantly made evident: and not only that
they maintained that every man had his
Genius, but every woman her *Juno* attending on her. All the greatest *Jewish* Rabbies of the three last Centuries, treading in
the steps of the learned *Porphyry,* and more
ancient *Jewish* Writers, held this doctrine;
and have sown it so thick in their works,
that a man knows not where to begin to
quote them, or where to end when he has
begun. They all agreed as one Man on this
head, and to this day it is generally maintained by the few among them that have
any learning. To go no farther than the
Patriarchs, they believe that *Adam* was often
conversant with, and governed by his Angel

*In his Lives of *Plato* and *Pythagoras.*

gel *Raziel*; *Sem* by *Jophiel*; *Abraham* by
Tzadkiel; *Isaac* by *Raphael*; *Esau* by *Scha-*
mael; *Jacob* by *Piel*; *Moses* by *Mitraton*;
and King *David* by *Michael*; as any one may
see, that will but look into their Writings
relating to these matters.

Nor are the instances in ancient Writers
of Men who had such *Genii*, and conversed
with them sometimes, infrequent. *Hermes*,
Socrates, *Numa*, *Cyrus*, *Scipio*, *Marius*,
Scylla, *Sertorius*, *Julius*, and *Augustus*
Cæsar, *Julian* the Apostate, and *Apollo-*
nius Tyanæus, are often mentioned on this
occasion; as well as *Aristotle*, *Dion*, *Fl.*
Josephus, *Plotinus*, *Galen*, *Synesius*, *Por-*
phyry, *Jamblicus*, and even *Brutus*, *Cassius*,
and *Cicero*; though these three last indeed,
had no communication with them, till a
little before their deaths. It were endless
to quote all the testimonies of Authors, that
these great Men were allowed to have their
Genii, who either appeared to them, or
only assisted and watched over them privately: whoever reads their Lives or Works
will easily acknowledge it, and save me
much needless labour. But the evidence
for *Socrates* having such an one, is so universal both among the Philosophers and the
Fathers,

Fathers, that I can't but mention it particularly. Some of the latter have carried it
fo far as to fay, that from thence he had
an actual prefcience of our Saviour's coming into the World, and though darkly (as
Socrates words are very dark on it) yet he
forefaw both the neceffity and advantages
of his appearing among Men.

As to the Philofophers, both *Plato*[1], and
even *Zenophon*[2], who was no friend to *Plato* (and would willingly have contradicted
and oppofed him, had he writ a falfhood)
agree in this fact, and are worth a thoufand
other Witneffes (for *Maximus Tyrius*[3], *Apuleius*[4], *Antifthenes*[5], *Diogenes Laertius,
Cicero,* and *Plutarch,* all agree in it) becaufe both of them knew him intimately,
and were Men of the higheft veracity and
honour. Nay, this was fo uncontefted a
fact, that *Origen* fhewing the virulence and
rage of calumny, in Men of bad hearts and
malevolent fpirits, whom no innocence can
efcape, nor virtue filence; adds, that fuch
People will even make a mock of the Genius of *Socrates,* as a vain thing.

---

[1] *Plato de factis & dictis Socratis in Theage.*   [2] *Lib.* 4[to] *me-
morabilium & alibi.*   [3] *De Deo Socratis.*   [4] *De Deo
Socratis.*   [5] *In vita Socratis.*

Now as this is fo evident, as to *Socrates*, fo a few quotations of the like nature, would make it as probable, that the teftimonies producible for all the reft are as well grounded; and efpecially, when fuch undeniable Facts and Authors are brought for their vouchers: all which, however, to avoid confufion and a troublefome prolixity, we fhall omit, and pafs to the opinion of the holy *Roman* Church, and more modern inftances of this fort among men.

It has been faid already, and 'tis univerfally known and allowed, that feveral of the ancient Fathers were of this opinion, and (abftracted from proofs from holy Writ, which, I will own to my adverfaries, is perfectly filent here) it was indeed a natural confequence from their being generally *Platonifts*. There will be no need therefore, of appealing to quotations from their works, on this head; and for the fame reafon I fhall pafs by the Schoolmen, many of whom are fo clear on this point; and content myfelf to fhew, that fome modern Divines and Philofophers have not deferted the Fathers here, but rather have gone as much beyond them, as truth and prudence could poffibly allow them.

Let

Let us begin then (without mentioning *Kircher*'s good Genius, who carried him through the Planets in his *Iter Extaticum)* with that grave and wonderful writer, the excellent *Francifcus Albertinus.* I fhall introduce this Author firft, both as he is a Jefuit, and on that account alone deferves to precede all others; and becaufe in his admirable Treatife *de Angelo Cuftode* †, he has, on evident reafons, though too tedious to infert, peremptorily determined, that every Church, Temple, Monaftery, and Family, as well as every Man, is allowed a Guardian Angel, not excepting even Antichrift himfelf, which, fays he, is to keep him from doing greater mifchief. Nay, he does not only affure us, on his own unexceptionable credit, that the number of Archangels is greater than that of Angels, and that the crowd of thefe laft, exceeds that of all Mankind: but to put it out of any poffibility of being ever contefted again, he has irrefragably proved it by a divine Revelation made to St. *Bridget,* whofe words he quotes, *viz.* That if all Men that have been born fince *Adam,* to the laft Man that

S fhall

---

† Printed at *Cologne,* 1613.

shall be born in the very end of the World, should be computed, there would be found more than ten Angels for every single Man.

I will not urge here that all this wise and venerable Order, are so far from doubting of this great Truth, that they and their whole Church pray to them daily; *(Paul* the fifth having published *Officium Angeli Custodis,* with the Prayers to them) because my ill-natured Opposers may say, they pray to a number of Saints who never had, and who they know, as well as Monf. *Launoie,* never had a being. But I hope I may fairly insist on it, as a good proof, that the Jesuit *Schottus* must have believed their Existence, otherwise he had never dedicated his Book of Mathematicks to his Tutelar Angel, so solemnly as he did: for however a wise and learned Jesuit may pray, he would never dedicate his Writings (I speak as an Author) but to a real Being, from whose influence he might receive benefit, and advantage.

But let us pass from these great Men, and their sacred Order, whose probity, humility, and piety, I ever honoured, to the learned *Cornelius Agrippa*; who in his third book *De occulta Philosophia,* and the

twen-

twentieth chapter, declares, that no Prince or Nobleman could be safe, or Woman chaste, or Man in this Vale of ignorance (so he speaks) able to serve God, but for the assistance of their good Angel. That great Divine *Bartholomæus de Sybilla* *, goes yet farther, and avers, a good Angel is assigned to every one of us, from the moment we peep into the World; because, as he wisely and judiciously observes, the minute we are in danger of sinning, the care of the good Angel is necessary to defend us from the assaults of Satan; and that till we are born, we are sufficiently watched over by our mother's good Angel.

In another treatise †, he is so modest as to except our Saviour from this general rule, and determines that he had no guardian Angel: and though he proposes it as debateable, he gravely and learnedly maintains it, against all opposers, and overturns a seeming objection, of the Angel that appeared to him in the Garden, and shews that it was but a ministring Spirit, and not a guardian Angel: which last thought, as odd as it looks, was the opinion of no less

S 2   a

---

* *Peregrinarum Quæst.* p. 436.
† *De Angelorum Custodia.*

a man than St. *Jerome.* As the Devil when exorcifed will fometimes witnefs to the Truth, fo even one of the greateft Here-ticks that ever appeared in the pulpit in *Great-Britain,* is forc'd to maintain the doctrine of good Angels very ftrenuoufly, in his fer-mon on the Feaft of St. *Michael* the Arch-angel*; though he does not carry it fo far, as that eminent writer *Joannes Eckius*† does, in his feventh homily on the fame feftival. Indeed many grave Doctors of the holy and infallible Church of *Rome,* have ventured to affign to Men in high and publick Stations, not only an Angel, but an Archangel; and to the Pope, befides his Angel in ordinary, which he had a full ti-tle to from his birth, a couple of prime Archangels, to affift and direct him, hav-ing all of them enough to do, to keep him and his important affairs in tolerable order. And really to fay the truth, I cannot but think thefe tutelar Angels of his Holinefs, muft be wearied out of their very lives, by fuch a vaft variety of bufinefs, and a mul-tiplicity of Intrigues, Defigns, and Inte-refts, as they muft have daily on their hands, for

---

* Vid. *Tillotfon's* Sermons. vol. 3.
† Vide *Eckium in dicto locol.*

for the good of mens Souls, and the fervice of the Church. Poffibly indeed the
two Angels, whom *Lactantius* *, with fome
ancient Fathers, afferts, God appointed to
watch over Satan, might fave them fome
trouble, and make their Province lefs bur-
thenfome to them. But the good *Eckius*
is fo bounteous of thefe fpiritual Guardians,
that he declares in that Homily, a Man of
confequence may fometimes be allowed
thirty or more Angels; and that he cannot
think his Imperial Majefty (for whom he
has a mighty regard) ought reafonably to
be allowed lefs, his great cares and employ-
ments confidered, than a fingle Angel for
every Kingdom, Dukedom, or Province,
over which he prefides.

One would think the *Germans* were either flattered extremely by the Divines in
this point, or fuppofed to have more enemies below, or friends above, than all
other Nations, fince they are more than
the reft indulged in this affair by them. Nay
the learned *Carlo Fabri* † has been alfo fo
careful of their interefts, as to give us in
the lift of the Angels affigned to the feveral

S 3 Princes

---

* Vide *Lactantium*, lib. 2. chap. 15.
† *Carlo Fabri dello Scudo di Chrifto o vero di David.* lib. 2.

Princes of the World, those who watcht o-
ver the seven Electors of the Empire, when
he writ. He assures us, that the Angel
Michael waited on the Archbishop of
Mayence; *Gabriel* on the Archbishop of
Treves; *Raphael* on the Archbishop of *Cologne*; the Angel *Uriel* on the Count Palatine
of the *Rhine*; *Secaltiel* on the Duke of
Saxony; *Jehudiel* on the Elector of *Bran-
denburgh*; and the Angel *Farechiel* on the
King of *Bohemia.*

It is certainly an huge pity this same
Carlo Fabri's knowledge did not look forwards into future Ages, since by this means
he gives us no account of the two Electo-
rates of *Hannover* and *Bavaria*; so that
unless Providence has issued new orders
about them, they must be unluckily left
destitute, of the care and superintendance
of any good Angels; and must therefore
necessarily cost his *Britannick* Majesty, and
his said Electoral Highness, abundance of
more Pains, Money, Troops, and Coun-
sellors, to manage them, than any of the
other seven can want, that have such pre-
ternatural assistances to aid them.

But as this is fully sufficient to shew, that
the holy and infallible *Roman* Church declares

clares entirely for the opinion we have been defending, I shall not weary the Reader by quoting more Authors; and shall only name a few eminent Persons among the Moderns, who have been allowed to have had an intercourse with their Genii, as well as the Ancients.

And here I can't but begin with that famous Physician and Astrologer *Peter D'Apona,* because he had no less than seven entirely in his service, which also taught him the seven liberal Arts, as *Ludovicus Wigius* [*] tells us. We shall place *Cardan* [†], and *Scaliger,* those two great rivals, next to him, though they are both so modest as to own they had but one a-piece; which is the more humble in *Cardan,* because even his father *Facius,* as the son assures us [||], had one, which he conversed with about thirty years. *Boissard,* in his book *De Divinatione* [‡], tells us at large, that the renowned *Trithemius,* Abbot of St. *James*'s Monastery, had several Revelations and important Discoveries made to him by his good Angel; and

S 4 *Frois-*

Dæmonologia, Quæst. 16.
Cardan de vita propria.
De rerum varietate, lib. 16. p. 231.
P. 49, and 50.

Froiſſard‡, the Hiſtorian aſſures us, Côunt *Raimond* of *Gaſcony*, had a conſtant communication with his Genius, who informed him of all occurrences, and frequently gave him his advice, as to his conduct concerning them.

To theſe Gentlemen, beſides *Paracelſus*, who 'tis diſputable whether he had a Dæmon attending him, or was one himſelf, every one will agree to join the illuſtrious *Taſſo*; who as his intimate friend *Baptiſta Manſo* *, the Author of his Life aſſures us, (being a witneſs of one of his converſations with it) frequently had a communication with his good Genius. *Bodin* (to ſay nothing of his anonymous friend, of whom he gives the ſame account) is another inſtance among the Moderns of this ſort; though *Guy Patin*† ſeems to inſinuate, his converſation with his Guardian Angel went little farther than ſuch hints as were lent him, by the chairs and ſtools in his room being moved by an imperceptible hand, whenever any thing was propoſed to him that he ought not to agree to.

But

Froiſſard Annal. lib. 3. cap. 17.

* See *Taſſo's* Life by *Manſo* in *Italian*, and in *French* by *D. C. D. D. T.*

† *P.tiniana*, p. 6.

But to omit many other Foreigners, who have been famous on this account, we might find several instances of the same nature among our own People, if the modesty of some Families, who would be offended to be named on this occasion, did not confine us to those which are already publick. Among these, the Manuscripts of the reverend Dr. *Richard Nepier* (with which Mr. *Ashmole* has wisely enriched the *Musæum* at *Oxford)* are plain evidences of his frequent conversation with his Angel *Raphael,* whose answers he has there regularly set down, not only as to several polemical points in Divinity, but (as he was a Physician as well as a Divine) as to his Patients and Prescriptions, their Diseases, and Cures.

This was an intercourse extraordinary enough, and yet it falls very short of that which another of our Countrymen, Dr. *Dee,* (the great Mathematician and Astrologer) is known to have had with his aërial Spirit: as Dr. *Meric Casaubon,* has with equal labour and zeal shewn, in his dissertation and preface before his large folio *, entitled, *A true relation of Dr.* Dee *his actions with Spirits;*

---

* *London* Edit. 1659

Spirits; to which I would gladly refer the Reader.

With thefe evident inftances therefore, I fhall fhut up this matter; and though I could name fome great Men at Court, who it is impoffible could have our hearts and affe&ions fo entirely devoted to them, if they had not more good Angels at their command than any I have yet named: yet being loth to infift too far on this point, and having fufficiently made good already, what I undertook to prove againft my adverfaries, I fhall venture to leave it to the Reader's ferious confideration; who I doubt not is fully convinced of the abfurdity of this obje&ion, that there are no fuch Beings as good Angels affigned to Men.

But were this lefs clearly proved, let me ask thee, dear Reader, what motives, what confiderations, what reafons, could move me to fay, I received this work from my good Genius? Would it not be much more to my honour, to foretell all thefe things (which will certainly in due time be verified) by the force of my own Learning, and Wifdom, and a happy Forefight into future events? Would it not be more glorious to my memory, that all Pofterity fhould fpeak

of

of me in future Centuries, (when they fee, with aftonifhment, the verification of all I have here prefented to them) as *Nepos* does of *Cicero* *, *Sic enim omnia de ftudiis Principum, vitiis Ducum, ac mutationibus Reipublicæ perfcripta funt, ut nibil in his non appareat; & facile exiftimari poffit, prudentiam quodammodo effe divinationem: Non enim Cicero ea folum, quæ vivo fe acciderunt, futura prædixit; fed etiam quæ nunc ufu veniunt, cecinit ut vates?* Would it not endear me infinitely more to After-ages, that I was the original Inventor and Author of this new and unexampled way of writing the Hiftory of future Times, than that I was the bare Tranfcriber, or Tranflator of this prodigious work? Yes furely, and confequently nothing occafions this honeft plain-dealing, and this ingenuous, this modeft confeffion, but the infinite weight which humility and gratitude ought to have with all Men.

I am fenfible the World has indeed been too frequently impofed on in thefe Matters; *Lycurgus* pretended his Laws were dictated to him by *Apollo*; *Draco*, and *Solon*, by *Minerva*; *Charondas*, by *Saturn*; and *Mi-nos*,

* *Nepos in vita Attici.*

nos, that his came from *Jupiter*, with whom he convers'd familiarly, nine years together, which was a pretty long Dialogue, for a Mortal to hold with a God.   *Zaleucus* afcrib'd his Laws to *Minerva*'s Revelations; and *Numa* pretended to owe his to his clofe and intimate Converfations with the Goddefs *Ægeria*, which he had with her in the Night-time; a very fufpicious hour for her communicating fuch Favours in! But thefe were the little Arts and Contrivances of Governours of the People, fet on fire with a poor ambition, of enlarging their power; whereas all I propofe to publifh, are a few naked Facts, which if they bring me any honour, when confirm'd by the event, I difclaim, as not belonging to me; and the difgrace of which, if falfified by time, I muft entirely bear with Pofterity, without any advantage at the prefent, but what I can reap from the envy and malice of an ungrateful Age.

Befides, what is it I fet up for?   I pretend not to entertain fuch hopes, from any correfpondence with my good Genius, as *Kepler* did on *Tycho Brahe*'s death, that nothing new fhould happen in the Heavens, unknown to him!   No! all I pretend to, is

to

to be the bare Publisher of just so much and no more, as he has been or shall be pleas'd to communicate to me: and if I do this candidly and sincerely, without obtruding any vain Fancies of my own on the world, I hope the least I can expect in return, is to be absolutely trusted and believed, in what I put into their hands. And indeed it would have requir'd such an unusual Fund of Imagination, to have struck out so many vast Inventions in all Arts and Sciences, and such infinite Scenes of Events, as are contain'd in the six Volumes I propose to present the world with; that I am sure this will serve as the fullest proof, (and a very modest and humble one) that I must have received them from the hand of a superior Being, since my talent that way, is so very confin'd. But this will be still further enforc'd, when my dear Reader perceives, that he finds so little in this Work, which ever was contain'd in Books and Authors, as being a subject entirely untouch'd and unthought of by mortal Man; and consequently he'll plainly discern things in every part of it, too transcendent for the little narrow roads and beaten paths of such low groveling Creatures as I am; and only fit to be the produce of

I

that

that enlightned Mind, whence I fortunately receiv'd it.

But I haſten to another malicious Objec-tion urg'd againſt this Work, which is, that allowing my Communication with my good Genius, it is impoſſible that he, or any ſuch Being, could be able to foretell Events, which are ſo contingent and uncertain. But this Ob-jection is very ill grounded; for firſt, it is againſt Matter of Fact, both in our own days and in ancient times: ſecondly, againſt the opinion of the holy and infallible Church of *Rome*: and thirdly, againſt Reaſon.

It is againſt Fact, even in our days; for, not to mention ſeveral unconteſted proofs of the like nature in *Lapland*, the *Eaſt* and *Weſt-Indies*, and many foreign Countries, we ſee at home here how common it is in *Wales*, to have the Death of particular per-ſons evidently foretold, as well as the place of their departure and burial, by the means of thoſe ſurprizing Apparitions, call'd Dead Men's Candles; which are as frequently ſeen walking their rounds in that Country, as our Watchmen are with their Lanthorns every night in *London*. Nay, we find in the Weſtern Iſles of *Scotland*, by the af-ſiſtance of ſuch aërial Spirits, not only Men

and

and Women, but even Children foretell
things to come, with the greateſt certainty;
nothing being ſo univerſally known and
practiſed there, as the learned Mr. *Martyn*
has ſhewn the World in his Hiſtory of thoſe
Iſlands; the veracity of which, no man
has, will, ſhall, may, or can preſume to
queſtion.

But ſecondly, it is againſt Fact in ancient
times; in as much as we have the teſtimony
of both the Hiſtorians and Philoſophers, that
the Oracles of the Ancients, in numberleſs
places, for many Ages, did on all occaſions,
when regularly conſulted, give ſuch undiſ-
puted proofs of their ſufficiency herein;
that both *Greeks* and *Romans*, who were
moſt capable of, and intereſted in diſcove-
ring the cheat, if it had been one, entirely
acquieſced in all they deliver'd; and found
it ſtill confirm'd by the Succeſs. Nor was
this perform'd only by the Heathen Prieſts
and Prieſteſſes, aſſiſted by their *Dæmons*,
at *Delos, Delphi, Thebes, Libadia, Mileſia,*
and a thouſand other places; but if we believe *Callimachus* and *Pindar*, the famous
brazen Bulls in *Rhodes*, on the Mountain
Æthobyrius, (probably directed and inſpir'd
by particular Dæmons and Spirits, like their

bns   Oracles)

Oracles) ufed to give the *Rhodians* fufficient warning of all impending Evils, or remarkable Accidents.

It were eafy to enlarge here, on many inftances of the like nature, if there were occafion for them, and to bring in the prophetick Cow at *Memphis,* the Crocodiles at *Arfinoe,* and the Doves and Oaks at *Dodona,* mention'd by *Herodotus*; as well as the Ox *Apis* in *Ægypt,* whofe oracular Faculties *Pliny,* and all the Ancients fpeak fo much of. The *Teraphims* of the old *Chaldæans,* which ufed to foretell future Events to them, by the means of the informing Dæmon, is an evident proof herein, as well as their Teleftick Science, which by certain Rites and Ceremonies, procured them the Converfation of their good Genii or Dæmons, at Mr. *Stanley.** informs us. Even amongft the *Jews,* we fee by all our accounts of them, this was a method of Divination or Prophecy, too frequently practis'd. The learned *Rabbi Kimchi* declares he believes *Laban's* Gods were of the fame nature, and a kind of *Teraphims,* that by the means of their Dæmons, were endued with a prophetick Spirit.   St.

* *Vid. Stanley* of the *Chaldaick* Philofophy. Ch. 4, 5, and 6.

St. *Auſtin* * is of the ſame opinion, as
well as · our Learned *Selden* in his Traƈt
de Diis Syriis; and *Philo Judæus* has the
ſame ſentiments, ſpeaking of the *Teraphim*
of *Michal* the Daughter of *Saul.* Nay, this
laſt-cited Author does not content himſelf
with advancing this as his opinion, but has
confirm'd it in another place, by that remarkable Hiſtory he has given us, of *Ma-
nachemus* the *Eſſæan Jew,* who he aſſures
us foretold, by the aſſiſtance of his good
Genius, that *Herod* (at that time an Infant)
ſhould become King of the *Jews.*

It was ſo generally known and believed
among the Ancients, that all Dæmons were
endow'd with this faculty, that *Homer*
makes *Elpenor*'s Soul in his 11th *Odyſſea,*
(lin. 69.) propheſy to *Ulyſſes*; and *Scipio* in
Silius Italicus, Tyreſias in *Statius, Æſon* in
Valerius Flaccus, and *Erichtho* in *Lucan,*
are all introduced as conſulting the Souls of
the Dead on things to come.

The famous *Pſellus* † gives us the preciſe
manner, how they were to obtain exaƈt An-
ſwers to their Demands from the Dæmons
and Genii; and preſcribes their manner of
preparing the Altar, and ſacrificing the
T Stone

---

* St. *Auſtin* in *Geneſ.*   † *Pſell. de Orac.*

Stone *Mnizuris* on it, which had the power of evocation over them : all which abundantly proves, what we have afferted on this point.

Thus Fact is againſt my Objectors. But further, the Opinion of the holy infallible *Roman* Church is againſt them; which ought to ſilence theſe ſilly Reaſoners.

All her Divines, and what is more, all learned Jeſuits allow unanimouſly, that even evil Dæmons can foreſee and foretell many things, not only as the Devil in *Samuel's* ſhape did, with regard to the impending Judgment of *Saul's* death, but of diſtant accidents, by interpreting the Prophecies in Holy Writ, more ſkilfully than even the Fathers, or Popes and Councils are able to do. Hence it was, ſay they, that the Devil foreſaw *Alexander* the Great (who is darkly pointed at by *Iſaiah* and *Daniel*) would conquer the World, and told him ſo by his Oracle at *Delphos :* and much more may we ſuppoſe Angels, and good Spirits, able to perform in the ſame way. Nor indeed do they only foreſee the riſe and fall of Empires, and who will be the inſtruments therein; but alſo what the Means, Manner and Time will be, and the Cauſes

Caufes and Confequences, and even the mi-
nuter Effects that accompany them. But if
any one defires to be more fully fatisfied in
thefe matters, let him read *Eufebius de Præ-
paratione Evangelica* *, and alfo St. *Auftin's*
Treatife *de naturâ Dæmonum*, where they
will find feveral reafons affign'd, for their
being endow'd with fuch powers.

Laftly, Reafon is alfo on my fide ; for
as fome by the advantages of greater knowledge, parts, age and experience, can fee
much further than other Men; as he that is
placed on an heighth, has a more extended
profpect and view, (efpecially if he has better Eyes and a fharper Sight) than he who
is in the vale: fince even wife Men, as the
excellent *Marcus Antoninus* † obferves, may
by looking back on paft times, and the
changes of Empire, forefee in fome meafure what will happen for the future; fince
even the humble *Loyola,* as *Maffæus* tells
us in his Life ‖, was a remarkable inftance
of this kind, fo much more can thofe fpiritual Natures, who are unincumbred with
bodily Organs, and have thefe and many

T 2 other

---

* *Lib.* 6. *Cap.* 1.
† *Lib.* 7. *Cap.* 4. *Gataker's* Edit. with *Dacier's* Notes,
Lond. 1697.
‖ *Ignatii Vita per Maffæum, Lib.* 3. *Cap.* 14.

other advantages, to infinite degrees above us, be suppos'd to be endow'd with such powers, in proportion as they rise higher, in the unbounded Scale of celestial Beings. Who can say, what unimaginable helps they may borrow, from their intimate acquaintance, if not with the very Decrees, yet at least with the ways of Providence, (whose Agents and Ministers they frequently are, in the great Changes and Revolutions below) as well as from their perfect knowledge of the natural Byass of our Tempers, the Influence of Education and Principles, of our Humours, Appetites and Passions, and from the perpetual course of Causes and Effects, since the Creation. What assistances may they not gain, even as bare Historians, contemplating all the various Accidents of Time, lying naked and undisguis'd in one view, before their piercing Eyes; as Physicians, judging as it were of the Constitution of the World, by the feeling its pulse; or even as meer Astrologers, surveying the immense Revolutions of the celestial Planets, in their different aspects, and the wide train of consequences produced by them, in the vast rotation of Events, in this Scene of things below.

But

But as this point is not worth infifting on further, I fhall now proceed to an Objection, which gives me infinitely greater trouble, which is, (*horrefco referens*) That it is entirely by my deep skill, in the worft fort of Magick, (or the Black Art, as the Vulgar fpeak) that I have attain'd to the amazing knowledge in Futurity, difcover'd in this Work.

An Objection, which if my Adverfaries themfelves fincerely believ'd to be juft, they would not dare to make, for fear of expofing themfelves to my refentments, and that power and art they pretend I am mafter of; and which therefore, as I might content my felf with barely denying, and they could never prove againft me, fo I fhall only anfwer for the fake of Philofophy, as *Apuleius* fpeaks, *ut omnes apertè intelligant, nihil in Philofophos non modo vere dici, fed ne falfo quidem poffe confingi, quod non ex innocentiæ fiducia, quamvis liceat negare, tamen habeant potius defendere.*

I am not ignorant from what quarter this afperfion comes; and if it continues to fpread, fhall not fail to name my unjuft Enemies, (as eminent and learned as they think themfelves) to the world, and expofe

T 3   them

them to the publick refentment, as wretches
of a malign and envious fpirit; who, like
the people about Mount *Atlas,* as *Herodo-*
tus tells us, curfe the rifing Sun, for the
prodigious heat and fplendour he lends
them.

I well know the only grounds they go
on, next to their envying the little Learning and Glory, which has fallen to my
lot; and as *Furius Crefinius,* when accus'd
at *Rome* of having by Magick drawn away
the richnefs and fertility of his Neighbours
Farms to his own, clear'd himfelf by bringing into Court his Rakes, and Spades, and
Plows, which alone produced his large
Crops; fo I hope my fincere confeffion of
the Celeftial Source, to which only I owe
this knowledge of Futurity difcover'd here,
will fufficiently overturn this wicked Objection, tho' I did not frankly lay before the
Reader, as I am refolv'd to do, all that the
malice of Men or Devils can contrive to
urge againft me on this head.

It is certain then, that in my retirement
in *Yorkfhire,* I did read the more innocent
branches of Magick, and apply'd my felf
much to underftand thoroughly all the
myfterious Arts of Divination, practis'd by
the

the Ancients; and that I am in fome degree skill'd in the *Anthropomantia*, or divining of Men, the *Cyathomantia* and *Oino-
mantia* by Cups and Wine, the *Chiroman-
tia* by the Lines of the Hand or Palmiftry,
the *Arithmantia* or divining by Figures,
the celeftial *Aftrologia* by the Stars, the *Clei-
domantia* or Bible and Key, the *Stichoman-
tia* by different kinds of Verfes; befides the
ufeful Art of *Phyfiognomia* and *Metopofco-
pia*, by the mien and perfons of Men: all
which indeed I was not meanly vers'd in.

I got alfo a thorough infight in the *Gaf-
tromantia* or divining by the Belly, the *Hip-
pomantia* by Horfes, and efpecially Hun-
ters, Race and Coach-Horfes; the *Rabdo-
mantia* by the Rods or White Staves, much
ufed at Court, where I both taught and
practifed it, as many Great Men* can vouch
for me; and which I think fully as valuable, the *Coskinomantia* or Art of managing
the Sieve and Sheers. I made alfo fome moderate progrefs in the famous *Cubomantia* or

T 4   *Alea-*

---

* I appeal to my very good Lord the Earl of *R—*, my
Lord *C—*, my Lord *L—*, and my Lord *G—* for the
Truth of this Fact; and am content to let the Credit of this
Work entirely depend on the report their Lordfhips, in
their great Judgment and Goodnefs, fhall give of my Abi-
lities herein.

Aleatoria, the Art of divining by the Dye, a Myftery which if well underftood would prevent numbers of our Gentry and Nobility being daily ftript and plunder'd with impunity, by thofe judicious and fagacious mortals, the Knights of the Induftry; not to mention the *Copromantia*, as the *Greeks* call it, or in plain *Englifh*, the Art of divining from the Dung of Creatures; a matter I wifh from my foul, the fage infpectors of our Clofe-Stools, were a little better skill'd in, than our Weekly Bills of Mortality fhew they are.

My Knowledge and Practice in thefe things, made a little too much noife; efpecially among the poor party I was then engag'd in, and who had little elfe to truft to, but a few monthly Predictions I difpers'd for them, and fome good Prognoftications once a year, from *Rome* and *Bologna* : But that my Skill, even in thefe little Outlines of Magick, went any further, than helping people to ftolen Goods, calculating Nativities, or giving fome fmall helps to Almanack-makers, as to Wind and Weather, and predicting a little Treafon now and then, from a few Eclipfes, Sextiles, Trines, Oppofitions, and Conjunctions of the Planets,

3 purfuant

purſuant to the Configurations of the celeſtial Bodies, and their mutual Radiations,
or in the leaſt border'd upon the infernal
Branches of Magick, (which I renounce and
abhor) I utterly deny.

There is nothing I do abominate more,
or hold in greater deteſtation, than all evil
magical Arts: and tho' I know the great
Hermolaus Barbarus rais'd the Devil, to
conſult him, on the meaning of *Ariſtotle's*
unintelligible term, Εντελεχεια ; and that the
learned Jeſuit *Cotton* had him examin'd, at
the famous Exorciſm at *Loudun* in *France,*
on ſeveral abſtruſe points in Divinity; yet I
muſt own, I cannot even think of ſuch
practices, but with the greateſt abhorrence.

Far be it from me therefore, to deſerve
ſuch horrid Imputations, as my envious Maligners would gladly throw on me: and if
by any extraordinary inſight into theſe deep-
er Myſteries of Divination, uſed by the
learned Ancients, I have heedleſsly given
ſome ſeeming grounds for this malevolent
Accuſation, I hope this candid confeſſion
will largely attone for it, and ſet me right
in the opinion of this honeſt and ſcrupu-
lous Age.   It has too often been the fate of
the greateſt Names of Antiquity for Virtue
and

and Knowledge, as *Naudæus* fhews us, to be blafted with this vile and grofs afperfion: and if fuch divine Perfons *(Heroës celeberrimi nati melioribus annis)* could not efcape it, I may the better defpife this invidious Objection, in thefe evil days into which I am fallen; and poffibly the next Generation may join my name with thofe illuftrious Perfonages he has defended, in fome future Edition of that learned *Frenchman's* Apology.

There is another Objection, fomewhat allied to this, which I fhall now go on to confider: and that is, an Infinuation fome people have whifper'd about, as tho' I borrow'd all the vaft Scenes of future Events, from my underftanding thoroughly the Celeftial Alphabet, which many of the greateft Rabbies affure us * is wrote by the divine Finger of the Creator in the Stars, plac'd in the Heavens in *Hebrew* Characters, and which contain all the various accidents which fhall ever happen below.

I am not fo difingenuous to deny, that I have been very converfant with the works of feveral of the *Jewifh* Doctors of note, as *Maimonides, Nachman, Chomer, Aben-Ezra,*

---

* *Vide Bafnage's* Hiftory of the *Jews, Book* 3. *ch.* 25.

Ezra, Kimchi, Jomtoff, Levi, Capor, and *Abravanel,* who have ſtrenuouſly maintain- ed this opinion; and aver'd that a true A- dept in this heavenly Science, may by it predict every change and revolution in Na- ture and Empire, in this inferiour World. I acknowledge, the learned Jeſuit *William Poſtell,* has not only confeſt the truth and infallibility of this Science, but has alſo cal- led his Creator, in the ſolemneſt manner, to witneſs his having read in Heaven (in the Stars thus diſpoſed in *Hebrew* Characters, which *Eſdras* has given the Key of) what- ever is in Nature. I confeſs, if that will ſatisfy my enemies, that *Picus,* the learned *Picus Mirandola* maintains, that ſeveral of the *Jews* hold this opinion as unqueſtion- ably true; and I own that even the illuſtri- ous Rabbi *Chomer,* embraced this Sect ſo far in the 17th Century, as to foretell the ruin of the *Turkiſh* and *Chineſe* Empires from it. Indeed, the great *Origen* is juſt- ly taxed by *Sixtus Senenſis,* in the ſixth chapter of his *Bibliotheca,* with maintain- ing it; and every one knows, *Plotinus,* by thus foreſeeing things, hindered *Porphyry* from killing himſelf: and the judicious *Flud,* whoſe Works I am ſo fond of, was

as

as deeply skilled in, and in all future accidents by it, as *Poſtell* himſelf.

Nay, that I may conceal nothing from
the Reader, and as I love to bring all learned remarks as cloſe to the eye of common
obſervation as I can; I ſhall not deny but
one of the moſt skilful and ingenious Writers of Almanacks among us, my honoured
and eſteemed friend Mr. *Vincent Wing*, has
plainly given into the ſame opinion, as appears by that fine Lemma he prefixes to all
his Almanacks;

The Heaven's a Book, the Stars are Letters fair;
God is the Writer, Men the Readers are.

But alas! does this prove that I am a fol-
lower of their Doctrines, and reduce them
to practice, becauſe I have been converſant
with thoſe Writers who hold them, and
have foretold ſome few things by them?
Is it reaſonable, or indeed honeſt, to infer,
that becauſe I may perhaps be more than
ordinarily acquainted with ſuch Books, and
have profeſt to eſteem them, and the immenſe erudition of ſome of their Authors;
that therefore I am tainted with all their
opinions, and have given into the whole of
their

their Hypothefis? No, furely! and above
all, fince I truly and fincerely aver, though
I have feen and ftudied *Gaffarell's* * *Tables*
of that celeftial Alphabet, and his Expla-
nation and Defence of them, yet I have not
got the leaft affiftance to this work from
thofe Syftems; and that what time foever
I may have fpent that way, which I candidly own has been too much, I have only been
able to difcover from them, that they know
lefs of that matter than *Patridge* and *Gad-
bury* did, in their little way of ftar-gazing.
Nay, I muft go further, and declare that
I have found fuch palpable errors in the
whole of their Doctrines, as makes me entirely diftruft and defpife them; and tho'
the reverence I had for the learned *Poftell*,
(whom ftill as a Jefuit I muft ever honour)
kept me a while in fufpence about them; yet
I foon abandoned both him and them, when
I found him fo intoxicated with Enthufiafm,
that he was firmly perfuaded a *Venetian*
Religious, whom he calls Mother *Jane*, was
fent into the World to fave all Woman-kind,
as every one may fee in his famous Treatife
(which for the fake of that bleffed Order I
blufh to mention) called, *The moft marvel-
lous*

---

* *Vid.* Gaffarell's *Curiof. inaudita,* c. 12.

lous Victories of Women, printed at *Paris*
in 12ᵐᵒ, in 1553.

This ˙ ſtumbling-block therefore, which
malice would lay in my dear Reader's way,
being thus happily got over, I ſhall proceed
to mention another envious inſinuation,
which ſome, who by the indulgence of my
friends perus'd this work in manuſcript,
have ungenerouſly ſpread againſt it. For,
ſay theſe judicious Perſons, if theſe Memoirs were indeed the performance of a
Guardian Angel, they would carry unqueſtionable marks of their high Original, and
the Style, and Matter, and Manner, would
evidently ſhew ſomething celeſtial in them,
and above the ſtinted force and skill of human wiſdom and learning.

It becomes not me, my dear Reader, nor
that unexampled modeſty I have ſhewn in
theſe Prefaces, to expoſe the want of Taſte
and Judgment, that appears in this falſe, this
groundleſs, this inhuman method, of at-
tacking ſuch a conſummate performance.
Let Men uſe me and it as they pleaſe, I am
reſolved to poſſeſs my Soul in patience, and
ſmile at their malice; and eſpecially ſince
I know 'tis as vain and impotent, as if they
laboured to tear down the Sun from Hea-

3   ven,

ven, becaufe their purblind eyes, dimm'd
by his fplendour, and unable to furvey fo
glorious an Orb, pretend to difcern a few
fpots in it. I fhall therefore filently and
quietly pafs by the illiterate ignorance of
fuch Barbarians; who thus refemble the Negroes of *Africk*, that murder all *Europeans*
for the deformity of their white complec-
tions, and not coming up to the hideous
ftandard of beauty which they have eftablifhed. I fhall; for my part, make no other
return to the ignorance and ill-nature of
fuch Cavillers, than my prayers for their
reformation; and fhall contentedly, in this
matter, chufe to refer myfelf to the better
informed Judgment and Tafte of the learned World, and leave them to decide how
unjuft a furmife this is, which they bring to
difcredit thefe Papers.

This only I muft fay, which with all modeft and candid perfons, and efpecially all
good Catholicks, muft have great weight;
That though there might appear fome flight,
fome very flight grounds for this objection,
yet the defects they are built on, ought to
be imputed to the alterations, interpolations,
omiffions, difguifes, or miftakes, I neceffarily, or poffibly a little injudicioufly, have
been

been guilty of, in preparing it for the Prefs; and were even thefe faults to be imputed to my good Genius and not to me, yet I never heard it objected againft the many Crucifixes and Pictures ador'd in the holy and infallible Church of *Rome*, as being made by Angels and Apoftles, and fuch celeftial hands, that they fell very fhort of the Works of many famous Sculptors and Painters among Men. It is enough that we are well affur'd of the Celeftial Hands that produc'd them, and that fingle point ought in juftice and modefty, to be fufficient to filence the filly criticifms and affected cavils, of fuch felf-conceited Examiners, who would call them down to the common rules of Art and Science.

And thus having————But 'tis time to let the wearied Reader fleep, who when he has refted himfelf, may (after the delightful entertainment of the remaining Letters, and the vaft fcenes of future times contained in them) either read at the end of this volume what is to follow in my third Preface; or flight it and throw it by, like the fag end of a Cloth, which ferves only to wrap up the reft of the piece, and preferve it from the dirt that would otherwife fall on it.

My

My Lord,

London-Chelsea, Feb. 2. 1997.

I AM aſhamed to acknowledge ſo late, that through a load of affairs of impor-tunate People, that engroſs my time and thoughts, I have ſo long referred you to Mr. Secretary, and am but now returning my thanks for two of your Excellency's Letters from *Rome*, one of *November* the ſeventh, and another of *January* the ſeven-teenth ; for both which I am indebted to your care and goodneſs, beyond all poſſi-bility of repaying you.

The account you gave of your reſpectful and honourable reception there, is very a-greeable to us in *London* ; and as his Impe-rial Majeſty's health is ſpoke of by the laſt Let-ters (as well as the diſagreement of the Elector of *Cologne* with the Court where you are) in ſtronger terms than ever, I doubt not we ſhall manage our Negotiations ſo happily, as to ſecure the Peace of *Europe*, and defeat the aſtoniſhing ambition of the Empire of the *Vatican*.

U   It

It is certain, we ſhall ſtand in need of our utmoſt efforts to accompliſh this, becauſe the reſt of the Proteſtant Powers are far from being well united, through the artifices of this See ever watchful to divide us, and even buy off the venal Faith of ſome of them from our Communion to hers. Moreover though the Proteſtant Intereſt is greatly increaſed in *Europe*, and in ſpite of all her ſnares, ſtronger this laſt Century than ever; yet they are ſo diſtruſted by their jealous Neighbours, that all offers to humble the Papal Power, are but conſidered as attempts, to throw their Kingdoms into confuſion and rebellion.

Beſides, the Popiſh Princes have by their furious Quarrels and Wars among themſelves (which this See has ever fomented) given the Pope great opportunities to raiſe his temporal Power, and ſpiritual Authority on their Weakneſs. Hence he has acquir'd ſuch large acceſſion of Subjects, Wealth, and Territory in *Italy*, that they are cow'd and over-awed by his prodigious Strength, and the intereſt he keeps up even in their own Kingdoms and Councils; and ſeem only deſirous of good conditions, to become

come as it were provincial Tetrarchs to this Lord of the Earth, and Vice-gerent of Heaven.

However, as this violent Jealousy of the Emperor, and the Scheme of introducing the Inquisition into *France*, are likely to unite us more than ever, in opposing her designs; and as our prodigious Naval Force has kept all the Islands in the hands of their old Sovereigns, and both prevented the *Venetians* being entirely swallowed up, and holds the Pope, by the means of his Sea-Coasts, Ports, and Trade, in great awe; I do not despair, but we may be able to humble his aspiring hopes.

The confirming *Civita Vecchia* a free Port, restoring all our Privileges, and declaring by his Bull that none of his Majesty's Subjects shall be liable to his Inquisitors, are great points gained, and also shew the fear he has of us, which I hope your Excellency will improve to weightier purposes.

Your accounts of the monstrous growth of this vast Empire, which has risen these two last Centuries, like a huge Mountain, from the unnatural fires and eruptions in the bowels of the Earth, have occasioned many reflections in my mind, on the blindness and folly of our Ancestors, who with

U 2   proper

proper care, might have prevented the confufion and oppreffion this age labours under.   If inftead of dreading the *Bruta Ful-
mina* of *Rome*, they had oppofed their cannon to her thunder, and inftead of attack-
ing her with a filly paper-war of Books and
Writings, they had by refiftance and arms
contracted her power; if inftead of increa-
fing her Riches and Wealth, and loading
her with the very Lands, and the Tribute, and
Spoil of their Nations, they had kept her
within her own bounds, humble, pious, and
juft; the Princes of the World, and *Italy*,
had not worn her Chains, and groaned
under her bondage now.   We had not
feen in thefe our days, her Armies and
Forces under the command of Cardinals,
and her Generals, that are Priefts and Jefuits in fecret at leaft, and *ex voto*, as they
call it, haranguing her armed Troops, and
turning the old word *Concio* (which figni-
fied the fpeech of a Commander to his Le-
gions, to the Senate, or People, upon affairs of State or War) to its original fignifi-
cation again, and fhewing themfelves the
true Sons of the old Soldier their Founder.

It is true, what our Anceftors did, proceeded from a laudable Piety; and the
Wealth

Wealth, and Poſſeſſions they poured into her lap, were paid by a ſincere reſpect to their religion. But what has been the good-ly conſequence? only this, *Religio peperit divitias, & filia devoravit matrem.* The Chriſtian Biſhop has been entirely abſorbed in the Temporal Prince; as the *Cæſars* of old ſunk the *Pontifex Maximus* in the *Imperator.* In the mean while through a thirſt to ſecure the Power of the latter, the holy Fathers have ſtuck at no Crimes or Wickedneſs, even of the blackeſt dye: And to hinder the Gates of Hell from ever prevailing againſt the Church, too many of her Popes, I fear, have gone thither, as eternal Hoſtages for her faithful alliance with it.

Your Excellency, who is ſo well read in her Hiſtorians before the ancient Reformation of Religion, is perfectly acquainted with many of the deteſtable Lives of theſe creatures, who ſtile themſelves the Succeſſors of St. *Peter.* A name they have no other title to, than that as *He* contradicted and ſhamefully oppoſed the truth, of what our bleſſed Saviour aſſerted twice, and afterwards denied him thrice; ſo they have ever ſince been acting the ſame part, and while they are openly renouncing him, have been violently mak-

U 3   ing

ing ufe of the Sword, and fhedding blood, under pretence of defending his caufe.

I fhall not rake in the filth of Hiftory, to mention to your Excellency the foulnefs of the Crimes, fo many of them were confef- fedly guilty of. Your Excellency and the learned World, are but too well acquainted with them: and would to God, for the ho- nour of Chriftianity, they were as fully a- niended as known! Indeed, fince the fa- mily of the Jefuits have fet up for the royal Line of this Empire, the crime of Whore- dom has been lefs frequent among them; but they have fo far excelled their Predecef- fors in all others, that it were to be wifhed we had fuch Popes again as *Paul* the third, *Pius* the fecond, and *Gregory* the eighteenth, who, with the beft titles of all others to be called Fathers of the Church, were, with all their Baftards, much better Popes than thefe laft ages have feen.

And yet thefe are the great pretenders to Infallibility, and to being directed immediate- ly by the Holy Ghoft; though furely common reafon would allow a Man to believe as ea- fily what a known Hiftorian tells us (abfurd and blafphemous as it is) in *Peter the Her- mit's Crufade to the Holy Land,* that a Goofe

he

he kept was believed by the Crowd to be the Holy Ghoſt; or what the *Turks* ſay of the ſame nature of *Mahomet*'s Pigeon; as that he ſpeaks by the mouth of ſuch vile and evil Popes, as theſe which the Jeſuits have given us.

Certainly if your Excellency conſiders their lives and hiſtory, you will be of an opinion I have often maintained, that nothing has more fatally contributed to that dreadful Deiſm which has infected our Gentlemen, and ſo long ſapt the foundations of our Faith, than the actions, or in other words, the Crimes of thoſe holy patrons of it. For where Men of ſenſe and figure evidently ſee, ſuch flagitious wickedneſs daily practiſed by them, under ſuch ſanctified profeſſions, they enter into a diſtruſt of their Religion, as ſome do of Phyſick, when they behold ſo many die by it: and as theſe laſt think the ſhorteſt way to health, is by plain conſtant temperance, ſo the others think the beſt and ſureſt way to pleaſe God, is by a plain, honeſt, moral conduct, without regarding particular Syſtems of Revelation and Rules of Faith.

It were eaſy to prove the weakneſs of this way of reaſoning, and to ſhew by experi-

ence

ence (to carry on the allufion) that both of them, when Age and Sicknefs overtake them, call for the Prieft and the Phyfician: but this I need not meddle with at prefent, having only hinted at the caufe, not the remedy, of that vile and infectious evil. The very Jefuits themfelves are fo fenfible of this truth, that they trouble not their heads to perfuade thefe Rulers and Pharifees to believe our bleffed Religion, provided they are filent and quiet. They only aim to gain the Crowd and Rabble of Mankind, and have calculated all their conduct, as *Terence* fays he managed as to his Plays, *Id fibi negotii credidit folum dari, populo ut placerent quas feciffent fabulas.*

And indeed, what other management could be expected from the inferior Clergy, or opinions in the fenfible Laity among them; when the Popes have on all occafions fhewn, that they judged themfelves under no obligations to keep the facred Commandments of Chriftianity inviolably, whenfoever they found the good, that is, the temporal intereft of the Church, advantaged by breaking through them. It is true, fome of the beft of them, as *Gregory* the twentieth, and *Pius* the tenth, as Popes, were blamelefs

and

and worthy Men, and careful enough not to break through thofe facred fences of our holy Faith; but even they, as Sovereigns, were feldom obferved to regard them, where reafon of State made it advifeable to diftinguifh between their private and publick Characters.

Whenever your Excellency, or any impartial judge, looks into the hiftory even of their reigns; you will find their Religion, as Temporal Princes, to be a Syftem in which they and their Predeceffors have ever moved, like flaming Comets, each in its different Orbit, not to be reduced to any known certain rules by the beft Aftronomers.

Like them you will find them menacing in their progrefs, ruin and deftruction to the wretched Sons of Men, and even feeming to be no otherwife influenced by God's Power, Laws, or Will, in the circle of their Lives, than Comets in their revolutions are by the Sun; which fometimes they approach fo near as to be heated, and violently fet on fire by its flames, but which generally they keep themfelves at fuch a diftance from, as to be not only cold and unaffected by its beams, but even unenlightened by its rays and fplendor.

But

But this I write to your Excellency, not as the Statesman, and my Royal Master's Servant, but as your old Intimate and Friend. You may blame yourself for my dwelling so tedioufly on the subject, by the long detail you have given me of their Power and Arts to sustain it, which my heart has been too much affected by, not to let it overflow a little in my pen. Your catalogue of the Relicks, and their intended sale of them, has equally surprized and scandalized his Majesty; and he is pleased to direct you to purchase some few of the moft remarkable, that will come cheapeft, but not to exceed ten thousand pounds in the whole. He inclines you should employ some skilful and able hand in bidding for them; and take care to have all their pretended vouchers and certificates exactly preserved, and sent over with them, with the utmoft care; that we may have here the strongeft evidences, of the superftition and vile conduct of this See at the same time, and try if the droufy eyes of some of our zealous Catholicks, can bear so glaring a light, without opening them effectually.

I admire their ufual caution and subtlety has not restrained them, from so manifeft a
breach

breach of all the Laws of decency, which they do not break for unimportant reasons; but I suppose, as your Excellency observes, the greatness of the gain this sale will produce, to supply the vast expence of the Cardinal-Nephew, has drawn them to these measures. For a small profit they would hardly have taken such a step; being like the Negroes in the *Guinea* Coast of *Africk*, who hold themselves obliged by their Religion, as *Bosman* tells us, not to eat a lean Fox, but that it is lawful to eat a fat one. I am confident however, it will strangely offend the *Italian* Gravity, and make them think on occasion of this Cardinal's conduct, of a certain proverb of their Country, relating to their good Lords the Popes, that *when God denies them Sons, the Devil sends them Nephews.*

Your account of their allowing no books in History or Divinity to be licensed, but such as are wrote by the publick Professors, is what I was no stranger to, nor the grounds of their policy in it; for 'tis plain, by this method, that the two great keys of Knowledge, as to the Will of God, and the Actions of Men, will be hung at their girdle. This they do under pretence of the love of truth,

truth, and to prevent falshood; though in fact, 'tis but to impofe it on the World their own way. I muft own *(entre nous)* I am not fully fatisfied, if it were to be wifh'd as to Hiftory (for as to Divinity I am certain it is) that the truth of every thing was known; for poffibly, if the fecret fprings of the actions of fome of our neighbour Kings of late years, the cabals of Minifters and Courtiers, and the trivial piques, humours, and paffions, in thofe Princes, that occafion Wars, and the deftruction of millions of their fellow-creatures, were nakedly and fincerely laid open to our eyes; I fear there could not be a readier way to turn the hearts and heads of Men, to hate or defpife thofe that rule them.

But thefe are fecrets only for your Lordfhip's ear: which as I believe I have pretty well tired on this fubject, I fhall return to one that will furnifh us with more agreeable fcenes of things, I mean our happy Country. As it is a great while fince your Excellency heard from me on that fubject, I think I may venture to tell you, as news, that about ten weeks fince our Parliament was diffolved, and laft week a new one called. Before their diffolution, after difpatch-
ing

ing tne publick Bufinefs with all poffible regard, both to his Majefty's affairs, and the intereft of their Country, they paft feveral Laws, which I cannot but congratulate you upon, as publick benefits.

The firft of them was an Act for tranflating all our Writs from the old unintelligible *Englifh* of the eighteenth Century, into our prefent modern Tongue; and alfo for the regulating and afcertaining the Fees of all Offices and Officers, Counfellors of Law, and Attorneys; and obliging thefe two laft named, to fwear, when they take the ufual Oaths on being admitted to practice, never to be concerned in any bafe, wicked, or evidently unjuft Caufe. The fecond was a Bill for eftablifhing a publick Bank for lending fmall fums of money to the Poor, at the loweft intereft, to carry on their trades with; fuch as the *Monte della Pieta* at *Rome:* but by this Act no fum larger than ten pounds, or lefs than twenty fhillings, can be borrowed, and it muft be lent upon fufficient Pawns, or City-fecurity.

The third was an Act for erecting the Bifhopricks of *London* and *Briftol* into Archbifhopricks, and enlarging their Revenues to five thoufand pounds *per annum*; and

appro-

appropriating a fund to raife all the Parifhes in *England* under thirty pounds, to fifty pounds the year. A fourth was the fo much talk'd of Law, for new modelling, and farther confirming and enlarging the two Corporations of the Royal Fifhery and Plantation Company, and their Rights, Privileges, and Prœmiums, as eftablifhed in the Reigns of *Frederick* the firft, and *George* the third.

Another, was an Act to prevent any Judge, Bifhop, or Archbifhop, to be preferred, or tranflated, from any See or Place to which they were firft promoted: and alfo one for the fettling four thoufand pounds *per annum*, for the founding a School and College, with proper Officers, for the advantage of Experimental Philofophy, according to the excellent fcheme propofed by Mr. *Abraham Cowley*, the famous ancient Poet.

The laft I fhall mention (though feveral others were paft) is an Act for explaining and amending an Act in the tenth of *Frederick* the fecond, and the eighth of *William* the fourth, for taking away all privilege of Parliament, in cafe of Arrefts for Debt, or Lawfuits, when the houfe is not fitting. And indeed, the amendments made in this Law are

are so favourable to the rights of the Subject, that it will endear the memory of the Contriver of it to Pofterity; and will keep up that veneration for Parliaments with the People, which the burthen and abufe of Privileges, had too far undermined and fupplanted.

I have not time to enlarge on the vaft advantages, thefe feveral Laws will probably derive to Pofterity; though indeed I could dwell on them with great delight, if I had more leifure, and were not writing to oue of your Lordfhip's great difcernment, and intimate acquaintance, with both the excellencies and defects of our Conftitution in Church and State.

At your Excellency's requeft, I fend you an exact Lift of all our temporal Peers, fummoned to meet at this Parliament, to be held at *Weftminfter* on *Tuefday* the 25th of *March* 1997, which the old Act againft creating more than one Peer in a Seffion, has contracted to a fmall number.

His Royal Highnefs G E O R G E Prince of *Wales*. His Royal Highnefs *Frederick* Duke of *York*. *John Scrope,* Lord High-Chancellor of *Great-Britain*. *John* Earl of *N--w,* Lord High-Treafurer of *Great-Britain.*

Wil-

William Herbert Duke of *Pembroke,* Lord Prefident of the Council. *William Fitz-roy* Duke of *Grafton,* Lord Privy-Seal. *Charles Seymour* Duke of *Somerfet,* Lord Steward of his Majefty's Houfhold. *George Sackville* Duke of *Dorfet,* Lord Chamberlain of the King's Houfhold. *Henry Lenox,* Duke of *Richmond. Charles Somerfet,* Duke of *Beaufort. Richard Beauclair,* Duke of *St. Albans. John Pawlet,* Duke of *Bolton. George Wriothefly Ruffel,* Duke of *Bedford. John Churchhill,* Duke of *Marlborough. John Manners,* Duke of *Rutland. George Montague,* Duke of *Montague. Charles Graham,* Duke of *Montrofe. William Ker,* Duke of *Roxburgh. George Hamilton,* Duke of *Hamilton. Frederick Pierrepoint,* Duke of *Kingfton. William Holles Pelham,* Duke of *Newcaftle. George Bentinck,* Duke of *Portland. John James Brydges,* Duke of *Chandos. George Campbell,* Duke of *Greenwich* and *Argyle. Charles Egerton,* Duke of *Bridgewater. George Compton,* Duke of *Northampton. Frederick Stanhope,* Duke of *Chefterfield. Robert Boyle,* Duke of *Burlington. John Slingsby,* Duke of *Warwick. John Davers,*
Duke

Duke of *Andover*. *William Bridgman*, Duke of *Guilford*. *Joseph Williams*, Duke of *Hargrave*. *Robert Halsey*, Duke of *Preston*. *John Bacon*, Duke of *Dunsmore*.

MARQUISSES.

John Stanley, Marquifs of *Derby*; *Henry Clinton*, Marquifs of *Lincoln*; *John Hales*, Marquifs of *Brompton*; *George Edward Turner*, Marquifs of *Allerton*; *George Walpole*, Marquifs of *Walpole*; *John Parker*, Marquifs of *Macclesfield*; *Edward Vaughan* Marquifs of *Richley*; *John Coke*, Marquifs of *Hilton*.

EARLS.

Henry Howard, Earl of *Suffolk*; *James Cecil*, Earl of *Salisbury*; *Charles Sidney*, Earl of *Leicester*; *Basil Fielding*, Earl of *Denbigh*; *John Fane*, Earl of *Westmorland*; *Charles Finch*, Earl of *Winchelsea* and *Nottingham*; *Philip Stanhope*, Earl *Stanhope*; *Charles Tufton*, Earl of *Thanet*; *George Spencer*, Earl of *Sunderland*; *Frederick Mountague*, Earl of *Sandwich*; *Charles Howard*, Earl of *Carlisle*; *Henry Lee*, Earl of *Litchfield*; *James Berkeley*, Earl of

X   *Berke-*

Berkeley; *John Bertie*, Earl of *Abingdon*; *James Noel*, Earl of *Gainsborough*; *Richard D'Arcy*, Earl of *Holderneſs*; *Frederick Lumley*, Earl of *Scarborough*; *Robert Booth*, Earl of *Warrington*; *Francis Newport*, Earl of *Bradford*; *William Zuleſtein de Naſſau*, Earl of *Rochfort*; *George Van Keppell*, Earl of *Albemarle*; *Thomas Coventry*, Earl of *Coventry*; *George D'Auverquerque*, Earl of *Grantham*; *Sidney Godolphin*, Earl of *Godolphin*; *Hugh Cholmondeley*, Earl of *Cholmondeley*; *James Sutherland*, Earl of *Sutherland*; *Robert Leſlie*, Earl of *Rothes*; *Robert Hamilton*, Earl of *Hadingtown*; *James Campbell*, Earl of *Loudon*; *Thomas Ogilvy*, Earl of *Finlater*; *George Hamilton*, Earl of *Selkirk*; *James Hamilton*, Earl of *Orkney*; *William Dalrymple*, Earl of *Stair*; *William Campbell* Earl of *Ila*; *Robert Hume*, Earl of *Marchmont*; *Charles Paget*, Earl of *Uxbridge*; *Frederick Bennet*, Earl of *Tankerville*; *John Mountague*, Earl of *Hallifax*; *Thomas Cooper*, Earl *Cooper*; *Robert Sherrard*, Earl of *Harborough*; *George Farmer*, Earl of *Pomfret*; *George Byng*, Earl of *Torrington*; *Charles Townſhend*, Earl *Townſhend*; *Henry Ray-*
mond,

mond, Earl of *Raymond*; Frederick *Offley*, Earl of *Stafford*; Edward *Scrope*, Earl of *Avington*; Harvey *Westley*, Earl of *Newington*; Joseph *Milton*, Earl *Milton*; John *Temple*, Earl of *Beverley*; Jacob *Tilson*, Earl of *Westbury*; Roger *Richmond*, Earl of *Malmsbury*.

VISCOUNTS.

William *Fiennes*, Viscount *Say and Sele*; Thomas *Lowther*, Viscount *Lonsdale*; George *Obrian*, Viscount *Tadcaster*; Frederick *Temple*, Viscount *Cobham*; William *Boscawen*, Viscount *Falmouth*; Robert *Grosvenour*, Viscount *Grosvenour*; James *Wentworth*, Viscount *Wentworth*; William *Jones*, Viscount *Wandsworth*; Robert *Smith*, Viscount *Langston*; Edward *Wynn*, Viscount *Marston*; Robert *Dean*, Viscount *Hedesworth*; Richard *Wardell*, Viscount *Wardell*; John *Morecraft*, Viscount *Alston*; Thomas *Clerk*, Viscount *Dorington*; Frederick *Holmes*, Viscount *Rainsford*.

BARONS.

George *West*, Lord *De la War*; Charles *Fortescue*, Lord *Clinton*; John *Ward*, Lord

Dud-

Dudley and *Ward*; *William Maynard*, Lord *Maynard*; *George Byron*, Lord *Byron*; *Robert Berkeley*, Lord *Berkeley* of *Stratton*; *George Carteret*, Lord *Carteret*; *Charles Waldgrave*, Lord *Waldgrave*; *William Afhburnham*, Lord *Afhburnham*; *Richard Herbert*, Lord *Herbert* of *Cherbury*; *Robert Gower*, Lord *Gower*; *Edward Boyle*, Lord *Boyle*; *Henry Windfor*, Lord *Mountjoy*; *Charles Granville*, Lord *Landfdown*; *Henry Bathurft*, Lord *Bathurft*; *George Onflow*, Lord *Onflow*; *John King*, Lord *King*; *George Edgecombe*, Lord *Edgecombe*; *Charles Morgan*, Lord *Tredegar*; *Henry Hobart*, Lord *Hobart*; *William Doddington*, Lord *Gonvill*; *George Pulteney*, Lord *Heddon*; *William Bowes*, Lord *Stretham*; *Edward Child*, Lord *Wanfted*; *Richard Dutton*, Lord *Sherborne*; *Thomas Bateman*, Lord *Bateman*; *Edward Monfon*, Lord *Monfon*; *Robert Coke*, Lord *Beverley*; *John Methuen*, Lord *Methuen*; *Thomas How*, Lord *How*; *Arthur Worfley*, Lord *Worfley*; *Henry Fortefcue*, Lord *Borlace*; *Robert Davers*, Lord *Clifton*; *George Windham*, Lord *Windham*; *John Mowbray*, Lord *Danvers*; *Thomas Edwards*, Lord *Harfton*; *Peter Strickland*, Lord *Ridgeway*; *Frederick Bam-*

Bamfield, Lord *Brereton*; *Joseph Lane*, Lord *Walton*; *John Pierce*, Lord *Rolston*; *Henry Hatson*, Lord *Elsington*; *George Gore*, Lord *Walford*; *Edward Beaumont*, Lord *Stoughton*; *Robert Bagot*, Lord *Cranston*; *Frederick Long*, Lord *Upton*; *John Pritchard*, Lord *Castleton*; *George Pitt*, Lord *Woodcote*; *John Stapleton*, Lord *Bromfield*.

I have been comparing this List, with the ancient ones that remain on record with us, and I am ftruck with the deepeft melancholly, when I fee fo many great and noble Families, that once made fuch a figure in our Country, wafhed away by the devouring Flood of Time; without leaving any more remembrance of their vaft Fortunes, ftately Houfes, and magnificent Equipages, than there is of the very Beggars, that in their days were refufed the fcraps and crumbs of their Tables. When they flourifhed, and diftinguifhed themfelves by their Wealth and fplendid Living, and immenfe Eftates, furrounded with Power and Intereft, Relations and Children, one would have thought they muft have lafted in their glory for ever; and yet, alas! in a few years of a Century or two, how are they and their Generation

fwept

ſwept away, like the Leaves of the Foreſt by the Winter's Storms.

It is true, indeed, ſome few among them have left Monuments of their merit and virtue, by good or great Actions, that make their names dear to us, and will carry down their Memories with honour and eſteem, to future ages. A few others, by the bleſſing of Providence on them, and their real ſervices to their Country, have left Poſterity behind them, that to this day reflect back part of the glory they receive from their Anceſtors: but alas, your Excellency will perceive how few they are, to thoſe whoſe Families and Fortunes have been hurried down the high and ſteep abyſs of time. *Apparent rari nantes in Gurgite Vaſto!* I am perſuaded, that of near twelve hundred Families that have been ennobled ſince the Reign of *Henry* the firſt, to theſe days, there will hardly be found above eighty who were Peers before the great Revolution, in the end of the ſeventeenth Century. I cannot but put your Excellency in mind here, of our favourite *Pliny*'s reflection on the like occaſion, when he was ſurveying a vaſt Aſſembly of the higheſt Court of Judicature at *Rome*, in his old age, and comparing

paring

paring them with the same Assembly, when he had first appeared in it a young Man; and considered within himself the terrible ravage, which so great a tract of time had made, among them and their Fortunes. *Tantas conversiones aut fragilitas mortalitatis, aut fortunæ mobilitas facit. Si computes annos, exiguum tempus, si vices rerum ævum putes:* and then follows that noble moral reflection, *Quod potest esse documento nihil desperare, nullius rei fidere, cum videamus tot varietates, tam volubili orbe circumagi.*

There is something of Madness sure, in the passion that Men are generally possessed with, of spending their days in care and anxiety, to build up mighty Fortunes, and raise a Family by their toils and labours; (and too, too often, by the most flagitious actions, and the vilest, and the most dishonest conduct) in hopes that they and their Descendants shall last for ever, and at worst, enjoy their Possessions for many Ages. But they calculate that matter so ill, that generally all they are able to do, is to feed the extravagance and pride of two or three Descendants for a while, till Luxury and Debauchery have brought all the dwindled, sickly Race to the grave; as Gaming, Build-

ing

ing, and Equipage, had put an end to their Wealth and Fortunes.

Now I am got into this serious way of thinking, what if your Excellency allowed me to carry it on farther, and obferve to you, that even the great Empires of the World, that fet the ambitious Spirits of Mankind on fire, are, in proportion, of as fhort-liv'd a duration, as thefe little private Families. For after all the Blood and Buftle, which they coft their mighty Builders and Founders to rear them up, we fhall find five hundred years may be reckoned the grand Climacterick of moft of them, as much as fixty-three to Men. In the Government of the Kings of *Judah*, beginning with *Saul*, the firft Kingdom continued to the Captivity of *Babylon*, which was five hundred years, and pretty nearly the fame fpace of time may be affigned from the Captivity, beginning at *Efdras*, and reckoning down to *Vefpafian*, who utterly extirpated the *Jews* and their Empire. The *Affyrian* Empire in *Afia*, was of juft the fame duration: and the *Athenian* Commonwealth, from *Cecrops* to *Codrus*, lafted four hundred ninety years, and then was changed to a Democracy. The Common-

wealth

wealth of the *Lacedemonians* lasted about that time, under the Kings *Heraclides*, till *Alexander* the Great swallowed that up with many other States. The consular Government in *Rome* flourished about five hundred years, till *Augustus*'s Monarchy; and the same period is observed from *Augustus*'s reign, till the fall of *Valentinian*, the last Emperor of the *West*, and that then the *Western* Empire failed. The same number of years were remarked a little after, from the time that *Constantine* the great transported the Empire from *Rome* to *Constantinople*, until *Charlemain*, who restor'd the Empire to the *West*, having chased the *Lombards* out of *Italy*. I could easily produce many other instances of the like nature, to shew that five hundred years has been frequently the age assigned to Empires by Providence. It is true, many have hardly subsisted so long, and some of them have flourished somewhat longer; yet the first of these we must consider as being formed and produced with unhealthy Constitutions, and that had naturally in their first conception, such *mala stamina vitæ*, that they perished in their infancy, and were not able to live out half

their

their days: and the others we muft look on
as we do on men of hardy, athletick Conftitutions, which are thereby enabled to out-
run the common periods of life, that generally are affigned to their neighbours. Of
thefe fhort-liv'd ones we may reckon that of
the *Perfians*, from *Cyrus* to the laft *Darius*,
continued but about two hundred thirty
years: and the Monarchy of the *Greeks*,
founded on its ruin by *Alexander*, and de-
rived from him to the Kings of *Egypt* and
Syria, lafted but two hundred and fifty,
and then funk under the *Romans*. In *France*,
from *Syagre* the laft *Roman* Proconful, who
was depofed, to *Clovis* the firft Chriftian
King, until *Pepin* Father of *Charlemain*,
and then after until *Hugh Capet*, was but
two hundred thirty-feven years; and fo of
many more. And on the other hand, the
Carthaginian Commonwealth, when de-
ftroyed by *Scipio*, had lafted feven hundred years: and even the ruin of the *Roman* Liberties, if we reckon in the feven
Kings (as we juftly may) which was compleated under *Julius Cæfar*, continued full
that time.

All I mean to deduce from this long
detail of things, is a very plain and obvious
infe-

inference, which I am sure your Excellency makes before I mention it; and that is, what little, mouldering, tottering Cottages, these boasted Empires seem, which yet are the utmost efforts of human pride and ambition, with seas of Blood, and ruins of Wealth. After all, the building up noble Families, or founding great Kingdoms, are in the eye of reason as trivial performances, as the baby-houses and puppets of Children, in comparison of those generous schemes and foundations, Wealth and Power might provide, to relieve the distressed and the miserable, the poor, the sick, and the unfortunate part of Mankind, and to instruct the ignorant, or reform the savage, the brutal, or the wicked among Men. In short (for we may trust such a dangerous truth to a private Letter) all the empty noise, and pomp, and shew of Life, which Men aim at with such infinite expence and folly, is not worth one action greatly generous, humane, or honest.

Well! by this time I suppose your Excellency is willing, to give me a full discharge for the two Letters I was indebted to you, when I begun this, which I believe you think is never to end: for fear therefore of
enlarg-

enlarging too much, I will foon put all my excufes for it in a very fhort and a very fincere compliment; and that is, that as full as our Court is at prefent, I do not find there every day one like you, that I unbofom myfelf to, on fuch fubjects with pleafure, being very much,

My Lord,

Your Excellency's, &c.

N----n.

I refer you for his Majefty's new Inftructions to Mr. Secretary's enclofed Pacquet, which I fee is above half of it in cypher; and which I heartily recommend to your care.

To

To the Lord High-Treasurer, &c.

My Lord,

Paris, Feb. 8. 1997,

MY last from this place to your Lord-ship, was of *December* the sixteenth; and I have since, pursuant to your commands, given Mr. Secretary the trouble of twoLetters, of the first and thirteenth of last Month. I now return, because you are pleased to have it so, to go on with the long account of Affairs here, since I have sufficiently answered all other particulars, relating to our Negotiations at this Court, in those two former ones.

When I broke off this subject in my last, I had acquainted your Lordship with the addrefs of Monf. *Meneville*, and the present Minifters, in remedying the Diforders of their Predeceffors conduct; and by Places, Preferments, and Penfions, to take off the edge of the factious Leaders of the People, and bring both the Clergy and Nobility, to the legal reftraints of Duty and Allegiance to the King. I obferved, that this had fuc-ceeded as it ufually does, where Men mean nothing by their Clamours for the good of

their

their Country, but to build up their own
Fortunes, and make themfelves confiderable: but I muft add here, that this would
have been doing their work but by halves,
if they had not cut off all occafion for new
Complaints and Patriots, by remedying the
evil that occafioned them. As the great
difeafes they laboured under, were the want
of Trade and People, and fcarcity of Money, frequent dearths of Bread-corn, the
defrauding the Kingdom in the accounts of
the Publick Money, and the extream Debaucheries of the Gentry; they endeavoured to remove them all, by fevere Edicts a-
gainft the Caufes of thefe Grievances.

As their Trade and Manufactures had
fuffered by an idle affectation in the Nobility,
of wearing and ufing every thing that was
foreign, high Taxes were laid on all Com-
modities not of the growth of the Kingdom: and as his Majefty fet an example to
his Subjects, by obferving this rule himfelf,
as to wearing Apparel particularly, fo no
Perfon that had any Office under him, or
that ever appeared at Court, was allowed
to wear any thing of foreign growth.
By this fingle point of management, the
tide of the fafhion was turned entirely in a
new

new channel, to the great advantage of the *French* Manufactures, and to the faving immenfe fums of the Cafh of the Kingdom, which ufed to go out to feed the pride and folly of the People of condition, to the utter impoverifhing of the Poor.

The fame care was taken to redrefs an evil that had gained ground extremely among the *French* Gentlemen, of travelling abroad. This, by a fevere Tax of the fifth of all their Eftates, and by being alfo difcountenanced by the King, in a little time was quite laid afide; and remittances of near a million of Money prevented, befides a deftructive importation of foreign fafhions and luxury. At the fame time as the long Plague, their unfuccefsful War, and the Dearths and Confufions of the times that followed them, had made a vaft confumption of their hands, and made their People, and efpecially their Gentlemen, very averfe to marrying, and taking fuch an encumbrance on their Pleafures and Debaucheries upon them; an Edict was paffed, by which no unmarried Perfon, if paft thirty and under fifty, could hold any profitable employment, or Penfion whatever; and all of them were taxed a fifth part of their yearly Income, if

Gen-

Gentlemen, and all others ten shillings a head. This was sufficiently strict, and yet the latter part of this Edict was more severe: for after remarking that it was unreasonable, he who ravishes a Woman, and only hurts her honour, shall be hanged; and he who debauches her by flattery, and ruins her Soul, shall be often admired by the Women, and envied by the Men, as a fine Gentleman; it enacts, That in all such cases, the Woman shall be entitled for life, on full proof of the fact, to the third part of the Person's Estate who debauches her.

Your Lordship may easily guess what a compleat alteration for the better this has produced in the *Beau Monde*, as well as the inferior People; and I am persuaded *France*, in half a Century, will owe one seventh part of its inhabitants to this cause; at least in conjunction with another Law, that soon followed it, by which severe Penalties were laid on all voluntary Abortions, or unwholesome Nurses; and freedom from several Taxes to all who had ten living Children, or a proportionable reward for all who had a smaller number, if above six.

The

The next Evil they applied themselves to remove, was the frequent Dearths; which they also effectually remedied by taking off the Taxes on plowed Grounds, and laying them on all such Trades as are nourished by our Luxury, and prove unprofitable to the Commonwealth; as Perfumers, Confectioners, Embroiderers, Wig-makers, Vintners, Jewellers, Lacqueys, Lawyers, Toy-shops, Foreign Lace, and gold and silver Lace-shops; by which means numbers were kept to Agriculture and Husbandry.

At the same time they kept publick Gramaries in all considerable Villages; by which means, by borrowing and saving from the plentiful Crops, like *Joseph* in *Egypt*, they have now near two years provision before hand, to supply their necessities, and relieve the low condition of the Poor in times of Famine, whenever this Judgment of the Almighty happens to visit this Nation, in vengeance for their sins.

The last evil this Ministry has prudently remedied, was the preventing the continual Frauds in the managing the Finances, and over-reaching the King and the Nation, in the Receipts and Disbursements of

Y

the

the Publick Money, and the Accounts of
the national Taxes and Funds.

Judge, my Lord, what notions I muſt
have, of his integrity and honour who is to
read this, when I ſpeak with abhorrence
and deteſtation, of the vile arts theſe Finan-
ciers, and Bankers of the Treaſures of the
State, made uſe of to enrich themſelves,
and impoveriſh their Prince and their Country. For it is evident by the faɗs, that have
ſince their diſgrace been proved on them,
and by the immenſe Fortunes they ſo ſuddenly raiſed, that there never were greater
Robbers or Villains employed, under a care-
leſs and laviſh King, and acunning Miniſtry.

To prevent ſuch baſe and diſhoneſt management for ever, there was an excellent
Ediɗ paſſed, conſtituting ſeven Commiſſi-
oners, with eighteen thouſand Livres yearly Salaries to each of them, ſworn to examine with the ſtriɗeſt care and fidelity, all
publick Accounts of the Nation; and with
their utmoſt induſtry, by their examining
all Officers (from the higheſt to the loweſt)
on oath, to diſcover all errors. Theſe Accounts, with all proper Vouchers annexed
to them, they were obliged by the firſt of
March, to publiſh and print annually for the
pub-

publick view; with their notes and obfervations upon them, and to mention all errors found in them, and the feveral Officers who had committed them, whether by
fraud or miftake. All fuch fums fo difcovered, the particular Officers and their
Securities, were to make good; and the
Commiffioners alfo, to have the entire benefit of fuch fums, paid to them by the
faid Officers and their Securities.

But this did not end here, for if after the
publifhing and printing the faid Accounts,
any other Perfon fhould prove and make
out, any fraud or miftake omitted by them;
then fuch Perfon was to be adjudged the
whole of the faid Sum, as a reward for his
diligence, half to be recovered from the
Commiffioners, and half from the offend-
ing Officer, who by fraud or corruption had
paffed it over.

By this means, it is hard to be believed
with what honeft feverity, regularity, integrity, and œconomy, the Publick Finances
here have been managed of late: while in o-
ther Nations, whoever robs a private Subject
of five fhillings, is hanged, and thofe who
can with dexterity rob their Country of a Million, are honoured and rewarded, if not ennobled for it.

If

If we add to this the publick Regiſtry, for all Conveyances of Lands and Settlements, and Deeds affecting the real Eſtates of this Kingdom; I believe your Lordſhip will ſee in theſe Regulations, as great care and conduct ſhewn, to retrieve this People from all their misfortunes, as has been known in this Kingdom, ſince the days of *Richlieu* or *Mazarine*.

I ſhall now take leave of this part of my obſervations, and ſhall proceed to ſuch others as I have not yet touched on; if poſſibly I can communicate any thing of this kind, that may deſerve your notice.

And the firſt I ſhall mention is the low ebb of Religion in this Country, which is indeed in a very dead and languiſhing way, between the blind Infidelity of the Laity, and the cold indifference and want of Zeal in ſome, and the immoral and luxurious Lives of others of the Clergy.

As the firſt of theſe is greatly occaſioned by the latter, ſo *that*, I fear, is too much to be charged to the conduct of the Court and the Miniſtry. For finding in the late conteſts with the Pope, that the Clergy univerſally preferred the intereſt of the Empire of the *Vatican*, to that of their own Country; it has been a conſtant maxim ever ſince, to ſink their credit
with

with the People, by encouraging them in a want of Zeal for Religion, and a scandalous looseness of Life and Morals, and preferring either the most lukewarm or the most luxurious and debauched among them, to all Sees, Abbeys, &c. in the gift of the Crown.

By this conduct, their influence on the Laity and the State, is perpetually sinking: and as such heads will probably prefer Men like themselves, to the Cures of Parishes in their several Diocesses, the credit and interest of the Clergy, and consequently of the Pope, must necessarily decrease; and all that they lose, must as naturally revert to the Crown, as the Power and Estates of Rebels, that are forfeited for Treason.

It is grown so much the fashion here, to treat them with contempt on all occasions, and despise them, that the great Men shut them out generally from their conversations; and even at their Tables they have always a Page or *Valet de Chambre*, to say Grace, (which for fashion's sake some of them keep up as an old custom in their Families) that they may not be disturbed by the Priest or the Friar.

And indeed, notwithstanding the general decay of Learning and Virtue, in the Ecclesiasticks of this Century, I believe there can hard-

Y 3   ly

ly be found fuch notorious and flagrant inftances of this nature, as in this Kingdom. Many of them are as nice and effeminate, as if,
(as we read of the Clergy of *Formofa*, who
are all Females,) they were entirely of a different fex from the Laity; or like the Pro-
phetefles of *Caria* in *Afia Minor*, who, as
Ariftotle tells us, were bearded Women.
But I am fure they live with fuch foftnefs,
nicety, and woman-like delicacy of manners, as fhew their fenfe and notions of
things, muft be mean and fenfual. Numbers of them are funk and drowned, in the
good Wine and Cheer of *Paris*; wallowing
in the Bottle and the Difh, as the chief
pleafure and joy of life, and are fo given up
to their bellies and gluttony, as if they
thought our blefled Saviour was born at
Bethlehem, becaufe the word in *Hebrew* fignifies, The Houfe of Bread; and was de-
figned to exprefs thereby, that they fhould
ferve him chiefly on that account, and feed
by him, Is it not a melancholy profpect,
my Lord, to fee the facred repofitory of the
divine Will, fhut up from the eyes of the Laity, and confined to fuch defpicable creatures, as ftewards and difpenfers of it to
others?

So

So far, indeed, they may be called faithful stewards of it, as they bestow its Treasures entirely on their neighbours, without keeping any share of it to themselves; being too often, and especially the Jesuits, in this case like Miners, who are perpetually employed to dig out the Riches of the Earth, for the use of the World, while they preserve not the least portion of it for their own service. The truth is, the pretended heads of this Church are not, as formerly, Men who by an eminence in Parts and Learning, and a Sanctity of Life and Manners, are chosen out as fit Overseers of the Christian Sheepfold, to increase their numbers, cure their disorders, and prevent their straying; but are picked out to disunite and disturb it, in hopes thereby to shake the foundations of the Papal Power. They are not, my Lord, so properly Archbishops of *Paris*, or Bishops of *Auvranches*, as Temporal Peers, and the Dukes and Barons of those places; who have these Preferments bestowed on them for life, as Pensions to oppose the Pope, and maintain the Quarrel of the Crown. How far true Religion can be served by such Creatures, or Learning, Virtue, and Piety, be kept up in this Kingdom, is

Y 4

easi-

eafily forefeen; and efpecially, when neither the outward decencies of publick Preaching or Praying, or even appearing in their
Churches, unlefs on great Feftivals, is made
ufe of to palliate their irregular Lives, and
corrupted Morals.

A reflection, which while I make with
forrow and anguifh of heart, on the State
of the Church here, I cannot without pleafure and tranfport turn my eyes on our own
Church; where we are fo happy to fee the
greateft purity of Faith, joined with a primitive fimplicity and fanctity of Manners,
and an eminency in both thefe, made the
fureft road to Promotion and Preferment.

Another point of policy which the new
Minifters have put in practice here, in relation to the Clergy, and which deferves to
be locked up *inter arcana Imperii*, is, for-
bidding all polemical Works from the Prefs,
or Difcourfes of that kind from the Pulpit.
For as fuch Difputes and Party-wars of the
Pen, have been ever obferved to heat, and
keep up the zeal and fpirit of the Clergy,
above all other things; fuch ftimulative and
awakening Medicines are by no means
judged proper by thefe State-Empiricks, for
that Lethargy and droufy Stupidity they

ind

find it their interest to keep the Ecclesiasticks in.

It is certain, by this means the peace and quiet of the State, as well as the Church, is the more secured, and many eminent Genius's employed in nobler pursuits, to the great advantage of the Commonwealth of Learning. But at the same time, this introduces a sensible decay and indifferency in all points of Faith, that lie like the Fortifications of Towns, on the Frontiers of a Country, where we are secure to have no War; mouldering, and falling away daily, being neglected, and ill maintained, in too profound a Peace.

Along with this part of their conduct they have joined another, and lest in any future disputes with the Pope, they should want able Pens to defend the Rights of the Crown; they have in several Universities, and especially in the *Sorbonne*, appointed Salaries for learned King's Professors of Divinity; though indeed their true title should be, Professors of the King's Divinity. These are the best Pens and the ablest Men they have, who are retained, like Lawyers, to plead the Cause of *France*, against the Usurpations of the Papal See, as they have

often

often done, though never fo fuccefsfully, as when they have had the Armies of the Crown for their Seconds.

The truth is, they have taken up fuch an averfion to Learning here, from the mif-chiefs it has occafioned, in their difputes with the Pope; that I am perfuaded I could not do them a more agreeable piece of fer-vice, than to contrive a Plan to model all the Schools and Colleges in this Kingdom a-new, in fuch a manner that they fhould be entirely employed in teaching Children Nothing, educating them to Nothing, and breeding them up to read Nothing. By this means, they might have the rifing Genera-tion, ready to receive any impreffions they pleafed, unbyaffed by the reigning prejudi-ces in favour of the Pope's Supremacy. If I fet up this Scheme here, I muft aim to in-troduce the famous *Chinefe* Sect of *Bonzes,* who affemble their Followers in the Fields, where every one is furnifhed with a pair of Drum-bones between his fingers; and when-ever the *Bonzes* learnedly prove to them, that all the Opinions, Pleafures, Sorrows, Hopes, and Fears of this World are *Xin,* that is, (in their Language) Nothing, which word ends every fentence; the whole Croud rock

their

their Bodies to an extafy of tranfport, and rattle their Drum-bones, crying out in confirmation of their beloved Doctrine, *Xin, Xin, Xin!*

I muft alfo of a certainty fend for fome Profeffors, from the Academy *Gli Infecondi* in *Italy,* who write Nothing; and for crouds of *Spanifh* Schoolmen, *German* Poets, *Dutch* Divines, *Englifh* Politicians, *Mufcovite* Sea-Captains, *Italian* Patriots, *Jewifh* Rabbies, and *Turkifh* Dervifes, who have above all Men the happy art of amufing others, and employing themfelves in that amiable myftery, of writing, and thinking, and doing Nothing. We fhould have fome trouble in watching carefully over a few buftling, inquifitive tempers, who are poffeffed with that devilifh fpirit, of doing, thinking, or writing fomething. But the ufual croud of the School or the College, might be left to the conduct of their gentle, eafy Genius, and by the amiable inactivity of their Indolence, would naturally arrive at Nothing. By fuch a model as this, great things might be done here, to drive out the impertinence of reading and ftudy; and in a few years we might fee this Reign, rival that of *Lewis* the feventeenth, when Learning, and Religion,

gion, and Arts, were fo happily banifhed that Kingdom; and Infidelity united all its divided Schifms and Parties, in one general League of Irreligion and Ignorance, againft Superftition, Pedantry, and Prieftcraft, or in other words, Piety, Virtue, and Knowledge.

But it is time to prefent your Lordfhip with fome obfervations of a different nature, as to the Humour and Temper of thefe People. I formerly took notice of the prodigious Luxury that reigns here, amidft the confufion of their affairs; which fhews it felf in all the amufements and diverfions of the better fort, in fuch an infinite variety of things, that it is impoffible to defcribe the half of them. It would be very entertaining to write an Hiftory even of the Fafhions, for the laft five years I have refided here, and I am confident it would make a little folio, to go thro' them in all their different reigns and feafons. High Stays, low Stays, no Stays, fhort-waifted, long-waifted Stays; fhort, mid-leg, all-leg, no-leg Petticoats; broad Lace, narrow Lace, *Flanders* Lace, *Englifh* Lace, *Spanifh* Lace, no Lace, Fringes, Knottings, Edgings; High-heads, Lowheads, three Pinners, two Pinners, one
Pinner;

Pinner; much Powder, all Powder, little Powder, no Powder; Mantua's with a Tail, want a Tail, false Tail; four Flounces, three Flounces, two Flounces, no Flounces; wide Sleeves, strait Sleeves, long Sleeves, short Sleeves; many Ribbons, all Ribbons, few Ribbons, broad Ribbons, narrow Ribbons, rich Ribbons, plain Ribbons, flowered Ribbons, stampt Ribbons, no Ribbons. Such a noble and important work as this, with the dates and rise of every Fashion, the Councils that decreed it, the Authors and Inventors, and the vast Revolutions it produced in the polite World; and dedicated to the lovely Dutchess of *Monbazon*, who is able, my Lord, to prescribe what Fashions she pleases, both to her own Sex and ours; would, I am sure, raise more Subscriptions here, than the Works of *Cicero* or *Livy*. I fancy an History of their Breakfasts at *Paris*, for these last thirty years, would be almost as diverting; for as the quickness and inconstancy of the fair Ladies Fancies, are ever on the wing for new Entertainments for us, it is comical to consider the various successions they have contrived, since the days of cold Meat and Wine of their Ancestors. How have these lovely Cooks rung the

changes

changes with Tea, Coffee, and Chocolate,
Chocolate, Coffee, and Tea, backwards
and forwards, fometimes drinking their Tea
infufed long in cold water, fometimes in
hot; and when they were driven off the
ftage, what new fcenes have they furnifhed
out, between Sweetmeats and Creams, Ty-
fans and Sherbets, Milk cooked in twenty
different methods, Bitters for the Stomach
of a thoufand forts, Wine mull'd and brew'd
in feveral fhapes, Jellies and Fruits of all
kinds, Broths and Caudles dreft up in various difguifes, and Poffets, Syllabubs, and Gru-
els, in as many; till at laft they have returned to Manchets and Butter, with frefh Eggs
and Whey, or Milk from the Cow, which
their Fathers ufed about three hundred
years ago, in *Lewis* the thirteenth's time.

One of the reigning Fafhions at prefent is,
in all their Affemblies, or Vifiting-days, to
entertain their Company with Conforts of
the beft Mufick, and to perfume all the A-
partments but the Anti-chambers, which
are at the fame time adorned with the moft
exquifite Pictures *Great-Britain* or *Italy* can
furnifh them with. I take this to be the moft
natural and agreeable method of receiving
great People with refpect, that can be thought
of;

2

of; for besides regaling you with many kinds of Wines and Sweetmeats, almost all the Senses are gratified at once, and the everlasting, unmeaning rhapsody of Talk, that prevails in mixt Conversations here, is removed; and the Ear, Eyes, Taste, and Smell, entertained in the nobleft manner. If your Lordfhip will allow me to mention one reigning Fashion more, that seems established here, I shall detain you no longer on this subject; and that is, the keeping Mutes in all great houses, which they generally import from *Turkey* at exceffive rates, and employ as *Valet de Chambres* and Waiters at Table. I fancy this humour is likely to reach some of their neighbours in time: and indeed, where half the World act, and the other half talk things, that ought to be buried in everlasting filence, I wonder it has not been introduced among us long fince. In some Provinces of *France* this has obtained so far, that they as commonly cut out the Tongues of Infants, as in *Italy* they make them Eunuchs; and the prices for them run so high, these having the advantage of hearing, which many of those that are imported want, that it is probable in time, the number of Mutes among

Ser-

Servants, will bear a higher proportion than they do in the letters of the alphabet. In the mean time, to encourage us to give into this practice in our Country, it is to be confidered, we may furnifh ourfelves much cheaper with very tolerable Mutes from both our Univerfities; who befides, are generally happy in a more grave and fheepifh Modefty than thefe Foreigners, and can fometimes alfo, on an extraordinary occafion, utter an odd monofyllable now and then, which is rather an advantage in my opinion, than otherwife.

I am forry, my Lord, that I muft lengthen this tedious Letter with two pieces of news, neither of which, I fear, will be agreeable. The one is the death of Monf. *Le Fevre,* whom your Lordfhip honoured formerly with managing fome bufinefs for you here. He was a chearful, well-natured, honeft Man, but he talked immoderately; and though he fhewed a great deal of wit in his Converfation, he ufed to laugh fo much at his own Jefts, that his mirth was feldom accompanied with *Sarah's* blefling, who faid, *God had made her to laugh, fo that all that heard her laughed with her.* I mention this the rather,

ther, becaufe I was with him the day he died; and as he had raifed his fortune from nothing, by your Lordfhip's bounty, fo he fpent it extravagantly, and died almoft for want. He took notice of this rife and fall in his Circumftances, and defired me to tell your Lordfhip, he died your humble Servant; and that for the change in his fortune, it was but in the way of the World, and according to the old axiom in Philofophy, *Ex nihilo nihil fit*.

But I have another lofs to acquaint your Lordfhip with, which will touch you more nearly; and that is the *Danifh* Envoy here, Mr. *Pleffenburg*, who died laft night of an Apoplexy, as he fat at fupper among a great many friends. He had no Will by him, to the ruin of a numerous Family; for his whole Eftate goes to his eldeft Son, a Man not worthy even to inherit his Name. Your Lordfhip knew him perfonally fo long, and lived fo intimately with him, when he was Envoy at our Court, that I need not draw his Character. He ferved his Prince faithfully, and was an honour to his fervice, and a credit to his Country; and indeed, we may fay in this cafe, that the Servant was greater than his Mafter.

Z

He

He was a most religious Observer of his Promise, of which he gave a glorious instance lately; when being pressed by the Nuncio to prefer a friend of the Society to a Troop in his Regiment, and put by one he had promised it to, he told him, he would not break his word to serve the true friends of Religion, and much less to serve its real enemies, the Jesuits. 'Twas an answer worthy of Mr. *Pleſſenburgh*, of whom I cannot say a greater thing, than that he had the honour of your Lordship's friendship, and deserved it.

In my last dispatch to Mr. Secretary, I gave so full an account of the state of my Negotiations here, and the high professions they make of their obligations to his Majesty, for interesting himself in the affair of the Inquisition; that I need not report a matter to your Lordship, which I know Mr. Secretary, with his usual care, has long since laid before you.

I expect very soon to have an Audience of the King, in which I hope to find their measures concerted and resolved on, pursuant to what I was instructed to lay before them, for their approbation. When it is over, I shall give your Lordship an exact account

count of it, and what is likely to be the refult of thefe counfels, which you fo happily direct, and fo worthily prefide in.

By our laft Letters by the way of *Vienna*, we have received frefh affurances, that his Imperial Majefty is fo well recovered of his afthmatick diforder, that he has ventured out to take the air in the Park, and to fee his Hawks, (which the Grand Seignior lately fent him as a prefent from *Conftantinople)* kill two or three brace of Woodcocks. However this may be relifhed at *Rome*, I am fure it is very agreeable news at *Paris*, and I hope will be as much fo at *London*; where I wifh you all the Honour and Happinefs you deferve, and am, with the greateft deference and regard,

My Lord,

Your Lordfhip's &c.

Herbert.

Z 2

To

To the Lord High-Treasurer, &c.

My Lord,

Constantinople, April 16, 1998.

IN my former Letters I believe I gave you a fufficient furfeit of my political obfervations on this great Empire, and its prefent Condition, Laws, and Cuftoms; and I fhall now furnifh another kind of entertainment for you, if any thing I can fend your Lordfhip can be juftly called fo. I fhall chiefly confine myfelf at prefent to give you fome imperfect accounts of my Telefcope's performances, and of feveral converfations I have had on it, with the Grand Seignior in perfon; in thofe fecret receffes of his retirement, the Apartments of the Seraglio, and the lovely Gardens with which it is almoft furrounded, to the very Banks of the Sea.

I have formerly told your Lordfhip, how extremely affable and courteous, not to fay obliging and affectionate, I have on many occafions found the Grand Seignior to me; infomuch, that I am really confidered here as the greateft Favourite, of any Ambaffador that has appeared here from a Chriftian Prince,

Prince, for thefe many years. This, I be-lieve, has been chiefly occafioned by my fpeaking the *Turkifh* Language to fome per-fection, and by my ftudying to gratify, as far as I could, his great paffion for fuch Curi-ofities, as I could furnifh him with from *London*; fuch as Globes, Maps, Clocks of all kinds, and Watches; Dogs, Guns, Barges, Coaches, and, in a word, whatever I found him moft defirous of.

It is certain, by thefe means I have in-gratiated myfelf mightily with him; fo that when he refufes Audiences to other Minif-ters, he often *fends* for me, and will make me fit in his prefence, and difcourfe of *Eu-rope* and my Travels, with a familiarity ve-ry unufual to this Court.

Since my laft Letters by Mr. *Biron*, I re-ceived his commands to wait on him, and found him in one of his Gardens, after our *European* Models, with Grafs, Gravel, Por-tico's, and Fountains, by the fide of one of which he was repofing himfelf. He told me, he had heard of the wonderful Tele-fcope your Lordfhip had fent me, and that he was impatient to fee it, and try if it an-fwered the furprizing relation the Grand Vizier had made him of it; and defired to

know,

know, if it could be set up in that place immediately. I answered every one of his demands, in the manner I knew to be most agreeable to him; and as I had been prepared for it by the Grand Vizier, I told him, I had brought it by some of his Highness's Slaves, who, with my Servants directions, should soon set it up, and regulate it. As he expressed a great desire to make trial of it immediately, and as the Evening was very serene and cloudless, I gave my People proper directions, and with a very little time and trouble, the necessary Apparatus for it was set in order; and then, without delay, it was brought in, and made ready for using. All this time he employed in examining me about it, how much it magnified, and if it were possible we could discern Mountains, Hills, Seas, and Rivers, in the Moon by it.

w I assured him I had tried it, and though in the last age few magnified more than two hundred, I found it magnified Objects many thousand times bigger than they appeared to the naked Eye; and that we could not only discern Hills and Rivers, but even objects like Towns and Forests in the Moon; and that, if the Inhabitants there

there were as large as some great Astronomers conceived them to be, I doubted not
in time, our Glasses might be so far im-
proved, as to see even Men and their actions there.

He repeated all this after me with vast
surprize; and after musing on it, he turned
to me, and said with some concern, Seignior *Stanhope*, do you think there can be
living Creatures, and above all, Men in
our Moon? I told him, I had great and
weighty reasons to be persuaded of it; and
as he himself would see Hills and Woods
in it, Clouds and Vapours surrounding it,
though they are very thin and small, and
also actual Waters, Seas and Rivers in it, I
durst undertake he would be of the same
opinion. For since she is found to resem-
ble our Earth in all such Conveniencies,
what is more natural than to suppose she
must have Fruits and Herbs also, as we
have; and if those, unquestionably Animals
to live on them; and above all others, Men,
since Nature does nothing in vain.

That it was absurd to suppose such a
beauteous Work of God, should be so ami-
ably and usefully adorned, and yet be furnished to no purpose, with such vast Con-

veni-

veniences, which might be fo pleafant and
ufeful an Habitation, for rational, intelli-
gent Beings; who might there enjoy with
fo much happinefs, the Beauties and Delights of the Place, and with due praife and
gratitude look up to the excellent Author.
That though our Eyes did not convince us
by fuch evident appearances, that there
were fo many refemblances in the Moon,
of what we fee on our own Earth, yet it
was abfurd to fuppofe, the wife Maker
would have formed fuch immenfe, folid,
opake Globes, rolling by rules, and in Orbits he has prefcribed them in the Heavens,
as bare ufelefs Heaps of Matter, and un-
wieldy Lumps of Rock or Clay, to no end,
but to give an imperfect Light to our fyftem,
and to be looked at by the Eye. And if this
is not to be imagined as to the other Planets, much lefs as to the Moon, who enjoys the Heat and Light of the Sun, to
much greater advantage than feveral of
them, and almoft as well as our Earth. I
faid a great deal of this fort to him; to
which he made feveral flight objections, that
were eafily got over: and perceiving our
Telefcope was, by this time near ready,
I prefented him with the vaft Map of the
Moon,

Moon, which I had from *London*, with all the Seas, Rivers, Mountains, Hills, Valleys, Forests, and the supposed Towns that are so accurately laid down in it by the Selenographers; and especially by the *Savilian* Professor Dr. *Bertie*, who has divided it into its several Kingdoms and Provinces.

He examined it with abundance of care, and was delighted with the prodigious size, as well as the beauty and exactness of the Performance, asking me many questions on it; and appeared particularly pleased to see *Stamboul*, and his own Dominions (which I shewed him) set down in it. But by this time our Telescope being perfectly settled, I begg'd his Highness to let his own Eyes answer his curiosity better than I could, and to compare the Map with what the Telescope would shew him; the Moon being just at the Full, and the Heavens clear and serene.

He immediately set himself to make his observations, and with the greatest surprize and transport, one while applied his eye to the Telescope, and then to the Map, surveying all the different ranges of Mountains, Hills, and Valleys, the vast Surfaces of Seas, Lakes, and Rivers, in the Lunar Globe,

Globe, tracing out every thing with the greateſt ſagacity.

It is hard for your Lordſhip to believe the amazement that appeared in his Face all this while; and as the faithful Teleſcope repreſented every thing ſo plain and diſtinct, and brought the Objects he ſurveyed ſo clear and cloſe to his eye, that he could not be more convinced of their exiſtence, had he walked on the face of the Earth he was ſurveying, he would ever and anon break out into ſome expreſſions of admiration.

He ſeem'd, indeed, to doubt a little as to the darkneſs of the vaſt Plains of the *Pontus Euxinus*, the *Caſpian*, and *Mediterranean*, and the *Baltick*, and *Eaſt* Seas, and the great Rivers that roll into them, by ſo many mouths; and ſuppoſed the Sea would rather appear with a lucid brightneſs, and even outſhine the everlaſting Snows and Rocks of Mount *Taurus*. But I ſoon convinced him, without troubling him with the philoſophical reaſons of things, with putting him in mind, that the Earth and Sea had juſt this appearance from the elevated heights of his own Mount *Olympus*, where he ſo often had been. The only ſcruple that remained with him, was as to the

the great *Hyrcanian* Foreft, and the refemblances, to call them no more, of the
feveral Cities, fuch as *Rome, Stamboul, Pa-*
ris, Vienna, and *London.* As to the Forefts, I made him obferve the vaft difference there was between the appearance of
the bright even flats and plains, and that
dusky,brown roughnefs that fwelled up in the
middle of thofe extended fields; and that
as all the higher grounds in the furface of
the Moon's Globe wear a remarkable brightnefs, compared with thofe vaft levels; it
was impoffible thefe, being fo dark, could
be high Downs, or Hills, not to infift on
the even Level that their tops appeared with,
which hilly Countries never have.

That it is certain, befides all this, that
allowing there are Woods and Forefts in
the Moon, (and fuch fhe muft probably
have, in fo many different Soils as he faw
there) they could appear no otherwife than
they did here, becaufe they imbibe the Sun's
rays through fo many apertures of their
Boughs and Shades, and therefore cannot
reflect them back, as the furfaces of hard,
folid bodies would: and fince it is plain,
there muft be Woods and Forefts there, and
if there, they muft appear in the fame man-

3   ner

ner he faw them; it is moſt reaſonable to call them, and ſuppoſe them ſuch.

For the Cities, I muſt own, my Lord, I had not much to ſay; and though it is true, the running of Rivers cloſe by them, the white circles that like Walls ſeemed to ſurround them, and the different heights and hollows, as it were Houſes and Towers, and Shade and Lights, that reflect from them within thoſe circles; and above all, that blackneſs, that like a thin cloud hung over the largeſt, and looks like a vaſt collection of ſmoke, ſuch as we ſee about Cities here; all which make it poſſible, they may be what the Map calls them: yet I cannot but think, they may be rather white Rocks, ſhaded by Woods on them, or ſome neighbouring Hills, than real Cities. However I endeavoured to convince the Grand Seignior, that the reſemblance was ſo ſtrong, and agreeable to what one would imagine Cities would make to us, if they were built there; that one could not charge the compoſers of the Map, with over-great raſhneſs or folly, for aſſigning ſuch denominations to them.

The Grand Seignior ſeemed pretty well ſatisfied with what I ſaid to him, and con-

3   tinued

tinued some hours surveying and contemplating the beauteous Object he had before him, till the interposing of some clouds, and a little rain that fell, put an end to this agreeable amusement I had furnished him with. We retired from the Garden into the gerat *Kiosc*, or Summer-house, where he often spends the Summer Evenings, and the beginnings of the warm Nights, with his chief Favourites and Baffas, drinking Sherbets and Coffee, and smoaking Tobacco. He made me sit down on the Sofa, and begun a long discourse with me, of the wonderful instrument I had brought him, which, as he expressed it, drew down the Heavens to the Earth, and made us as it were neighbours to those celestial Orbs, which the great Author of them had placed so remote from us. He asked me of the distance between us and the Moon, and when I told him it was generally computed by Astronomers, that her mean distance was about sixty semidiameters of the Earth, he seemed astonished that our Telescopes could bring her so near us; but he was a great deal more so, when I acquainted him with the much greater distance, betwixt us and the other Planets of our system, some

of

of which I told him I would fhew him, whenever he could have leifure for it; and, if he pleafed, the next day about evening, if the Sky was ferene and cloudlefs. He feemed much rejoiced with my undertaking, to procure him that fatisfaction fo foon; and telling me, he would not detain me any longer for that night, he in a very gracious manner difmift me, and left me to retire to my houfe, where I immediately haftened; much pleafed that I had the honour, of being the firft that had introduced the *Turkifh* Moon,(the Arms of this Empire) into the acquaintance of her great Mafters, that had oftener alarmed the World, with her appearance in their Standards, than ever fhe had been able to do, with all her Eclipfes.

Early in the evening of the next day, I returned to the Seraglio before it was dark, the weather being very favourable, where I found the Grand Seignior attending my coming. He immediately began to tell me, that as he was convinced by what I had faid, and what he had feen the night before, that the Moon muft be inhabited, he had been confidering with himfelf, what fort of Men they muft be that were placed there.

there. I told him, that, was what no one could pretend to account for, but that probably they muſt in many things reſemble us pretty nearly, and in all likelihood be not much more different from us, than many Nations of the *Indians*, which the Ancients had diſcovered in *America*.

But, ſays he, I am perplexed with a great ſcruple, that I know not how to get over; and that is, as we know of a certainty that *Mahomet*, in his paſſage to Heaven with the Angel *Gabriel*, touched there, I cannot conceive, had there been Men there, but he muſt have communicated his Law to them; and if he had done ſo, he muſt have mentioned it in that holy book his *Alcoran*, which he has left us. Now as he has not taken the leaſt notice of ſo important a point, I am perſuaded there cannot be ſuch Inhabitants there, as you and your Philoſophers have diſputed for.

I ſaw the danger immediately, of touching on this point, and therefore ſhifted it off, by ſaying, that there were ſo many Worlds more, as thick planted with ſuch Colonies as the Moon was, that it was probable he choſe to leave them to themſelves, ſince had he undertaken to viſit them all, they

were

were fo infinitely numerous, and fo infinitely diftant, it would have taken up many millions of years, to have gone through
with them.   Your Highnefs, continued I,
will allow there is fome weight in this reafoning, fince it is as probable that every
Star we fee in the Heavens, and an immenfe number we cannot fee, even with
our Telefcopes, are every one of them fo
many Suns, in the centre of as great and as
noble a fyftem, at this which we are placed
in, all the Planets whereof have the fame
pretenfions to be inhabited as the Moon.
This, I obferved to him, was a point which
all Aftronomers contend for, as in the higheft degree reafonable; not only from the
fame arguments that evince the Moon's being replenifhed with living Creatures, and
rational Beings, which I already touched
on; but alfo becaufe, in the firft place, all
the denfer Planets are feated neareft the
Sun, in regard that the denfer matter re-
quires more heat, to render it capable of natural Productions; and fecondly, becaufe
the nearer fuch Planet is to the Sun, the
greater is the velocity of its motion, and
confequently, the viciffitudes of its Seafons
are rendered the quicker, as it is highly pro-
                                        per

per they fhould be, in order to favour the productions of Nature in it, of what kind foever they are. And really the prefumptions on thefe accounts, and many others, are fo exceedingly ftrong in favour of this opinion, that I think we muft leave the Aftronomers, in poffeffion of this favourite Doctrine of theirs, till we can bring better arguments againft them, than I have ever yet heard of. I perceived he was going to reply, and as I had a mind to avoid the dialogue, I told his Highnefs, if he pleafed, we would leave thofe enquiries, to fee what information we could get about it from *Jupiter*, one of the nobleft Planets of our fyftem; which, fays I, (pointing to it) fhines fo brightly yonder, as if he had fpruc'd himfelf out in order to fhew himfelf to us, and entertain your Highnefs in the beft manner, his great diftance from the Sun and our Earth will allow him.

Accordingly, I immediately applied my Telefcope to him, and as I had feldom feen him fo bright, he made a very glorious figure, dreft up with all his Belts, and Spots, and Satellites about him. I laid the fine Map your Lordfhip fent me of him, before the Grand Seignior, with the imaginary

Regi-

Regions, Mountains, and Seas, which thefe admirable Glaffes have furnifhed us the profpect of.

I pointed out all the moft confiderable tracts on his mighty Globe, and efpecially the bright Mount *Olympus*, and *Athos*, and the wide *Atlantick* Ocean, and *South* Sea on his *Weftern* Limb, and the vaft Iflands here and there difpers'd in them.

I then made him turn his obfervations, to fuch of his Satellites as we were able to obferve, and explained to him how thefe attendant Moons, ferved to enlighten the darknefs of his Inhabitants, and to make him fome amends, for their being fo far removed from the warmth and fplendor, of that fole fource of light and heat in our fyftem, the Sun. He attended to both their appearances, in the Map and the Heavens, and the explanatory hints I added to all, with infinite furprize and delight; every now and then crying out, how wonderful it all was, and what a pity, that fo immenfe a Globe, fhould be confined to fo dark and gloomy a fcituation!

To remove his concern on this account, I told him, that though *Jupiter*'s People, certainly received but the twenty-fifth part

of

of our light from the Sun, and that his days were but five hours long, yet it was plain, by the very brightnefs he now fhone with, and by the fplendor of fo many attendant Moons, he had abundant light to make every thing agreeable, and pleafing to his inhabitants; who had probably more light and warmth than our Polar Regions, and were certainly fo formed as Moles, Owls, and Batts with us, to take more delight in the gloom of the evening, than the dazling glare of the broad-day. That poffibly in *Jupiter*, they meafured not their days by fun-rife and fun-fet, but by feveral fucceffions of them, and called them only fun-hours, and moon-hours; after fuch a proportion of which, according to the ftrength of their bodies, they divided their times of reft and labour. * * * * * * * * * *
* * * * * * * * N. B. *There were here some new, and (in the Editor's and Tranflator's poor opinion) some beautiful hints given the learned World, in relation to* Jupiter, *and the reft of our Planets. But as feveral of our greateft Aftronomers, whom I will not name, for fear of expofing them to the rage and refentment of Mankind, have been pleafed to threaten, they would lay out all their*

their skill, in publickly oppofing the new fyf-
tems, which had been communicated to him,
it has been thought proper to fupprefs them
for the prefent. A method which the Tranf-
lator has the more willingly complied with,
for the fake of peace, and to prevent new
Schifms, Feuds, and Factions, between great
and learned Men; and efpecially, fince fuch
amicable methods have been propofed, that
there is good hope all points may be fo fairly
adjufted, that thefe vaft difcoveries, in
this new fyftem of things, may, to the fatis-
faction of all parties, be communicated to
the World in the fubfequent Volumes. Ac-
cordingly, the Tranflator has modeftly defer-
red his Publication of them, and in the
mean time, has fo carefully connected the
paragraphs in this admirable Letter, that
there will appear no material interruption
in the fenfe. * * * * * * * * * * *
* * * * * * * But certainly, fays he,
how contented foever they may be with
their Light, they muft fuffer feverely by
cold; nay, I am afraid their Waters are
conftantly frozen. I told him there was
no fear of that evil, if we either fuppofed
their Waters of a warm nature, like our
mineral Springs, and Hot-Wells, or the
inha-

inhabitants fo fram'd, as to delight in a cold climate, and abhor a warm one, as our northern nations do the heat of the Line; or if warmth, like ours, muſt be ſuppos'd neceſſary for them and their plants, &c. poſſibly as *Jupiter*'s Diameter is 20 times greater than that of our earth, and all of it baſk'd in the ſun's beams, the warmth of the ſun might be greatly increaſ'd there by *Jupiter*'s ſo frequent rotation round its own axis, and by its acting on ſo much greater an extent of ſurface; which anſwer, however your Lordſhip may think of it, paſs'd for very good reaſoning at the Seraglio. But, ſays he, I fancy I am the more ſenſible of their being pinch'd by cold yonder, becauſe I find the night air grow very uneaſy; and as we have fully obſerv'd theſe wonders of the heavens for this time, let us retire to our former ſhelter in the Kioſc, and talk over our coffee of theſe amazing Diſcoveries.

We were hardly ſet down on our Sofa's, when he began to ask me, whether the Aſtronomers in *Europe*, or elſewhere, were often thus employ'd, and to what uſes their labours ſerv'd? I told him, unhappily Aſtronomy had been confin'd to *Europe* to its great diſſervice; having been baniſh'd *Egypt*, and thofe regions in his Empire, that by their ferene skies and air were fitteft for her obfervations, and where fhe firft appear'd, and for many ages flourifh'd confiderably. That in *Europe* our Aftronomers were perpetually taken up in watching the Stars, Comets and Planets, adjufting their places, and obferving their motions. That by their labours we both difcover the harmony by which the immenfe works of the Creator are knit together in the great Univerfe, the motions of the heavenly bodies, the degrees of their magnitudes, light, heat and motion, and how they act on each other, their natural intercourfe and regulated circulations, with their certain returns and periods. That by their obfervations on each and all of thefe, we are oblig'd to confefs and adore the infinite magnificence, power and goodnefs of the great Mover and Former of them all; of which we could before have no true notions, till thefe his glorious works were thus reveal'd to us to our equal convenience and pleafure.

That befides thefe advantages, we alfo were indebted to the labours of Aftronomers, for the clearing up the now eftablifh'd fyftem of all the Comets in their immenfe

2

Orbits,

Orbits, as well as the perfection of our Geography and Chronology; both which would be made up of mere fables and guesses without their assistance. Nay, that we owe to the same means, that our navigation is become so safe and secure thro' the vast seas and pathless oceans through which our commerce is extended. That his Highness might have some notion hereof by those very *Satellites* of *Jupiter* which he had been so long observing that night, the observation of whose frequent Eclipses alone, had ascertain'd the Longitude of many thousand places in our Earth, which before were utterly unknown; and had thereby made that noble Globe, I had presented him with from your Lordship, so admirably compleat, as I had often shewn to him.

That besides many other things, by the observations of their Eclipses, as I had explain'd them to him, men had demonstrated, by their being seen earlier when the Earth is nearer, and later than calculation when it is remoter from *Jupiter*, that Light was not propagated to us instantaneously, but by a successive motion; and that we can measure out its journeys from the Sun and the Planets to us, as by a stated scale, which

was

was about 500000 miles in a minute. We
had a vaft deal of converfation on thefe fubjects, in which as I gave him accounts, that
probably our Earth, by its fmalnefs, had
never yet been obferv'd from *Jupiter*, and
that *Jupiter*'s Moons, to fay nothing of *Venus*'s, which are vaftly fmaller, were as large
as our Earth, and that as their days were proportion'd to their revolutions round their
Axes, fo they were in fome of them double, and in others 16 times as long as ours.
We fell again into a long difcourfe, whether
thefe vaft Orbs, no ways inferior to the Earth
in bulk, ought not to be allow'd inhabitants
as well as our Moon. As to *Jupiter*, the
very beholding him thro' the telefcope with
his feas and mountains, made it fufficiently
probable to him: but tho' I urg'd to him,
that it was abfurd to fuppofe that an infinite
Creator would have fuch glorious parts of
his Creation void and empty of proper claf-
fes of his creatures, like an extravagant
builder raifing more edifices than he was
able to place fitting furniture in, and ufed
many arguments, which I need not repeat
to your Lordfhip, I could hardly make him
confefs, that he thought it very probable
that they muft be inhabited.

I   How-

However, I had the pleasure to find that my hopes had not deceiv'd me, and that what I had said now and formerly of Astronomy's being driven out of *Egypt*, and those parts of his Empire, which Nature had, as it were, cut out for an Observatory for this lovely Science, had made great impressions on him. In short, before we parted, he order'd the Visier to take care directly for chusing a fit place there, and building and endowing an Astronomical College, as I should direct; and desir'd that I should send for some of the best Professors in *Europe* to settle there, with large and honourable provisions.   I can assure your Lordship this is already settled so far, that a large quantity of ground near *Grand-Cairo* is set out, and by this time actually building; and as I am persuaded no delay or obstacle will arise from hence to compleat this noble design, I intreat your Lordship to give such orders, that some excellent Astronomers may be prevail'd with to set out with the next fleet for *Turky*, whose provision and protection to their full content, I do hereby, on sufficient warrant, bind my self to be answerable for.

Judge, my Lord, what progresses we shall be able to make in this noble Science, when

the

she is reftor'd to her native Empire, and the ferene and cloudlefs skies of *Egypt*, where neither rains nor vapours, nor the exhalations, mifts and fogs of our Northern Climate fhall once interrupt her divine Contemplations. What difcoveries fhall we not make in the Heavens of new Stars arifing, old ones decaying, unobferv'd Comets, with new Suns and Planets in their feveral fyftems, arranging in the thoufands and ten thoufands of the yet undifcover'd hofts of Heaven, in the beauteous order and array of Glory, in which their omnipotent Creator has plac'd them in his infinite Wifdom and Power?

But I muft leave this fubject, my Lord, left I run out into too great lengths on it; and tho' I have often fince attended the Grand Signior, to fhew him the reft of the Planets, and particularly *Saturn* with his Ring, and his Satellites, which he was infinitely pleas'd with; and had many farther converfations with him on their Eclipfes, one of which I fhew'd him; and alfo on the new difcoveries and improvements in Aftronomy, and the new College for its Profeffors in *Egypt*; yet as the repetition of them would be needlefs, after what I have

said

said on them here, I shall not trouble you with them.

On my return home from the Seraglio, I met your Lordship's dispatches of the 28th of *December*; but as my last of the 25th of *Febr.* effectually answer'd all their Contents, I shall make no other return to them here, than my humble thanks for the care you express so obligingly for me, and to make my compliments to Mr. Secretary for the huge Pacquets of *English* News Papers he was pleas'd to inclose to me. It was really a surprize to me, to see such a vast spawn of the productions of these insects, that thus float and feed upon the air we breathe, and have no appearance of existence but in their constant buzzing about, hearkening out, and attending and list'ning to the noise and motions of their neighbours. They seem to make their ears as useful to them, as the Pigmies which * *Pigafetta* tells us he saw in the Island of *Aruchet* near the *Moluccas*, who liv'd in dark high caverns (like the garrets, I suppose, of these Authors) and lay upon one ear as a bed, and cover'd themselves by way of warm bedcloaths with the other.   B b 4   I send

* Viaggio del sig. Ant. Pigafetta, &c. Racolti da Ranusio, *p.* 368. *Venet.* 1588.

I fend your Lordſhip, as a little return for all your favours, a very excellent ſtatue of *Conſtantine* the Great, which was lately dug up near this city by ſome *Greek* maſons, and with great difficulty preſerv'd from the barbarous hands of the workmen, who maim all ſuch ſtatues as they meet with any where. It is the more curious, becauſe it is repreſented with a croſs to it; which (tho' the Eccleſiaſtical Writers aſſure us there were many ſuch erected to him) is, I believe, the only one to be found now in *Europe*. Your Lordſhip will obſerve, that it perfectly agrees with the Medals of this Emperor that are ſtampt with it, of which I ſend your Lordſhip two very fair and well preſerv'd. . He is crown'd by a victory on the reverſe with this Inſcription, *In hoc ſigno Victor eris*; and I am rejoic'd I have got ſuch a treaſure to adorn that admirable collection you have made, and are daily increaſing.

Every thing here continues on the ſame happy foot as when I laſt wrote, and our merchants are treated with the greateſt favour and regard we can poſſibly deſire. As I have few correſpondents, I have no foreign news worth ſending your Lordſhip, unleſs the late death of his *Poliſh* Majeſty, who,

who, after the moſt intemperate Life, died at (I think) near eighty. A great age for any one to arrive at, and eſpecially a King; it being obſerv'd by hiſtorians, that of all the *Roman, Greek, French* and *German* Emperors, but four liv'd to eighty, and but five Popes; and none of thoſe in any late Century.

He was ſo given up to his belly, one would have thought he could not have liv'd to fifty, unleſs the devil had kept him alive to procure credit to intemperance. He was a ſowre, ill-natur'd man, but an excellent King; for it made him inacceſſible to flatterers, and not to be practis'd on by favourites, and the ſkilfulleſt courtiers, who could neither lead or blind him. He had ſo little Religion, that he infamouſly gave up that which he was born in for his Crown; and us'd to ſay, as it was neceſſary to profeſs ſome kind or other, if he was not a Prince, he would have lik'd that of the *Jews* beſt, becauſe it allow'd railing at all the reſt, and was never believ'd or minded by thoſe that profeſt it.

As that Crown is ſoon to be ſet to ſale, I hear there are already as many new Kings ſet up among them, as ever were made on

a twelfth-

a twelfth-night for diverfion; and will probably have the fame fate, and be unking'd
again, when their parties that fet them up
are tir'd of them and their filly play, and
fick of the poppets they created.

I beg the continuation of your Lordfhip's
undeferv'd favours, and to believe me, with
all poffible gratitude, my Lord,

Your Lordfhip's, &c.

S T A N H O P E.

To the Lord High-Treafurer, &c.

Mofcow, March 8. 1997.

My L O R D,

SINCE mine of the 29th of *November*
and 17th of *January*, I have receiv'd
but one fhort one from your Lordfhip of the
26th of *February*, in which you acknowledge
the receipt of mine, and are fo good as to
defire the continuance of my correfpondence, and to exprefs fome fatisfaction in the
accounts I have hitherto had the happinefs
to fend you.

You are pleas'd alfo to defire the beft information I can procure you, in relation to
the Jefuits practifing Phyfick here with furprizing fuccefs; which, you are told, has

contri-

contributed to their intereſt in this Court, as much as any one method I took notice of to your Lordſhip, in relation to the prodigious growth of that Society in *Muſcovy*.

As I have endeavour'd to prepare myſelf to obey your Lordſhip's commands on this head, I ſhall begin ſuch accounts as I have been able to procure for you, with ingenuouſly confeſſing, that I quite overlook'd that particular; which was chiefly occaſion'd by my conſidering them only as Eccleſiaſticks, and omitting the diſguiſes they wear here, and in all Courts, in every kind of profeſſion that can give them intereſt and favour.

And indeed it muſt be allowed, that their great application to the ſtudy of this profeſſion has been of infinite credit and ſervice to them, by the prodigious ſucceſs they have had in their practice at the Czar's Court, and throughout his Empire; and tho' this is aſcrib'd, by common report, to the prayers of the Society, that bring a bleſſing down on all their preſcriptions, yet I fancy I ſhall have no difficulty to perſuade your Lordſhip, that 'tis owing to their employing ſome of the moſt learned and ingenious men of their whole body in the buſineſs of this profeſſion. For as by the *Athenian* Law, all

mean,

mean, illiterate people, and flaves particularly were forbid to practice Phyfick ; which, if put in force now, would exclude numbers of bafe, fervile, mercenary creatures, who follow that employment, and would force them to turn Horfe-farriers and Rat-catchers; fo thefe Fathers have taken care that none of their body fhould ftudy this branch of learning, who were either of mean parts or griping fpirits. By this means, what between vaft reading and a generous neglect of fees, as well as clofe attendance on their patients, and feveral new methods they have eftablifh'd, it is hardly credible how few that have recourfe to their medicines, have fail'd of being recover'd, where old age, or a weaknefs of nature, or a long courfe of intemperance and debauchery, did not occafion it. I have as little faith in the common run of Phyficians as moft people, but I muft own I have alter'd my thoughts on that article, fince I have feen fuch effects of their skill; and I fancy were the ingenious *Petrarch* now living, he would not write in the title page of his *Hippocrates*'s Aphorifms, as he did in his days that odd Axiom, *Nulla certior via ad falutem quam medico caruiffe, caruiſſe,* for the reverſe of it is now become true.

There have of late years prodigius genius's in phyſick appear'd in *Great-Britain,* who, like new ſtars, have enlightned the darkneſs of the laſt age, and have plainly ſhewn, not to ſay demonſtrated, the reaſons of the ſeveral virtues and operations, by means of which their preſcribed Medicines produce ſuch vaſt changes in our bodies. Nay, Dr. *Turner,* in his *Treatiſe de principiis rerum,* has found out evidently the fountain and firſt principle of life and action in all animated and vegetable bodies, which formerly appear'd ſuch an unfathomable myſtery to our Anceſtors, who were wandering about and groping in the dark after knowledge ; or, at moſt, wiſhing in the dawn of its morning for that bright and glorious Day that has ſince broke out upon us.

The Jeſuits have ſtudied the works of theſe great men with no ſmall application, and by improving their hints, and introducing ſeveral new methods and rules, have been of vaſt ſervice to the publick ; ſome of theſe I ſhall now lay before your Lordſhip,

ſhip, as I have obſerv'd them my ſelf, or have been appriz'd of them by others.

And I ſhall begin with that excellent one of prohibiting all Apothecaries to practiſe on the ſevereſt penalties. For beſides the want of skill in a profeſſion they can never be ſuppoſed maſters of, it is certain thoſe Gentlemen uſed to beſtow their attendance on the poor *Ruſſians*, merely with a view to be well paid for their drugs, (that would otherwiſe have rotted on their ſhelves) juſt as Vintners give a funday's dinner to their cuſtomers, provided they pay for the wine they drink. After all, my Lord, there is methinks as good ground for this Law, as for one we have in *Great-Britain*, that forbids Drovers to be Butchers, it being unreaſonable that the ſame perſons who provide the cattle we are to make uſe of, ſhould alſo have liberty to kill.

Another method they introduc'd here, and which produc'd a great care in the phyſician of his patient's recovery, was, obliging the Doctor to refund half his fees in caſe of the death of the ſick perſon. This ingratiated them much with the people, as it ſhew'd a generous neglect of gain in the college that eſtabliſh'd the rule, and alſo alfo fpurr'd on all practitioners to do their utmoft to ferve their patients, or to pay a reafonable fine for their want of fuccefs.

In the next place, all that were licens'd to practife, were oblig'd to keep regular Diaries of every fymptom in their patients from the leaft to the greateft, and to have the Friends and nurfe-keepers that were about them write down all things obfervable in their abfence, and to give copies (if demanded) of their prefcriptions, in cafe the fick perfon died, to the cenfors of the college, where any ignorant or faulty conduct was fineable. By this means the hands of thofe dangerous animals, officious Phyficians as well as ignorant ones, were feverely tied up, and caution and judgment made neceffary in prefcribing.

But further, all were obliged to fee their prefcriptions made up themfelves, and that right and good drugs were only ufed ; by which means thoufands of lives were fav'd,that us'd to be facrific'd to the knavery of Apothecaries, who gave bad ones, or the ignorance of their apprentices, who often gave wrong ones ; both which evils were thus effectually prevented.

Another

Another method they were oblig'd to observe, was, that each practitioner was sworn to report to the college and censors all such extraordinary cases as occurr'd in his practice, and his observations on them, and at least three each year; out of which a choice collection was made, and annually publish'd for the service of the publick, with proper notes and reflections: and this occasion'd great helps to the advancement of the Science in general, and the improvement of each member of the college in particular.

In the next place the Czar, at their request, gave the college the lives and bodies of so many condemn'd Felons as they pleas'd, to try all such experiments on, which they judg'd useful to improve their Science. By this means many thousands of such experiments were made, to the vast emolument of the world, and at the same time the lives of as many thousand honest *Russians* sav'd, that us'd to be sacrific'd to the folly, the curiosity, or rashness of their Doctors, by substituting Malefactors to be purg'd, blooded, and vomited, and to run thro' all the ordeal fire of experiments, in their room.

But

But again, the college having divided all diseases incident to the human body into four parts, each member was oblig'd, after ten years practice, to confine themselves entirely to the lift of such diseases, as they judg'd themselves best qualified to succeed in the cure of, and all the rest of their lives to meddle with no other distempers, unless in case of necessity. By this means their studies and experience being thus entirely apply'd to a narrower province, they grew in time so absolutely masters of all that lay within their own district, that they frequently perform'd cures in the most desperate cases, and were able to exert the whole force of their art in that particular branch which they apply'd their studies and practice to. And certainly, my Lord, it is to this regulation of the Jesuit Physicians in *Russia*, as much as any thing I have observ'd, that we have found out since the 19th Century so many wonderful specificks for the Jaundice, Bloody-Flux, Small-Pox, Dropsy, Green-Sickness, and Cholick, which otherwise would never have been discover'd, or at least not so soon. With the same sagacity they have introduc'd the use of scales into their practice, and the weighing Urine with greater caution than

C c

Bankers

Bankers do Gold; from whence in many cafes what advantages have arifen, is known to all. Nor with lefs care and judgment have they brought Mufick into ufe in particular diforders, which before their cultivating this Science, was never once thought of any fervice, even in melancholy or phrenetick diforders themfelves.

But I muft not pafs by unmention'd another fingular method they have ever ufed this laft forty years here, and that is, curing feveral diforders by milk of goats and affes, which they have brought to prodigious perfection by feveral methods that are referv'd to themfelves. One of thefe I know by experience, is dieting the animal whofe milk they prefcribe with particular kinds of herbs, whofe juices and qualities they judge moft efficacious and conducive to the circumftances of the diftemper. The fervice, (the miracles, I may fay) they have done in this way is perfectly prodigious; and indeed as they firft introduc'd the skilful ufe of the admirable *Chinefe* Root Ginfeng with fuch fuccefs in moft cafes, fo they are obferved as much as poffible to deal in the fimpleft medicines, and frequently reftore men to health with as much eafe as *Afclepiades* did, who

I

only

only ufed cold water and wine in his method of cure.

This fingle circumftance in the practice
of Phyfick is furely of vaft importance ;
and as one of the prayers in the wife
Italian's Litany, is, *Da Guazzabuglio di
medici* ; fo certainly that terrible hodge-
podge of drugs, powders, and a thoufand
compounded recipes we are obliged to fwal-
low for a little eafe or health, is as hazardous
and as unpleafant a circumftance as I know
in all their method of prefcribing. I remember to have read in a great phyfician's
works, that what naturalifts affert, that
whoever draws the root of *Moly*, *Cynofpaftus*,
or Mandrake, out of the earth, will die
foon after, is a meer vulgar error ; but I
wifh he could as eafily convince us, that
thofe who take their roots and drugs in-
wardly, are not often feiz'd with death for
their pains. And indeed there is nothing I
admire more in their conduct, than their
banifhing thofe heaps of drugs which ufed
to enter into the prefcriptions of moft phyficians, and which formerly many of them
were obliged to keep up, *propter metum Judæorum*, tho' thereby they facrific'd our
lives to the difhoneft gain of thofe vermin

the

the Apothecaries, whom they were afraid to difoblige.

Their gentlenefs and caution to avoid violent courfes, is much applauded alfo. Some phyficians purge, bleed, blifter and vomit with fuch hafte and fury, that they may be faid rather to murther the difeafe than to cure the man, who is left weak and fpent may be for life ; and, like a Country where the King gets the better by a bloody civil war, they fave the man, by ruining the happy conftitution he enjoyed before. This is what the Jefuits are remarkable for avoiding, unlefs where it is abfolutely neceffary indeed ; which, as they manage matters, feldom happens.

There is another particular, which is entirely owing to them, and which has been very ferviceable to thefe people, that I muft not forget to take notice of. Your Lordfhip has often heard how epidemical pleurifies ufed to be here, and what numbers they fwept away of the poor *Ruffians* every year, like the plague in *Turky.*

To remedy this, the Czar, at the inftigation of the Jefuits, introduc'd the cuftom of ufing linfeed-oil by the common people with all eatables, where olive or fallad-oil was formerly

merly ufed (on which laft he laid great duties;) and by means of this medicinable kind of fuftenance, they have fo effectually removed this reigning kind of peftilence, as I may call it, that it is feldom known to make any ravage among them now. This was at once reftoring the health of a nation, my Lord; there remain'd only to banifh the gluttony and drunkennefs of the Nobility and Knezzes, to have in a manner compleated the cure.

One would think, my Lord, I had reckon'd up enough of their performances, and yet I have one more to touch upon that is fufficiently remarkable, and that is, a pleafant Elixir which they have invented, a few drops of which, taken juft going to bed, never fails to give eafy reft, and, what is moft extraordinary, pleafant dreams. You fee, my Lord, their skill has contriv'd to reach to that half of our lives (which we give to fleep) that before lay entirely out of our power and theirs; and as they have invented a fpecifick, to make it not only eafy but delightful to us, I think they almoft deferve to have altars and monuments raifed to them.

But,

But, my Lord, after what I have faid to the advantage of thefe Gentlemen, I am forry to add one reflection that overturns all their glory; and that is, tho' they have made the practice of Phyfick extremely laborious to themfelves, and ufeful to others (beyond what it ever was known to be) by thefe methods and inventions; yet they have done it all with faulty views, to enflave thofe they pretend to ferve, and eftablifh the Empire of the *Vatican*, and all its fuperftitions and errors. Nay, my Lord, it is faid, that they watch the finking fpirits and the dying hours of their patients, to fcrew from them, by their follicitations and importunity, large legacies and confiderable donations to their fociety; and, what is ftill more deteftable, that they are as induftrious and artful to difpatch their enemies out of the way, as they are to preferve the health and lives of their friends. It is certain, there have not wanted inftances in this kind that have occafion'd fuch fufpicions; yet they have entirely furmounted them, and beat down all oppofition, by letting every one fee it was in vain to contrive any remedy againft their power; it being as ufelefs an attempt (in *Caligula's* words)

words) as *Agrippina's Antidotum verfus Cæfarem.*

But it is time to quit this subject, to acquaint your Lordship with something more material, and that is, the apprehension every one is in here, that the war between this Crown and *Sweden* is like to be carried on by both sides, with greater animosity and resolution than ever, this approaching season. They work night and day at *Petersburg* in their preparations to have their fleet in the *Baltick*, before the *Swedes* can be able to leave their ports; and indeed, if the frost were once gone, and the Harbours open, I believe we should soon see the *Muscovite* squadron at sea. They carry on their levies for their land forces with all possible application, and have made large remittances to *Poland* and *Germany*, to remount their cavalry; and tho' I am inform'd by a sure hand, that the *Swedes* are doing their utmost not to be unprepared for them; yet I am very doubtful they will not prove so good a match for them this campaign as they did last. How far his Majesty's mediation between the contending powers may be proper, your Lordship and the King are the best Judges; but I am privately assured, it would be very

useful

uſeful to the *Swede*, and probably not unacceptable to this Court.

I know not, while the Princes of the Earth are contending for theſe little corners of it, whether it may entertain your Lordſhip, to give you a little hiſtory of an honeſt Gentleman here, one *Rabbi Abraham Abrabanel*, who has very fairly put in his claim to the whole * of it.

He is a mad enthuſiaſtical *Jew*, who followed merchandize, and broke ; and after travelling over moſt part of *Europe*, ſettled here at *Moſco*, and was employ'd at laſt by the Czar, as his firſt herald, and got a good deal of money by drawing up genealogies for the *Ruſſian* Knezzes and Noblemen, whoſe pride he flatter'd, by tracing up the ſource of their families further than hiſtory or truth could carry them. He had a very numerous family, and as the *Jews* here paid him great reſpect, as being a deſcendant from the famous *Abrabanel* of the tribe of *Judah*, and the houſe of *David*; his pride and ſome loſſes in his fortune turned his head, and made him take up one of the oddeſt fancies that ever madman thought of, that

* *Vide Filmer*'s Patriarchal Scheme.

he

he is the direct defcendant from *Adam* in a right line by *Noah*, and has a full title to his father's inheritance, the world. Tho' he hehaved very oddly in his family and neighbourhood, yet no one ever difturbed him, till he went one day directly to the Czar's apartments, and making way for himfelf thro' all the crowd, humbly acquainted him with his pretenfions, and defired him to fet a good example to the princes of the world, by refigning his Empire to him.

The Czar was fo good as to compaffionate the poor creature's diforder, which he foon perceiv'd by his appearance and geftures, as well as his fpeech, and very gently defired him to give him fome time to fettle his private affairs, before he refigned his crown; and promifed him to have all poffible regard fhewn in the mean while, both to his perfon and remonftrances : But as he happen'd to fmile in fpeaking thefe words, *Rabbi Abraham*'s paffion was raifed fo high, that he called him a vile diffembling ufurper, and ordered the guards to feize him. Your Lordfhip may eafily imagine the confequence was, that they very bafely neglected his commands, and convey'd him with lefs refpect than became his ftation as Emperor

of

of the World, to the pnblick Bedlam where they confine madmen.

This affair has occafion'd much mirth; and as the Czar has order'd great care to be taken of him, I had the curiofity to pay him a vifit yefterday along with the *Danifh* Envoy here, to fee if we cou'd make any tolerable terms for our royal Mafters. We found him in a neat, clean room, where his wife was fitting by him weeping bitterly; but he was in no manner of concern, but writing a great many letters which lay in heaps before him. As he offends no body, we began to difcourfe with him of his affairs, and defir'd to know calmly what his pretenfions were; becaufe we were confident if the Princes of the World could be convinc'd of the juftice of them, they would rather come to an amicable treaty, than difpute it with him againft Confcience and Reafon, by arms. As he knew us both, and our characters, by feeing us often at Court, he feem'd mightily pleas'd; and pulling a prodigious long genealogy out of his papers, he bid us read them there, and we fhould find he was the lineal defcendant in the right line from *Adam,* and confequently had an undoubted title to every acre on the globe.   We

We look'd over his paper with great respect, and told him we should represent the
affair and his pretensions at our several Courts;
but would be glad to know, whether he was
not inclinable to compromise matters, and
accept some kind of tribute, by way of
acknowledgment of his title, and allow the
present possessors to hold their Crowns under him as Fiefs of his great Empire. By
the Crown of *David*, said he, it is a very
fair proposal; and tho' I have eight sons
who could fill the Thrones of *Europe*, to
say nothing of the rest of the Earth, better
than they have been for these five Centuries
past, if your masters and the rest of their
brethren will pay me 1 *s. per* acre, rough and
smooth, I shall give them no farther distur-
bance, nor trouble my head with writing to
my subjects on this dispute. It is true, says
he, finding the Czar trifling with me, and
putting off matters from week to week, I
was drawing up manifestoes to all my vassals,
and discharging them from owning their
pretended masters any longer; and I have
order'd all the inhabitants of the Earth to
pay no further rents, taxes or customs to
them; and if I can once cut off those sup-
plies of their power and pride, I shall soon
humble

humble them fo far as to fubmit to me. The truth is, fays he, taking me afide, and whif-pering me in the ear, I am under fome per-plexity what place to receive the money they bring me in; for having at prefent no one of my Territories in my poffeffion, if they fhould pay it me here, this Ufurper the Czar might be fo difhoneft and bafe, as to feize on it for his own ufe, and poffibly might hang up fome of my poor, faithful vaffals for their loyalty to me.

I told him very freely as his friend, that his doubts were reafonable, and that he fhould firft try to get into fome one of his Kingdoms by the way of treaty, before he order'd any of his rents or fubfidies to come into him, unlefs a few for his private occa-fions. He thank'd me very gratefully for my good advice, and told me he was re-folv'd to follow it; and in the mean time, fays he, I fhall fend four general manifeftoes to the four quarters of the World, and cir-cular letters to the feveral Princes and their fubjects, acquainting them with my title, and commanding them to acknowledge it. After all, faid he with tears in his eyes, God knows how far they may regard my remon-ftrances; but confidering how few of them
can

can pretend the leaſt title under my great
Anceſtor; and beſides that defect in their
titles, how much worſe they govern my poor
people than I ſhould, I think they might in
conſcience either ſubmit to me, or at leaſt
pay me a few millions of Rubles by way of
an annual tribute. Beſides, as I ſhould be
willing to take half thoſe taxes and rents
from my ſubjects which they extort from
them, it is certain the poor people would
gladly revolt to me if they durſt, and if I
had a tolerable army to maintain my juſt
title.

I told him he ſpake very reaſonably; but
it was ſo difficult an affair, either to conquer his antagoniſts by force, or convince
them by reaſon, that he muſt neceſſarily
manage with the greateſt caution and prudence to compaſs his ends. Sir, ſays he,
you know not the circumſtances of mankind as well as I do, who both from intereſt
and inclination have ſo long conſider'd their
hardſhips and oppreſſions, and their uneaſi-
neſs under their Tyrants, whoſe titles to their
Empire are only founded in blood and violence, and a few ſorry Laws which their
ſwords have cut out for their own purpoſes.
My people are torn in pieces by new Religi-

ons

ons of a hundred different cuts and fashions, by unjust Laws and worse Judges, by Poisons they call Physick, and Murderers they call Doctors, by Plunderers they call Landlords, and publick Villains whom they call Tax-gatherers. They have departed from all the good customs of their Ancestors before the flood, and after it; and have so far deviated from the right of succession in the lineal descendants, that I can maintain there is not this day in the world a single family that has the least title to the estates they enjoy.

There is no Prince in *Europe*, whose Genealogy I cannot trace up to people that were no later than 2000 years ago; either Pedlars or Tinkers, Lieutenants, Lacqueys or Lawyers, or at most menial Servants to several of my relations. There is not a Nobleman, Knight or Gentleman on earth, who is a lineal descendant from his own forefathers: I have search'd into their Genealogies, and I find them in their different successions the sons of Coachmen and Footmen, Soldiers and Courtiers, Priests, Friars, Jesuits, and Valet de Chambres.

Besides all this, they have confounded right and wrong, vice and virtue; they take

corrup-

corruption for juſtice, hypocriſy for religion, falſhood for truth, luſt for love, brutal
fury for courage, cheating and fraud for honeſt gain, prodigality for generoſity, pride
for greatneſs of ſpirit, ribaldry for wit, debauchery for pleaſure, purchaſes for legal
titles, cunning for wiſdom, ſlavery for liberty, and irreligion and infidelity for
ſtrength of reaſon and zeal for truth.

Nay, they miſtake the butchers of mankind for heroes, readers for ſcholars, baſtards
for heirs at law, ſoldiers for patriots, flatterers for friends, and honeſt adviſers for open
enemies; they look on atheiſts as moral
men: and in ſhort, their conduct in every
view is ſo equally abſurd and wicked, that
I am no longer able to bear with them; and
I ſee evidently I muſt take the government
of them into my own hand, to be able to
reform them as they ought to be. Neither
in truth do I reſolve on this from any intereſted views of power and profit to myſelf
and children, but barely for the general
good of mankind, being willing to ſacrifice
the unqueſtionable title I have to the Empire
of the World, to their ſervice, if I could
otherwiſe contrive any way to work a proper reformation among them in this depra-
ved ſtate of things.   I told

I told him I very much approv'd his generous intentions to serve the publick, and be as inftrumental as his high birth and ftation entitled him to be; but that I was apprehenfive his fetting up his title, how juft foever, might occafion prodigious wars and commotions in the world, which muft certainly be a great affliction to him. Dear Sir, fays he, what you fay would deferve my confideration, if I did not certainly know, that obliging men, even by force (if force muft be us'd) to acknowledge my title, would ftill deliver them from much greater evils. For be affur'd, fays he, (in a very important whifper) all the famines, peftilences, commotions, defolations and wars that have afflicted the world thefe laft 40 Centuries, have fallen upon men by the vengeance of a juft Providence, enrag'd to fee the fucceffion and claim of my family laid afide and neglected by a wicked and degenerate race of villains and traitors. He accompanied this with a flood of tears; and turning to his wife, My dear, fays he, if your Majefty will reach me thofe papers I have written, I think this will be an excellent opportunity for difperfing them through my fubjects; and Gentlemen, fays he, as

you

you are the firſt of my vaſſals who have ſhewn a ſenſe of your duty and inclinations to return to your allegiance, if you will ſend them to the ſeveral Princes they are directed to, and aſſiſt me to bring about the Revolution I have reſolv'd on, I ſhall both conſider your reſpective Maſters, and (tho' I can't part with any of my dominions in *Europe)* I hereby promiſe them the beſt Territories in my *Aſian* or *African*, or at worſt in my *American* Continent. But by this time the farce grew too tedious; and therefore deſiring a few weeks to conſider of his demands, we thought fit to retire, and leave his Imperial Majeſty to write his diſpatches without the help of Secretaries or Counſellors. I am ſorry I forgot to beg his Majeſty to take care of his precious health, and to be on his guard againſt his mighty rivals for the Empire of the World the Jeſuits, and the dangerous Monarchy of the *Solipſi*, who I fear are ſo jealous of all rivals in intereſt and power, they will be very apt, by fraud, or poiſon, or violence, to remove ſo dangerous a Competitor out of the way.

But I muſt make amends to your Lordſhip for this trivial amuſement, by a preſent that is really worth your conſideration and

regard,

regard, which I fend you by this bearer; and that is no lefs than fixty volumes in *Folio* of the late Czar's travels thro' *Europe*, who, as your Lordfhip knows, never ftirr'd out of his own Empire.   He was a Prince of great natural genius and abilities; but as he did not approve of his own or any great Princes travelling, he employ'd a number of the moft able and underftanding men he cou'd procure, to take that trouble for him, and travel thro' the whole tour of *Europe*, accompanied with excellent defigners, who at all proper ftations fhould graphically defign the face of nature, and the fituation of rivers, towns, palaces, caftles, mountains and plains, in the very manner the eye furvey'd them on the fpot.   Befides this, they were oblig'd to take draughts of all the fineft gardens and improvements, the moft famous performances in Architecture, Painting and Sculpture; and even the very habits, the very looks, fhape and air of the people of every country they pafs'd thro'.   Nay, they were to defign the very cattle, fifhes, birds; and, in a word, every thing that could deferve their notice in their journeys: all which they were to accompany with the beft notes, remarks and obfervations poffible.   But this

is

is not the only treafure that has enrich'd thefe
volumes; for here are all the rarities of the
beft cabinets in *Europe* for choice collections
in all kinds, exprefs'd to the life in admirable cuts, and explained by fhort judicious
differtations. In thefe, all the beft ftatues,
and their habits, medals, feals, intaglias and
baffo-relievos, infcriptions, vafes, maufole-
ums, facrificing inftruments and veffels, fe-
pulchral and other lamps, lachrymatory and
fepulchral-urns, idols, engines, and inftruments of war; rings, fymbols of cities and
countries, inftruments of mufick, and the
weights and meafures of the ancients, are
incomparably reprefented, as well as whatever relates to the temple and worfhip of
their Gods; not omitting all the modern
productions of art and nature in animals,
plants, minerals, metals, and the manual
improvements of the feveral Sciences. An
immenfe profufion of all thefe, digefted under their proper heads, are engrav'd on thefe
copper plates in a beautiful and regular order, where we may at once form the cleareft
notions of all fuch things, without running
the hazards of ill health, as well as the corruption of faith and manners, which travelling is generally accompanied with, and

have

have at leaſt all the benefits that one can borrow from the eye in performing the tour of *Europe.* The Czar has about 1000 Copies made of them, which are preſented as the greateſt favours to thoſe they deſign to oblige; and as I owe this I have receiv'd to your Lordſhip's friendſhip, by whoſe means I am fix'd here, I thought it a piece of juſtice to reſtore them to the hand, by whoſe mediation I became poſſeſs'd of it from the Czar's bounty.

If it were not for the Patriarch's death, who died here laſt week, I ſhould have no news of any conſequence to communicate to your Lordſhip. Tho' he was brought over, in the latter part of his life, to all the Jeſuits meaſures in modelling this Church to ſubmit to the Pope, yet he would have been an excellent Biſhop but for one fault, which I believe few men were ever guilty of before him. He was a learned, ſenſible, pious man, and with the greateſt zeal to ſerve the cauſe of Religion and Virtue, he had an utter contempt for that epidemical evil in the Chriſtian Church, the building up a fortune, and making a family. But as he ow'd his advancement to the Prince *Dolhorouky,* thro' a falſe notion of gratitude to the end of his

life,

life, he never ceas'd heaping preferments on every relation or friend, nay, on every dependant of that Prince, how worthless soever, (against all reason, nay, against his own) on the sole merit of their belonging to that family. This a little obscur'd the lustre of his virtues, and might teach us (but, alas! we do not want the caution) that we should not be too violently grateful; which is almost as dangerous as being too violently in love, and distracts and biasses the judgment as much. But we may forgive this excellent Person this weakness, which was compensated by so many great and shining virtues; and besides, there is so little danger of his example being infectious, that I fancy he is the first man in this age, who (in his character) fell a martyr to gratitude. He is to be buried with a great solemnity, which the Jesuits are to have the management of, as well as of providing him an humble, docible Successor, who, 'tis said, will certainly be the Bishop of *Novogorod*. One very unfit for such a charge, being an old, weak, injudicious creature, without will, or even speech or passions of his own, but as he is inspir'd and mov'd, like a puppet, by the hands of these jugglers behind the curtain; and so

notori-

notorioufly dull, that the *Knez Petrowisky* told him in a violent quarrel this winter, his head was fo barren (he is very bald) that it would not even bear hair.   Yet to thefe very defects, which ought to have prevented his promotion, it is that he owes his advancement: a thing, miferable and unfortunate as it is, that often happens in the world; thefe Jefuits being like thofe mungrel fort of curs, that would never find a mafter to own them, but for fuch poor blind wretches, who cherifh and feed them, that they may lead and guide them in the ways of the world.

But I detain your Lordfhip too long with thefe trifles, and therefore will not increafe their number by vain and ufelefs profeffions of being on a thoufand accounts, and by a thoufand ties,

> *My* LORD,
>> *Your Lordfhip's,* &c.
>>> CLARE.

My LORD,

London, Chelfea, Feb. 24. 1999.

I Had the pleafure of receiving yours of *December* the 16th and *February* the 8th, and have now the fhame of anfwering them together;

together; but if your Excellency considers the multiplicity of affairs that have been on the carpet of late, and in which I have been more than ordinarily engag'd; you will not take it unkindly, if I am more dilatory in my answers, than my strong attachment to your noble family, and my personal regard and esteem for your merit and services, may justly demand from me.

In the mean time, I have not been wanting in my care, as to those negotiations you are charg'd with, as the dispatches from Mr. Secretary *Bridges* will witness for me; nor in my respects for your brother, who is now one of the two Secretaries for foreign affairs. It is true, the salary, by increasing the number of Secretaries to four, is not so considerable as formerly, yet the credit and honour of the place will be of greater service than a more lucrative employment,

His Majesty expects with impatience the resolutions of the *French* Court, as to the affair of opposing the Inquisition. As you have receiv'd his instructions on that affair from his own hand, you will do well to return as exact an account as possible of your next audience, and to shew your utmost dexterity to spirit them up to vigorous

D d 4 　　　resolurefolutions on that matter, which may produce events of vaft fervice to that crown and this, in humbling the exorbitant power of the empire of the *Vatican*. Your care in reviewing our *French* feaports and garrifons, and the works carrying on in the harbours of *Dunkirk* and *Calais*, gave his Majefty much fatisfaction; and be affur'd, I fhall endeavour to improve the impreffions which your diligence and skill, in obferving the ftate of things where you are, have made on him, to the utmoft.

The ability and application of the *French* Minifters to retrieve the low condition a weak and unfortunate reign has reduced their country to, is very commendable; and as fhe can never recover ftrength enough in half a century to make her once more an object of our jealoufy, it is our intereft to fupport rather than diftrefs her, left fhe becomes a perfect province to *Rome*. *Cæfar* left her fo, and there are many cowled *Cæfars* beyond the *Alps*, and in her own bowels, whofe heads are as wife and bald as his, who would make her fo again, if the paftoral ftaff and crofier did not want fomething of the force and vigour of his fword. Our accounts from *Rome* leave us no fhadow

of

of doubt of this, as well as their deep defigns on *Germany* ; but I hope the recovery
of the Emperor, and a vigorous oppofing
the eftablifhment of the Inquifition, will
give us both room and time to lay fuch
invincible obftacles in her way, as fhe can
never get over.

But Mr. Secretary has fo fully enlarged
on this fubject to you formerly, that there
is no occafion for renewing any difcourfe
on it now to your Excellency, who are alfo
fo well appriz'd of the ftate of affairs in
Europe ; and therefore I fhall only add my
earneft defires that you may continue to do
fervice to the King and your Country, and
honour to the character you fuftain, by obferving and taking hold of every occafion that
offers, of making his Majefty's cares for the
fervice of the world more and more fuccefsful.

I obferve with pleafure (to pafs to another fubject) that while your Excellency is
thus follicitous for the fervice of the publick, you are perfectly regardlefs as to your
own intereft here ; and particularly, as to
the Royal Fifhery and Plantation Companies, in both which you have fo large a
ftock, and are fo deeply engag'd. As thofe
corporations have been entirely new modell'd
by

by the act paft this laft feffions, and much improv'd from the ftate they have been in, fince *Frederick* the firft and *George* the third's eftablifhing them, till now, I believe it will be a pleafure to you, if I acquaint you with their prefent circumftances.

I fhall begin with the Royal Fifhery, to which this act has affign'd fix new ports to the ten formerly appointed, and obliges the company to keep at leaft 200000 hands employ'd, either as Coopers, Shipwrights, Smiths, Cawkers, Sawyers, Sailors, Fifhers, and Sailmakers; or elfe in making nets, baskets, ropes, dreffing and fpinning hemp and flax, and weaving poledavies. Of thefe hands, there are to be at leaft 1600 lame and 1000 blind people employ'd in ropes and netmaking, and the hemp and flax articles. The company muft keep at the leaft 1000 Buffes employ'd, and one fifth of all their hands, boys from 11 to 16 years of age, and one third new men, who had never been at fea before, as a nurfery for feamen; and are to furnifh the royal navy, on forty days notice, with 4000 mariners. On thefe accounts it is enacted, that for the encouragement of the company, and thofe who enter into wages with them, and enabling them
who

who carry on the trade (tho' lefs gainful
to private perfons, yet more ferviceable to
the Nation than any other) to purfue
it vigoroufly, the fourth of all the Profit of play-houfes, fhows, prize-fighters,
operas, mufick - meetings and gaming-
houfes, fhall be paid to them for ever;
and alfo the 200th part of all money or land recover'd at law, and the fame
of all immoveables that are fold. That all
common beggars and vagabonds, and all
foundlings, when eight years old, fhall belong to the company, and be feiz'd by
them, and kept in their work-houfes for
feven years, allowing them cloaths and diet,
without wages. That no perfon fhall have
more than 10000 $l.$ ftock, nor lefs than one,
in the company's funds, except his Majefty,
who fhall have 20000 $l.$ embark'd therein;
and that the tolls and cuftoms for paffage
on the great canals cut by *George* III.
and *Frederick* II. from *Briftol* to the
Thames, from *Southampton* to *Winchefter*,
and from fea to fea from *Carlifle* to the
Humber, be paid alfo to them. That for
their further encouragement, each *Friday*
in every week no perfon fhall eat flefh, on
fevere penalties nam'd in the act; and eve-

ry

ry houfe in which are five inhabitants, befides children, fhall be oblig'd to take from
them one barrel of herring or other fifh, at
the market-price.

This is the main of the act, which by
the nearnefs of our fhores, and being furnifh'd with all victualling and fifhing ne-
ceffaries within our felves, without the taxes
the *Dutch* pay their mafters; and being
nearer the *Baltick*, and moft foreign markets,
enables us to underfell all our rivals in this
trade, to breed up every year feveral thoufand Seamen, and employ numbers of our
ufelefs poor, and import immenfe fums of
treafure to our happy Ifland.   But the great
advantages this new model of the royal
Fifhery has procur'd us, are beft feen by its
ftocks having rifen above five *per Cent.*
which your Lordfhip will be a great gainer
by.   The Plantation-Company for the new
Colonies in the *Weft-Indies,* is by the fame
act favour'd by great encouragements, as to all
duties of exports and imports, and a grant of
three millions of acres, to be laid out and ap-
plotted equally to all planters who fhall fettle
there, and build new towns.   They have alfo
large Premiums fettled for fuch limited quantities of iron, pitch, tar, hemp, flax, filk,
indigo,

indigo, wine or oil, as they fhall import from them hither. This has rais'd their ftock as confiderably as the former, and will probably, in a few years, make us utterly independent of our neighbours in the North for all naval ftores, which us'd to drain fuch immenfe fums from us.

I do not congratulate your Excellency on your particular advantage herein, but on the credit and honour you have gain'd, by being fo zealous for the welfare of thefe two glorious companies, and the prodigious addition they are likely to give to the ftrength and wealth of our native country. They will not only enrich us vaftly beyond any of our neighbours, (and they that are richeft, will be able to carry on a war longeft, and confequently tire out and fubdue at laft their enemies;) but they alfo vaftly increafe our naval ftrength, employ our ftarving poor, and will fo far enlarge and extend our colonies on the Continent (greatly encourag'd by our former laws) that our trade will be every day growing more confiderable. The very wine, oil and filk imported annually from them, is incredibly great already ; and tho' in *Frederick* the firft's and *George* the third's days, there

were

were hardly forty engines for throwing of
filk in this nation, it is certain there are now
above a hundred; and yet there are daily
new ones fet up by the company, which
throw more filk with two or three hands,
than by a vaft number of workmen in the
ordinary way. The demands for our goods
and manufactures there, are within this laft
century (as I am affur'd) rifen to double
what they were before; and I doubt not
but your Excellency will live to fee our
Thames like the famous River the *Tibifcus*,
of which it was faid, that one third of it
was water, a fecond fifh, and another fhip-
ping and boats.

The truth is, our colonies abroad have,
and are likely to acquire ftill fuch an increafe of hands and ftrength, that the greateft
care will be neceffary to keep the ftrongeft of them dependent; and yet to provide that the weakeft of them may not
live on the blood and fpirits of the mother nation, nor fuck, if I may ufe the
allufion, on her breaft too long. I am
confident as they will require, fo they will
well deferve, and fully repay this care.
Befides the advantages of the commerce
and navigation betwixt us, it is certain, they

3   gene-

generally in proportion produce greater, more fublime, and warlike fpirits ; as being compos'd of adventurous and daring people, or, at worft, of melancholy difcontented men ; which laft, to fay nothing of the other, (who muft evidently be of fervice to us) are the beft feed-bed for ingenious and inventive, as well as learned and judicious heads. It may indeed be objected to our foreign plantations, that they are in part made up of the filth and purgings of the nation, as felons and robbers ; but we all know *Rome* it felf built up all its courage and virtue on no better a foundation : and after all, even fuch offenders have often fuch refolution, fubtilty, ftrength, fharpnefs and activity, as make their pofterity, (by thefe qualities they derive from them,) fufficient amends for their defcending from fuch evil anceftors.

I am confident the new bifhopricks founded among them by the piety and generofity of his Majefty's anceftors, as well as thofe of *Carolina, Barbadoes* and *Bofton,* eftablifh'd by himfelf, will greatly contribute to the reformation of manners and principles in our colonies, and to the keeping them firm in their allegiance to the crown. Befides, as the

the fevere ecclefiaftical difcipline fettled there againft all profanenefs and fcandalous immorality in both laity and clergy, and the encouraging thofe two noble colleges, erected there by *George* III. have gone a great way already in their civilizing and improving them; fo I doubt not but a regular continuance of them, will fully amend what is yet wanting.

The melancholy profpect you have drawn, as to the corruption and debauchery of the *French* nobles, and the mifery and exceffive poverty of the lower people, muft furprize every one, who confiders the glory, virtue, and bravery of that nation in the laft centuries, that coft her jealous neighbours fuch treafures of wealth and blood to prevent the univerfal empire fhe aim'd at in thofe days. It is true, one would not fee fo dangerous a rival reftor'd to her former ftrength and vigour; but yet a generous enemy cannot fee her prefent misfortunes, without fome regret. However, a few years and a wife adminiftration may by degrees refettle her affairs, and bring her out of that weak and languifhing confumption that at prefent preys on her; but that deadly corruption and degeneracy of faith
and

and manners that infects her clergy and
laity, seems of a more desperate malignancy,
because it does not only prey on her vitals,
but is also encourag'd and increas'd by those
physicians, who are only able to undertake
the cure. Certainly while the King and
his Ministers find their account in imitating
the maxims of *Venice*, keeping the interest
of the clergy low, and their persons and character contemptible, Religion and the influence of the mitre will be utterly absorb'd in
reason of state, and the power of the crown;
and the subject must necessarily become
equally sceptical in their belief, corrupt in
their principles, and immoral in the conduct of their lives. Now tho' this will evidently lessen the unreasonable authority of
the Pope and the Church with the nation;
yet whether such measures will not at the
same time unloose the sacred bonds, by
which religion ties the allegiance of the
people to the supreme magistrate, and make
them bad subjects in proportion as they are
bad christians, is worth the consideration of
the mighty *Machiavels* of *France*.

Your Excellency, who is so well acquainted with the history of our own country, will be the better able to judge of such

E e   conseconfequences by the reign of *Frederick* III. in the 19th Century; when the miferable infection that had corrupted both the lives and faith of one part of our people, had almoft driven the other to an abfolute revolt in their allegiance and principles, to *Rome* and her fuperftitions. A confequence as natural in the politick, as a confumption to an old inveterate cough in the natural body; and if that wife Prince had not in time forefeen, how unfafe all foundations muft be, that were not built on a pious, prudent regulation of the eftablifh'd church, and by profeffing an abhorrence for libertinifm and fcepticifm, and a zeal for our religion, by preferring and honouring none that were known to think meanly of it as to their opinions, or that difhonoured it by their lives, I know not if we had not now been bowing to images, and adoring the Pope. The ftruggles and convulfions which that loofenefs of principles we were infected with, produc'd in his father's reign, are known to every body, that does but curforily look into the hiftory of thofe times; and certainly, nothing but the piety and prudence of his fon, could have reftor'd our peace and happinefs, whofe calm and rational zeal for our religion,

religion, in a few years wrought as great a change in the people, as ever happen'd on such an occasion since the days of *Constantine the Great*, when the sincere Christian triumph'd over the dissembling Pagan. But I will not follow this subject so far as it would lead me ; and shall only say, that I heartily wish our neighbours in *France* may not find some consequences from the maxims they are pursuing, very different from what they expect ; and that they are not tumbling into a greater, to avoid a lesser evil ; like him who run into the water for fear of rain.

But let us leave these melancholy prospects for other nations, and let us reflect a little on the happy condition of our own country, and what it owes to that glorious Line of *Hanover*, that has adorned its throne with such an uninterrupted race of Heroes. What blessings have they not deriv'd on us, and our posterity, by their counsels at home, and their arms and courage abroad in the field ; by giving us the best contriv'd and the best executed laws, and by raising the trade, wealth, power, and glory of our country to such heights, that our enemies may envy, but cannot lessen, and our friends may admire, but know not how to increase?

And

And certainly, as our anceſtors uſed to ſay, when they were torn in pieces by their ſenſeleſs and diſtracted factions, *That* England *could only be ruin'd by* England ; ſo we may as truly maintain, that our happineſs, and (that greateſt of all our bleſſings) our Liberties, as now ſettled under our excellent Prince, can never be deſtroy'd but by Parliaments ; and our Church, as it now ſtands fenced in by human Laws, and founded on the divine Law, can only be overturn'd by the Fathers of it the Biſhops. As neither of thoſe caſes can be ſuppoſed poſſible, unleſs men ſhould break thro' the moſt ſacred truſts ; and, in ſpite of the moſt ſolemn obligations that nature, religion, and honour, can bind them by, prove falſe to their Poſterity, their Country, their King, and their God ; I think we may be juſtly ſecure of their continuance, and bid adieu to jealouſies and fears !

I return your Excellency my thanks for your two manuſcript treatiſes, which gave me much entertainment for three days, which I ſtole from the hurry of affairs in this reſtleſs town, to give to my gardens in my beloved retirement at *Windſor.* You have ſo high a reliſh for the true rational

3   plea-

pleasures of life, which are to be found in the silence and solitude of the country, that I shall easily persuade you to believe me, when I aver, that a debtor releas'd out of the City-*Marshalsea*, is not more transported with his liberty than I am, when I get loose from the crowd of importunate great beggars, (that besiege our chambers and anti-chambers, nay, our tables, and even our very beds, that should be sacred to peace and rest,) to breathe a little free air in that private retreat I am so fond of.

This was ever my way of thinking in my best health and vigor; but I must own, it grows much upon me of late, now that I am in the decline of life, and find the business of the world increase upon me, with the additional load of age and its infirmities. You will smile at me, may be, when I tell your Excellency, that I sometimes think seriously of retiring betimes, and living no longer, as I have done this thirty years, enslav'd to the world, and the wretched business of it, but to be at last possess'd of that delightful wish, *vivere sibi & musis*; or, to translate it into better *English*, to live to my self, and the great Author of all things.

When

When or whether ever I fhall be able to put this in execution, I cannot fay; but if I do not tell you my fixt refolutions, I tell you at leaft my fincere defires, which lie nearer my heart than any thing elfe on this fide of the grave; where, I think, I find many hints given me every hour, that I am foon to retire. I am fure the unreafonable fatigue I am forced to undergo at Court, will hurry me thither the fooner; and I often reflect on the remark in the *Talmud, That there is no prophet in the Old Teſtament,* (as they paft their days without care) but they out-liv'd four Kings: and that *Joſeph* died before his brethren; *becauſe,* fays the *Talmudiſts, he was turmoil'd and harraſs'd by being prime miniſter to* Pharaoh.

But thefe, you will fay, are but the little fretful fallies of a mind fick of confinement, and thirfting after liberty; let us therefore leave them, without juftifying them further with the leaft complaint of the malice, the envy, and ingratitude of the publick, which, (tho' perhaps not very fuccefsfully, yet ftill) we endeavour to ferve; and return to the bufinefs of the world, and the worthy Creatures that make up the Crowd, and contribute to the noife of it.

The

The beft news I can fend you from it (you fee, my Lord, death and the grave are ftill in my thoughts) is the departure of Sir *John Wingford*, the beft lawyer, and the worft judge that ever appear'd in *England*. He was, at the bottom, extremely avaricious; he had long refus'd the place of chief Juftice, which his Majefty had offer'd him, on account of his prodigious abilities, for the fake of the immenfe fums he got every year from the crowd of his clients. But as the fevere act againft lawyers exorbitant fees, and the infirmities of a bad conftitution and a wafted body in the latter part of his life, at length oblig'd him to comply with the defires of his Majefty, and indeed of mankind, to accept of it; he did it with the worft grace imaginable, and as haughtily, as tho' he had facrific'd the intereft of his family to the good of the nation.

I muft own, with fhame for my ignorance, that I was no fmall inftrument in fettling that affair; and I can make no better atonement for it, than confeffing that I have now reafon to believe, this firft and greateft of our lawyers, (whofe memory and imagination, whofe learning and judgment feem'd

E e 4   by

by turns to outdo not only mankind, but themselves,) to the disgrace of human nature, prov'd the vilest and most corrupt of judges ; and found the way, as I'm told, to make a comfortable balance between the bribes given his wife, and the fees of a private pleader at the bar. But he's gone to appear before the great Tribunal of his Maker, and therefore we shall leave him to stand or fall, as he pleases to determine ; and I shall only add to the trouble I am giving your Excellency, since we are upon this subject, the death of a much honester judge, but a weaker man, my Lord Chancellor *Hoskins,* who died last week, a few days before him, of a fit of the apoplexy, which took him off in an instant.

Tho' his abilities were vastly meaner, yet his probity and honesty were infinitely superior to the others ; but he had so perverse an integrity, that if any one attempted, or appeared to attempt, to lead or wheedle, or influence him in his decrees, he was sure to go the contrary way, where-ever it lead him. He carried this so far, that my Lord *D*—— having a suit before him for a great Estate with Mr. *L——p,* in which he was sure to be cast, contriv'd to get a certain

great

great man, whom I fhall not name, to recommend Mr. *L——p*'s intereft to him, with
a kind of menace if he did not do him juftice; by which fingle expedient he fo turn'd
the fcales, that he run violently and head-
long againft Mr. *L——p*; and indeed againft
juftice, and reafon, and equity, to avoid the
imaginary guilt of being influenc'd and biafs'd.

It is true, fome of his friends have attempted to make an apology for this weaknefs, by afferting, that on his being advan-
ced to that bench, he had been mifled in
his judgment in one of the firft caufes he
heard, by Mr. *P——l,* a near relation of
his Wife's; and as he had been feverely
cenfur'd for it, like the fcalded dog, he was
afraid of the leaft fhower of rain that threatned to fall on him: but furely this was but
giving a ftronger proof his weaknefs inftead
of excufing him, and fhews more fully
what vile and wretched creatures we are,
when our poor fcanty portion of reafon is
influenc'd by our paffions or folly.

But I will quit this ungrateful fubject for
one that ought to be more agreeable to you
and me; and that is, my fincere affurances,
that as much as I have ever been attach'd to

the

the intereft of your Excellency, and your noble family, I have never been biafs'd by any other regard, than that evident merit and juftice, which oblige me both by inclination and judgment to be, with the moft reafonable paffion and affection,

My L o r d,

Your Excellency's, &c.

N----m.

My L o r d,

Rome, Feb. 28. 1997.

BY the laft Courier by the way of *Lyons,* I was made happy in the receipt of your Lordfhip's of the 2ᵈ inftant, for which I return you my moft fincere thanks; and as I hope I fhall never forget the friendfhip and kindnefs you have exprefs'd for me in it, fo I fhall make it the ftudy of my life to deferve them more and more, by all the little fervices I am capable of rendring you and my royal Mafter.

I was favour'd with two difpatches of Mr. Secretary's the week before within fix days of each other, to which I made the propereft returns I could in the prefent ftate of things; and as they will be communicated to your Lordfhip, I fhall not give you

ɪ   the

the trouble of a needlefs repetition of them here. I have, fince I made thofe anfwers, communicated the contents of them, and the advices and orders that occafion'd them, to the Imperial and *French* Ambaffadors here; who feem very unanimous in entring into all his Majefty's meafures, and exprefs greater refolution and refentment againft this Court, than I could have expected from the indifferent pofture of their affairs at prefent.

They have given me fuch peremptory af-furances of this kind, and of acting in con-cert with our Court, that I am fully con-vinc'd, if the Emperor's health continues to improve, we fhall be able to give a greater blow to the ambitious views of this Empire of the *Vatican*, than fhe has receiv'd fince *George* IVth oblig'd her forces to repafs the *Alps*, and leave *France* in peace, and the *Swifs* in full poffeffion of *Piedmont*, and that part of *Savoy* which they have ever fince been mafters of.

Your Lordfhip's reflections on the im-meafurable growth of the Papal Power, and the weaknefs and blindnefs of thofe who contributed to it, are equally becoming your experience and knowledge as a ftatefman, and the honeft zeal of a *Briton* and a Proteftant.

teſtant. If you expreſs ſome reſentment, it ariſes from a generous concern for the welfare and liberty of *Europe*, and the Honour of Chriſtianity; both which have been in the moſt daring manner endanger'd, not to ſay deſtroy'd, by the inſatiable ambition of this pretended Vicegerent of Heaven.

I am infinitely rejoic'd, that what I have hitherto been able to remit to you from hence, has been any ways agreeable to your Lordſhip; and ſhall therefore continue to ſend you ſuch obſervations of the ſame nature, as I think may entertain you. This I am ſure is a nobler uſe than any thing I am able to furniſh you with can deſerve to be applied to. The truth is, your Lordſhip has brought me ſo deeply in your debt by your laſt letter, that I fear all the diligence and means I can uſe, will be too little to balance accounts in any tolerable manner with you. However, I will depend on your goodneſs to accept of ſuch inconſiderable payments as I am capable of making you. To begin ſome attempt this way, I muſt acquaint your Lordſhip, that ſince my laſt letters to Mr. Secretary, according to my inſtructions, in concert with the two Ambaſſadors, I demanded an audience of his Holineſs the 20th inſtant;

to

to which I was immediately admitted, tho'
he was that morning something indifpos'd, by
a cold he had got the day before, by walking too late in his gardens.

I found him in his great chamber hung
with purple velvet, where he receiv'd me the
firft time I had audience of him; and as I
perceiv'd by his fmiling on me when I enter'd, and by the contenance he put on when
I begun to fpeak to him, that he either was,
or defir'd to make me think he was perfectly
pleas'd with me, I refolv'd both to deliver
the Memorial on the part of his Majefty in
relation to the Inquifition; and alfo to lay
before him, that in prefenting it, I not only
obey'd my Mafter's commands, but alfo in
every line of it fpoke the fenfe of the Emperor and his moft Chriftian Majefty. Accordingly I acquainted his Holinefs, that I
had demanded that audience on an affair of
the greateft importance to the reputation of
the *Roman* See, the happinefs of *France*, and
the quiet of all her neighbours, who were
deeply interefted therein. That his Holinefs,
by the fuggeftions of men of unquiet and
turbulent fpirits, who were better underftood
than nam'd, had of late made feveral extraordinary fteps to the fetting up the Inquifition

tion in *France,* where his Predeceffors had
never once thought of eftablifhing it; and
as fuch an attempt will infallibly be accompanied by feveral ill confequences, I humbly
befought him that he would, with that
calmnefs and goodnefs which diftinguifh'd
his character, allow me to lay before him
thofe preffing reafons, which made it at all
times improper, and at this time utterly impracticable. I obferv'd he blufh'd at thefe
words; and rubbing his forehead with his
hand, feem'd to be more than ordinarily
mov'd; and as I expected he would have
fpoke, I ftopp'd a little that I might frame
what I had to fay, as near as I could, to the
temper he fhould put on; but as he only
nodded to me, and bid me go on, I immediately proceeded.

That if thofe who prefs'd his Holinefs to
follow fuch counfels would confider the reafons that made fuch an attempt both now
and at all times unadvifable, they would not
fhew fuch warmth and paffion in carrying it
on, as they manifeftly had done. That
thefe reafons were founded, Firft, on the natural temper of the *French,* who being of a
free communicative difpofition, and wearing their hearts as it were at their lips, would
be

be expos'd to a thoufand accufations for words, that proceed from mere levity and gaiety of mind, rather than any guilt or wickednefs of the heart, where herefy can only be feated.

That in the fecond place, it was notorious that there was no nation in *Chriftendom* where hereticks had been fo effectually purg'd and driven out, even to the lofs of many millions of fubjects, as in *France*; and this both by open wars and private maffacres, as well as the fierceft perfecutions, tho' againft the folemn ftipulations of formal treaties, in which the honour of the Crown was conftantly facrific'd to its zeal for Religion, and its regard for this See.

That in the third place, as none of his Holinefs's Predeceffors had ever refolv'd on fuch an attempt before, it would be confider'd in *France* as the moft violent outrage againft the liberty of the fubject, and the honour of the Crown, that could be contriv'd by the greateft enemies of both: and as *France* abounded with difcontented people, and was ftill labouring under its late misfortunes, an innovation of that fort would be attended with fuch commotions and factions, as muft end in an utter fubverfion of

the

the Royal, if the Inquifition fhould be efta-blifh'd; or if refifted by force, and fuccef-fully oppos'd, of the Papal Authority. As I kept my eye fix'd on his Holinefs, I plain-ly perceiv'd his colour come and go at thefe words, that fhew'd an extraordinary emotion within; but as he put on a pretended fmile, and endeavour'd to difguife it, by coughing two or three times, and ftroaking his face with his handkerchief, and as I apprehended there was as much fear as anger in his contenance, I made no paufe, but continued my remon-ftrances.

That, fourthly, as the power of the Cler-gy had of late years been carried higher than ever, and that as his Holinefs had by the laft treaty poffefs'd himfelf of two of the ftrong-eft places of *Dauphine*, and almoft entirely mafter'd *Savoy*, and thereby, in effect, pof-fefs'd the keys of *France* as abfolutely as thofe of St. *Peter*, this new attempt would be confider'd as fetting up a Monarchy within a Monarchy, and opening the gates thereby to new violences, rapine and war.

That, fifthly, as fome (and his Holinefs beft knew who) have and do obftinately maintain, that the Clergy are not fubject to their fecular Princes, nor oblig'd to obey
their

their Laws, whether contrary to the Ecclefiaftical Eftate or no, the leaft Princes could
do, was to prevent their Lay Subjects being
liable to imprifonment, corporal punifhment,
and even torture and death, from this terrible tribunal of the Clergy, efpecially fince
fuch power was exprefly againft the laws of
the land.

That, in the fixth place, as there had
been high difputes between the moft Chriftian Kings and his Holinefs's predeceffors,
concerning the privileges, rights and immunities of the *Gallican* Church, and the extent of the Papal Authority; the Tribunal
of the Inquifition might be applied to extirpate fuch doctrines, and thofe who maintain them, as herefies and hereticks, to the
endangering the power of the Crown and
Church of that Nation. That moreover, as
the Ecclefiaftical Laws, eftablifh'd in 1897.
by *Paul* the IXth, had determin'd, that fubjects might refufe tributes and taxes to their
Sovereigns without fin, if they thought them
unjuft; and might difobey any other legally proclaim'd Law of their refpective Princes,
which they judg'd very inconvenient for
them to fubmit to; and as all loyal fubjects
in *France* were generally of a different opinion,

F f   nion,

nion, they might, on declaring their fentiments herein, be taken up and detained in
the prifons of the Inquifition as hereticks,
on account of their being loyal and good
Frenchmen.

In the eighth place, as to matters merely
fpiritual, fince many doctrines are taught by
certain divines (whom his Holinefs highly
efteem'd) as true, which the Chriftian Church
have been fo far from approving, that they
have violently oppos'd them as falfe, and
overturning the very foundations of Chriftianity; if the Power of the Inquifition fhould
be lodg'd (as it certainly would) in thofe very hands, the beft Catholicks might be imprifon'd and tortur'd by fuch as hereticks,
for holding the real doctrines of Chriftianity; which poffibly has been fometimes the
cafe.

Here his Holinefs, who had hitherto been
entirely filent, was no longer able to conceal his impatience; but looking with a
fix'd and ftern countenance at me, ask'd me,
if I had any thing further to offer to him?
To which I thought it beft to reply (cutting
off two or three lefs agreeable remonftrances, that I fhould not too far incenfe him)
that I had not. I have in command how-

I

ever, added I, to enforce all I have said to your Holineſs, with repreſenting it as the common ſentiments of the Emperor, as well as his moſt Chriſtian Majeſty and my Maſter; in all whoſe names I humbly beſought him to accept the Memorial I had in charge to deliver to him, (and therewithal I took it out of my breaſt, and in a very reſpectful manner preſented it to him) beſeeching his calm conſideration and favourable anſwer to it.

He took it ſomewhat haſtily, and put it into his pocket; and after a ſhort pauſe anſwer'd me very calmly (being, as I conceiv'd by his mien and geſtures, glad I had done) and told me, *imperatoria brevitate*, it ſhould be fully conſider'd, and as fully anſwer'd.

I ſaw evidently how diſagreeable an entertainment I had given his Holineſs; and being deſirous, if poſſible, to ſmooth his temper, which I had ruffled too far by ſpeaking more truth to him in half an hour, than probably he had heard in all his Pontificate before; I pulled out the Catalogue of our Nobility I had been favour'd with from your Lordſhip, very fairly copied and tranſlated, and told him, in obedience to his commands, I had procur'd him the Liſt of the *Britiſh* Peerage in the preſent Parliament.

He

He feem'd glad to have the fcene and the fubject fhifted; and taking it from me, and looking on the title, he ask'd me immediately how many Catholicks there were among them? To which I replied, after fome hefitation, that in his Holinefs's fenfe of things there was not one Catholick Peer in *Great Britain*; but that in our opinion, there was not one Heretick among the whole of our Nobility. He appear'd not a little furpriz'd, tho' he made me no anfwer; but look'd at me with an odd mixture of difguft and aftonifhment in his contenance, by which I plainly faw he was lefs acquainted with our affairs than I imagin'd. Immediately herewith, finding my attempt to remove his ill humour was likely to increafe it, and conceiving my retiring would probably be the moft agreeable compliment I could make him, (fince I faw him not a little perplex'd and difturb'd) I put an end to my audience with the beft looks and the beft *Italian*, I could get together for the occafion.

I made not the leaft mention, as your Lordfhip fees, of the other articles relating to the *Swifs* Cantons, and our trade and fleet in thefe feas; becaufe I judg'd it improper to infift on them now, when he appear'd in none of the beft difpofitions to anfwer me as I could defire. I hope therefore you will approve of my delaying them for fome happier hour, and the *mollia tempora fandi*, which I fhall not fail to watch for, and take hold of, and give an exact account of the anfwers I receive thereon.

I know not whether it may not be agreeable, after entertaining your Lordfhip with this audience, to give you fome account of the prefent Pope *Innocent* the XIXth; and though I doubt I fhall draw his picture very unfkilfully, I fhall at leaft endeavour to avoid two great faults of Limners, and fhall both give you a fketch that fhall refemble him, and yet one that fhall not flatter him. He is in his perfon a low, broad, ftrongmade man, and fomewhat of the *ftaturâ quadratâ Suetonius* gives to *Vefpafian*. He is of a faturnine complexion, and melancholy afpect, with large black eyes and a bottle nofe, a well-fhap'd mouth, but which appears with lefs advantage when he laughs, (which indeed is feldom) having very bad teeth; which however would fhew better had he more of them. He is reckon'd perfectly chafte as to women, his chief pleafures being eating and drinking a little too

volup-

voluptuoufly, and ufing much exercife either by hunting or hawking when he rides,
or walking long in his gardens. He is not
however much given to his bed, feldom
fleeping more than feven hours; and even
in the heats of the fummer avoids repofing
himfelf in the day time. He feldom minds
books any farther than to buy vaft quantities
of them, to crowd his favourite library; and,
after the *Italian* tafte, he is fond of filling it
with vaft collections of admirable pictures,
bufts and ftatues, being a paffionate admirer of antiquity in all its branches, as his fine
cabinets do plainly fhew. However, he
loves the company of learned men, but
chiefly thofe of his own Order, by whom
he is continually furrounded, and who
would willingly exclude all others from his
notice, as well as his favour.

He is about 52, and has been now fix
years Pope; and as he was chofen, as I may
fay, to the Pontificate before *Pius* the VIIIth
his predeceffor died, chiefly for his zeal for
his Order, he has not, fince he attained that
dignity, given away one confiderable Place,
Abbey, or Benefice, but by the advice of
the Cardinals in full Confiftory.

He

He has but one Nephew that he has ever shewn the least regard for, and to him he has only given the hat, and some benefices, which in all are worth but about 30000 l. sterling annual rent; but he is so very dissolute and debauch'd, and of such mean parts and abilities, (and especially since no Popes are elected till they are sworn not to lavish the wealth and preferments of the Church on their families) that it is thought he will do no more for him. All his other relations he is so cold to, whether in regard to his oath, or for want of natural affection, that he has not admitted them to come to *Rome* but once since his election, and that but for a few weeks, sending them home with very moderate presents.

He is a *Milanese*, of a pretty good family; his father Don *Mario Franzoni* having a considerable ancient estate in the neighbourhood of that city, to which his being heir, was the first occasion of his being entic'd by the Jesuits (with their usual policy) to enter into their Society, tho' they had conceiv'd great hopes of him for his talents and abilities, which were very extraordinary. When he grew up, he answer'd all their expectations;

and

and being made Secretary to the famous Cardinal of *Santineri*, who was employ'd in so many important negotiations, and afterwards as Nuntio at the Courts of *France* and *Spain* successively, (in the late wars between the two Crowns) he shewed what he was able to do, by gaining his esteem, who was one of the ablest and severest judges of men.

When his master was made Pope, he soon got the reward of his many and faithful services, being in two or three years time made Bishop of *Padua*, *Maestro di Camera* to the Pope, Archbishop of *Milan*, Legate of *Ferrara*, Nuncio to *Venice*, and at last Cardinal, with the title of *Santa Maria in Aquino*. In these posts he gained the love and admiration of all, both as an excellent master of Politicks, an upright Judge, and one whose prudence and wisdom knew how to influence every one, and be influenc'd by none. He has a great turn to business, is indefatigable in weighing and considering whatever he sets about, and finding out the best and easiest means to bring it to pass, determining nothing but on sure grounds, shewing the clearest head, and the firmest resolution in every thing he takes cognizance of, or sets himself to accomplish. There is

2   nothing

nothing too deep, too dark, or too weighty for the ftrength of his parts, having no de-fect but the want of learning, which he makes ample amends for, by that kind of knowledge which is moft cultivated by his fociety, a perfect experience of affairs, and a thorough infight into the nature of man-kind, who are the tools of their ambition and policy.

He is indeed fomewhat apt to give way to paffion, and to act with too little diffimu-lation with regard to others with whom he is offended; and efpecially in fpeaking againft thofe whofe follies, or irregularities in their conduct, difpleafe him. This had like to have loft him the Pontificate; but as that was concerted in the late Pope's life, his enemies were not able to put him by; and indeed they could hardly have chofen a man likelier to ferve the fociety, and preferve, if not enlarge their power, if it were poffible to carry it further. His fcheme to get himfelf chofen Emperor, is a manifeft proof of this, the fuccefs where-of is but too likely, if his Imperial Maje-fty fhould relapfe, before his defign can be fufficiently countermin'd.

He

He has few very intimate favourites, dividing his kindnefs equally among the ableft of the Cardinals, who are moft capable and defirous to ferve the fociety, which has been the inviolable maxim this See has obferv'd ever fince it became the inheritance of the Jefuits. But as I have taken up a great part of this difpatch with defcribing what I knew of this extraordinary perfon, I fhall defer giving your Lordfhip the characters of the moft confiderable Cardinals who are chiefly employ'd by him in his weightieft affairs ; and fhall now pafs to fome other matters that deferve your notice.

And the firft thing I fhall mention is, the extraordinary Bull which his Holinefs has juft publifh'd, in relation to keeping of *Lent* with lefs ftrictnefs than formerly. The original Bull in *Latin* is very voluminous, and therefore I fhall content my felf to fend fuch an abftract, as fhall take in the fubftance of the whole, only omiting fuch unneceffary forms as occafion its length.

It begins then with a fort of preface, in which his Holinefs *Innocent* XIX. addreffing himfelf to all true fons of the holy *Roman* church, takes notice of the univer-

fal

fal care of the faithful incumbent upon him, and the perpetual follicitude he is under, both for the falvation of fouls, and the eafe and happinefs of the chriftian world. He fervently exhorts all the faithful to exert their beft endeavours to prevent the daily revolts and falling off of fo many members of the catholick church, who in thefe evil, nay, worft of times, on whom the ends of the world are come, are deluded by hereticks, and led away by the Devil into the paths of error, and the dangerous infection of the northern fchifm.

After enlarging a good deal on this point, he proceeds to take notice, that whereas the fevere difcipline of the church, conformable to the zeal of the primitive times, concerning the abftaining from flefh in *Lent*, had been found to produce fundry great inconveniences to the fcrupulous obfervers thereof; (all which are enumerated and enlarg'd on with very pathetick complaints :) Therefore, fays the Bull, to lighten fuch burthens, which, like an heavy yoke, do gall the neck of our zealous catholick children ; and, to make the obfervance of *Lent* lefs painful to them ; we, by virtue

tue of the fupreme authority committed to us from above, have thought fit to pronounce and determine, and by thefe prefents do abfolutely determine and decree, that all wild fowl, and more particularly and efpecially thofe which refort to and generally live on the water, and frequent rivers, ponds, lakes and feas, be from henceforth deem'd and taken as fifh, and be ufed, underftood, receiv'd and taken as fuch, by the faithful for ever.

Moreover, that no doubt, fufpicion, or fcruple herein may remain in the minds of all true catholicks, concerning the deeming, taking, ufing, underftanding, receiving and eating the feveral kinds of fowl, for real and actual fifh, as we have and hereby do pronounce and decree by our fufficient authority and determination; we have thought fit to annex and fubjoin hereunto thofe cogent and weighty reafons and motives, that have determin'd our judgment in this matter, in which the falvation of fouls, our great and chief care, is fo deeply embark'd.

Firft then, whereas the original foundation of fifh being appointed to be eat in *Lent*, was greatly built on the opinions

of

of thofe eminent phyficians and philofophers *Galen, Hippocrates, Chryfippus,* and *Erafi-ftratus,* who maintain'd, that fifh do not nourifh any more than water, into which they are immediately turn'd, we do declare the fame to be falfe and abfurd, groundlefs and ridiculous. For tho' *Ariofttle,* in his fifth book, does maintain that opinion, whofe great authority, with thofe afore-cited, did too far influence the piety of the church herein; yet it is found by conftant experience, that thofe kinds, formerly only accounted as fifh, do rather nourifh the body more than thofe kinds, which we have, and hereby do allow to the faithful. It is alfo as vulgar and trivial an error, that thofe kinds of fifh were appointed to be eaten in faft-days, and in *Lent* particularly, be-caufe in the Deluge the fea and all kinds of fifh, efcap'd the general curfe that fell on other creatures, the earth and its pro-ductions; for it is certain, that curfe fell equally on all.

But, fecondly, our judgment hath been grounded on thefe other important reafons; firft, becaufe of the great and furprizing con-formity between thefe two fpecies of animals, the feathers of the one anfwering the fcales

of

of the other, as the clearnefs, fluidity and brightnefs of the water, the element of the one, doth to the air, the ufual element of the other; in both which elements alfo they do mutually live, as a fort of amphibious creatures, as the diving of waterfowl, and the flying of fome fifh, and the frisking and leaping out of water of all, do plainly manifeft.

But further, this conformity is found alfo in the fins of the one correfponding to the wings of the other, and that they agree in that remarkable circumftance peculiar to them, of moving the lower eye-lid only, and that many of them have a kind of holes in their heads for eyes and ears which no other animals have; and, which is ftill more wonderful, neither of them have bladders, or do ftale or urine like other creatures; and the very motion of the one in the air, (the tail ferving as a rudder to both) is nearly refembling that of the other in the water. But there is ftill behind a yet more furprizing proof of this great conformity between them, and which has been of great weight with us; and that is, that the globules of their blood are both of an oval figure, which is found in no other animals,

animals, as is evident every day to thofe who make ufe of microfcopes, which put this point out of all doubt.

But, thirdly, what has mightily determinin'd us herein, is the conftant ufage of all our predeceffors in the *Roman* See, who have ever allow'd the fea-fowl call'd the *Macreufe*, to be deem'd, eaten and taken as fifh; which is a plain Indication, that our prefent decrees and determinations are in all refpects bottom'd on the fame truths, and conformable to theirs. It is true, the learned *Naudæus* has pretended to prove that wild fowl, and efpecially the *Macreufe* aforefaid, cannot be reckon'd fifh, becaufe all animals that have necks, have lungs, and if lungs cannot be fifh: But this is fo vile and falfe a way of reafoning, that it deferves not to be confuted, fince both whales, and dolphins are fifh, and yet have lungs, as the learned * *Scaliger* plainly proves againft *Cardan.*

But, 4thly, we have made this decree alfo for the good of fouls, becaufe we continually find many, who, thro' the former feverity, are alienated in their affection to holy catholick church, and fall off daily to the hereticks; or at leaft, if they do

* Exercit. *p.* 224.   not

not revolt from us, endanger their fouls, by incurring our excommunication, and privately eating flesh, which is fo exprefsly forbidden on that terrible penalty.

In the 5th place, we have confider'd the tendernefs and delicacy of fome conftitutions, which are frequently endanger'd by being confin'd at that feafon from all forts of flesh ; and moreover, we find by experience, that there are fewer children got in *Lent,* which is much to be laid to heart in a church, which ever has, and we truft ever will, depend on her numbers. There is alfo lefs work and husbandry done then, from the fame caufe, men as well as beafts being then much weaker, by having been pinch'd by the bitternefs of winter, and at the fame time ftinted in their food ; many weaker husbandmen being alfo killed by the change of diet. Nay, this evil extends to their very calves, kids and lambs, which are frequently ftarv'd, or at beft ftinted in their growth, by having little milk left to fuckle them ; all which are heavy grievances, and produce many ill confequences to our catholick children.

Laftly, we have been mov'd hereunto by two fpecial reafons. The one is, becaufe
while

while our faithful fons are thus pinch'd and burthen'd, hereticks thrive, and are fatted by their loffes, keeping at leaft 9000 veffels in taking fifh, which they extort great rates for from our people, to the great detriment of our church, and the intolerable increafe of their naval power. But our other reafon is no lefs confiderable, and that is, that *Lent* is moft unequally fettled and appointed throughout the chriftian world ; for while the faithful in *Europe* are thus bow'd down to the grave, by the feverity of the church, others, in different regions of the world, have their *Lent* in fo favourable a time of the year, that their fruits and gardens load them with all kinds of delights. Of this laft point, *Chile*, and its fruitful country and climate, among many others, is a flagrant inftance ; and therefore it is but fit to bring all catholick chriftians herein upon a greater equality, and to prevent *Europe* from envying the advantages of the youngeft daughter of the church, *America*.

For thefe therefore, and many other as important reafons, which it is needlefs, or improper to infert here ; we, out of our paternal care of the faithful, have, and here-

G g

by

by do decree, that all wild fowl, and especially all water-fowl aforefaid, be from henceforth deem'd, taken, receiv'd, underftood
and eaten as fifh by all catholicks, of whatever region, country or climate ; and we
alfo, in tender regard to the faithful,
do allow all *Englifh* and *Dutch* Brawn to
be taken, eaten, receiv'd, deem'd and us'd
as Sturgeon, as well becaufe the flefhy parts
thereof, are fo macerated by the boiling,
pickling, and long keeping, as to have lefs,
and more wholfome nourifhment in it, than
any kind of fifh ; and alfo, becaufe as it is
entirely of heretick growth, it is probably
lefs nutritive, than the pooreft fort of viands
in chriftian and catholick countries.

Laftly, for the greater eafe, confolation,
and fatisfaction of all the faithful, and that
their bodies may not be worfe treated than
thofe of fchifmaticks and hereticks, when
their fouls are fo much better fecur'd and
provided for; we do further determine and
decree, that as well on all faft-days, as
throughout the whole of *Lent*, it fhall be
lawful to all our Nuncio's, Bifhops, and
parifh-priefts, and all proper officers duly au-
thoriz'd by us to that end, to iffue licenfes
to all fick people, or all that are afraid of be-

2

ing

ing fick, or otherwife incommoded, (or apprehenfive of being incommoded in their health or ftrength by abftaining from flefh, when the allowance of fuch fowl or fifh is not fufficienly agreeable to them) to eat all and every kind of flefh, that they fhall judge to contribute more effectually, to the fuftenance and comfort of their bodies, in their pilgrimage here. Provided always, that all fuch perfons do regularly take out authentick licenfes for the fame, and pay, if rich, for fuch licenfe, either for the whole *Lent*, or the year, the fum of twenty Scudi, or, if poor, the fum of two Scudi, and no more.

And to prevent, cut off, filence and confute for ever, all debates, cavils, difputes or objections hereon; we do hereby declare, that all and every perfon who fhall in any wife oppofe, contradict, argue againft, or in any fort contravene this our decree, is, and fhall be adjudg'd to ftand excommunicated, and cut off, as a rotten member, from the body of the holy catholick church; unlefs by his full and ample fubmiffion, repentance and retractation, he fhall be abfolv'd for the fame. Given under the feal of the Fifher, this 19th of *February*, 1998. and in the fixth year of our Pontificate.

Thus,

Thus, my Lord, I have perform'd my promife, and given you an abftract of their famous Bull, the political views of which will fufficiently employ your Lordfhip's thoughts. There is nothing more certain, than that this See has refolv'd on new modelling their church, finding by experience the abfolute neceffity there is for it. For altho' the power of the *Roman Vatican* is vaftly increas'd, it is evident their intereft with all catholick Princes is greatly funk. Indeed they are almoft on the wing to depart from her, if the vaft height of that deluge of riches, ftrength and intereft were but once fo far abated; that, like *Noah*'s dove, they could find a fafe place for even the fole of their foot to retreat to, and not be oblig'd to return unto the prifon of the ark, when they have taken their flight from it. The only hold this See has of them, is very different from that they had in antient times; for then fhe was reverenc'd as the real head of the chriftian church, arm'd with the divine authority; whereas fhe is now regarded as a temporal tyrant, who makes religion but the ftalking horfe to univerfal empire. How greatly this has fhaken her authority among the Princes of *Europe*, and alarm'd

I   their

their jealoufies, is perfectly known to your Lordfhip, as well as the vaft increafe of credit and reputation that the proteftant faith hath obtain'd hereby in the world. And tho' reafons of ftate, and their jealoufies of our trade and power, keep them too much eftrang'd from us; yet fuch a crifis of affairs may come, as may unite them all with us fo far, as to renounce the papal authority, and fet up patriarchs of their own, and as probably reform the faith, as alter the government of their churches.

Indeed the ill fuccefs of the *French* King, in attempting this, has kept them greatly in awe, together with the vaft power of the clergy in their refpective Kingdoms. For the chief ecclefiafticks being entirely Jefuits, or their creatures, do their utmoft to fupport the intereft of the *Vatican*, and to watch every motion of their fovereigns, that looks like the leaft encroachment on the papal authority. In the mean time, all poffible meafures are taken at *Rome*, to prevent either the people or their fovereigns, taking new difgufts at her towring ambition. It is this probably has occafion'd the Bull I have fent you; which, as ridiculous as the pretences in it are, will pleafe the people

extreme-

extremely; and will alfo hurt our royal fifhery, and leffen the numbers of our feamen, at the fame time that it takes off one great burthen that lay on the good catholicks fhoulders.

There is another point, which this See is as fond of correcting as the affair of *Lent*, and that is, the vaft damage they receive from the celibacy of the Clergy, and the numbers of hands which are every year cut off from them, by fhutting up fuch crowds in monafteries and nunneries. Thefe might bring an incredible addition of ftrength to the Church and all popifh Princes, if they had not, by fuch filly monaftick inftitutions, made them ufelefs to both. It is not to be denied, but that this method has produc'd great genius's in their Church, who, by brooding over their melancholy, and clofely purfuing their ftudies, have made a great figure, either for piety, abftinence and charity, or for learning and knowledge, (efpecially in divinity); the ableft pens for the intereft of this See having been pluck'd from the wings of the poor creatures that are fed, and fhut up in thefe hen-houfes. The Church has alfo found her account by encouraging celibacy, from

the

the great wealth many of thofe her unmarried votaries have left her heir to ; but the
fcandal that has fallen on her by the irregularities many of them, unable to bear
thefe reftraints, have daily run into, have,
in my opinion, largely over-balanc'd her
Gains.

Befides, I am perfuaded, for one great
genius in piety or learning her monafteries
and the celibacy of her Clergy have produc'd,
they have loft and buried ten, that would
otherwife have been ferviceable to the
Church or State : while, under a filly pretence of defpifing the world and its glory
as vain and finful, they have lull'd thoufands of excellent perfons afleep, and dead-
ned them to all regard for their Country,
or any ambition to excel in ufeful knowledge and practice of the Sciences, or employing themfelves in the civil arts of peace
and war, in which the good of fociety is
fo deeply concern'd. This is a prodigious
damage done to the publick ; but there is
another that fits heavier on them, which
they are more concern'd at ; and that is,
their occafioning an immenfe draw-back on
their numbers, and in proportion diminifh-
ing their ftrength and their power.

G g 4

Let

Let us confider this a little, my Lord, as to *France* and our own Country, fince the antient reformation of religion among us; excluding all confideration of the damage to Chriftianity in general for fo many centuries before. As I know *France* pretty well, I think I have grounds to fay, there were no lefs than 300000 churchmen and nuns under vows of celibacy at that time in that Kingdom; and probably not fewer than 120000 under the fame denomination in *Great-Britain* and *Ireland*; the breed of all which numbers we have gain'd for 500 years, and that of all their defcendants; and the *French* have loft, and confequently in propoortion, all other catholick Countries.

It is plain that this is of infinite fervice to one party, and of equal detriment to the other; and in a few centuries more, as their numbers muft daily fink, and their trade, wealth and manufactures in proportion with them, it is eafy to forefee that the balance will ftill be turning, and at laft decide in favour of the Proteftants; tho' the advantages of the evidence and truth of their doctrines, and the difcovery of the faults

and

and errors of the Papifts, fhould no way contribute thereunto.

I have feen computations that pretend to demonftrate, that by this fingle miftake in politicks, and cutting off the breed of fuch numbers, whofe real abilities and bodies might have rais'd fuch powerful recruits to their caufe; the Church of *Rome* has loft near 30 millions of fouls, whofe labour, trade and wealth, were they now in being, might have prov'd a vaft over-balance of the proteftant intereft and power. At the fame time, as tho' this was not enough, befides the tyranny of their Government and the Inquifition, they as it were ftrive to leffen their numbers ftill more ; by almoft daily fafts, pilgrimages, and annual *Lents*, and an unpardonable connivance at adultery and whoredom (not to mention the unnatural fin;) all which are vaft draw-backs and difcouragements to matrimony. As the Proteftants have wifely avoided thefe faults, it is evident what advantages we have over them, if we make a right ufe of them. And yet after all, it is to be fear'd, that the perpetual policy, induftry and application of this See, and the coldnefs and fleepinefs of our people, may be fo ill match'd,

match'd, as to give them too many occafions of breaking in on us, by our divifions and factions, and yielding them the
victory, which we indolently rely on Providence for, and they, by fo many plots, artifices, and engines of ftate, are perpetually
contriving to obtain.

But as I acquainted your Lordfhip, that
the Jefuits are very fenfible of the inconveniences we have been remarking on, I
muft do them the juftice to take notice of
feveral remedies they have of late apply'd to
this evil in *Italy*, and where-ever they have
intereft and power to put them in practice.

And in the firft place, it is generally believ'd, that they indulge numbers of their
Clergy in private marriages, who have not
the gift of continence ; but this is manag'd
with great addrefs and fecrecy, and cannot bring in very large recruits to them. In
the next place, they keep a fevere hand on
the admiffion of perfons into their monafteries, allowing much fewer than ever to be
harboured there, and only fuch as would be
ufelefs or troublefome to the world, if they
were in it. Nay, I am affur'd, that two or
three pious Bifhops having left lately large
fums

fums by their wills to the founding new monafteries; this Court order'd a ftop to be put to them, and divided the money among the neighbouring poor; which fhews their fentiments on this head. They have alfo of late made feveral laws, by one of which all unmarried laymen or women are oblig'd, if paft forty, to pay one fifth of their income to portion poor virgins and young tradef-men who marry. By another they have re-viv'd the *Roman Papian* law, by which all who were unmarried after twenty-five, are incapable of giving or receiving a legacy; and by a third they have re-eftablifh'd the *Jus trium liberorum* of old *Rome*, by which parents who have three or more grown chil-dren living, are favour'd with an exemption from certain taxes. Thefe have had extra-ordinary effects; nor have their allowing of divorces, in cafe of barren or very unhappy marriages, and obliging both parties to mar-ry others, and of late punifhing whoredom and adultery with great feverity; and above all, their obliging mothers to nurfe their own children, (by the neglect of hir'd nurfes, thoufands of infants being daily loft to the commonwealth) been of lefs benefit to
the

the filling their exhaufted Country with its trueft riches, numbers of fubjects.

Thefe, my Lord, are ufeful regulations indeed ; but as they are but of late date, and come like the prefcriptions of wife phy-ficians in an old confumption, where the lungs are too far fpent and wafted, it is very uncertain how far they may prove fuccefsful; and at worft, we have the pleafure to know, we have the benefit of them of a long time in *Great-Britain,* by the care of the wifeft legiflature, and the beft of Princes that ever watch'd over the publick interefts.

Before I conclude this fubject, I cannot but acquaint your Lordfhip with an anfwer I once had from a zealous Jefuit in this city, who, dif-courfing on it with me, maintain'd that the Proteftants, who glory in the increafe of their numbers, do multiply merely from the curfe of God upon them, that by a juft judgment he might have the more victims, to pour down his vengeance on, for their herefies, wars, and numberlefs fins againft the Church. For, faid he, in the zeal of his heart, had they kept up monafteries and nunneries, God had want-ed fome millions of facrifices, to fuffer for

the

the fins of themfelves and their parents. You fee, my Lord, how conveniently the charity of the good fociety would difpofe of us, tho' we increas'd fafter than we do ; they want but power fufficient to their wills, or they would enforce their opinions by real facts, and convince us abundantly, that Heaven had mark'd us out for vengeance. But I have enlarg'd too far on this fubject already, and fhall therefore increafe your Lordfhip's trouble no further, by fpeaking to fome other particulars mention'd in your laft, which I fhall chufe to referve for another occafion ; and fhall trefpafs no longer on your patience, than to affure you of my beft diligence, in anfwering the ends of my refidence here, and my fhewing my felf with a heart fully fenfible of all your favours,

My L o r d,

Your Lordfhip's, &c.

H e r t f o r d.

My L o r d,

London, Chelfea, April. 5. 1998.

NOtwithftanding the pleafure I have ever had in your Excellency's correfpondence, I am in pain to begin it to day,

day, with acknowledging, that tho' I have been honour'd with three of yours of *Nov.* 29th, *Jan.* 17th, and *March* the 8th, from *Mosco*; I have never yet been able to make my acknowledgments for them, except by a very short answer to the two first, which deserv'd a very different return. But the truth is, I have ever liv'd on such good terms, and with so entire an intimacy with your Excellency, that I am in less pain how to excuse my self to one, who hath ever lov'd even my faults; and will therefore the easier pardon any involuntary omissions of the respect which I owe you. I can the easier hope, to find your Excellency favourable in your construction of my long silence, when I tell you, I have had more perplexing and uneasy affairs on my hands of late, than I ever remember since I knew this Court.

As they are at last pretty well over, I hope I shall be able to prove a better correspondent now to your Excellency than I have been; by being for some time more than ordinarily engag'd, in endeavouring to be as faithful a servant to my royal master, as my infirmities and labours increasing together, would allow me. Besides, not

not to accufe my felf too far, I muft plead in my defence, that I have ever had my fhare in the trouble of moft of Mr. Secretary's difpatches to *Mofco*; fo that my offences are only perfonal trangreffions againft your Excellency's goodnefs, and which is a great matter for a minifter to have to fay, I have at leaft no national guilt to anfwer for.

That I may atone for the faults I confefs fo fincerely, I muft begin with my beft thanks for your account of the ftate of our affairs at your Court ; and as you have put our trade there on an excellent footing, I doubt not but our merchants will find their intereft in it, as we may fee already they do, by their having fent double the number of fhips, on the account of the increafe of that branch of our commerce, than they formerly us'd to do.

As his Majefty refolves to keep up the beft correfpondence poffible with the Czar, and to have a Refident at leaft, if not an Ambaffador, perpetually with him, to preferve a conftant mutual intercourfe of good offices between the two Crowns, and favour our traders thither all we can ; fo I believe nothing but your being wearied

of

of that employment, will incline him to recall your Excellency. I believ'd indeed by your long continuance in that Court as an Ambaffador, you were almoft chang'd into a perfect *Ruffian* ; but I never expected to fee your Excellency turn'd a downright *Laplander*, as one muft almoft fuppofe you, by the relation you give of one of the moft incredible things, that ever this or any age before it, heard of.

For my part, I fhall never difpute againft abfolute fact, and a fact your Excellency declares your felf an eye-witnefs of ; but I can affure you, his Majefty has not fo ftrong a faith ; and is of opinion, you have either a mind to laugh at us, or to make us laugh at you and your Sun-fhine. I therefore beg in your next, you may inform us if you have heard or feen any thing more, of the handy-work of thefe Sun-drummers ; tho' after all, they are only qualify'd to ferve us poor people of the northern Regions, and can be of no fort of fervice to thofe who are burn'd up in the South ; and whofe prayers, like the old *Jews*, are all for rains and dews, and rivers and fprings.

Your full and particular account of the intrigues of the Jefuits, in relation to the
Greek

Greek Church, and bringing it and *Ruffia* under the papal yoke, had the honour of his Majefty's notice and approbation ; but (as the King obferv'd in reading it) the Jefuits have been humble enough, to copy after fome part of thofe excellent plans, which his Majefty and his royal Anceftors, put in execution long fince here, to the infinite fervice of the *Britifh* Churches.

For fo long ago as the beginning of the laft century, *Frederick* III. eftablifh'd præmiums in our principal colleges, for thofe who gave the beft proof of their fcholarfhip; not to mention the royal college founded by him, and fo nobly enlarg'd by new endowments by his fucceffors, and particularly his prefent Majefty. Nay, the Jefuits have only imitated the zeal, of one of our beft Princes in the fame century, who at once raifed 400 poor livings to 50*l.* a year, by recommending their deplorable circumftances, to the care of the legiflature ; and we all know with how much nobler a munificence, our royal mafter has very lately taken care, of a provifion for all the reft of his poor and diftreffed Clergy. But whencefoever they have borrowed their regulations, I am perfuaded

H h of

of what your Excellency maintains, that
the *Ruſſian* Church muſt in a very little
time, become a province of the *Roman*
See, and embrace all her errors, ſuperſti-
tions, and idolatry, as the eſſential truths
of Chriſtianity.

But I ſhall not touch on this ſubjeɛt,
which lies ever uppermoſt in my thoughts,
and haunts my dreams, leſt I expatiate too
far upon it; and therefore ſhall only add
my ſincere prayers, (and by God's bleſſing
my beſt endeavours) that this over-whelm-
ing deluge that thus ſaps and privately un-
dermines, or violently in a torrent breaks
thro' all the mounds and banks, that human
induſtry and wiſdom would oppoſe to it,
may not, when it ſwallows up and covers
the reſt of the Earth, ruſh over and ſub-
vert the ſacred fences, of the Proteſtant
church and religion in the world.

Your relation of the extraordinary improvements they have made in the praɛtice
of Phyſick, was extremely welcome to me;
but, to ſay truth, many particulars in it
are criticis'd by our moſt celebrated praɛti-
tioners here, as leſs proper and uſeful than
your Excellency ſeems to think them;
but as you are no phyſician, and only report

port fuch facts as you have been inform'd
of, you are no way accountable, for any
miftakes they may be liable to.

For this reafon, I fhall not fend you
any of their objections, which feem befides
of lefs importance, than to deferve your
notice; and fhall rather chufe to return all
the miracles of your Jefuits, (in phyfick a-
mong the *Ruffians*) with one that in my
opinion exceeds them all, which *Great-
Britain* has alone found out the fecret of.
Your doctors therefore muft triumph no
longer, that they cure the Gout, and diffolve
the Stone, that they fubdue Fevers, and
reftore and heal Confumptions as eafily
as we cure Agues, or that they have
fecret fpecificks for the Jaundice, Small-
pox, Dropfies and Pleurifies; for we have
a skill in phyfick fuperior to all their performances, in a diftemper hitherto judg'd
incurable by all. A diftemper every one is
as certain to labour under as the Small-pox,
and yet fubject to have feveral times in his
life; a diftemper (which can be faid of
no other) that generally does moft harm
to the nobleft and worthieft fpirits in the
world; nay, a diftemper which I have
been told you have had fome terrible fits of,

H h 2   can

can your Excellency yet guefs at it, my Lord, it is that fatal and defperate malady, violent Love!

I fhould not offer to mention this to you, if I was not as certain of the truth of it, as that I am now in my chamber writing to you; for I have actually known two of my intimate acquaintance, my Lord *L*—— and Sir *Thomas D*—— who were dangeroufly feiz'd with it, cur'd within thefe fix weeks, and they are now perfectly well, as they have affur'd me with their own mouths. Nay, my Lady *B—y W*— my wife's relation, who, after a long courtfhip (which was bafely broke off) had engag'd her affections to my Lord *P*—— and was fo irrecoverably gone in it, that fhe could neither eat or drink, or fleep, or even fpeak, but with him, and his conduct in her thoughts, was alfo in a little time fo perfectly recover'd, that fhe made a vifit to his Lady, without the leaft palpitation of heart; and is fo indifferent to him, that fhe can even praife him. She is no longer fplenatick or melancholy, but receives and returns the vifits of her friends, goes to all publick places with the greateft gaiety and pleafure imaginable; and is fo good humour'd,

humour'd, that she has not turn'd off a
servant these two months. Your Excellency sees I do not write these facts, from
the general report that prevails here with
every body, but as cases within my own
knowledge and observation ; so that you
may depend on it, this art is arriv'd here
to its utmost perfection, and that the cure
of this terrible disorder is now become more
infallible, than that of the Ague by the Jesuits Bark.

Doctor *Howard* is the person to whom
the world is indebted for this admirable
secret ; and tho' by his Majesty's commands,
he has entrusted the methods of cure, for
fear of death, to three of the King's Physicians ; yet they are sworn not to discover
or make use of it, till he is safe in his grave.
I cannot therefore pretend to give your
Excellency the real secret of this prodigious
art ; but I shall tell you the method of his
prescriptions, as far as some of his own patients
have related it to me ; by which it is plain,
he treats it in the general, as they do several
other chronical distempers, having ever an
exact regard at the same time, to the particular constitution of the disorder'd person.

The

The firft thing the Doctor prefcribes to them, is, the taking a little Pill thrice every day for three days, with a fmall paper of powders, which tafte and fmell like powder of Crabs-eyes; both which 'tis conceiv'd fweeten the blood, correct the acrimony of the humours, and chear and recreate the fpirits extremely. After thefe three days, they bleed and blifter them feverely for about a week, as the cafe and the patient's conftitution allows them; this done, they take the pills and powders again for two days, then they give them violent purgatives to 8 or 9 ftools a-day for a week or longer, as the cafe is, with ftrong fudorificks to carry off redundant humours; all which is accompanied with drinking a kind of ptifan, and keeping to as low and emaciating a diet as the patients can allow, for at leaft ten days or longer, if they can bear it eafily. This method (the chief fecret of which, they fay, lies in the pills and ptifan) conftantly eradicates the diforder, in the moft inflammable conftitutions in a month's time; and in fome much lefs will do, and efpecially where they are not naturally, of a very rank or robuft conftitution.

I have

I have already hinted, that the chief secret is conceal'd in the pills and ptifan,
which alter the ftate of the blood and humours, and fortify the heart ; while the regular evacuations calm the hurry of the
fpirits, cool the body, and difcharge from
it all the vicious morbifick particles feparated
from the habit, till at laft that inflammable
difpofition is entirely remov'd, which is the
great fource of thefe kinds of diforders. It
is certain, that ever fince this method has
been follow'd by Dr. *Howard*, the violent
effects of this paffion or poffeffion, I know
not which to term it, have never difturb'd
the world as they ufed to do. For now
whenever people find their paffion is unfuccefsful and defperate, withot hanging or
drowning, fhooting or poifoning, which
was the ufual method, they calmly fend
for Dr. *Howard*, who immediately puts
them into the Love-courfe, as they call it, and
fo they get rid of it at once, and then very
quietly go about their affairs ; and as foon
as they have recover'd the cure, (which, as
in moft other cafes, generally takes up as
much time as the diftemper) they chufe a
more proper, or at leaft a lefs cruel perfon
for their adorations. It is univerfally agreed,

that

that the fincere and tender hearts of the
poor Ladies, are cur'd with much more
difficulty than the Men ; and fome of them,
as my Lady *R-----* particularly, died, after
fhe had been given given over for incurable;
but this does not happen one time in a
thoufand.

This I take to be one of the happieft difcoveries of this age; for tho' *Morifon*, in
his Itinerary *, affures us, that in his time the
baths of *Baden*, were made ufe of with great
fuccefs for the cure of this terrible diftemper,
hopelefs love ; yet I think he evidently took
up that ftory on very infufficient grounds.
For not to urge that if this were true, they
would have been the moft famous baths,
and the moft reforted to by all people and
nations in the whole world, (which is falfe
in fact); he overthrows his own affertion, by
maintaining, a few lines after, they were
of great fervice to women that were barren.
Now without appealing to the experience
of our Ladies and Gentlemen, who know
very well on what account they frequent
our Baths and Spaws; I leave it to common
fenfe to judge, how it is poffible thefe waters of *Baden*, could produce two fuch contrary effects, as curing Love and removing

* P. 26.

Barren-

Barrennefs; and confequently, I think, we may allow Dr. *Howard*'s prefcriptions, to be a blefling to his fellow-creatures peculiar to this age, and utterly unknown to our an-ceftors.

I fhall not trouble your Excellency, with many confequences with which this affair is, and will be accompanied in the world, but fhall pafs on to fomething more important; and that is, to return you my fincere thanks, for your noble prefent of the Czar's travels in fculpture, which have oblig'd me infinite-ly. However, as I think them too noble a prefent, for the library of a private fubject, you will allow me, after profefling my felf deeply indebted to your generofity, to give them, in your name, to his Majefty, who is you know extremely fond of fuch cu-riofities.

As to the propofal you make, of the King's offering his mediation between the Czar and the King of *Sweden*, who are both making fuch preparations for war, I muft acquaint your Excellency, that upon fome private hints from the *Swedifh* Ambaffador here, his Majefty order'd me to feel the pulfe of the Czar's Envoy at this Court; but he declar'd frankly, his mafter could

never

never think of a peace, or the leaft ftep towards it, while his enemies kept any part of *Livonia* in their poffeffion. Thus this affair is defperate, unlefs the bravery of the *Swedes* this next campaign, (as I heartily wifh) may reduce them to fpeak in a lower ftile. I am very forry I had not notice early enough, of the departure of the laft caravan for *China*, becaufe as the *Chinefes* we formerly brought over, and who have taught our people here to be as good potters, and to make as fine veffels as any in *China*, are growing old and crazy ; and as we would be the better, to have fome more skilful hands from thence, I muft beg your care to have twenty or thirty, of the beft that can be hir'd at any expence, fent to us by the return of the firft caravan. Our chief want is painters and bakers, tho' the truth is, we are already fuch mafters in this art, that we export vaft quantities of our manufacture for real China ; and it is, in my opinion, only to be diftinguifh'd from it, by its being differently, and perhaps I might fay, better painted.

I am now to acquaint your Excellency, that his Majefty has made a new regulation, as to that noble foundation of the three

Secre-

Secretaries of the Embaſſy, which *G.* III. appointed to accompany all his Ambaſſadors at his own expence, (of 200 *l. per Ann.* each) in order to breed them up to a perfect knowledge in ſtate-affairs, as you well know. The King is pleas'd to ſignify to all his foreign miniſters, that he has reſolv'd to add one to their number, and will allow no perſon to receive the ſalary of Secretary, who has not ſpent four years at one of the univerſities, and will not oblige himſelf to ſpend ſix years, at each Court the Embaſſy is ſent to, and to write in his turn all diſpatches ſent the Crown, and take the oath of ſecreſy and fidelity uſual in ſuch caſes.

Mr. Secretary writes this poſt, to have all theſe articles ſtrictly obſerv'd and comply'd with, and an exact account tranſmitted to the Secretary, of thoſe Gentlemen that are now with our Envoys, that any who do not come within theſe regulations, may be diſmiſs'd, and new ones nominated by his Majeſty in their places; in all which I doubt not, Mr. Secretary will find an exact compliance on your part.

It

It is certain thefe are very ufeful improvements of that noble fcheme; and as our Embaffies have by thefe means, prov'd excellent nurferies to us for able Statefmen, and prevented our being the dupes and bubbles of other Nations, in matters of negotiation and treaty, as we too often were in the days of our anceftors; his Majefty and hisMinifters abroad,cannot be too exact, in feeing his orders duly executed. There is alfo a particular article added to thefe inftructions, which is, that if any one of the Secretaries of the Embaffy, be ever known to be guilty of any indecency in his manners, or offends againft fobriety, modefty, truth or honour in his conduct; he is immediately to be confin'd and difplac'd, till his Majefty's further pleafure be known.

It is faid, the famous Duke of *Cumberland*, fo celebrated in our hiftories, who was fon, or grandfon, I forget whether, to that excellent Prince *George* the II^d, was the firft inventor of this project, which has almoft been as ferviceable to our Country as ever his fword or counfels prov'd; and I am perfuaded few of his many great actions, endear'd him more to his countrymen than this, tho' it was not actually put in execucution

cution, till *George* the Third's halcyon days.

As Mr. Secretary gave you a full account, of the diffolution of the laft Parliament and the calling of this, I muft now acquaint you, that they met laft week, and are fallen to the difpatch of all matters recommended to them, with great diligence and application. As this was the firft time of their fitting in their noble new Parliament-houfe in *Hide-Park*, I went with his Majefty there to fee them; and indeed I think I have not beheld a nobler fight, than that beautiful room which has been built for their fitting in, and the auguft crowd of Lords and Commons, that met his Majefty in the houfe of Lords, which is no ways inferior to the other, except in fize.

As the Peers were all in their robes, and the Commons in their *Venetian* Senators habits, you may imagine how glorious an affembly this was, with one of the greateft Princes at prefent in the Chriftian world, or which is more, of the royal Line of *Hanover*, fpeaking to them from the Throne, with all the fpirit and elegance of *Cæfar* to his Senate, without his ambition and tyranny. For my part it mov'd me fo ftrongly,

2   that

that I was as little able to hide my tears then, as to conceal the pleafure it gave me, from your Excellency now; and tho' I have feen the States of *Hungary*, the Parliament of *Paris*, the Diet of *Ratisbon*, and the Senate of *Venice*, they look'd in my thoughts like boys in a fchool or a college, to them. The *Venetian* habit, which *Frederick* the II^d introduced, gives a vaft air of folemnity and gravity to the Commons; and certainly how venerable a figure fcever the Parliaments of our anceftors make in our imaginations now, they muft have made a very abfurd appearance to the eye, that furvey'd them in fo many party-colour'd habits, white, black, red, blue, grey, and with as many other variable dies as the rainbow, as 'tis plain from hiftory they ufed to wear in their debates. Some have imagined, they ufed this method to diftinguifh their particular divifions, parties, and leaders by, like the factions of the *Prafini* and *Veneti* of old among the *Romans*; and there are fome paffages in our ancient *Englifh* Poets and Hiftorians, and particularly one in *Pope* that looks a little this way; but yet it is certain there is nothing of truth in this conjecture; and that the different colours in their cloaths, proceed-

I

ed

ed merely from the humour and caprice of every member. And tho' some late authors maintain, that 'tis ridiculous to suppose an assembly, that so often determined the fate of Empires and Nations, would meet together in such an odd variety of different coloured suits, (like a regiment of Train'd-Bands, that were not able to cloath themselves one way) unless there were some politick view and meaning in it; or, at least, that they design-ed to distinguish their several religions by their colours; yet I can produce very clear proofs that all this is entirely mistake and fancy, and that what I have asserted, is the real truth of the matter.

I am sorry that they have abrogated the good antient custom of printing their votes, and that they now keep their debates and resolutions, so private and secret as they do, or else I should have had the pleasure of send-ing them all to your Lordship. However, I shall tell you one remarkable part of their proceed-ings, and that is, their voting that no person shall sit in that house that is not past 25, nor against whose conduct any thing criminal, dishonest, or immoral, can be evidently proved before the Secret Committee, which is always appointed to examine into petitions

ons of this nature. At the fame time to prevent the attacks of private malice, whoever
petitions againft a member on this account,
is oblig'd to give fecurity to prove his allegations, or be imprifon'd for five years, as an
infamous and fcandalous informer. If two-
thirds of the Committee vote the allegations
duly proved, the member has his choice of
having his cafe heard before the whole houfe;
or, if he declines that, of withdrawing privately, and upon his non-attendance, his
feat is declared vacated, and a writ is iffued
for electing a new member. Nay, they have
bolted the doors of that houfe, againft all
who are engaged in many law-fuits, or either diftreft in their affairs, or involv'd in
debt, or that have not been feven years poffefs'd of the eftate that qualifies them to be
elected, if the faid eftate be purchafs'd by
fuch members, and not defcended to them.
The reafons on which thefe important votes
are grounded, are almoft felf-evident; and
they have further added to them, that none
fhall be capable of fitting in that houfe, who
is not at leaft two months of the year, refident in the Borough or Country that he re-
prefents; and who receives any pay or falary,
of any kind or nature foever from the Crown;
both

both which are moſt uſeful and admirable reſolutions concerning the elected; and indeed thoſe concerning the members attendance in the houſe, on the great truſt repoſed in them by their country, are fully as important. Theſe votes are, that any one abſent one half of a ſeſſions, without proof by affidavit of a proper cauſe approv'd by the houſe, vacates his ſeat; and every member who on the Speaker's circular letter, giving warning of an approaching weighty debate, preſumes to abſent himſelf without ſufficient cauſe, ſhall be reprimanded on his knees by the Speaker. Nay, they have voted that any one who, during ſuch debates, ſhall leave the houſe, or that ſhall preſume to vote without hearing them, ſhall, at the bar, demand pardon of the houſe for the ſame.

To enforce theſe yet farther, they have reſolv'd that the houſe ſhall be called over every *Tueſday* and *Friday*; and all that are abſent twenty days in the ſeſſion without leave, or ſufficient cauſe ſhewn, and above all, when important matters are debated, ſhall be ſeverely cenſur'd by the Houſe for the firſt and ſecond fault, and on a third commiſſion of it, expelled. It is believ'd they will ſoon

order

order heads of a bill to be brought in, to make all thofe votes and refolutions pafs into a law; and indeed it feems of great confequence that they fhould.

I muft confefs, as a publick minifter, I am lefs fond of fuch fevere regulations; for tho' the loyalty and tranquillity of thefe times, make them lefs to be feared at prefent, yet fuch divifions and difcontents may arife hereafter, as may make them lefs favourable, not to fay pernicious to the intereft of the Crown. But when I confider, as a friend to my country, of what infinite fervice they would be to the banifhing corruption, and mean-interefted fervile hirelings from that houfe, that fhould be facred to truth, honour, loyalty, and the love, the eternal love of our country, I cannot but incline to them.

I have a thoufand times weigh'd the chief arguments, for and againft this important point in my own mind, and I muft own I have ever found the certain advantages, fo much tranfcend the poffible inconveniences, that the ballance has ftill turn'd in favour of fuch regulations. Indeed our Houfe of Commons thus modell'd, would prove fuch a bulwark againft rapacious or defigning minifters,

nifters, as well as againft Princes of too enterprizing or ambitious fpirits in future ages,
and wou'd be fuch a fecurity, to preferve the
rights and prerogative of the Crown, and the
privileges and liberty of the People, in the
fame equal channels in which they now run,
pure and unmix'd; that I am perfuaded his
Majefty could not confult the happinefs of, his
fucceffors or people more, than by turning thefe
votes into a law. As the King feems to think in
this way, poffibly this may be done; and if
not in this parliament, at leaft in this reign.

Your Excellency will be furpriz'd, after
profeffing that thefe are my fentiments, when
I tell you, that there is a numerous faction,
ftarted up already in this very parliament,
to oppofe all the meafures I am taking for
the publick good, and mifreprefent the
whole of my paft adminiftration. To mortify me the more (if fuch trivial changes in
the moft changeable of all things, the heart
of Man, could mortify me) I find the faction is fupported underhand by Sir *J*--- *C*---
and Mr. *L*. two perfons that I little expected, and much lefs deferv'd fuch ungrateful
returns from, after all I have done for them.
In the mean time, as they keep behind the
curtain, Mr. *M*---- is the perfon who leads the

faction;

faction; and indeed his great abilities entitle him to it, for as your Excellency well knows, 'tis with Men as with Deer, the beſt headed leads the herd. Yet this very Man have I favoured enough, to have tied him to my intereſt for ever; nor do I know any cauſe for his forſaking me, but that I have oblig'd him beyond a poſſibility of return; and when that is the caſe, * *Tacitus* will tell us the natural conſequence. The great outcry is rais'd about the publick accounts, and I know not what millions that are clandeſtinely ſunk and evaporated into air; as I doubt not I ſhall ſee all theſe clamours do, when I can properly clear myſelf, by laying my accounts before the houſe. Sir R----*d* B---- is as loud as any, and rails with his uſual blundering eloquence, but he has not talents even to ſerve a good cauſe; and tho' his abuſive tongue can bruiſe like a cudgel, it wants edge to wound his enemy; or, as *Du Hailan* the *French* Hiſtorian ſaid, he can blacken like an old cold cinder, but cannot burn.

In a few weeks, I ſhall ſee how far this blind and groundleſs malice will lead them, and ſhall give your Excellency an account

* Pro gratiâ odium redditur.

of what thefe worthy intrigues produce. In the mean time, let me fpeak it without arrogance, I am fecure, and almoft carelefs of what may happen; for, believe me, my Lord, I am more willing to return to Fortune the trifles fhe has lent me, and refign the mighty envied pofts which they purfue me for, (if my royal Mafter would approve of it) than ever I was to receive them. It is long fince I have learn'd in this fchool of the world, where fo few are educated, without feeling feverely the fmarting corrections of their mafter's rod; that there is little to be got in it worth the pain and trouble, and above all, our virtue, which we generally pay for the knowledge and experience we lay up there. Judge therefore, if when one finds malice, and rancour, and envy, are conftantly the returns which are made thofe who happen to fucceed better in it; if one can avoid being weary and fick, of the filly purfuits we are fo eagerly engag'd in there, and fond of retiring from its noife and hurry. This is not the language of the Courtier, but of the Man and the Friend, whom your Excellency has known a little too long to miftruft his profeffions, or imagine he can dote at this time of life on the filly fopperies of place,

preferment

preferment and power, which in the vigour and fun-fhine of his days, he never put in balance with peace and retirement, with innocence and honour.

But I begin to grow grave, and therefore it is time I fhould take my leave of your Excellency, to whom I wifh all the happinefs, profperity, and favour this world can give you. I wifh them not to you as real folid bleffings, but as pleafing imaginary fatisfactions, and the beft kind of appearances of happinefs here, to blunt the edge of fo many real evils as we continually labour under. Above all, I wifh them to you becaufe they now and then afford us, the fubftantial delight of doing good to others, of relieving wanting merit, pulling down the oppreffor, ftripping the profperous villain of his fpoils, drying up the tears, and defending the caufe of innocence in mifery.

May I live (for the few years I can yet live) to fee this the chief employment and bufinefs of your life in this world; and may not the errors and fins of mine, prevent my feeing you crown'd with the glory of it in another. I am, my Lord,

Your Excellency's, &c.

N-----*m.*

To

To the Lord High Treasurer, &c.

Paris, March 4. 1997.

My LORD,

I Was honour'd with your Lordſhip's of *February* the 24th from *London* yeſterday, which brought me new proofs, of that undeſerved affection and regard, with which you have ever honour'd me. I know not whether to applaud moſt, your Lordſhip's care of our Country, or affection to your friends and my family, or to make my compliments to you as the beſt of Miniſters or Patrons. But I hope you will believe me honeſt enough to wiſh, that our family ſhould rather be depriv'd of your favour, than our Country ſhould ever be robb'd of ſo able an head, or ſo ſincere and zealous an heart, to conſider and purſue her intereſt. If I do not deceive my ſelf, I think I don't ſay this, with any little view to my brother's being made one of the Secretaries for foreign affairs (how greatly ſoever I am oblig'd by it) but from a real ſenſe, of what the happieſt Nation and the beſt of Princes owe you, for the labours of an illuſtrious life waſted in their ſervice.

I 4

But

But your Lordſhip's mind, and the obligations you lay on your friends as well as
your country, are above the little returns
of words and compliments; and therefore
I ſhall take a method to pay you my acknowledgments, that will be more agreeable
to you, by ſhewing you that I have endeavour'd to diſcharge the truſt, you have
repos'd in me here. Purſuant to your
commands therefore, and my inſtructions
from the Secretary by his letters of the ſame
date, on *Tueſday* laſt I demanded an Audience of his moſt Chriſtian Majeſty; to
which I was immediately admitted, tho'
that morning the Pope's Nuntio, and the
Spaniſh Ambaſſador were both put off, with
excuſes of his Majeſty's indiſpoſition. Upon
account of theſe excuſes, (as I ſuppoſe) his
Majeſty receiv'd me in his bed-chamber,
where I found him accompanied with none
but Mr. *Menezville*, his chief miniſter, who,
as you know, leads him as he pleaſes. He
receiv'd me, with a very great appearance
of good humour and franknefs; and as
he had the memorial in his hand which I
had given him the *Sunday* before, as he came
from maſs, he immediately cut off the
formality of a prefatory introduction to what
I had

I had to say, by telling me he had carefully read and consider'd with Monsieur *Meneville*, the memorial I had presented him with, on the part of his *Britannick* Majesty, my Master. He told me he was perfectly convinc'd of the terrible train of consequences which must attend the establishing the Inquisition in *France*; and as he well knew the motives that made the Pope press for it, were only to increase his power, and that of the Clergy who adher'd to him in his Kingdom, he was willing and desirous to take any measures he could to prevent it. That he conceiv'd those propos'd in the memorial were well concerted, and would be of great service; but that he thought there was an omission in it, that was absolutely necessary to be supply'd, if we resolv'd to deter the Pope, from such a dangerous and insolent outrage on the honour of *France*, and the liberty of his subjects. As he spoke all this very quick, and with a good deal of action and emotion, as his manner is, he made a short pause here; and seem'd to expect my reply. Upon which I told him, that I was so confident of the King my Master's zeal, to lessen the unreasonable power of the

Empire

Empire of the *Vatican*, and at leaft, prevent any new encroachments, as to what
regarded *France*, that I was certain his
moft Chriftian Majefty's propofals, for additional meafures for that end, would be
chearfully embrac'd. I would have gone
on to defire that his Majefty would confider, that as all the extraordinary fteps
taken by my Mafter, were barely for the
intereft of *France*, I doubted not but all
poffible regard would be fhewn, as to any
further demands, to avoid unneceffary expence to *Great-Britain*; but he ftopp'd
me with his ufual eagernefs and quicknefs,
to tell me, that the omiffion he complain'd
of was, that of fending two Squadrons on
the Coafts of *Italy*. I was fo glad to find
there was nothing further infifted on, that
I told his Majefty, without hefitation, that
he might depend on that affiftance, whether matters came to an open rupture with
the Pope or no. That his Majefty of
Great-Britain feldom fail'd to fend a fmall
one into the *Mediterranean* every year for
the protection of the trading part of his
fubjects; and that I doubted not but he
would fend two much ftronger and earlier
than ever, to any ftations which fhould be
thought

thought neceſſary for the ſervice of *France.*
He ſeem'd extreamly pleas'd with this de-
claration, and turning about to Mr. *Mene-*
ville, he whiſper'd him ſo loud, that I
plainly heard him ask him, have I any
thing more to ſay? To which the other
having anſwer'd ſo low, that I could hear
nothing; his Majeſty inſtantly turn'd to
me, and laying his hand on his breaſt,
ſaid, I am deeply indebted to his *Britan-*
nick Majeſty, I am much indebted to his
Britannick Majeſty. He repeated theſe expreſſions at leaſt thrice; and then, as I found
he continued ſilent for ſome time, I pull'd
out the laſt Memorial which I receiv'd in
Mr. Secretary's diſpatch, and told his Majeſty, that I was commanded to preſent it
to him on behalf of my Maſter; and to
let him know, that it was a copy of the
ſeveral heads of things which our Ambaſſador at *Rome* was charg'd with to repreſent
to his Holineſs, againſt the eſtabliſhment of
the Inquiſition in his territories. He took
it from me, and juſt looking over the title,
he gave it into Mr. *Meneville's* hands, ſaying, it is long; you muſt make an ab-
ſtract, and report the ſubſtance of it to
me; upon which words, Mr. *Meneville*
ſaid

said nothing further, but put it in his pocket, whispering something into his Master's ear. His Majesty then turn'd to me, and ask'd me, whether our Ambassador at *Rome*, had already deliver'd that Memorial to his Holiness, and obtain'd a favourable answer to it; to which I could only answer, that I look'd on that as certain, but as yet I had no account of it; and that when I had, I should immediately acquaint his most Christian Majesty with my intelligence. To this he made no reply; but turning his discourse on the sudden to the ambition of the papal See, he said, with surprizing emotion to me, they think to make my Kingdom a Province to *Rome*; but, says he, striking his hand on his heart, not till I and half my Army are first cover'd with the sods of *Dauphine*; meaning, as I conceiv'd, that he would first die fighting on his frontier to *Savoy* and *Italy*. I told his Majesty, I hop'd neither of those unfortunate accidents would happen. I know not, said he, but I am sure one shall not happen without the other. If Providence had not disappointed all my best concerted projects, I had long before now secur'd the peace and honour of

France;

2

France; but it so pleas'd Providence, that every thing went contrary to my just designs. I did my best, and used my utmost endeavours; but all was to no purpose. Every body knows the event; I can blame no-body but Providence; Providence would have it so, and I was forc'd to submit to its decrees. I observ'd he dropp'd some tears with these last words, and as I saw him in a great deal of trouble and concern, and having nothing further to speak to him on; I only begg'd Mr. *Meneville* I might soon have an answer to my memorial, and put an end to my audience, and immediately withdrew. The complaints against Providence, that made up the whole of the latter part of my audience, seem'd to me something very extraordinary, and brought to my mind the behaviour of *Francis* I. a predecessor of this King's, about 450 years ago, in somewhat the like circumstances. For when he saw his rival *Charles* V. had taken St. *Difier*, and was resolv'd to besiege him in *Paris*, he broke out into violent complaints against Providence, repining at its decrees; and said to his wife, my Darling, (for so he us'd to call her) go pray to heaven, that if

against

againſt all juſtice *Charles* V. muſt be favour'd thus, that at leaſt its partial providence, will allow me to die fighting in the field, before I live to be beſieg'd in my capital. After all, theſe fine complaints of theſe mighty Lords of the world, that dare thus repine againſt and reproach the juſtice of their Maker, ſeem to me as impudent and ſilly, as the conduct of *Sorbiere*'s * Abbe St. *Cyran*. That old Author tells us, the Abbe, as he was one day eating cherries in his room, endeavour'd ſtill as he eat them, to throw the ſtones out of the window, which often hit againſt the bars, and fell on the floor ; upon which he ever and anon flew into a fury, crying out, ſee how Providence takes a pleaſure to oppoſe itſelf againſt my deſigns. And indeed, my Lord, the mightieſt undertaking of theſe rivals of Heaven, are, in the eye of infinite power, neither greater or nobler than the good Abbe's cherry-ſtones, that he was directing with ſo much care and prudence. I have hinted enough to your Lordſhip of the weakneſs of this Prince in my former letters; and as in Princes more than in other Men to be

* Sorberiana, *p.* 74.

weak,

weak, is to be unhappy; I believe there
are few among his fubjects, (as wretched
as the fubjects in *France* are) who are more
uneafy in all the chief circumftances of
life than he is. Indeed, by what I have
been able to obferve of the world, and
the mighty monarchs of it, whom we envy and admire fo much; I am perfuaded
this is oftner the cafe than we are apt to
imagine. Crowns are fuch weighty, troublefome ornaments, that there are but two
things that can make them fit eafy on
the wearer's head; either an ardent defire of doing great and glorious actions,
and deferving well of mankind; or the
fenfelefs vanity of feeing one's felf fo high
above others, as to the fopperies of power,
riches, palaces, high living, and all the
little tinfel fhew of pomp, pleafure and
luxury.

The firft of thefe are feldom found,
but in a few great fpirits, who appear
now and then like comets, to the amazement of the world; and are to be ex-
cepted from the general rules that others
move by. The other indeed is often to be
met with; yet fo high a degree of it,
and good fuccefs with it, is neceffary to
fweeten

sweeten the cares of Princes ; and so many disappointments and misfortunes in publick and private life befall them, and often such ill health, and other accidents, that level them with the rest of mankind ; that we must believe them seldom at ease, tho' we should not take into the account the prodigious expectations they entertain, which are therefore the harder to gratify ; and the violence of their passions with which they pursue them, which makes the least ill success the more insupportable.

However, this Prince has one good quality, which will make him serviceable to our present views, in spite of his weakness and unhappiness ; and that is, a good degree of courage ; which, with the help of two or three ill ones, much obstinacy, and a violent unforgiving temper, will probably cut out more work for his Holiness than he can easily manage. The whole Nation is in great expectation what the event of our councils will be ; and I perceive the Jesuits are in prodigious apprehensions, seeing so terrible an alliance likely to be form'd against them, as *Great-Britain*, *France* and *Germany*. They set all

all engines at work, to defame and asperse
our sovereign and nation as hereticks and
monsters, that are odious to God, and all
good men ; and they are as busy to ex-
pose and ridicule his most Christian Majesty, by spreading vile reports as to his
personal frailties, and all the errors and
mistakes imputable to him, as a Man or
a King. They have writ two dangerous
pamphlets lately, which are handed about
in manuscript ; one of them is a virulent
satire against this King and his first Minister, *Meneville*: It is a sort of diary of
his life for the last *Lent*, of which I
shall transcribe you two days. First day
of *Lent*. Got up betimes from Madam *Du
Vall*, confess'd to Father L——— a *Dominican*, and got absolution ; forgot to go
to mass, and eat my breakfast ; dress'd by
the Duke of *C*—— the Count of *D*——
and Mr. *P*—— went to Mr. *Meneville's*,
and ask'd leave to go to council ; could
get no answer, till he had consulted the
British Envoy ; got his consent, and went
thither. Resolv'd on a war with the Pope,
swore the ruin of the Church to the hereticks, past an arret against schools and colleges, as opening peoples eyes too much.

K k

Another

Another againſt popular preachers and zea-lous biſhops; went to dinner as ſoon as Mr. *Meneville* was ready, eat till I was ſick, drank till I was fuddled —— Mr. *Meneville* ſwears the Pope is an heretick —— deſerves to be burnt, chain'd to *Trajan*'s pillar, and make the Churches in *Rome* ſerve for fag-gots. Grew very merry, ſent for Mrs. *Du Vall*, ſcolded her, forgot going to con-feſſion. Went to cards, my old luck, loſt every thing I play'd for; cheated by Mrs. *Du Vall*, bubbled by Monſieur *Meneville*, laugh'd at by every one, pitied by no body. Went to the opera, ſix foot-ſoldiers cried *vive le Roy*, pleas'd to ſee ſuch proofs of my people's love. *Britiſh* Ambaſſador bow-ed very civilly. Several of my own ſer-vants carry'd with much reſpect to me. Very fine muſick, and a world of com-pany. Madam *Du Vall* the fineſt woman I could ſee there —— went home, ſupp'd upon fleſh, got fuddled, threatned the Pope, ſwore heartily, commended the brave hereticks of *Great-Britain*, and their almighty fleets, talk'd over the great feats I would do when they help'd me, loſt my tongue and my ſenſes, ſent for Madam *Du Vall*, and was carried to bed.

Second

Second day ; made Madam *Du Vall* get up firſt——— call'd for Father *L*——— the *Dominican*, confeſs'd, and abſolv'd ; heard maſs in my chamber, while I eat my break-faſt——— ſick in my ſtomach, my head out of order, drank ſome brandy, took the air at *New Marly*, at noon ; out of ſorts, took a cordial, ask'd Mr. *Meneville*'s advice, and took another cordial, grew better, got home, and din'd on fleſh, could eat lit-tle, drank the more. The *Britiſh* Ambaſ-ſador came to wait on me. The Pope a villain, Biſhops raſcals, Jeſuits rogues, and Catholicks fools. The riches of the mona-ſteries and convents, and the Lands of the Church, the beſt fund to maintain a war with the Pope——— Monſieur *Meneville* will manage all. Mrs. *Du Vall* ſhall make the campaign with me, will give her an eſtate in church-lands ; much pleas'd, heard a fine conſort of muſick, order'd a new tax upon *Guienne* to pay the band of muſicians ; ſaw Mr. *Le Blanc* dance ; gave him a regiment for it ; a great pity he's no ſoldier——— *Bri-tiſh* Ambaſſador went home. Call'd for ſupper, bad ſtomach, ſwallow'd wine enough, and eat ſome *Portugal* hams, to ſhew I was a good Chriſtian, and no *Jew*. Made

K k 2   Madam

Madam *Du Vall* fing, and Mr. *Meneville*
dance. A fine gentleman, a faithful fubject, and an able minifter; might get his
bread by dancing, better than *Nero* by his
fiddling. Drank abundance, talk'd more;
begun to think, grew dull and melancholy,
fell afleep in my chair, dreamt I was drinking with the *Britifh* Ambaffador and the
Devil; waken'd in a fright, carried to my
apartment, fate on my clofe-ftool, and rail'd
at the world, went to bed, and ventur'd to
lie alone.

The reft is all of the fame nature, very
malicious; and, like all true malice, very
dull. For this reafon, I fhall not trouble
your Lordfhip with any more than a few
fhort hints of another; in which they pretended to prove his *Britannick* Majefty
and his Parliaments are the publick incen-
diaries of *Europe*. That his Majefty has
erected the houfe of commons into a fort
of grand prerogative-court, where the wills
of all the crown'd heads of *Europe* are
to be firft duly prov'd and enter'd, with a
*falvo jure magnæ Britanniæ Regum fi illis
aliter vifum fuerit*; and the next heir is
to be admitted or rejected, as beft fuits the
convenience of the prefent ftate of things,

2   and

and the inclinations of the good people of *Great-Britain*. That no fuch will is to be deem'd authentick, unlefs the deceas'd takes care to have 100000 arm'd witneffes, to prove the validity thereof. That in cafe fuch will be pronounced valid, it fhall not be conftrued to extend to bequeath to the heir, or his fubjects, any foreign trade or naval power ; but fo far as they fhall be dependent on, and fubfervient to, the interest and commerce of *Great-Britain*, and no further. That in cafe any prince or potentate, nation or people, fhall prefume to conftrue it otherwife, the faid prerogative-court do iffue out a writ, call'd a *Claffis major quæ fcire faciat* ; and fettle all points of the faid will thereby, as they judge proper ; fubftituting a convenient decree and will of the faid court, in the place thereof, of which the known rule is, *falus Populi fuprema lex efto*. That the faid court has pretended to compute, by their political arithmetick, that fince the 16th Century to the 20th, the Princes of *Europe* have facrific'd the lives of above 100 millions of the bravest of their fubjects to Wars, begun and carried on for the moft frivolous filly excufes imaginable ;

K k 3 and

and fometimes, for little trivial piques of minifters and favourites againft each other, for which an honeft heretick would not turn off a footman. That therefore they have made a decree, that no monarchs in *Europe* fhall prefume to go to war till their quarrel is tried in the faid court, and fentence pronounc'd there for war or peace ; and to act accordingly. There is abundance of fuch aukward malice in the pamphlet, which is not worth repeating. I fhall therefore omit it, to acquaint your Lordfhip with the refentments of a particular perfon, who may be able to do us more prejudice, with a few words to his mafter, whom he rules and governs as he pleafes, than all the pens of the Jefuits, who think to govern the world.

I need not tell your Lordfhip, that I mean Mr. *Meneville*, who expoftulated with me yefterday in a very calm and civil, but at the fame time in a manner that fhew'd a great deal of conceal'd refentment. He met me at court, and afk'd me to walk with him in the King's garden ; he talk'd to me a little on the Memorial I had given his Mafter, and then began a long expoftulation, that has made me apprehenfive we

may

may have difgufted him too far. He told me, I very well knew the *French* fea-ports had never remain'd in our hands, or the laft treaty of peace been fign'd between *France* and *Great-Britain*, but for him; which God knows, fays he, I did not do for the fake of the penfion then fo folemnly promis'd me, or to provide for my family, but to ferve my country, that was tearing in pieces. That your Lordfhip and I both knew he had not got it accomplifh'd, if he had not ruin'd the Marquis of *M——* who was violently for carrying on the war with *England*; and perfuaded the *French* King he was a penfioner of the Pope's, tho' the faid Marquis was Mr. *Meneville's* good friend, and as faithful and wife a mi-nifter as ever was in *France*. That three years after he had thus gct the peace fign'd, his Majefty would have broke it again, but that he offer'd him a thoufand arguments againft it, and fav'd *Great-Britain* from that ftorm; and now he kept him firm to the fcheme of our ccurt, for humbling the Pope, and oppofing the Inquifition; which laft point, however, he infifted the lefs on, becaufe it was the true intereft of the Kingdom. That I very well knew how

ill

ill his penſion had been paid, ever ſince it
was firſt promis'd him ; that there was now
two years and an half due, and not a penny offer'd him. That your Lordſhip, (you
will pardon the freedom of reporting this)
manag'd your maſter's treaſures like a banker,
rather than a prime miniſter ; and that if
the friends of *Great-Britain* in foreign
Courts were always thus us'd, we would
find the ſcene chang'd ſuddenly. I would
fain have interrupted him here, but he
would not let me ; ſo he went on to ſay,
that if he could think of deſerting *Great-
Britain*, he might find his account much
better with the Pope's Miniſters, where he
had been offer'd near double what we contracted for ; but his Maſter's honour, and
the intereſt of his Country, were too near
his heart. However, as the forgeting real
ſervices, and remembring ſmall diſobliga-
tions, often made the beſt friends enemies,
he deſir'd I would conſider well of it, and
without a uſeleſs waſte of words and reaſons ; (which, ſays he, you are ready to
give, and I will not receive) take care to
anſwer theſe complaints, with the ſingle argument, that can only juſtify your conduct to
me. The inſtant he had ſaid this, he left me
with-

without allowing me time to reply; and as I have faithfully related the whole of his expostulation, I humbly recommend it to your Lordship's consideration, to have the arrears of his pension instantly paid him. I am persuaded, the Pope's Ministers would give him vastly more than we do; and tho' he must, to oblige them, run counter to his Master's inclinations, and the body of the people; yet he has such an ascendant over the King, that he is able to manage him, and every thing by him, as he pleases. I shall add no more on this subject, but to beg I may be instructed very suddenly how to answer Mr. *Meneville*, with something more than good reasons and great promises, or my credit here will be but short-liv'd. In the mean time, I am persuaded, if he be kept our friend, all will go well, and we shall probably mortify the Pope sufficiently. Indeed his most Christian Majesty, has so vastly improv'd the strength of his frontier towns in *Dauphine*, by their new-invented method of fortification, that the strongest places in *France*, fortified after the old manner, are not strong enough to keep sheep from wolves, or geese from foxes, when compared with them. All the

troops

troops are ordered to be compleated without delay throughout *France,* and money
is fent to *Swifferland* for remounting the cavalry; fo that every thing here looks like
preparations for war, and the Jefuits and
their numerous party are evidently under
great apprehenfions of its breaking out.
However, probably their interefts in all
Courts is fo prodigious, and they have fo
many fpies that lie within the bofoms of
their enemies, that they will manage fo, if
poffible, as to make all this ftorm blow
over. A few months will clear up this matter, and I fhall redouble my efforts to bring
every thing to bear; being perfuaded, fuch
a crifis, when both *France* and the Emperor are warmly inclin'd to a rupture with
the Pope, and to concert proper meafures
to curb his ambition, is not eafily found.

In the mean time, my Lord, allow me
to pafs to lefs bufy fcenes of things, and to
tell you, that after I parted with Mr. *Meneville* yefterday, I went to fee the magnificent entry of the old Marquis *del Carpio,*
Ambaffador extraordinary from *Spain.* He
had an infinite train of rich liveries, coaches
and attendants, and made an appearance
becoming that Monarchy in its higheft fplendor;

dor; but as he is a violent enemy to *Great-
Britain*, and will certainly serve the Jesuits,
(whose creature he is) all he can, I heartily
wish him and his fine shew in *Madrid*. I
knew him when I was in *Spain* very well,
his name is *Haro*, and he has very considerable
estates in *Andalusia*; and is on that
account, and his zeal and bigottry, much
consider'd by the Jesuits; but otherwise,
he is both in his person and understanding,
infinitely despicable. This entry cost him
a vast sum of money, which I suppose the
Jesuits, whose errands I am sure he comes
on, will answer for him. The very coach,
which he rid in cost near 6000 *l.* and
brought into my mind the rich shrines for
relicks, (to say nothing of some great noble-
mens palaces) which are so glorious and
splendid without; and yet within, contain
nothing but the decay'd remains of some
worthless creature, which must now be reverenc'd as sacred, and regarded almost
with adoration by the crowd. I shall leave
no stone unturn'd, to get as early intelligence as I can, from the best hands, of the
design of this embassy, which I am sure
are no ways auspicious to our present views;
and shall give your Lordship notice of
them

them with all poſſible expedition. It is
certain, that one part of his buſineſs is, to
influence this Crown to give no ſort of encouragement or aſſiſtance to the *Portugueſe,*
in the diſpute which is ariſen in *America,*
between them and the *Spaniards,* and is
likely to be carried on with prodigious violence. As the affair is perfectly new, and
the whole of it ſufficiently curious, I ſhall
let your Lordſhip in a few words into ſo much
of it, as I could learn at preſent. 'Tis a
matter likely to be attended with prodigious
conſequences, and to engage both the pens
and the ſwords of the two nations, with all
the rage that either glory or profit, can
ſtir up in them ; for the quarrel is about
nothing leſs than the bounds of their ſeveral Empires in the vaſt Continent of *Ame-*
rica. Your Lordſhip muſt remember to
have read, how Pope *Alexander* VI. in the
the 16ᵗʰ Century, when the diſcovery of
the new World was thought little of, divided
it into two hemiſpheres, the eaſtern and
weſtern ; the firſt of which he beſtow'd
on the *Portugueſe,* and the laſt on the *Spa-*
niards. For the firſt three or four Centuries, every thing was very calm and quiet,
neither Nation having been able to pene-

trate

trate and difcover, much lefs to plant and occupy, the inmoft parts of that prodigious Continent. But as of late years, *America* is grown vaftly populous, and the inhabitants for this laft Century, by the help of the natives, have carried their colonies and plantations thro' the remoteft provinces; it happen'd the *Portuguefe* and *Spaniards* frequently met, and had furious contefts and engagements, about the boundaries of their dominions. The *Portuguefe* maintaining, that the *Spaniards* have intruded too far, and the others denying it, all the Geographers of each Nation, and the Mathematicians of *Europe*, have been engag'd of one fide or other with the utmoft fury and paffion; and yet cannot agree about fixing the Longitude, differing, many of them, about 19 degrees. It will, in all probability, coft much blood and treafure, before this difpute be determin'd; and 'tis generally faid, the Jefuits in *Paraguay*, who are jealous of them both, blow up the coals, and ufe all their arts to put things in a flame; which is no difficult task between two Nations fufficiently warm and refentful, and that have fuch vaft tracts of a very rich fertile country, to contend about.

The

The *Spaniards* have loft a great friend in the Duke *de Richlieu*, who died here laft week, in fpite of all the heaps of wealth he had rais'd, by cheating the Nation, and ruining 8 or 10000 families. However, he died very comfortably among his Jefuits, to whom he left 10000*l.* out of near fifty times that fum, to pray his foul out of purgatory. It is currently reported here, my Lord, that he had violent difputes with his confeffor, what the value of his fins might be computed at, and the maffes requifite to pray his foul cut of danger. Tho' he was much afraid of going there, and heartily fuperftitious; yet he lov'd his dear money fo well, that 'tis faid it was not without great uneafinefs he inferted that fum in his will. After all, there are fo many people who wifh him at the Devil, that I am terribly afraid, they will be apt to out-vote a few priefts, who endeavour to pray him into Heaven; and that the curfes of thofe he has ruin'd, will probably drown the found of the prayers, of thofe he has paid.

Your relation of the vaft improvements in the royal Fifhery and Plantation-companies, were extreamly agreeable to me,

on

on account of the advantages which our
Nation, and the glory your Lordſhip's ad-
miniſtration, will reap from them ; but as
to my private affairs, they were of no ſort
of benefit to them, having unluckily ſold
out about two months before. 'Tis incredible, my Lord, with what regard and honour you are conſider'd in this Nation,
upon the new regulations you have eſtabliſh'd about thoſe two companies, and in
what terms they mention the whole of your
miniſtry, and his Majeſty's reign. As I am
convinc'd, there never were praiſes better
deſerv'd, it gives me infinite concern to find
your Lordſhip's ſtile ſo much chang'd from
its uſual ſpirit and force, and to hear you
talk in ſo deſponding a manner of the infirmities of age, your wearineſs of the
world ; and, which I fear is neareſt your
heart, the envy and malice of a degenerate
race, and an unthankful age. But your
Lordſhip's ſpirit is of a nobler turn, than
to let your virtue be alarm'd from its own
ſhadow, envy ; which is ſo far from in-
juring, that it is ornamental, and a necef-
ſary help to it, and rather ſerves than
hurts it. 'Tis true, your Lordſhip ſtands in
need of no ſuch aſſiſtances ; but in other
people,

people, the fear of its lashes makes them watch over their frailties, and avoid running into a thousand miftakes, which otherwife they would fall into. By this means, 'tis fo far from hurting virtue, that, like the clipping of the fheers to the hedge, it makes it grow thicker and ftronger from its wounds. Your Lordfhip has been too long ufed to it, not to know that it accompanies the actions of the great; like the dragons, gryphons, and other beafts and monfters, which the heralds give them, not as blots and deformities, but for the ornaments and fupporters of their coats of arms.

May you live many years to triumph over the groundlefs malice of your enemies, and enjoy the well-deferv'd gratitude and praifes of your friends; may your Lordfhip long continue to ferve his Majefty and your Country; and at laft, in a good old age, loaden with years and honours, retire to that grave, which you think of fo often, and I hope will wait for fo long; which is the fincere wifh of, my Lord, your Lordfhip's, *&c.*

HERBERT.

To the Lord High Treaſurer, &c.

Conſtantinople, May 1. 1998.

My LORD,

SInce I wrote to you the 29th of *February*, and the 16th of *April*, in return to yours of the 29th of *November*, I have never heard the leaſt account from you; which is owing, I am ſenſible, to a want of ſhips ſailing to this port, and no neglect or diſregard of your friends, of whom your Lordſhip is but too obſervant and careful. In a few days, I flatter my ſelf, I ſhall be made happy in your letters; and to know what hopes you can give me, either of the chief Phyſician for the Grand Signior's own ſervice, or the profeſſors of Aſtronomy, for whoſe ſalaries and proviſion I became reſponſible. I therefore hope there will be no heſitation or delay in procuring ſome worthy Gentleman to come and ſettle in the *Grand Cairo* college, which is at laſt ſo happily eſtabliſh'd by my intereſt with the Grand Signior.

It is incredible, with what zeal and expedition ſuch things are diſpatch'd, when the order is once iſſued by the Port; for

L l   then

then all hands are at work, and in a few weeks they are able to raife very extraordinary ſtructures. The College at *Grand Cairo*, and the Aſtronomy-ſchool, I am inform'd, were entirely finiſh'd in this manner in a few weeks, tho' there are ſpacious apartments, two large halls, and a noble obſervatory built up, purſuant to the incloſ'd plan I tranſmit to your Lordſhip.

I am impatient to hear ſomething of the dogs I formerly wrote for to your Lordſhip; for I have been ask'd a thouſand queſtions about them, their perfections, and their performances, by the Grand Signior, whenever he ſees me; and he often ſends for me, when they are the chief affair of ſtate, he wants to ſettle with me. I am forc'd to anſwer him at random, as near as I can, to what I imagine will be the truth; and, as any diſappointment would be intolerable and inſupportable, I muſt conjure your Lordſhip, that all poſſible care to gratify his Highneſs, may be taken herein. I muſt repeat the ſame thing, as to a Phyſician, which is of vaſt importance: and may oblige, if complied with, conſiderably, and if neglected, may produce terrible conſequences for ſo ſmall a trifle.

Since

Since I wrote laft to your Lordfhip, I have been three or four times at the Seraglio with the Grand Signior, entertaining him with your tellefcope, in which he takes more delight each day than other; and is grown fo familiar with every one of the planets, that he vifits them now by himfelf, without ftaying for any introduction of mine. Tho' he is not very fond of travelling upon the Earth, he frequently makes the great tour of the Heavens, and vifits all the conftellations in their turns; and begins to be confident, that in another age, we fhall not only be able to fee the inhabitants of the Moon, which would be ufelefs, without any other benefit, but to invent engines to carry us thither.

I am fo often fent for to the Seraglio on thefe accounts, that I am frequently call'd there the Sultan's Aftronomer; but as I have made as many delightful excurfions by Land and by Sea, as well as in the Air and the Heavens, your Lordfhip muft allow me to defcribe fome of them to you. One of the firft I made this fpring with him, was, to the Ifles of *Papa-Adafi,* (as the *Turks,* or the *Princes,* as the Chriftians call them,) in a gilt barge, row'd by

eighty

eighty flaves ; and as the barge was entirely built for rowing, it is incredible with what prodigious fwiftnefs we flew along the water, going at leaft three or four leagues an hour. As we went to hawk and fhoot on thefe lovely Iflands, the Grand Signior had feveral other barges, with his fowlers, oftragers, and falkners, and a vaft number of fetting-dogs, fpaniels, and many cafts of hawks of all kinds,, who followed us at fome. diftance. The Sultan keeps feveral families on the great Ifland, who plow and fow entirely to feed the wild fowl, letting a vaft many acres of grain rot every year on the ground, that they may make their haunts there ; and it being death to fhoot one of them, but when the Grand Signior is on the Ifland, it is incredible what prodigious quantities refort thither. There are of all forts and kinds on it ; for even thofe that are of a weak wing, and make fhort flights, as patridge, pheafant, quail, &c. and which could not eafily fly hither, are by the Sultan's order carried there to breed. The Iflands lie at the extremity of the *Propontis,* and tho' they are not many leagues round, have great variety of grounds. In the largeft, towards the north, there is a fort of mountain ;

and

and as all the plains and valleys, and even the mountain itſelf, abound with natural woods, mix'd with fine vineyards, and arable lands and paſturage, beautifully chequer'd, there is not poſſibly a lovelier ſcene to be met with.

We came there early, and they having had notice the day before, the Sultan's horſes which were kept there, were all at the ſea-ſhore, waiting for him and his attendants. We landed oppoſite to his magnificent hunting-lodge, with great ſilence, and in an inſtant we were all mounted, and the ſelect band of his ſportſmen, with their dogs, hawks, and guns, attending us. When we were got up into the Country, this great band divided itſelf into eight or ten ſeveral parties, which were for different kinds of game, and then all fell to their ſport with ſuch agreeable confuſion of entertainment and pleaſure, as was perfectly ſurprizing. I am perſuaded, both their falkners, fowlers, dogs and hawks, are infinitely more skilful than ours ; for I ſaw not one that did not perform their parts to admiration all the while we were in the field ; and tho' both at our own and the Emperor's Court I have been often delighted

L l 3 with

with fuch fports, yet I never faw any thing comparable to thefe.

I will give your Lordfhip a fhort account of two or three paffages, that gave me moft pleafure, that you may judge if I am un-reafonable in applauding them fo highly; and as you ufed in your youth to be fond of fuch entertainments, I hope it will ftill be agreeable to you, to hear of thofe of others.

I obferve they ufe the fame diverfion as we do in *England*, of daring the larks with the Hobby, foaring over them aloft in the air, while the dogs rang'd the field till the nets are drawn over the poor birds that lie clofe to the ground, and are afraid to truft to their wings; but then 'tis their cuftom that the moment they are taken, they are car-ried in a cage to the Emperor, who imme-diately gives them their life and liberty. Their gofhawks fly the river at malhard, duck, goofe, or hern, and the feveral kinds of large water-fowl; and all the time we were in the field, I never faw them fail to kill them at *fource*, as they call it. But what was more furprizing, was, a large kind of falcon, which is fo couragious, that I faw them feize on the fallow deer and wild

But

goats, faftning between their horns, and
flapping their wings in their eyes, till they
run themfelves dead, and the huntfmen
come in and cut their throats.

But their fowlers are yet more extraordinary than their hawks: I faw one of them,
call'd *Ibrahim*, who drove a covy of patridges into his nets, as our fhepherds would
drive fheep into a pinfold; which, as it was
a method unknown to me, I fhall defcribe
to your Lordfhip.   He had an engine made
of canvafs, exactly cut and painted, like
an horfe, and ftuffed with feathers or hay;
with this horfe and his nets he went to the
patridge-haunts; and having found out the
covy, and pitch'd his nets below flopewife
and hovering, he went above, and taking the
advantage of the wind, drove downward.
Then covering his face with long grafs, and
holding the engine fo as to hide him, he
ftalk'd towards the patridges very flowly, raifing them on their feet, but not their wings;
and driving them juft before him at pleafure.
If they chanc'd to chufe a road contrary to
the path he would have them take, he crofs'd
them with his horfe, and by artfully facing
them, forced them into the path that led to
the nets, to my great furprize and pleafure.

But

But I saw this same man with more delight, taking the whole eye of pheasants, both cock, hen, and pouts, to the great entertainment of the Sultan and my self, who obferv'd him from the top of a neighbouring hill. He had an excellent pheasant-call, all the different notes of which he underftood, and made use of with such perfect skill, that having pitch'd his nets in the little pads and ways of the wood, which they make like fheep-tracts in the places where they haunt; and taking the wind with him, and his canvafs horfe, for they ftill run down the wind, he drove the whole eye, or brood, into his fnares, and brought them to the Sultan, who was much pleafed, and rewarded him for his skill and diligence with a purfe of money. It were a vain attempt, to think of defcribing the twentieth part of the diverfion and fport we met with; but if your Lordfhip will reprefent to your felf, a vaft number of fwallows in a fummer's evening, on the bank of a lovely river, hunting for their prey, and purfuing with infinite fwiftnefs and skill, the little flies and infects floating on the air or the water, or the tops of the grafs, you will have a tolerable image of our fport, and the ifles of *Adafi* this delightful day.

After

After all, your imagination will fall vastly short, both of the numbers of the pursued and the pursuers, and the transports and delight of the beholders: All nature, not excepting the great Lord of Nature the Sun, labouring to pay its share of tribute and homage to the Grand Signior's pleasure. But as I never should have done, if I attempted to describe half the diverting scenes and adventures of that day, I will shut them all up, with giving you an account of one of the last of them; when the Sultan being wearied, retired to a noble tent that had been set up for him, where in the shade we continued to enjoy the prodigious prospect, (for it was open from the bottom a few feet) and to refresh ourselves with drinking sherbet, chocolate and coffee. His Highness immediately order'd all the game we had kill'd that day, to be laid in their several heaps before him; deer, chamois or wild goats, on one side; and on the other, wild geese, duck and mallard, herns, cranes, pheasants, patridge, grouse, snipes, quails, rails, and a number of birds, that I know not how to name, being foreigners to our country, unless I make use of the *Turkish* language.

But

But as the Grand Signior refolv'd to wait for the Vifier, whom he had fent three days before, to infpect the Architects and Engineers he was employing in the ifland *Tenedos*; juft as we had fufficiently, like true conquerors, refrefh'd ourfelves on the field of battel, pof-fefs'd ourfelves of the plunder, and reckon'd the flain, the Grand Vifier came. He gave his Highnefs a very particular and agreeable account, of that ftrong and noble Arfenal and Magazine, which he is building with fuch vaft expence, by that harbour. It is true, the Port is very ordinary; tho' even that is im-proving, by the vaft mole he is running out into the fea, oppofite to the ruins of old *Troy*. The Arfenal, when finifh'd, will be of great importance, and put a bridle, as it were, on the mouth of the *Hellefpont*, the *Propontis*, and *Thracian Bofphorus*; and will contribute a good deal to preferve the do-minion of the *Archipelago*, that is, fo much as our excellent Prince is pleas'd to allow him in thofe feas.

We had hardly receiv'd the Vifier's rela-tion of the fortifications there, when we were all order'd to embark in our feveral fta-tions and barges, where our Gally-flaves re-ceiv'd us with their ufual falutation; and in

a little

a little time, by the help of so many well-
plied oars, brought us to *Conſtantinople.*
However, as the night overtook us in the
middle of the channel, and the wind blew
very high, tho' without danger, I obſerv'd
the ſea-water perfectly ſeem'd to flaſh fire,
with the violent motion againſt the ſides of
the barge; ſo that I read plainly by it, to
my great ſurprize. It put me in mind of
Moſes's expreſſion in the firſt of *Geneſis,*
where he ſays *the Spirit of God mov'd on the
face of the waters*; and then follows, *God
ſaid, Let there be light, and there was light*;
and made me wonder ſome have not fan-
cied, that as man was created out of the
earth, ſo light was form'd out of the waters,
and the divine motion given them, as ſuddenly and brightly as the flame ſtarts out of
gunpowder, when touch'd by the fire.

I forgot to take notice to your Lordſhip,
that as the Viſier brought with him the new
plan of the *Dardanelles,* the Sultan bid me
take notice of the *Romeli-iskiſſar,* (or the
Caſtle that guards them on the ſide of *Europe)* which has been built up of late
years very fine and ſtrong, and fortified
with the largeſt cannon in the world; and
ask'd me, if I thought the ſhips of my King
would

would be able to batter down that, as they had done the old one in his great Uncle's time? I was a little furpriz'd at the queftion; but I avoided anfwering it directly, as civilly as I could, by faying, I doubted their being able, and was fure they would not be willing. But as we landed immediately at the Seraglio, the Sultan only anfwer'd me with a fmile, and a courteous nod; and ordering the barge to convey me fafely crofs the water to *Galata,* I took my leave of this goodnatur'd and generous Sultan, who wants only our Education and Religion, to make a great figure in the world. I got to my lodgings about two hours after fun-fet, much pleas'd with the magnificent variety of one day's diverfions; and was hardly fet down on my fofa to repofe myfelf, after fo agreeable a fatigue, when my old Druggerman or Interpreter, *Abraham,* a learned *Jew,* whofe converfations often entertain my folitary hours, came to me with a good deal of furprize and amazement in his face. I immediately faw fomething extraordinary had happen'd, and enquir'd of him what was the matter? My Lord, fays he, I bring you an account, which if it proves true, will make the enemies of my nation, and

the

the despis'd *Jewish* people, glad to lick the dust of their shoes. Here is Rabbi *Solomon* just come from *Tunis*, who is sent to warn our brethren, that the ten Tribes are discover'd in the middle part of *Africa*, where they retir'd in the days of their Captivity and affliction. He says they have a vast Empire there, and are very powerful, having near 50 millions of souls under their Kings, who are most observant of the Law, and have preserv'd their language pure and unmix'd, as well as their rites and ceremonies. The said Rabbi *Solomon* avers, that the great Messiah is risen among them, and hath chosen out an army of 500000 pick'd men, all as valiant as the *Maccabees*; that they have left all the strong holds of their Empire of *Gangara* and *Seneganda* well garison'd, and are in motion from the frontiers of those kingdoms, to cross the desarts of *Borno* and *Guoga*, and pass the *Nile*, seize on *Egypt*, and then the land of *Canaan* their Inheritance, and build up the fallen glories of mount *Sion* and *Jerusalem*. As I had a map of *Africa* in my room, I immediately search'd it for the kingdoms and desarts, my good Druggerman had settled his friends in, and found so far all was right; but desiring

to

to know what authorities he or Rabbi *Solomon* had for this report, he gave me two letters from the Synagogue of *Tunis*, directed to the faithful *Jews* of *Stamboul* and its Provinces, willing them to be on their guard, and behave like men, for the Kingdom was about to be restor'd to *Israel*. Along with these he communicated to me, under the solemnest promises of secrecy, the Messiah's Manifesto; in which he exhorts his subjects and brethren to prepare to rise, for the restoring both the sword and sceptre, into the hands of the faithful and chosen of heaven; and commands them to be ready, to depart for *Jerusalem* to the solemn sacrifice, so soon as they had certain intelligence from him, of his being possess'd of *Egypt* and *Grand Cairo*. I read them all over (that is, the *Turkish* translation of the *Hebrew*) with much admiration; and asking *Abraham*, if he believ'd these to be genuine letters? he answer'd me very hastily and angrily, as genuine as the Talmud; and that it was universally known to all the *Turks*, and the merchants in *Stamboul*, that these things were true; and it is certain, I had heard for several days, of some commotions in the inland parts of *Africk*, of a strange people

I then

I then ask'd him, what the *Jews* determin'd to do? Even, says he very eagerly, to obey the commands of their Messiah; and so soon as he hath conquer'd *Egypt*, to depart from the four winds under heaven, and be gather'd unto the brethren of the dispersion at *Jerusalem*, at the solemn sacrifice. He said this with tears in his eyes, and such emotion of heart, that I could not chuse but pity him, and his deluded people, who are as credulous as malice or love; and will probably, throughout this vast Empire, be standing with their ears prickt up, and, like birds, ready to take wing with all they can carry with them, if the news of this Revolution continues.

He had hardly done talking of this new-risen Messiah, when the Chiaus from the Grand Signior entred my apartment, with I know not how many slaves, loaden with part of the spoils we had taken that day, and which in his Master's name he presented me with, by his order. Your Lordship may believe, my thanks were not the only payment I made, in return for this prodigious favour; but I must own, it gave me so honest and reasonable a pleasure, to receive so extraordinary and publick a mark of the Sultan's

I

regard

regard for me, that I thought it cheaply purchas'd. I made the Chiaus fit down by me; and, as if fome revolution planets were rifen on the world, he began to tell me, that fince the Sultan had come to the Seraglio, the Grand Vifier had told him two furprizing pieces of news. Upon this the Chiaus related *Abraham*'s ftory, very much in the fame manner I have told it your Lordfhip; but with this addition, that the new Meffiah was the ftrongeft and moft beautiful man upon earth.

The other account he gave me was, that according to a belief they ever have entertain'd in *Perfia*, a great Prophet had lately appear'd there, who calls himfelf *Mahomet Mahadi*, the fon of *Hoffein* fecond fon of *Ali*, who folemnly avers to the people, (who fo many ages have been expecting him) that he lay hid all this while in a cave of the mountains of *Georgia*. He declares he is come from *Mahomet*, and is deputed and authorized by him to refute all errors, and reunite all in one belief, that there may be no more divifions and fchifms, among faithful Muffulmen and true Believers.

He preaches on horfeback, and made his firft fermon in the city of *Maradel*; and
feiz'd

feiz'd on the horfe, which for fo many Centuries has been kept for him there at the publick coft, * ready faddled and bridled. The Chiaus, who told all this with the graveft air in the world, faid that he was followed by great multitudes; and that it was expected the *Turks* and *Perfians* might by his means be united in Faith and Doctrine; but that the Prince of *Bafora* and he were like to have violent ftruggles. As I defir'd he would explain the occafion of their difference, he told me, that the Prince of *Bafora* ‖ had all along pretended to an hereditary fucceffion in the good graces and peculiar favours of the holy Prophet *Mahomet.* That in virtue of that intereft he had in him, the Prince and all his anceftors had conftantly, for fuch rewards and fums as they could agree for, given written affignments on the Prophet in heaven, for fuch places there, as the Prince recommended perfons to him for. This privilege his anceftors and he, like our Popes, had poffefs'd undifputed, till now that unfortunately the new Prophet *Mahomet Mahadi* avers, that he is commiffion'd to declare, that the holy Prophet has abrogated the Privileges, formerly allowed to the Princes of *Bafora*, they having recommended many unworthy

* *Vid.* Ambaff. Trav. in *Perfia.*   M m   people
‖ *Vid.* ditto Ambaff. Travels.

people to his beſt poſts in heaven; and that now the ſaid privileges were entirely tranſ-ferr'd to *Mahomet Mahadi*, the ſon of *Hoſ-ſein*, the ſon of the bleſſed *Ali*. I aſk'd the Chi-aus, if theſe accounts were well vouch'd and confirm'd? He aſſur'd me they were; and that all men were alarm'd with them beyond imagination, expecting vaſt revolu-tions would attend them, unleſs ſome un-foreſeen accidents ſhould intervene and pre-vent them. That the Grand Viſier, by the Sultan's deſire, had ſent for the Mufti to conſult with him hereupon; being appre-henſive very dangerous commotions may ariſe on the ſide of *Perſia*, if the utmoſt care be not us'd in it; and that it was be-liev'd the Grand Signior would be ſummon'd, to give an account before the new Prophet, of the fatal ſchiſm between the *Turkiſh* and *Perſian* Muſſulmen. The Chiaus having ended his extraordinary hiſtory, was pleas'd to withdraw; and as the good *Abraham* re-tir'd along with him, they left me to my own reflections on the amazing credulity, ſuperſtition and blindneſs of mankind. If either of theſe two accounts from *Africa* or *Perſia* prove true, it is poſſible thoſe po-pulous territories, may be laid waſte and

deſtroy'd

deftroy'd in the flame they may kindle. But
the *Jews*, my Lord, are above all other nations foolifhly credulous; this *Abraham* my
Truchman, is really more knowing and judicious than moft of his Tribe, and yet he
reads the *Talmud*, the *Mifnah*, and all the
fabulous myfteries of the *Cabbala*, with as
much veneration as the Pentateuch. He
is as much perfuaded that our tears were not
falt, till *Lot*'s wife was chang'd into a pillar
of falt; that fhe has ftill her *Menfes*; and that
fhe was thus chang'd, becaufe that out of malice
fhe would not put down the faltfeller on the
table to the angels; as that *Sodom* was burnt.
He believes ftedfaftly, that before the Deca-
logue was given the *Ifraelites*, God defiring
it fhould not be confin'd to them, went to
mount *Seir*, and offer'd it to the *Idumæans*
defcended from *Ifaac*; but when they heard
the fixth commandment, *Thou fhalt not kill*,
they got up and refufed it; for that it had
been faid to their anceftors, (*Gen.* xxviii.) *By
thy fword thou fhalt live*. That upon this God
offer'd it to the *Ifhmaelites* defcended from
Abraham by *Hagar*; but when they heard
the feventh, *Thou fhalt not commit adultery*,
read, they refus'd their obedience to that
command, fince they had receiv'd a contra-

ry one, namely, *Thou fhalt increafe and multiply*; upon which (he avers) God was forc'd to offer it the *Jews*, who took it without exception.

Nay, I've heard him maintain, that at his leifure hours in the fixth day, God created ten things privately; 1st, the earth that fwallowed up *Corah*, *Dathan*, and *Abiram*; 2dly, the whale that fwallowed up *Jonah*; 3dly, the rainbow which he hid in the clouds; 4thly, the ram which was facrific'd for *Ifaac*; 5thly, the rod with which *Mofes* wrought his miracles; 6thly, the manna for the *Jews*; 7thly, the ftone of which the tables of the Law were made; 8thly, the devil and his accomplices; 9thly, hammers and pinchers, which men cou'd never have invented; and 10thly, the head of *Balaam's* afs. He has been ftill of opinion, (among a thoufand other as abfurd opinions) that as women cannot be capable of the covenant of circumcifion, fo they cannot be entitled to happinefs in the next life; and that at the day of judgment, which will be on a *Friday*, *Adam* muft be compleat, and therefore will reaffume his rib, and fo *Eve* will ceafe to be; and all women defcended from her will be contracted into that rib, and be no more, and confequently not judg'd.

2

But

But it were endlefs to reckon up the traditions he holds; and I only quote thefe few, to fhew your Lordfhip the wild fuperftition and credulity of this people, who make a mock of our faith as abfurd, and yet are capable of ruining the welfare of their country and families, by following the firft Impoftor that fets up for a Meffiah, and begins a rebellion that for a few months appears fuccefsful.

But we will difmifs him at prefent, to fpeak on fomething more agreeable; and to acquaint your Lordfhip, that I here tranfmit you the names of fuch of the *Greek* Popes and Bifhops, &c. as are averfe to fubmit to, and unite to the Church of *Rome*, which they look on as a fuperftitious and idolatrous ufurper; and who have join'd unanimoufly in the Remonftrance, to which their names are annex'd, in petitioning for his Majefty's powerful protection againft her. As it is highly reafonable, to make fome provifion for the neceffities, and even the eafe of thefe deferving men, I do earneftly beg, that fuch a moderate ftipend fhall be annually fettled on them, as may prevent their fuffering too far, from the power and oppreffion of the Jefuits, for their maintaining the truth of

their

their doctrines, and the equality, if not the preeminence of their Church over *Rome.*

But your Lordſhip muſt accompany me with the Grand Signior, in another excurſion we made by water, for freſh air and the diverſions of the field, a very few days ago; which may poſſibly give you ſome amuſement to read, as it gave me infinite delight while I was enjoying it. I was ſummon'd laſt *Tueſday* by the Sultan, to attend early at the Seraglio the next morning; when accordingly we got aboard the ſame barges, with all the Falconers and Fowlers, Guns, Dogs, and Nets, that were neceſſary to make our diverſion fully compleat. Your Lordſhip has heard of that little wonder of the earth, for beauty and riches, the Grand Signior's new houſe of pleaſure, known by the name of the *Fanari Kioſc,* which he has finiſh'd with ſuch immenſe expence at the lovely Promontory near *Chalcedon.* 'Tis built ſomething after the manner of the King of *France's* houſe of pleaſure at *New Marli,* but adorn'd with vaſt expatiating porticos of the fineſt pillars, and over them with cloſe galleries of his Sultana's apartments. The whole is built in the middle of the fineſt garden, after the *European* manner, that is to be met

with

with in the world; cut out into regular plantations of fruit and foreſt, and parterres of flower-gardens, mix'd with ſo agreeable an extravagance, that it ſeems to ſtrike the eye and the imagination of the ſpectator, with too forcible a ſurprize. For the extent of the gardens is ſo unbounded, the plantation of trees, both fruit and foreſt, are ſo numerous and ſo large, and the whole ſo skilfully interſpers'd, with a vaſt profuſion of parterres and compartments of flower-beds, fountains, caſcades, vaſes, obelisks, temples, viſtas, porticoes, walks and alleys; and all ſurrounded with ſo perpetual a ſerenity of the heavens, and fertility of the earth, that it looks like the Paradiſe, which God planted for the Lord of the world to dwell in. The gardens are ſo vaſtly extended, that they conſtantly allow deer to graze among them; but they are ſuch as they breed up, and prepare for this purpoſe, by hamſtringing them, ſo that they can't run faſt; and gelding them when their heads are grown, ſo that they never herd with other deer, nor caſt their horns, but ſtill wander about the gardens; where they ſtrike the fancy very agreeably, with ſeeing ſo unſual an inhabitant of the parterre, browſing among the knots of flowers. The pro-

ſpect

spect from this great height is as astonishing,
as all the other circumstances; for from
hence we have a compleat view of the
Grand Seraglio, its buildings and gardens,
of the vast dome of *Sancta Sophia*, and the
chambers of the Divan; the lovely Isles of
the *Princes*, and the smooth glassy face of
the *Propontis*, as well as the haven of *Chalcedon*; the beauteous bason and gulf of *Nicomedia*, and the rich hills and plains of fertile *Bythinia*, that lie below its view, in the
finest irregular level that the eye can dwell
on.

Nay, the whole city of *Constantinople* rising in its beauteous terrasses, street above
street, and dome above dome, with all its
gilded minarets and steeples, towers and cupolas, and mix'd with the surprizing verdure of the groves and gardens, and shades
of cypress, and other ever-greens, which
beautify the prospect of that city, lies perfectly under its command; with all the
crowds of shipping, saicks, skiffs, boats and
barges, that perpetually cover the face of the
sea below it, and by their constant motion
heighten the prospect extremely.

To this earthly paradise were we carried,
my Lord, the *Bostangi Bassa* steering us, as
his

his office obliges him ; and as it is not over four or five miles from the Seraglio, we flew there in our vaft row-barge in an inftant, and found it furrounded by a high wall of full twenty miles circuit. This extent of ground is kept entirely under all kinds of beafts, both of foreft and chafe, and all forts of wild fowl ; having vaft natural lakes, and artificial canals and rivers, for thofe that delight in the water, and great ranges of plow'd fields fown, and woods and coppices cut into walks and avenues, for the other kinds. Being never difturb'd, but juft on odd times when the Sultan comes to hunt and fowl, the frequency and tamenefs of the game is furprizing ; both birds and beafts ftarting and flying before you for a little fpace, and then ftopping their flight, and ftanding at a gaze about you, till the murdering hawk or gun, or the treacherous dog, teaches them to avoid the arts and fnares, that Man is contriving for their ruin. Nay, in all the noife and confufion of the field, when fuch numbers were hunting on the one fide, hawking on another, fetting in this field, and fhooting in fome adjacent one ; yet the herds of the beafts, and the flocks of the fowl, never attempted to be-

take

take themſelves to the open country, but kept ſtill within their belov'd confinement, and the delightful boundaries of the park-walls. Judge, my Lord, how lovely a ſcene this muſt make to one, who has ſo high a reliſh of the ſports of the field, as the Grand Signior; where in every inclo-ſure or coppice, you ſee new game riſe be-fore you, and find freſh employment for the faulkner, the huntſman, and the fowler. The truth is, we were marvelouſly enter-tained, for the three or four cooler hours of the morning; but as we wanted the deli-cious breezes of the *Papa-Agaſi* Iſlands, and (beſides the calmneſs of the day) there be-ing not a cloud to be ſeen in the whole hemiſphere, the Sun was ſo violently hot, tho' ſo early in the year, that one would have thought it had been in *July* or *Auguſt*, and made it impoſſible to move, under the violence of its rays, with any eaſe. We therefore retreated to the great *Salone* of the royal *Kioſc*, where in the fine porticoes to the north of the *Salone*, liſtning to the murmuring water-falls of one of the fineſt fountains in the World, we ſate cool and undiſturb'd by the Sun-beams. We ſtaid a good while here, ſitting on the *Sofas*, and

muſing

muſing after the faſhion of the Turks, without ſpeaking to each other, but now and then a few monoſyllables; when we were agreeably ſurpriz'd, with the Boſtangi-Baſſa's approaching us with above 100 ſlaves, all loaden with different kinds of viands, the ſpoils of the field and the foreſt, the earth, the air, and the water. If there had been living creatures in the other element, the fire, as Ariſtotle pretends there are, I believe he had brought them too, and laid them as he did all the others, at the feet of his mighty Maſter. While we were at our ſports in the field, the Boſtangi Baſſa had taken the ſlaves and barges, with all the nets, and had brought the tribute of the ocean for his part, mix'd with the ſpoils of the garden, in a great many baskets and diſhes, loaden with cherries, ſtrawberries, apricots, melons, and other of their early fruits. The Sultan was much pleas'd, and as it was near dinner-time, he order'd they ſhould get it ready with all expedition ; and as the Turks live on the ſimpleſt kind of food, that is as eaſily dreſs'd as 'tis digeſted; in a very little time it was ſerv'd up, in the north portico of the great Salone, where we were ſitting. The Grand Signior, with his uſual

good-

goodnefs, commanded me to dine with him; which I did with infinite pleafure, being delighted to receive every day, new proofs of his more than ordinary regard for me. Our meal, tho' it was chiefly rice, boil'd in the broth of different kinds of flefh, or elfe mix'd with bits of mutton, or the flefh of our pheafants and patridges, relifht very well; having the *Turkifh* fauce to it, temperance, and heighten'd with (the more ufual one of the Chriftians) exercife.

We had fome difhes mix'd up with a fort of curdled milk, call'd Joghourt, and differently colour'd with faffron, or the juice of pom-granates and rafpberries, and feveral other in-gredients; and fome fifh and roaft meats, or Kiabab (as they call it) of our venifon and wild fowl, which we hardly tafted. To this we had the moft delicious and wholfome drink, that ever the earth pour'd out of her breafts to her children, plain water, from the foun-tain we fate by, with a little frefh bread, (for they never eat it ftale) to give it the higher flavour. Thus, without taking as many hours to it, as our gormandifing *Britons*, and other *Europeans* do, we finifh'd our light, and therefore our pleafing and healthful repaft; which, however, was a little

little lengthned out, with a lovelier defert of fruit, than I had ever feen fo early in *May*.

And now I cannot but take notice to your Lordfhip, of a fafhion that obtains here in all meals of fruit-kind, which I heartily wifh were the mode in *Great-Britain*; and that is, the placing on the table a large *China* bowl, with a cover to it that flopes down into the veffel, with a wide aperture in the middle of the defcent. Into this every body throws the melon-parings, the ftalks and ftones of the cherries, and the cores of pears and apples, the skins of goofeberries, and the ftones of damfins, plumbs, &c. all which we Chriftians, in fo odious and filthy a manner, take out of our mouths flaver'd with our fpittle, and lay expos'd to every ones eyes, on our plates or the table: Whereas this neat and cleanly veffel hides all that vile filth, and hinders the eye from being fhock'd and offended with fuch heaps of naftinefs. They call it *Ordoma*, which I know no word we have to anfwer; but it fignifies a pot or *Privy* for the *Mouth*; and it is fo univerfal of late among them, that thofe who can't buy *China* ones, have earthen ones of common potters ware; the *Turks*
above

above all things, ſtudying neatneſs and clean-
lineſs.

But it is time, my Lord, to haſten to the
ſea-ſhore and our barges, whither the cool
evening and the declining ſun is calling us.
Here you muſt now ſuppoſe us embark'd,
and floating on the lovelieſt of all the baſins
in the earth, the ſmooth ſurface of the *Propontis*; flying with the incredible force
of ſo many oars with vaſt rapidity on its
cryſtalline boſom, unruffled with the ſmalleſt breeze. As we ſate in the boat, I aſk'd
the Grand Signior, if the accounts of the
Jews ten tribes being diſcover'd in *Africk*,
and marching with their Meſſiah for *Egypt*,
and of the Prophet *Mahomet Mahadi* appearing in *Perſia*, were true. He ſeem'd a
little ſurpriz'd with the queſtion ; but as he
had no mind to puniſh my curioſity with
a harſh reply, he told me I muſt wait for
the lame poſt, to be ſecure of the truth
of ſuch great events ; by which I found
plainly, there is more in thoſe reports than
I imagin'd, tho' probably leſs than *Abraham*, my Interpreter, and the Chiaus would
have me believe.

Imagine us now, my Lord, landed at
Conſtantinople, and retir'd to our different
habita-

habitations, and the trouble of this letter
ſhall laſt but a very little longer, than while I
deſcribe to you the exact figure and perſon,
of one of the *Turkiſh* Santones or Derviſes,
as they are generally call'd.   I found this extraordinary creature, ſitting in my hall when
I came home, from whence he would not
retire by fair means, for all that my ſervants
could ſay, till I came and gave him a piece
of ſilver, to procure the favour of his quitting my territories.   He was not one of
thoſe kinds of Monks, who live together in a
particular community, under certain regulations ; but a vagabond member, that coun-
terfeited abſtinence and ſanctity; and a
ſcorn for the World and all that was in it,
in order to be admir'd and rewarded.   He
was a little creeping wretch, with a long
red beard, that he continually ſtroak'd, and
had cover'd his head with a tall ſugar-loaf
cap of blue linnen, with black ſtrings and
fringe ſow'd to it, which hung down to his
neck.   He wore two ſheep-skins for a coat,
ſow'd together like a ſack, with two holes
for his arms at the ſides, and at the top
and bottom for his head and feet : This he
had tied about his middle, with a Buffaloe's
tail, which was ſtrung round with ſeveral
little

little rings of red and white marble. He had a bracelet of the fame creature's hide about his arms, and in his right hand he carried a wand, with a piece of ivory at the end, like a faw, to fcratch his back where he could not get at it to claw it with his nails; to which fplendid equipage, he had join'd a long thick club, as a weapon of defence, and an horn that hung over his fhoulders by a ftring, to found upon occafions, and gather the good Muffelmen about him. Behold, my Lord, the drefs of religion run mad, or putting on the mask of hypocrify! would to God fhe never look'd better when fo difguis'd, and we fhould have fewer of the Jefuite tribe cloaking the wickednefs of their actions, under the fanctity of their habits; and yet fewer, who out of a furious zeal againft fuch difguifes, would ftrip religion as naked as the Savages of *America!* I wait with impatience for your next letters, and am,

My L o r d,

Your Lordfhip's, &c.

S t a n h o p e.

P R E-

PREFACE the IIId.

By way of *Poſtſcript* to the Criticks.

WHEN I laſt parted with thee, my dear reader, with all the civility of a man that was in hopes never to meet thee again; I was juſt ſhutting up my defence, againſt all the objections that envy or ignorance cou'd bring, to hurt this ineſtimable performance. I little imagin'd then, that after having ſo entirely driven my enemies out of the field, they ſhou'd be able to bring any freſh forces againſt me. But, alas! I find that many-headed monſter, an ingenious reader, is like the dreadful Hydra; and that no ſooner an author, with the labour of an *Hercules*, has cut off one envenom'd head, and laid it groveling and ſenſeleſs at his feet, but inſtantly a crowd of others, as poiſonous and ſpiteful, riſe up in its place to attack him. Accordingly I am aſſur'd, ſince I finiſh'd my ſecond Preface, that there is ſtarted up one formidable objection, which I am oblig'd to anſwer, as it carries an air of truth with it, and is grounded on this; that theſe vaſt diſcoveries and improvements, theſe changes and revolutions of things below, which are mention'd in the ſubſequent let-

N n   ters,

ters, cannot poffibly happen, nor confequently be true, many of them are fo improbable.

To which I anfwer, in the firft place,
that for that very reafon, becaufe they are
improbable and unlikely, I give credit to
my good angel's prediction of them, and
am confident they will come to pafs. I
will not fay with *Tertullian, Certum eft quia
impoffibile eft*; but I will fay, with all fubmiffion and modefty, that had my good
genius defign'd to impofe on me in thefe
matters, or I upon the wife, the judicious
and wife reader, they would have been contriv'd with a greater approximation, (as the
learned fpeak) and verifimilitude to truth.
If they were mere fables invented to deceive,
they would have been model'd, to as near
a conformity as poffibly they could, to the
leaft difputed realities, and would have put
on the drefs of probability at leaft, in order
to impofe on the credulity of mankind.
There is a vaft extent in invention and imagination; and if falfhoods were defign'd to
be obtruded on the world by thefe papers,
they might eafily have been cook'd up, in
the common appearances, and refemblances
of fuch things, as are frequently found out,
and difcover'd every day.   The

The small regard therefore that is shewn here, to such little tricks and subtilties, in many prodigious discoveries in arts and sciences, travels, revolutions and alterations of all kinds, and especially in the 4th and 6th volumes, ought to stand as an evidence of their truth; and that they are not forgeries and impostures, but real facts, which time will produce, and which are delivered to mankind with the carelesness and simplicity of an honest publisher; more sollicitous to reveal actual facts and events, as he receiv'd them, than to disguise them so craftily to the world, as to seem more likely to happen, and easy to be believ'd.

Were there occasion for it, and were I not apprehensive of enlarging this Preface too far, I could say a great deal here on that famous observation, *Aliquando insit in incredibili veritas, & in verisimili mendacium*; and convince my readers, how little weight any objection ought to have with him, that is bottom'd on this sandy foundation. But I hope I need not dwell much on this point; and indeed whoever are knowing and learned enough, to be acquainted with the infinite incredible verities in the world of science, the vast numbers of improbable

and

and unimaginable truths, to be met with there, and the heaps of plaufible errors and delufive falfhoods, that men are fo ufually led away with; will never confider the improbability of fome relations in this work, as an argument for any thing, but their being more unfeign'd and genuinely true.

But, 2*dly*, I have to anfwer, that there is nothing foretold here, which will really feem fo very improbable, to thofe who know the infinite power of the great Source of all events below; who have confider'd the vaft operations of nature, the force of our minds when fet on work by ambition and emulation, and the ftrange changes and chances, the revolutions, alterations and improvements, which attend all things here; as well as the vaft fields of art and knowledge, which the new world hath brought forth among us, by the labours of different voyagers. Let fuch ignorant objectors therefore, that are buried in the prefent ftate of the earth, and think it will continue in a manner unimprov'd and unalter'd, let them, I fay, look back, if they know any thing of it in former ages. Let them confider how abfurd and incredible it would have appear'd, if a man, for example, at the building of *Rome*, had (thus enlighten'd)

lighten'd) foretold the vaft growth of that
Monarchy, the overturning all others by that
embryo ftate, the majefty of the pagan religion there, the birth and rife of the Chriftian, the breaking of the *Roman* Empire
into feveral little fcraps and pieces, which
are now mifcall'd Kingdoms; the fpreading
conquefts of the Pope and his Monks, their
difpofing of crowns and fceptres, and temporal and eternal happinefs at their pleafure,
the reformation of Religion, and all the
wars, factions and revolutions, which that
fpiritual Monarch occafion'd, to maintain
his Empire on earth, and his interefts and
pretended alliances with heaven : Let them
reflect, I fay, if fuch a relation (or prediction) would not be receiv'd as more ridiculous
and impoffible, than thofe that are mention'd in thefe fix volumes.

But the truth is, whoever knows any thing
of the hiftory of this globe, or the little
wretches that crawl on it, and call themfelves
men and lords of it, would never raife fo
weak an objection. For what is it, but one
conftant fcene of the moft furprizing and
incredible changes? How have the very face
and features of it (if I may fo fpeak) been
perpetually torn and difmember'd, by delu-

ges

ges and earthquakes, by vulcanoes, tempefts and inundations? as every one knows,
that is acquainted with geography, or natural philofophy, or that will read the accounts
of fuch matters, in good authors.

Strabo particularly in his firft book, and
Pliny in numberlefs places *, will inftruct
us fufficiently on this point; not to omit
Diodorus Siculus, and efpecially where he
gives us the account, how the vaft overflow-
ing of the *Pontus Euxinus* laid the whole
Archipelago under water, deftroying all the
inhabitants, tearing up the mountains by
the roots, and forming a new world of
iflands, that here and there peer up their
rocky heads, amidft the deluge.

As to the amazing alterations, in the
manners and cuftoms of particular nations,
who is there that is ignorant, how power
and politenefs, how arts, and arms, and
learning, have been, from age to age, changing their feats, and, like the ocean, gaining
ground in one place, while it lofes it in another? How is *Greece,* the feat of freedom
and knowledge, philofophers and patriots,
become

---

* *Vid.* Plin. lib. 2, 3, 4, 5, *and* 6. *See alfo* Refleffioni
Geografiche del P. D. Vitale Terra Roffa à cap. 13. ad
22.

become a neft of flaves and ignorants; and inftead of thofe renowned Architects and Sculptors, that for fo many ages crowded her cities with the nobleft palaces, and taught her animated marbles almoft to breathe and move, fill'd with ruftick builders of clay cottages and huts, and cutters of faltfellers and mortars, as *Tournefort* calls them? How is the mighty *Rome* grown the mother of fuperftition, cowardice and cruelty, who was once the chief nurfe of the oppofite virtues among men? In a word, not to dwell too long on fo painful a fubject; how has fhe fallen from her once exalted character, and exchang'd the generous fentiments and conduct of her ancient heroes, for the impious dreams of vifionary Monks, the furious rage of Bigots, the little craft of Hypocrites, and the filly dotage of her mitred Monarchs?

As to the ftate of learning, to look no farther back than the laft two ages; how is *Ariftotle*, the father of fcience in former times, degenerated, in many refpects, into the character of ignorance and infancy in this? How are the fchoolmen, who gave laws to heaven and earth, depos'd and rejected, and

N n 4 their

* *Vid.* Tournefort's Voyage, *Vol.* 1, *p.* 156.

their wrangling doctors fucceeded, by the great improvers of knowledge, who have made fuch important and fuccefsful difcoveries, in this wide world of matter and life, which the others had fo long kept us ftrangers to? Befides, if we confider how few years are paft, fince we improv'd Aftronomy by a true fyftem, verified by demonftration, and founded Philofophy on actual experiments, not on imaginary notions and opinions; fince the compafs and the needle trac'd out the mariner's unerring road on the ocean, and war join'd fire to the fword, or mufkets banifh'd bows and arrows; fince the invention of printing gave new lights and aids to the arts; fince mufick and painting had a new birth in the world; fince regular pofts were firft invented, and fet up by *de Taffis* * in *Spain*, and trade and correfpondence got wings by land, as well as by fea; fince Phyficians found out either new drugs or fpecificks, or even the fecrets of Anatomy, or the circulation of the blood; fince our own nations learn'd to weave the fleece of our fheep, or that even one half of the earth had found out the other; and above all, if we reflect, that the fmall compafs of time,

* Strada de bello Belgico, Dec. 2. lib. 10.

time, which all thefe great events have happen'd in, feems to promife vaſt improvements in the growing centuries; it will not appear furprizing, and much lefs abfurd, that fuch difcoveries and improvements are allotted to our pofterity, in thefe volumes.

Even as to trade, riches and power, how has the new world prov'd the great nurfery and prop of the old, which was fo long a weak and fickly infant, hardly thought worth the rearing or owning, tho' it is now grown one great fource, of the ftrength, wealth and profperity of thofe kingdoms, who almoſt grudg'd its fupport? Nay, as to Politenefs and Literature, and the arts of Peace and War, to look no farther back than our own doors, and our own homes; how is *Great Britain*, within a fmall fpace of time, tho' once fo defpis'd and neglected in *Europe*, grown, under the care of a few good Princes, the feat of trade, and power, and learning, and the glory and admiration of the whole earth, even at this prefent hour; to fay nothing of that progrefs foretold in this work, which fhe will daily make, (except under fome adminiftrations and reigns, and certain years of reigns) and is now actually making, of growing ftill
greater

greater and more confiderable? Away therefore with thefe objectors of improbability,
who deferve as little to be regarded, as
thofe who infinuate that I have copied all
this work, from the famous *Mazapha
Einok*, or *Enoch*'s Prophecy, which *Ægidius
Lochienfis* brought *Peireskius* * from *Æthio-
pia*, and which was fuppofed to contain
the hiftory of all things, to the end of
the World; tho' I folemnly aver, I neither
handled, nor faw, or even believed fuch a
work was, or is in being, whatever fome
learned men, both of the *Jewifh* and Chriftian perfuafion, alledge for its exiftence.

The truth is, this laft infinuation is
fo trivial, as well as falfe, that I had
not thought it worth mentioning; but
that I might omit nothing which my
friends, (to whom I entrufted the communication of the manufcript to others)
affur'd me, the moft ill-natur'd of their
correfpondents, objected againft it. As
I have always thought, malice fhould
never be difregarded, how blind or ftupid
foever it appears; fo I have left none of
the filly remarks, of my oppofers uncon-
futed;

* Vita Peireskii per Gaffend. Lib. 5. *p.* 395.

futed ; tho' if one takes a view of thefe objectors, the beft of them will appear but like a child playing at blindman's buff, where the hood-wink'd trifler, catches at every thing he can, and runs about, the fool and jeft of all around him, in a violent fume and hurry ; and after guefling wrong at whatever he blindly ftumbles on, is forc'd to let it go, and then falls to again, with the fame fuccefs, and lays hold on another.

Without attending therefore any longer, to the anfwering the ftupid malice of objectors, I fhall proceed to give my friends, the learned world and pofterity, fome cautions about this work, and fo conclude, and let it take its fortune.

And the firft caution I fhall give them is, that tho' I am confident all things deliver'd in thefe fix Volumes, will inevitably come to pafs ; yet left hereafter any bafe *attempts might be made*, on the lives, honours, or fortunes, of fome illuftrious perfons mention'd in them, in order to overturn fuch predictions, as feem to relate to them ; I do hereby forewarn pofterity, not to entertain any defigns, of deftroying the credit

credit of thefe papers, by fuch indirect methods.

As I freely own, I chiefly intend this caution, for my dear friends the good fathers the Jefuits, who may be too free with their pens, or their penknives, with fuch views, I think it would be in vain to urge againft them, the *Wickednefs* of fuch a procedure; for their zeal and piety is fo prodigious, that if they believe it for the good of the Church; that fingle argument, will fufficiently fanctify any meafures, which Men lefs holy and religioufly given, would foolifhly boggle at. I therefore fhall only put them in mind, of the *Folly* of attempting fuch an impoffible project, as the removing privately out of the way the perfons, or publickly ftabbing the reputation of fuch people, as are doom'd and foretold here to be their enemies.

Let me then beg of them, and all that are capable of acting, with their honeft and furious zeal or artful wifdom, to confider, that befides the vanity of fighting thus, againft unavoidable events, I have alfo in many places purpofely fo difguis'd Mens actions and characters in this work, that it will be impoffible for them. to difcern the real

perfons,

perfons, till the very facts themfelves, difcover them to the World.

In the next place, I do hereby declare before-
hand to *Pofterity*, that if fome things fhould
feem, not to fall out exactly as they are
foretold, that they, and not thefe incomparable productions, muft bear the blame
of it. Let them be affur'd, that thofe appearing failures, happen from one of thefe
two caufes. Firft, that either they do not
underftand what is or appears to be written,
thro' the difguifes I neceffarily made ufe of,
or that people may put, on their own or
others actions, in order to elude fuch predictions; or, 2dly, Men are deceiv'd, either by reports of others, or their own fal-
lacious fenfes, perfuading them they have
feen things happen otherwife, than they
really have, and confequently the bare appearance of events, ought not to be fet up
in oppofition, to the undoubted truths here
difcover'd to them.

I remember well, an impertinent objection of this nature, was once made by
the Queen of *Poland*, to a very renown'd
and illuftrious Prophet of the 17th Century *,
who

---

* Vide *Bayle's* Dict. in the letter M on *Defmaretz*.

who had dedicated to her an admirable
work, in which he had foretold the ruin
of the *Mahometan* Empire, by the arms of
Lewis XIII. and *Urban* VIII ; nor shall
I forget the wife and judicious answer he
gave her. For on his presenting his book
to her Majesty, she pretended to censure
one mistake he had run into, by not having
known, that *both* the Heroes of his Prophecy, hapned to be some months dead,
without having attempted what he foretold of them ; to which the Author replied, (as I beg leave to do, to all silly objections of the like nature, which Posterity
may raise against this Work) that pretended
facts, are never to be set in competition,
with unquestionable Predictions ; and those
that offer to do so, are not fit to be disputed
with.

This therefore I request of them, in return for my labours in presenting them with
these Volumes, that they fully assure themselves, that all I have or shall publish is
true, and then let them depend on it,
that whatever comes to pass, will in due
time, (sooner or later) be accommodated to,
and be found to tally with every thing foretold in them.

But

But I muft go yet further with my cautions, and that I may conceal nothing from pofterity, I fhall own, that I am in much lefs pain, for the verification of any Predictions in thefe letters, than I am left the few copies I print of them, may thro' envy or folly, or an utter ignorance of their worth, be entirely loft or fupprefs'd, before thofe times, when their truth and value will be confirmed. I therefore beg all, into whofe hands thefe Repofitories of truth, thefe invaluable Anecdotes of hiftory fhall fall, to preferve them with care, till the days of which they fpeak fhall appear, tho' like the Prophet *Micaiah*, they are kept ever fo clofe prifoners, till their truth or falfhood be manifefted to all. Befides, as it is much to be fear'd, my dear friends the Jefuits, (of whom, like that ill-boding prophet, thefe papers, to my great concern, do never prophecy good, but evil) may buy them up at immenfe prices, in order to fupprefs them; I muft beg of pofterity, that fome Law may pafs, that authentick copies of them, may be fafely preferv'd in our publick libraries, and, like the Sybilline oracles, be confulted on the emergencies of ftate; and that it may be death or banifhment,

for

for any perfon to apply the leaves of them, either under pies or pafties, to pack up groceries, to line trunks, or cover band-boxes, or make ufe of them in any mean filthy office whatever.

As to the *imitatorum fervum pecus,* the little tribe of copiers, who will endeavour to foift their fpurious writings on the pub-lick, for the fequel of this I have now ho-nour'd the World with ; I am not much in pain, for any damage their maim'd pro-ductions may bring, to thefe immortal Ar-chives of futurity. The truth is, I look on this fort of writers in the fame light, as thofe filly kind of birds called *Dotterels,* which Mr. *Camden* * tells us, by aping the motions and actions of the cunning Fowler, and imitating all he does, are foon caught hold of and deftroy'd by *him,* whom they endeavour to mimick. Poffibly the fublimity of that fuperior genius, which has enrich'd this nation with thefe treafures, may deter fuch creatures, from attempting fo vile an infult ; tho' alas when we hear the ingenious *Stephen Pafquier* ‖, complain-ing fo gravely and judicioufly to *Ronfard,* that

---

* In his account of *Lincolnfhire.* ‖ Les Lettres d'Eftienne Pafquier, *p.* 17. à Lyon. 1607.

that no fooner *Jeane la Pucelle**, puſh'd by a divine inſpiration, and as it were delegated from Heaven, came to ſuccour the arms of *Charles* VII. but immediately two or three impudent wretches ſtarted up in *Paris*, and pretended to be commiſſion'd, in the ſame celeſtial manner as ſhe was; how can I hope this performance, will not meet with the like treatment, from baſe counterfeits.

However, at the worſt, I am prepar'd for this little misfortune, if it muſt be born; and tho' it is certain, that there ſeldom appear'd a glorious work, but it occaſion'd a ſpawn of creeping plagiaries, to forge ſomething as like it as they can; yet it is ſome comfort to conſider, that the ſame thing which gives them birth, deſtroys theſe little abortions; and that like *Moſes*'s rod, it ſoon devours the falſe ſerpents, that pretend to imitate the miraculous product, of a ſuperior power.

But really this ſort of ſcriblers, does not alarm me half ſo much, as another race of impertinents, who are call'd Commentators, and pretend, (tho' with very different ſuccefs) to improve books, juſt as Gardeners do their fruit-trees; upon which

O o   they

* The Maid of Orleans.

they graft and inoculate, all that their filly tafte and fancy can furnifh them with, while the mother-ftock is quite loft and hid in the exuberant growth, that too often converts all its wholfome juices, to feed a barren fuperfluity of leaves. As I have great apprehenfions, the vaft reputation of this work, will occafion feveral learned blockheads of that tribe, to attempt fomething of this nature upon it, I do hereby in the face of the World, enter my proteft in form againft fuch proceedings; and all notes, obfervations, remarks, explanations, conftructions, caftigations, emendations, or various readings, which thefe animals may pretend to affix, to the native fimplicity of the original text, of thefe venerable volumes.

I am loth to be particular on this head, for fear of giving offence, by reflections that may look too national; and efpecially where a people honeftly zealous for their country's liberties, and that have fo long been our good and faithful allies, may feem ill-treated. But as it is too fhamefully notorious, that the *Dutch*, above all the Earth, have a moft violent turn to play the fool this way, I do hereby folemnly aver, let what

what will be the confequence, if any man among them, like a new *Mezentius*, thinks to tie the dead carcafe of his comment, to this living work, I fhall give him reafon to wifh, that his hand, like *Scævola's*, was on fire, when he employ'd it in fuch an attempt.

At the fame time that I think it proper, to lay the world and them, under this fevere reftriction, I am ready to make them abundant amends, for my extraordinary fenfibility in this point, by my eafinefs and condefcenfion in another; and that is, by allowing a free liberty, for all nations and languages, not only in *Europe*, but the reft of the world, to tranflate it as often as they pleafe, into their mother tongues, how rude or barbarous foever they may be. Far be it from me to wifh, much lefs to endeavour, to confine that day-fpring of knowledge, which by my means is about to rife upon the world, unto any particular corner of the earth, unto any little nation, fect, or tribe of people whatever! No! I have not fuch a narrow mind! Let it have its full courfe! Let all mankind make their beft ufe of it! provided thefe two conditions be punctually obferv'd: Firft, That fome *Englifhman*, who

under-

underftands *French*, and, like the reft of our
countrymen, can fearch to the bottom of
things, may only be employ'd to tranflate
it, for that fuperficial people of the other
fide the channel; and, fecondly, That all
judicious Catholicks do engage, (in return
for my thus freely communicating it to
them) that they will read it without bigotry
or prejudice, or any filly fears of the Pope's
authority, when he places it (as my good
Genius has affur'd me he will) in the *Index
Expurgatorius*, and prohibits the reading of
it, under pain of lying half a century in the
devil's * oven, or, which is much worfe, in
the prifons of the holy Inquifition, fo juftly
rever'd by all good Chriftians.

And now, moft dear Reader, (begging thou
may'ft not be afflicted at it) I muft haften
to a conclufion of this *Geryon*-like monfter
of a Preface, which poffibly, in fuch a nation as this, made up of Authors and Cri-
ticks, may never be read; or if it be, may
have little weight with thee. Be that as it
may, I cannot but wifh, for thy fake, and
what it introduces to thee, it were equal
either to that of *Calvin* before his Inftituti-

ons,

* *A new name, which my good angel has given Purgatory
in the originals of thefe Letters.*

ons, or *Caufabon's* to his *Polybius*, or *de Thou's* to his hiftory, which are juftly efteem'd the three mafter-pieces of all prefatory difcourfes.

I have ventur'd on the publick, and muft ftand to the fentence of that ever-changing Camelion, that lives only on what it catches with its tongue, to which I expect to become a prey. Yet am not I without hopes, that tho' fome may be fufficiently ignorant and malevolent, to fay this work I have given them, is like *Euclio's* houfe in *Plautus*, *quæ inaniis oppleta eft & araneis* ; yet others, *quorum ex meliore luto finxit præcordia Titan*, whofe minds are more enlighten'd, and capable of judging of the true value of things, will have nobler thoughts of it.

I have taken due precaution for its protection, by dedicating it to the fervice of the world, thro' the hands of that illuftrious Perfon, who will one day prove an ornament to thefe nations in his life, and a blefsing to mankind, in the Heroes that are to defcend from him; and am refolv'd not to proftitute the fubfequent parts to any but Patrons, that, like him, underftand what a treafure I prefent them with ; left I feem to copy the filly authors of this age, who dedicate

dicate their books to fuch ungenerous and
infenfible creatures, that one would think
they were imitating *Diogenes*, who us'd to
beg of ftatues, to teach him to bear the
coldnefs and negleƈt of thofe perfons, to
whom he applied for relief, proteƈtion and
favour.

Neverthelefs, I would not be thought in
publifhing this admirable performance, to
have aim'd at fo poor an end, as making the
great men of *Europe* pay court to me, for
any advice or inftruƈtions I may give them;
or to oblige thofe who fit on the thrones of
the world, to pay me tribute and homage,
as they us'd to do to the famous *Peter Are-
tine.* On the contrary, I declare before-
hand, neither Kings or Queens, Princes or
Princeffes, Noblemen or Ladies, Knights or
Gentlemen, Minifters of State or Merchants,
muft expeƈt any favour from me, or direƈti-
ons for their future conduƈt, and true interefts of their defcendants, but as they fhew
themfelves real friends to my native Country,
and the civil and religious Rights, of thefe
happy Nations.

To have done; As I appeal to Time, the
great parent of truth, for the verification of
all I publifh, and to Pofterity, (which, as
Tacitus

Tacitus speaks, *decus suum cuique rependit*) for that honour and deference, which I already behold them paying, to my faithful labours; so I appeal to all the sensible, the learned, the judicious and worthy spirits of the present age, from the judgment and censures, of the common herd and mob of mankind; that is, Lawyers without probity, Physicians without learning, Soldiers without Courage, Citizens without honest industry, Knights and 'Squires without common Sense, Clergymen without piety, Noblemen without honour, Senators without regard to their country, Patriots without integrity, and Scholars without genius, judgment, or taste!

F I N I S.